THINGS I
WROTE ABOUT

KELSEY HUMPHREYS

© 2023 Kelsey Humphreys
Things I Wrote About
First edition, February 2023

Magnamour Press
magnamour.com
kelseyhumphreys.com

Editing: Shayla Raquel, shaylaraquel.com
Cover Illustration: Shana Yasmin

ISBN: 978-1-959428-03-9

For the sensitive ones who experience massive emotions and have found the courage to face and feel each one.

And for Sarra.

AUTHOR'S NOTE

While this book is a fun, hilarious romance, it does deal with the death of a loved one and the grip of addiction. At the time of this writing, I am over eight years sober. I would like to give mad props to everyone who comes face-to-face with the substances they are trying to avoid, within their healthier outlets for escape. Television, movies, and books all feature alcohol seemingly constantly—content warnings not required.

If you are newly sober, you are a warrior and a champion. You're amazing, and I'm so proud of you. However, parts of this book may be difficult for you.

Kelsey

PROLOGUE

THE PRESENT
DALLAS, TEXAS

I cannot believe the nerves I'm feeling right now. I might actually be sick. *It's writing, Sadie! You do this every single day—get a grip!* But the header of the website, my own website, taunts me.

SADIE CANTON, AMERICA'S PARAMOUR.

Yikes.

The little pink hearts dancing around my name?

Gag me.

I should've taken that down years ago, even if the press is stuck on that nickname. Gwyn insisted, though. She loves it. But as much as I adore her, Gwyn may not be entirely right in the head. She's in marketing, after all.

Every time I'm mentioned in the media, good or bad, I can track the adrenaline hitting her bloodstream. Her eyes bulge from her skull, and she starts to salivate, literally. In those moments, she always reminds me of a French bulldog—adorable and just a little bit deranged.

She hates what I'm doing now. She wants television interviews, podcast tours, the works. But I don't want to put this into sound bites. I need to write it out.

Lorelai and Tash agree, my sisters agree—I have to do this my way.

The cursor flashes there, waiting.

Ugh, this is going to hurt.

I swallow and start to type.

Dearest Readers,

I'm not sure how to even begin this post. I'm aware no one reads blogs anymore. But this is important and can't fit into an Instagram caption. And I want to write to you directly.

I guess I should start with the debacle in the Caribbean and the stint in the hospital a few weeks ago. That was all blown wildly out of proportion by the paparazzi, I assure you. I'm fine. We're all fine. Although, again, I apologize sincerely to my sister Samantha and my new brother-in-law Emerson.

And I apologize to you, my beloved friends.

I feel I owe it to you, even if—truly—the words I wrote spiraled beyond me, grew bigger than me. You all felt the change, inspired it, even. Still, we've shared so many pages, you and I. You choose to hold my rambling thoughts in your hands, when you could hold so many other things, to give my stories your time and attention, and that, to me, is precious.

So I'm sorry.

Because I asked my publicist how many interviews she thinks I've done over the years to promote my dozens of romance novels and my handful of movie adaptations. She told me the number is well into the hundreds. If you've seen some of them, you know my famous one-liners, you've heard about my own romance, you know my stories.

The thing is, for over a decade, in every one of those interviews . . .

I lied.

CHAPTER 1

I can do this. I will do this. I can do this for Samantha. I can do this for Emerson. I can do this for myself.

I play the mantra on a loop as the little rusty cab bumps me along the winding road to Cielo Escondido. When Sam told me she and Emerson were going to do a destination wedding, I was surprised. The destination weddings I've been to have all been intimate, low-key, barefoot-on-the-beach affairs. Charming, romantic, and small.

Silly me.

Nothing Samantha does is small.

And we are Cantons. While we still feel like a somewhat normal family of Okies with a greeting card business, Canton Cards International has expanded beyond the wildest dreams of my father and grandfather. We are listed in articles about "American Royalty" alongside the Fords and the Waltons.

But we've got a big fat load of nothing on Samantha's fiancé. Emerson Clark is the oldest son in one of Great Britain's billionaire families, as beloved as actual British royalty.

So when these two say "destination wedding," what they mean is "we've bought out a secluded resort on a private island for six hundred guests for an entire week."

As my ride pulls past the gate into the palm-lined drive, I see the appeal. The lush grounds boast every color of the rainbow, in every type of flower, shrub, and tree. Each bloom is bigger and more saturated than the last. Leaves of every shade of green sway in the breeze, and I spot lemons, oranges, mangoes, and coconuts as we wind toward the hotel. The land looks wild yet kept. Bursting yet meticulously manicured. Peaceful yet thrilling too.

We pull up to a sprawling main building, an ivory stucco palace that is almost blinding in the afternoon sun. Windows and doors are open, birds and insects harmonize their songs, and the heavy air smells like plums and tree sap. The name of the hotel translates to Hidden Heaven. I get it, I do.

But for the next week, this place is, without a doubt, going to be my personal hell.

Me: Showtime [Crying emoji]
Tash: You are one of the strongest badass bitches I know.
Tash: You got this!!!!
Lorelai: You're a queen, Sadie. Head high, heels on. Consider this week already handled.
Me: It doesn't feel handled . . .
Lorelai: Feelings are liars, darling, you know this.
Me: True. Wish me luck.
Tash: You don't need it.
Lorelai: Who needs luck when you have us? [Kiss emoji]

I take a breath and switch to my other text thread. I hit send, ripping the Band-Aid of this week right off.

Me: I'm here
Sam: YAS!!!!!!!!!!!!!
Sam: Now the gang's all here!
Sam: Sade, come straight to the Honeymoon Villa.
Sam: The rest of you meet us there ASAP!!!
Skye: Since it's her wedding week, we're letting her run wild with exclamation points and all caps.
Sam: YEP!!!! =D =D =D
Sam: Just like how on your wedding week, we all left you alone.
Sam: Radio silence for days, remember?
Skye: I do. It was glorious.
Sam: Weirdo!
Sam: !!!!!
Sally: Skye's face twitches every time her phone buzzes.
Sally: It's hilarious.
Skye: Not as hilarious as you last night after ONE drink, pip-squeak. I have video.
Sally: What I meant was, can I bring you anything? Drinks for everyone?
Susan: Oh yes please! I'll have a few of whatever you had last night.
Me: A few? Already? What have I missed?
Susan: The wedding planner's flights have been delayed. Guess who's pinch-hitting as coordinator?
Sam: And I love you so much for it!
Sam: And Sal, I already have Juan bringing us various drinks with little umbrellas.
Sam: SO ALL OF YOU JUST GET OVER HERE!

I smile at my crazy sisters and hustle to Sam's suite as fast as I can with direction from the concierge. I've got a ball cap pulled down, sunglasses on, and an oversize sweatsuit to complete my Hobo in Hiding look. I don't want to run into anyone, especially not before I freshen up.

Since we have the whole island to ourselves, I didn't bring my bodyguard, and I'm already missing that layer of insulation between me and the world. Dean needed some time off. And really, this isn't *the world.* This is mostly family and close friends.

Mostly.

I walk faster.

A tan, fit, positively radiant Samantha opens the door just as I am about to knock.

"Sadieeeee!" she cries as she hugs me hard around my arms before I can lift them.

"She's in rare form, even for her," Skye jokes from somewhere beyond the door.

"I am, I really am." Sam smiles wide as she takes my bags from me. "I'll have someone take these to your villa down the path. You and Sally and Janie are together. How were your flights?"

"Fine, sorry I couldn't come in yesterday with you all."

"We get it, Hollywood. Set life and all that, so glamorous!" Susan says as she meets me with a hug. Sally and Skye join in right after. As I walk deeper into the villa, we make quick work of catching up about everyone's flights and Susan's kids' shenanigans so far.

I finally see the view from Sam's private patio. It's unreal. As in, must be photoshopped. The bright aqua ocean kissed by sand so white it hurts my corneas. The beach seems to extend forever in front of us *and* on either side, interrupted only occasionally by palm tree clusters. This must be the best view on the whole property.

"Okay," I sigh, staring. "I see how you got Emerson to agree to this."

"That's what I said too." Skye is my most introverted sister, and our soon-to-be brother, Emerson, is even more extreme. He and Samantha are a true grumpy-sunshine-opposites-attract situation that I couldn't have written better or sweeter if I'd tried. And I might try, if she lets me. My modern retelling of our parents' love story has become one of my most popular novels to date.

"This view, a few certain bikinis, unmentionable sexual favors"—Sam laughs, and we all cringe while laughing too—"and the promise that he could go hide alone somewhere on this island as much as he needs to or wants to, aside from the rehearsal dinner and actual wedding."

"And is that where he is now? Hiding up a tree somewhere?" I turn to her, still half giggling and enjoying my mental picture of Emerson Clark hiding from his own friends and family behind a tree trunk. Samantha's face falls, and the room goes painfully quiet.

Okay, here we go.

"He and the guys are playing volleyball," she says quietly. Susan and Skye stare at me, while Sally looks between all of us.

"Right. Listen, let's not be weird about this," I start, forcing myself to keep my voice calm and my face cheery.

"Sadie, you know Emerson doesn't have many friends. We couldn't—"

"Sam." I dip my chin and almost glare at her. "I know that. Of course. This week is about you guys, not me."

"Wait, what are we talking about here?" Sally asks.

I put a reassuring hand on the bride's shoulder. "I'm fine with it. I mean, all of it was like a decade ago! Give a girl some credit!" I widen my eyes indignantly. I turn to Sally. "Shep." I shrug a shoulder.

"Shep . . . Riggs?" Sally's eyes go wide at me.

"Not many other Sheps in the world . . . fortunately."

Sally takes a hair of a step backward. "Gummy bears Shep Riggs?"

My chest immediately aches as Susan nods quickly.

Skye clears her throat. "And Dennis too."

I sigh. "And Dennis."

"Wait." Sally joins us in the miserable reality that is my life. "Two of the groomsmen are your ex-boyfriends?!"

"Ex-boyfriend and ex-fiancé," Susan mutters, eyeing me. I'm sure she's imagining how terrible this is for me, and she is spot-on. But I won't show it.

"Yes. But we are all adults now, and my relationships with both of them are ancient history. Neither of them is bothered, and I'm not either. Really, I can't believe you guys were worried about this! You know me. I've done allll the internal work. I'm fine!" Again, I pretend to be offended at their lack of faith in my total fine-ness. They buy it and take a collective breath. Well, three out of the four. Skye isn't sure.

Not only is she the most perceptive of my sisters, but she was also in New York with me. She saw some of the carnage, as much as I tried to hide it. In fact, she may have seen more than even I saw myself at the time. I force away the memories as Sam starts to babble.

"Oh, whew! Good, okay. Great! I really was worried because we've never really talked about it, and like here they are and here you are and hey-o how about a week stranded on an island together—woohoo!" She laughs, and I do too, feeling my will to live wither with each fake chuckle.

"I knew you'd be fine. It's not like you haven't dated or uh, hello! Been engaged! Since then." Susan starts to relax as she passes us each a drink. I appreciate that while mine is a nonalcoholic cocktail, I still get a paper umbrella.

"Exactly." They don't know the whole truth, and they don't need to. It's over. The memories, the confusion, the grief, even

THINGS I WROTE ABOUT

the hatred—it's all in the past now. "Moving on," I say, walking back across the gorgeous villa. "I come bearing sister gifts!"

Samantha gasps. "You did?"

"Yes!" Sally pumps her fists as if she knew this was coming.

"You don't have to do this every time," Susan says half-heartedly.

"Yes, she does, we expect it now!" Skye counters. "Gimme!"

I pretend to huff at her. "K, so yours is going back."

"Going back where?" Skye huffs too. "We know you get these things in your celebrity gift bags, and we're fine with it. Please give us your Hollywood hand-me-downs."

We all laugh, and I start passing things out of my big tote bag.

"Sally, a hookup from my agent," I say, handing her an envelope.

"Holy shit!" Sally yells.

"Language," Susan says automatically.

"Thank you!" She squeals and hugs me hard after she discovers the four tickets to a Harry Styles concert in Dallas. I don't personally understand her generation's obsession with him, but I'm happy to host her and some friends at my apartment after all their concert dreams come true.

"Suze is next, and Skye is right, this was from a goody bag." I don't say it was from the Oscars because they will tease me to no end about it.

"Sadie! This thing isn't even on the market yet! I looked it up!" She gasps as she pulls out a UV light face mask contraption that is supposed to be better than Botox.

"I know. And sister, it's legit, let me tell you. I got an extra for myself," I admit.

"How many Darth Vader–type contraptions do you two own at this point?" Skye teases but then adds, "And can you give me any you don't use anymore?"

"Same!" Samantha says.

"Skye, these weren't from one of my goody bags, because I don't get invited to the Grammy's." I hand her a small box.

"Another pair of noise-canceling headphones? How many does she need?!" Samantha squawks as Skye pulls them out of the packaging.

"These aren't just any headphones. They're like the Rolls-Royce of headphones. And!" She pulls them out of the protective sheath. "They're neon!" We all ooh and aah over them.

"Lastly, the woman of the hour," I say, handing Samantha a wide flat box. I watch her face with glee. I had my illustrator, who creates all the wonderful couples that don my book covers, draw Samantha and Emerson. They're in London, he's wearing a suit, she's in her bright yellow dress, it's gorgeous.

And she's weeping.

"Sadieeeeeeee, I love it so much!"

"You love my book covers, so I thought it might be special for your own happily ever after." I sniff into her neck as she hugs me tight.

"Damn. I feel bad for everyone else who bothered with wedding presents," Skye says as she, surprisingly, turns the moment into another group hug. "No gifts can compare to Sadie gifts."

"Facts," Sally says.

My heart warms. I am not around as much as I should be, and I wasn't around when they needed me the most. We lost a few precious years that I can never get back. But I do see my sisters, and I know them. And giving gifts is a way to remind them of that. To remind them I *still* get them and accept them. I'm still on their team, and hopefully express that, even though I've failed before, from here on out, I'll always drop everything and run if they need me.

I pull out of our hug and grab my glass. "Okay, enough sappy stuff. Here's to an amazing couple and a weeklong party all about this gorgeous bride!" All five of us call out cheers and gush over Sam. She is ecstatic. *Peak Samantha*, as my mother would've said. She starts to go over the activities for the week. There are many.

Um, have I been transported to some kind of billionaire-wedding sleepaway camp?

Each day has adventurous excursions in the morning and relaxing methods of recovery in the afternoon. There are classes, various group mealtimes and food options, different entertainment each night, and set quiet hours. Just like summer camp.

Maybe I should have used my *I have to be on set* excuse for a few more days.

Especially since every single night there's a themed dinner, starting with tonight. The theme for tonight is the color yellow, and we're all supposed to meet at the main restaurant in just a couple hours. *Ugh.*

I excuse myself to get ready, and Sally joins me. I know she wants to ask for more details about Shep and myself. Dennis she doesn't know, but she's seen Shep on and off throughout the years, since Susan's husband, Adam, Emerson, and Shep were best friends in college. That's how Emerson got the job in accounting at Canton Cards' offices in New York: because he and Susan are friends. We all went to OU together, even though I was a few years behind them.

Since Sally is still at home in Oklahoma near Dad and Susan and Adam, she's probably seen Shep around quite a bit. I'm not sure. But instead of asking or volunteering more information of my own, I claim fatigue and duck into my room. She lets it go, thank goodness.

I shower and start to prepare. Mentally, emotionally, physically. I pray too. I need strength. I need peace. I need more hairspray to fight the island's crazy humidity.

I decide to surrender and go with beach waves. My long, dark blond locks don't look nearly as nice as they would if my glam team were here, but they'll do. As will my own makeup job and the tight yellow dress I picked up for this evening.

Funny.

I'd rather face all of Hollywood. Or a live 6:00 A.M. spot on *Good Morning America*. Or even one of those dreadful Reading My One-Star Reviews segments on one of the late-night shows. Even an awkward dinner with Dennis discussing our failed relationship.

Any of those options sound better than coming face-to-face with Shep Riggs.

———

I look at myself in the mirror. I stretch my spine and push my shoulders back. Unaffected. Content. Successful. Happy. New York Times Bestseller. Producer. Celebrity. Sadie Canton, America's Dadgum Sweetheart. That's who I am. That's who I have to be to get through this.

I slip on my wedge sandals, grab my clutch, and make my way out of my room. Sally and Janie—Skye and Sam's close friend from New York—must've already left. I hold my chin up as I walk the path to the lobby alone. But it doesn't take long to bump into people from the guest list. Friends of my parents, a distant cousin, a Canton Cards franchisee who's been with us from the beginning.

Everyone gawks at me a little bit. I understand, as I've met almost all my heroes in person now. They never quite live up to my vivid imagination. So I can't help but wonder if those around me are thinking things like, *Her face has a lot more fine lines in person than on Instagram* or *Her teeth aren't as white in person as they are on TV* or *I wonder why she got dumped by that sexy actor from her movie.*

I focus on the kind things actually coming out of their mouths rather than the crazy thoughts I put inside their heads. Really, no one is all that worried about me. They're wondering what crazy thoughts I'm thinking about them. The more I study humans, the more I find we're all a bunch of raging, insecure narcissists. Yay, humanity!

I do love chatting with Aunt Lee, though, one of my mother's best friends, who is going on and on about my last movie. She hates the way they changed the ending from how it was in the book. *I know, Aunt Lee, you and everyone on the internet.*

I see the main dining area coming up ahead of us and excuse myself. I want to shake off these conversations and put on the most genuine smile I can muster before heading in there, so I duck into a small bar off the main lobby. One wall is lined with windows overlooking a pier where some of the resort boats are docked. It looks peaceful out there. I debate pulling off my shoes, throwing them over my shoulder, and making a run for a small boat. I could man it, right? Push off into the sunset, alone?

No. This is for Sam. I take a deep breath.

But the breath catches, before my ears even hear the words behind my back. My whole body senses what's coming before my brain does. As my mind catches up, my heart constricts. There's a hint of stupid excitement, almost lifelong wonder, but mostly, the grip on me is one of dread.

"There she is, America's Paramour." His voice is deeper and rougher than the last time I heard it. His small-town accent is all but gone now. But the hairs standing on end all over my skin confirm it's him.

Emotions rush through me as my whole being reacts, hopefully invisibly. I see a slideshow of all the moments with him passing through my mind like a video stuck on fast-forward. Only the first few images are happy. Then there's only pain.

Shep. *Shep.* My best friend, my first love, my antihero, my ruin. My everything and then my enemy. I don't allow myself to startle or gasp or adjust my posture at all. Not one iota. This will not be like last time. I simply turn with a small smile and greet him with his new nickname, like he's done to me.

"And you, A Wolf in Shep's Clothing."

My voice sounds so calm! Easy breezy! Unbothered!

Hell yeah! Good job, Sadie. You got this.

Then I actually see him.

Oh.

He looks amazing. I don't let my eyes wander past his face, not that it's hard to keep them there. He still reminds me of a missing Hemsworth brother but with sharper features and blonder hair. Like a Viking. Like a hero. Like a grown man.

Why, God? Why do men get hotter with age? Is he taller somehow?

The small crow's-feet? The tiny wisps of gray in his sideburns? *WHY?*

I ignore the irritating, cocky half smile he gives me. I pass over the scar on his forehead and the stubble on his chin. I make myself look square into his eyes.

They're the same. Damn it. Damn him. One look in the bright green, and I'm caught, trapped in his gaze, frozen. I'm right back there, that night.

I'm fourteen all over again.

CHAPTER 2

18 YEARS AGO
TULSA, OKLAHOMA

This is going to work. I'm doing it. Country music is blaring, so no one hears me slip into the big ranch-style house owned by Cody Bills's parents. It smells like boys, pizza, and beer in here. I smile, excited. I adjust the wide leather belt hung low over my layered tank tops. Susan's old Daisy Duke shorts fit perfectly, and even if she spots me here tonight, I doubt she'll miss them from the back of her closet.

Chin up, Sadie, you should be here, just like everyone else.

"You shouldn't be here," a voice says to my right.

Dang it! I've barely made it past the front door. I turn and face the voice.

It belongs to the cutest boy I've ever seen. White-blonde hair, tanned skin, and bright eyes. I can't tell their color in this dim lighting, but they're not brown. Blue? Gray? I can't look away from them.

He smiles a smile that tells me I'm caught. Not at the party. Caught liking him, admiring what I'm seeing. He may be the cutest boy in the whole city, but unfortunately, he knows it.

Meanwhile, I'm frozen. Should I run into the house? Should I turn and leave?

"What?" I croak out after an eternity.

He takes a step toward me, his boots clunking on the entryway wood floors as he does. Boots? Not sneakers or flip-flops? That's weird. His eyes flick down to my legs and then back up. He gestures toward me with his red Solo cup. "Look, little Bambi, I'm not sure what in the cow-tippin', backwoods Sam Hill was fixin' to happen here, but you've been caught in the headlights and you need to go on home."

It takes me a moment before I remember to stick to my story. I straighten my spine. "I'm a freshman."

He is unmoved. "Nope."

"Yes, I am. I go to Union, that's how I knew about the party."

He juts his chin up at me. "Ha, nice try, but I actually *do* go to Union, so I know you don't."

I feel myself start to deflate. "You do?"

His smirk spreads into a smile. "I'm the new wide receiver, that's how I know you don't go there. If you did, you'd already know all about me."

Recognition flares in the back of my mind. I did overhear Susan and her friends talking about a new country boy all the freshmen and sophomore girls were drooling over. Yes. And Dad piped in at dinner about some star that the coach had gone and plucked from a small town . . .

"The guy from Poteau?"

"In the flesh." He flexes his substantial arm muscles as if posing for photos. I might be impressed with him if he weren't already so impressed with himself. His eyes go wide, and he laces his voice with mock awe. "And you can run home to your little junior high friends and tell them aaaalllll about how you met me! They won't believe it! Now git."

Angry, I laugh hard. *At* him. "*Git?* That explains why I can barely understand a word you say. Here in the big city, not everyone cares about silly football. Now, if you'll excuse me."

I take a small step, but he doesn't move out of my way. And he looks like he's getting just as mad as I am. I stare him down, even though I have to look up at him. He shakes his head, which enrages me all the more. Everyone at this party is underage—what does he care if I'm here too? And who made him the party police?

"Sorry, I forget jocks need small, slow words. Move. Out. Of. My. Way!"

"Sadie?" I hear a shriek from somewhere behind the blond wall before me. "Sadie Lynette Canton! What are you doing here! You're going to get us in so much trouble!"

I roll my eyes and barely keep from groaning like a toddler as Susan joins us in the entryway. She turns to the giant. "Sorry, Shep, my—"

"Shep, like Shepherd?" I cut in because I can't help myself. I want to know more. I want to know everything.

"Nope. Just Shep."

Susan's smile tightens, and she scolds me through her teeth. "My little sister was just *leaving*."

"Seriously, Suze? You won't even know I'm here."

She shakes her head. "I'm not supposed to be here either, but if Mom and Dad find out? Not that big of a deal. If they find out *you* were with me? I'm dead."

I feel my already blushing face darken with embarrassment as the beautiful wall of a boy—Shep—watches us. My sister is only three years older than me but makes it sound like I'm just out of diapers or something. This is so stupid and unfair. I direct all my emotion at those eyes . . . that aren't watching us.

They're watching *me.*

"Why are you still here? I'm sure there's a game of beer pong with your stupid hick name on it."

His gaze darkens at my jab.

Susan gasps. "Sadie!"

"Don't worry, Suze." His grin is wicked. "She's cute, your lil' baby sister. Reckon you better make sure she gets home before her bedtime."

Then he's gone, and I'm so irritated I could spit. I am mortified that he saw all of that. And disappointed at how familiar he seemed with my sister, calling her Suze, like they're close. And yet I kind of want to go after him, if nothing else than to see what other crazy things come out of his mouth.

And to figure out what color his eyes are.

———

Green.

The brightest green eyes that ever were or ever will be, until the end of days. I will them to look at me from where I sit in the stands. I'm with a group of friends down the bench from my family, above the student section where all the high schoolers are.

My dad played football, and Susan is a cheerleader, so it's not unusual for our family to come to the games. It is unusual for me to actually watch. Watch is not the right word. I was . . . enraptured? Enthralled?

Whatever the word, the new kid was as amazing as advertised tonight. Dad was reeling about how Shep Riggs changed the entire football team and would carry the school to a state championship. How he'll play at the University of Oklahoma or some other big football university and go on to the NFL. Dad was giddy. I believed every word.

I watch Shep now on the sidelines below. The only thing brighter than his green eyes under the stadium lights is his wide smile. He's feeling good about his game, clearly.

Oh.

I notice the cheerleaders, drill team dancers, water girls, and even some band girls flocking to him on the sidelines.

Yep, he's feeling good about his game, in every sense of the word. I don't see one specific girl approach him to stake her claim, so he must not have a girlfriend. Which means he can have his pick of the very willing litter. There are junior and senior girls throwing themselves at him even though he's just a sophomore.

One pom girl has such a gleam in her eye as she bites her bottom lip in his direction, I wonder if she might start stripping naked on the ground before him, entire town be damned. In fact, I'm starting to wonder if she's all right. She might need medical attention, this girl. She's looking unstable, pulling on her uniform top like she wants to rip it open She-Hulk style in a rush of lust. Jeez! *Medic! We need a medic down there!* I shout in my head. Pathetic.

That's a bit mean. Honestly, I think I dislike the display so much because I can relate.

But with all *that* going on, he's not going to notice me. It's fine. I'll be a freshman at Union next year, maybe he'll notice me then. Suddenly my eighth-grade year before me seems like an arduous eternity.

The crowd is still going wild over the win. Everyone is yelling at the players and the coach. My father calls out, "Good game, Shep!" Somehow, his voice is heard by the MVP below. The green lights Shep uses to see veer up to find my father and then, for a moment, they land on me.

He cocks his gorgeous head to the side as if to say, *I told you so.* I roll my eyes and try my hardest not to smile. I manage to keep it to a tiny grin. I feel my cheeks start to burn, but luckily he's looked away already. I've never noticed or wanted to be noticed by a boy like this before.

One more year.

It will be fine.

Just a year.

It'll fly by.

. . . *A whole year! I hate my life.*

———

Not a whole year, just half.

It's February, it's freezing, and I'm walking home. My friend Annie lives in the neighborhood next to mine, which didn't sound like a long walk when we were chatting on Messenger. It didn't feel long when I was walking toward her. It feels like an epic trek now as I walk back.

But when a beat-up pickup pulls alongside me and a pair of bright green eyes stare me down through the window, I warm instantly.

"Hop in, Bambi, you'll catch your death out here."

"You say weird things."

"My gramma always said that. Get in!" He shivers from the breeze of his open window. I smile and climb in.

I look over at him. "You headed to Cody's?"

He nods.

I move to blow on my hands and remember I'm clutching Annie's copy of *The Chronicles of Narnia* in my hands. I set it down on the console between us to rub my hands together.

"That'n's pretty good."

It takes me a moment to process what he's said. "Y-You've read it? Which one?"

"All of 'em."

"You read?" It comes out as if I'm asking if he teleports.

He shrugs. "Not much else to do in Poteau." I stare. "I like sci-fi better. *Foundation. 1984.*"

I can feel that my mouth is hanging open. My surprise is on full display, and I can't rein it in. He laughs. "You gonna trap flies in there, girl."

"Sadie." I shake myself out of my stupor. "My name is Sadie."

"I know."

Filled with warmth that he remembers my name, I blurt out, "Are you going to the Sweethearts Dance next week?" I quickly add, "It's all Susan can talk about."

"Haven't decided yet." He glances over at me with a wide smile, and I quickly look away. "Why, you figure I should take you?"

"No!" I say, convincing no one that that wasn't exactly what I was thinking. I really thought I'd gotten good at masking what my mother calls my very big feelings. I am too emotional, my sisters tell me often, and I was thinking I'd become pretty skilled at hiding how affected I am by everything. Until now.

He huffs a little laugh. "You're not ready for me yet."

"Psh, get over yourself." Embarrassment chokes me as I open the door with the truck still moving. We're near enough to my house. "Here's fine, thanks."

"Hey, I said *yet!*"

"In your dreams, you hillbilly!" I say it with force as I walk across my lawn, but my lip is trembling.

Crap!

I hold in my whirling emotions for the whole walk up the porch steps. And when I get inside. And for the whole evening with my family. I hide it all until I'm alone in my bed, late into the night. Then I let myself cry stupid tears over a stupid boy in a stupid truck with a stupid name.

I enjoy the rest of eighth grade just fine.

CHAPTER 3

1 MONTH AGO
THE CARIBBEAN

I am not affected by this man. I am not. So, as a completely unaffected person, I look away from his eyes. I take a moment to peer around the little bar and then up his frame. It's a quick glance, like I'd take in anyone. Normal acquaintance behavior.

Bad idea.

He's in a navy suit that I know was tailored to hang perfectly around his still-intact wide receiver muscles. He doesn't have on a vest or tie. His pale-yellow shirt is unbuttoned at the top, as if it can barely contain his raw masculinity.

My heart should not be flipping over in my torso. I've seen him in a suit. A tux, even. It must just be that he's still so striking. After all these years, again and again, he still pulls at me like a magnet.

No, not a magnet.

A black hole.

I'm annoyed at how aware of myself I suddenly am. I am rarely self-conscious anymore. I've been picked apart by every gossip blog and fashion TikTok account. Even before fame, my parents, while loving, could've been described as hyper critical. And let's not forget I have four sisters. Not much affects my self-esteem anymore.

Yet I feel, I physically register, his eyes as they take their time looking me up and down. I decided to be subtle and polite with my perusal. He has not. I can't let myself blink or start to blush. He'll pounce on any signs of weakness.

I am unaffected. Un. Af. Fect. Ted!

"Well, I'd better get in there." I give him a tight smile and begin to walk around him, giving him as wide a berth as I can without being obvious.

But he reaches out and touches my forearm. Gently. So gently I almost don't feel it. Except for my skin recognizes his fingers, flashing me back to the library that night. Fresh searing pain explodes across my brain. I should keep moving past him. Nothing good can come of this. But my feet immediately stop moving and my entire arm goes up in what my brain perceives as scorching flames. Pleasant ones.

"You look different." His voice is low, but his tone jabs. It's not a compliment like the parking lot. *You look better.* Another night I'd rather forget.

I can tell he means different as in old. Different as in too much Botox. Different as in sad or thin or who knows. Who cares. Not me. He means different in a bad way.

So what? I can do this. It's all ancient history now.

I smile, it's a nice smile, mostly sincere. I hope it doesn't look sad, even though it feels sad when it hits my cheeks. "You look the same, Shep." I exhale. "You look great, actually." I move my arm and start to walk. "It's good to see you."

Yes! Suck it, Shep Riggs, because I am the bigger person! I am mature now! HA!

Finally, I'm past him. My arm cools even as I feel his gaze on my back. I'm to the lobby area, almost home free.

"Bullshit," he says behind me.

I freeze and turn. He wants to rile me, as freaking always. Tonight, I won't be riled. I'm not a kid anymore.

I raise one shoulder. "This week is for them, so we might as well make the most of it. Maybe we can even come out of this as friends." I look away and start walking. I want to sprint the hell out of his sight and into the throng of people. But an unaffected person doesn't hurry. My pace also allows me to hear him, just barely.

"Yeah. Fat chance, honey."

He sounds so bitter. I'm still baffled by him to this day. How can *he* be so angry with *me?* It's ridiculous. Yes, I left, but I was broken, and he and I both know it was him who did all the breaking. The man shattered me. It took years for me to put myself right. Then he was angry that I had . . . that I had moved on. I wouldn't have even had to move on if he hadn't . . .

Never mind. I feel the familiar rage building in me as I walk through the crowded dining area. Rage I can't let out with running or writing or pounding glorious shots of alcohol so strong it could be used as industrial cleaner. *Don't go there, Sade.*

The nerve of him. The nerve of myself, letting him make me an internal mess. I've already worked through all this!

I'm distracted by smiles and greetings as I pass through the room. The hotel's main restaurant, a wide room covered in subtle tropical prints and beachy creams and tans, is clearly not equipped for this many people to dine at once. Dinner is in two shifts, the first of which is for family, the wedding party, and closest friends. I look for my sisters, assuming I have a saved seat.

Apparently not. There are a few spots at a family table off to the side. I spot my cousins and their kids and make my way over, eager to sit down and blend in. I greet everyone and take a seat, grabbing a water and sucking it down, wishing it were wine.

No, Sadie. You're strong enough for this.

"Whoa! You're Shep Riggs!" my cousin's daughter Lucy cries out, her eyes above my head.

Okay. Maybe I am not strong enough for this.

"I am indeed. This seat taken, little lady?" he asks her, as charming as can be. I smile up at him and don't let myself scoot away. The smile he gives her turns to a venomous baring of teeth when he looks down at me.

So. Tonight is going to be just like the benefit. *Great.*

All my internal organs squeeze like a fist. This is going to be the longest, hardest week of my life. Not that he'll know it. I just told him we could be friends. It's fine if he sits by me. Totally fine.

He thumps in his chair. He's too big for the small space beside me. Too big for the table. Too big for the room. He's only 5'11" but he's spent most of his life in weight rooms, and it shows. And Shep is just . . . larger than life. He always has been.

But I sure as hell am not going to shrivel next to him, that's for damn sure.

"I can't believe we ended up at the celebrity table! I've seen both of you on TV! This is so cool!" Lucy gushes. I think she's about eight years old and I wonder what exactly she's seen or heard. I smile, and Shep laughs. My cousin Kat coughs nervously.

"Will you guys take a selfie with me? Or Sadie, do you have any books here? Oh! Could you sign something for my best friend Ellie? Mama says I'm not allowed to read books with naked men on the front, but she has all of them in her room! Like a million!" Well, apparently Lucy is a little conversation train that's just left the station and is running right off the tracks. "Ellie would just die. I showed her a ton of videos about you on YouTube, but she doesn't even believe you're my mom's cousin, did you know that?

"And my grandpa always points you out on Esspin, Mr. Riggs. Every time." I realize she means ESPN. Shep and I are both caught up in the awkwardness, just staring at this girl. She's got bright blond hair with almost ginger coloring to her, but with huge, signature Canton teal-ish eyes. "I can't believe this! And look how white your teeth are! Do you go to the dentist all the time? My mom says braces are really expensive, right? Did you both have braces? You're both rich, though. I wonder which one of you is richer!"

"I am."

"I am."

We say the phrase in unison. Both scoffing, as if the question is ridiculous.

"Lucy!" My cousin finally reins her in. "I'm sorry, she'd yaw the hind leg off a donkey once she gets going!" Kat laughs as her face turns fuchsia. She pretends to lecture Lucy while Shep glares down at me.

"You think so, Sadie? You know I have four separate deals with Nike. Four."

I am a rock. I am an island. I am quoting Simon & Garfunkel to myself. Wow.

"I'm not sure even Nike can compare with Disney," I say casually into my glass of iced tea before taking a sip. I try to keep the conversation between myself and The Asshole and not the entire table, which is totally captivated by the pissing contest currently happening.

His eyes hold mine with almost glee. "Maybe so, but Nike, Under Armour, Gatorade, *and* ESPN?"

I set my glass down and sniff, as if to load the barrel. "I'm just grateful to still be landing deals for my own work."

Shots fired.

I wince internally. It's hard to believe this man *used* to bring out the best in me.

I feel his arm nearest to me stiffen, just barely. I know I've landed a bull's-eye on his chest. Because he's not an athlete anymore. Those aren't his deals; those are the endorsements he's secured for his clients. He's just an agent now. The best agent in the entire sport of football, maybe, but still, he himself is on the sidelines.

His turn to talk into his water glass. "And why wouldn't you? No one can resist the Canton name."

Okay.

That stings. It's a predictable bullet, but it's pierced my armor. My father and his business had nothing to do with the success of my first book, which led to the entertainment empire I have now. It's a truth that no one believes. Apparently not even Shep.

Unaffected, Sadie.

"It is quite a name," I concede, relaxing my posture and letting him and his assumptions win.

"Must be, since you can't seem to give it up," he mutters. I don't respond but focus a considerable amount of energy into my fingertips. It's a weird trick I use to redirect blood flow when I think I'm going to be flushed. Even if I'm not blushing, I bet he's happy to have won this round. I'm not positive, because I look away. Thankfully, as I do, my father stands and taps his glass with his fork.

Shep shifts in the seat next to me, as if he's trying to align his body with the central table where Dad stands. But that's not what he's trying to do. He's trying to kill me.

His thigh pushes into mine under the table. Then his calf encroaches too as he stretches out. The luxurious fabric of his pants might as well be a line of lit matches along my bare leg.

That's not enough for him, though. Again acting as if he merely needs the room, he widens his arms. He puts a hand on the top of the backrest of my chair. For one second, his knuckles touch my shoulder.

It's too much too soon.

I'm captured and strangled. I pray he doesn't notice it as I gasp for air.

A sharp, deep inhale.

There's not enough air. This is it. I'm going to die here.

Death by a knuckle brush.

———

I finally spot my moment. Shep, after an excruciatingly slow meal filled with small talk around the table with anyone but me, has excused himself to the restroom. I am up like The Flash. I give Skye a look that says *I'm done.* She nods, having watched me persevere having to sit within elbow-knocking distance of Shep for the last hour. A distance he took advantage of, shoving his bulky arm into my space like I was invisible. He's two beers in now, and I cannot and will not stick around for what comes next.

I see the lobby area at the back of the dining hall where I came in earlier. Is the doorway glowing? Because it's an oasis in this hot, awkward, sexually charged desert. I'm almost running.

But as I hit the doors, so does Shep, from the other direction. He smiles in absolute triumph.

"Trying to escape already?"

I relax my posture. "Not at all. I was headed to the restroom."

"Well, these are closed for cleaning, so we'll have to go to the others on that side of the room." He points behind me into the dining hall I just left.

I pause. I desperately do not want to turn around and go back in there. I can't. But I don't want him to know that. I look past him to see if there are, in fact, cleaning signs. There are. He is staring, waiting, like a snake about to strike.

He laughs. "Liar."

"What? Why would I lie to you?"

"I don't know, why haven't you turned around to go use the bathrooms I just pointed to, Paramour?"

I don't react to the name, which he says with such disdain he might as well have just called me America's Slut. I have an urge to squint at him, to sigh. I do neither.

"I just really have to go, so . . ." I turn and use the excuse of bodily function to bolt with urgency like I'm launching off starting blocks. He mutters something bitter under his breath, and I decide it's the last damn straw. I look back to say—

SMASH!

I collide with a pimply teenage-looking server holding a tray of . . . full champagne glasses. I'm now cold and slick and fizzy. The crack of that many smashing glasses stops all the conversations. The entire room comprising almost everyone I know is staring, startled. I am now drenched. The guy is awkwardly holding me and the tray is dripping too and . . . no.

No! Our feet are slipping outward on the marble floor. I can't get traction on the polished surface, and neither can he, like a couple of dogs on iced sidewalks. We flail like a cartoon, trying to leverage the other for help. But there is no help. His eyes go wide at me and I shake my head at him and *Oh, heaven help me, we are both going down!*

We do. We go all the way down.

I twist at the last second to avoid splitting spread eagle and smack my tailbone so hard on the floor I cry out. No one can hear me over the clang of the silver tray that the server released when our bodies parted. It is now gonging, announcing our demise on the shards of glass, in case people all the way back on the coast of the United States didn't hear the first crash.

The poor server hops up, less mortified than me. He apologizes as he helps me stand, but it's as if he's yelling because the room is still frozen. Every mouth hangs slack. Except for one.

Shep is laughing.

The bastard is a foot away, watching and laughing.

He could've stopped us, helped us. He could've helped me up. He's right there! He's biting his finger and holding in what I'm sure is a huge guffaw because his shoulders are shaking badly.

I look away from him and face the lesser evil—an entire room that's just watched me bite it, hard. They can now see through my yellow dress, I'm sure. Some are clearing their throats. Sam's eyes are as wide as her plate, and Emerson is looking away, purple with secondhand embarrassment.

I grab a glass off the floor. It's empty but not broken.

"Well, here's to starting this week off with a bang, everybody!"

I raise my glass and the whole freaking world exhales with relief. People laugh, glasses are clinked with forks. Some yell "Cheers!" Everyone is ecstatic to have been told how to react. *You're welcome!*

The server hands a couple cloth napkins in my direction, but I wave them off as I hand him the empty glass. No point in trying to cover myself now. I have to get out of this dress, away from the potent champagne and the sound of Shep's stifled snicker.

I straighten my spine to walk out of the room. I look at Shep and give him a shrug and a little chuckle as I go. He looks surprised. He thought I'd avoid him or look angry.

That's right! I'm not embarrassed or ashamed or concerned with you at all, Shep Riggs!

I am, however, getting the hell away from him right this second.

Unaffected my throbbing, champagne-soaked ass.

CHAPTER 4

17 YEARS AGO
TULSA, OKLAHOMA

High school. Huge, bustling, limitless high school. Finally!

There's a weird law of nature within the high school caste system that dictates if you have an older sibling in school who is cool, or even just not a total loser or a psycho, you are deemed cool by default. I don't understand this law, but I'm grateful for it.

Because I hit the freaking jackpot. Susan is not just cheer captain and her senior class president, but she's also student body president—voted in by the entire school. Everyone loves her. She is friendly, driven, organized, smart, and pretty.

I would be jealous except she's made my little freshman life so great, I am genuinely happy for her. I wouldn't want to be student body president anyway. I'd rather star in the musicals and win all the talent shows. Or maybe be valedictorian.

Even marinated in my sister's general awesomesauce, I am still a nervous wreck for the first couple weeks. It's high school. It's important to get started on the right foot. Our school is the size of a small college, and the schedule is hectic. It takes me some time to adjust.

Of course, I spot the star of all my dreams and fantasies over the last year in the halls. And in the parking lot. And in the cafeteria. And dancing with the rest of the starting lineup at the football assembly from my seat in the gym bleachers. I watch him from afar, but he doesn't see me.

Until today.

It's early, and I'm sitting in the lower cafeteria going over my notes for my first class. I'm alone at a table, but there are a few other early birds in this area of the caf. It's a commons-type area that's near the main entry from the student parking lots.

"Well, look who finally goes to school here." He nudges Cody Bills, the quarterback whose home we met in a year ago. A couple more players trail behind them, all looking at me. I blush. I was hoping for a *Wow, you look so grown up, you're ready for me now, want to go out on a date tonight?* Not quickly picking up where we left off, jabbing back and forth. I barely look up from what I'm doing, as if him coming over to me isn't the most exciting thing since the Christmas morning that my parents surprised us with a trip to Disney World.

"Poteau."

The nickname doesn't faze him anymore that I can tell. No, he's a man among boys here, a football phenom who's as handsome as he is talented. I sigh, realizing his head has grown exponentially, judging by the smirk he gives me.

"You gonna make me a poster for the game, Bambi?"

I look back to my notebook. "Why? You wouldn't be able to read it."

"Ohhhhhh!" His teammates cry out in a chorus of howling and cursing, ribbing their superstar.

"I know a jealous girl when I see one. You want one of my jerseys to wear too? I have a few extra. They aren't just for the cheerleaders, you know, the *popular, older* girls. You can wear one too, even if you're knee-high to a grasshopper."

My eyes jerk back up, confused. "If I'm what?"

"Even if you're just a lil' nobody baby freshman."

Now all the boys look to me, waiting. That stings. I don't want it to, but it does. It doesn't even make sense, logically, because I'm not some unpopular pariah just because I'm a freshman. I'm likable enough, pretty enough.

My family says I'm oversensitive "to the nth degree." But I'm learning more and more how to hide my strong feelings. So now, with a group of cute, smelly, teen boys glaring me down, aside from a blush on my cheeks that was there when they walked up, there's no visible reaction. I don't cower or break eye contact. I maintain my grin.

"Now . . . what would be the point of wearing it, when I won't even be at the game?"

He blinks, and I take that moment of victory to stand and gather my things, trying to keep my face blank.

He balks. "Bullshit. Everybody goes to the games."

"No, Poteau. Not everybody."

"I've seen you at games."

I find my smile. "You notice all the *lil' grasshoppers* at your games, Hotshot?"

All the boys' eyes look back to their leader.

"Only the ones that think I'm a hotshot."

Crap! My smile is gone, but I manage to shrug casually. "My dad dragged me there." I turn and begin to walk away. I call back, "Good luck tomorrow, though."

"Don't need it, but thanks anyway, Bambi."

The way he says the nickname shows that he knows how much I'm affected, even as I try to hide it. I want to turn and run at him and slap the stupid grin off his face. I want to scream that I'm not some doe-eyed baby girl. I want to flip him off and cuss him out.

I simply walk away.

———

Now it's Friday night, and as badly as I want to go with all my friends, I can't actually go to the game.

Idiot!

I watch the local broadcast at home with my younger sisters, Skye, Samantha, and Sally, letting my parents make a date night out of the home opener. I'm sure they went to Red Lobster beforehand and are now at the game cheering for Shep Riggs like he's their own son. At least my dad is. My mother watches games in a more scientific way, searching for patterns and tracking data in her big genius brain.

And here I am trying to hear the game over my sisters screaming about shared Barbie accessories and Sally singing along to Nick Jr.

I sigh.

I do learn a lot from watching football on TV, however. Having the commentators explain things is helpful. Their reaction to Shep's two missed catches at the end of the third quarter clues me in to why Shep looks so pissed on the sidelines. The team wins the game, but Shep's smile isn't as wide as usual. He's mad at himself.

The local broadcast shows all the postgame activity on the field and even some of the postgame activity in the locker room. During an interview with the head coach, I notice Shep in the corner in the background.

It almost doesn't look like him. He seems small, young. Someone is talking to him, at him. With the broad build and blond coloring, it has to be his dad. I look closely.

The man appears to be verbally ripping Shep into pieces. Shep nods in agreement, keeping his head tucked down. The players around them look away, making me think Mr. Riggs is spewing some seriously vile words at his son.

I instantly loathe the man.

I want to go to wherever Shep is, hug him, tell him "Good game," tell him he's a beast out there.

But not long after, the local reporter actually interviews the hometown star himself. He showers Shep with praise, lobbing him easy questions and fawning all over every answer. Shep is cocky, unaffected, happy. When he runs off-screen after the interview, I hear the cheers of his horde of female admirers, and other fans too.

Poteau seems totally fine.

I file all this information away for later.

———

"Well, you missed a hell of a game."

It's Tuesday, well past the end of the school day. I stayed late for the fall musical audition rehearsals. I'm in the lower cafeteria again, waiting on Susan. He saunters over to me, leaving the pack of players that are passing through to head to the parking lots. They must have just finished afternoon practice.

"I heard you've had better."

He barely flinches. It's a tiny reaction, but it's there.

"Uh-huh. Like you didn't watch it. You need a ride home?"

"Eh, Susan will be done with student council stuff eventually."

"C'mon." He turns and motions with his hand. "I can take you now."

It takes me a second to gather my things, and as I do, a couple teammates gravitate back to Shep's side. I rush to catch up to them. To my surprise, Shep is giving two younger players a coaching session of sorts.

"No, see, you're thinking that in those few plays you're gonna run the route the exact same, but you're not. There's a two-, three-, five-second difference. You can't rush it."

"You're telling me run slower?" one guy asks Shep.

"I'm telling you watch and get where Cody needs you to be. Every single time." Both of the teammates scoff in response. Then they thank him before peeling off to their own cars.

"So?" he says, once we're in the car and on our way. "I had practice, and I know you didn't have detention."

"How do you know I didn't have detention?" I huff. I'm tired of him acting like he knows me so well. Like I'm a little cherub or something.

He glares right back at me. "Did you?"

"No. Fall musical auditions are coming up, so there are rehearsals to learn the material."

"You sing?"

I nod.

"You any good?"

I shrug. "We'll find out after auditions, I guess."

"Don't do that. You know you're good. I can see it on your face—just tell me so." He's wearing a grin that is impossible to say no to.

"I'm pretty good."

He looks at the road and back at me. "Sing something."

"No!"

"C'mon, just a line of something."

I hesitate, but I know I'm going to give in. I can't refuse him. I think quickly about what he'd like. It's an easy answer: anything country. I sing the chorus of the LeAnn Rimes song, "Nothin' 'bout Love Makes Sense."

I don't look at him as I sing. I definitely don't look at him after I'm done singing. The silence hangs for a couple seconds.

"Well, shit." He whispers the words. I hold back a smile that is sure to be goofy and ridiculous as he composes his thoughts. "So, that's what you're gonna do then, right? Be a singer? Like a country star?"

"Maybe Broadway."

"New York?" he asks. I nod. He stares out the windshield in thought for a beat, then adds, "I like New York."

His simple statement feels huge, massive. My goofiest goofy smile breaks free.

"You could do country too. Or be a pop star."

"Eh," I reply. "I think I like acting better."

"Hm." The grunt sounds different, so I look over. He shifts in the driver's seat.

"What?"

He looks back at me. "Seems like it'd be hard to trust someone's good at actin', I think."

He studies me, and I study him back. The dumb jock who reads more than I do, who's happy all the time, unless no one is looking. I raise an eyebrow. "Takes one to know one, I think."

He cocks his head, considering my point. We're only a minute from the house now, so the country music takes over the car. He doesn't glance back at me. But I watch him.

I watch him for most of my freshman year.

I find myself watching everyone, studying people for character research with my various drama assignments, but him most of all.

He is always smiling, and I suppose he has a lot to smile about. But beyond just easygoing, he seems to be flippant about everything other than football. I hear through the rumor mill that he goes on dates but never has a girlfriend. He must make good enough grades to stay on the field, but I've never seen him stressed or studying or even carrying a book around.

A couple times a month, we find ourselves up at the school after hours, and he always offers to take me home. They are my favorite little pockets of life, those minutes with him. I try not to show it, but I save up questions to ask about his favorites (spaghetti, Kit Kats, country music, the color crimson, large Sprites from Sonic Drive-In) and his life (he and his younger brother get along okay, his dad is a jerk, his mom is long gone).

Near the end of the year, I run into him after school. This time he's not alone or with teammates. He's surrounded by cheerleaders. It must be some cheesy off-season ritual because they're all wearing shirts with his jersey number. I decide not to approach, turning instead toward the library where I can wait for Susan or Dad to pick me up.

A few minutes later, he finds me among the bookshelves.

"Need a ride?"

I look up from my phone, then hold it up as an explanation. "Susan's coming."

"Text her back then. I can take you."

"Okay."

As we walk out, he grabs at my shoulder to take my backpack from me. His rough knuckles touch my arm. It's the most thrilling three seconds of my existence. Better than a roller coaster or acing a test or the first bite of a fresh cookie.

I am about to stop walking, shocked, but his loud voice snaps me out of my trance.

"Good gravy! What you tryin' to do, bulk up like a linebacker? What you got in here, Bambi?"

I sigh at the return of that stupid nickname. It ticks me off, so I revert to our default mode.

"These things called textbooks. Nonfiction. Some of us want to *learn* things, things for real life, not just how to throw a ball around on some grass."

"I *catch* the ball," he retorts, holding up his palms, "and these sticky hands are gonna pay for my college."

"More like butterfingers," I snipe.

"Damn it, Bambi. You ever gonna quit bein' ugly to me?"

"Will you quit calling me Bambi?"

Neither of us says anything the rest of the walk out, but we're both smiling like fools. We make it to his car right as I'm about to ask about his future, beyond college football. I open my mouth, but he opens his door and we're both shocked by the sound of candy wrappers. Mounds of Kit Kats fall from his truck down onto the concrete. Laughter and cheers erupt from under the awning, where his gaggle of cheerleaders stands watching.

Shep curses under his breath, but he's blushing from ear to ear. He looks up into the cab, which is covered in streamers and posters and overflowing with candy. He climbs in part of the way and then out again. "Your side's clear, you can get in."

I get in, but I do a crappy job of hiding my disgust. Not just at the obscene amount of candy, but also the number of girls giggling at him. So many girls, all the time. After he gathers up all the candy and throws it behind his seat, he climbs in. I don't say anything and neither does he. I can feel him watching me, though.

Eventually, he chuckles. "Don't get so worked up."

I jerk my head back. "I don't care."

"Your face is red somethin' fierce."

"My what? Can you just speak normal English, Poteau?! Ugh!"

He laughs. "They're just girls, Sadie."

It is with Herculean, mind-bending, world-changing strength that I refrain from responding and look out the window. *I'm a girl, aren't I? Do you see me as a girl? Am I just like them? Am I different from them? How? Why?*

I say nothing.

Instead of letting me out on the curb like he usually does, he pulls into the driveway.

"Don't you have like a million little sisters?"

I laugh a bit, happy to let some of the tension out. "Three."

"Want to go get a Walmart sack so you can take some of this? I can't eat crap, so there's too much even for me and Buck."

I nod and head in to get the bag.

When I come out, Shep is surrounded.

By three little Cantons.

Oh no.

"You're Shep?" Samantha bats her eyelashes at him as only a curious ten-year-old can.

"Yes, ma'am." He gives my sisters his full-court-press smile.

Sam returns the smile. "Oh, so are you Sadie's boyfriend?"

Holy crap! What!

He laughs. "No, just her friend."

"But she has your name up in her room, with hearts all around it." Samantha cannot help herself. Skye is no help, just watching and eating a Kit Kat like she's at a matinee show.

"Is that right?" He turns to me, looking so smug, so cocky, he— well, he's . . . he's an asshole. The A-word. That's what he is in this moment. I scramble.

"That sign says STEP! Steps, like I'm learning for the musical!" I lie. I never lie. I will ask for forgiveness on Sunday morning. I can't just let him know I'm still swooning over him. *Why, why didn't I take that silly sign down?*

"No," Sally says to my lie, confused. She's only five, and her confused face is maybe the cutest thing ever.

Shep squats down to her level, filled with glee, while I ask God for a tornado. A freak lightning strike. Earthquake. Any natural disaster right here, right now will do just fine. Unlikely, since I just sinned with my white lie. I groan.

"No. T for twain. H for hat." She sticks a tootsie roll pop in her mouth. "H for hat. It on dere."

"Yeah. There's no H in step. That'd be Shtep!" Sam starts laughing. "That'd be sho shuper shilly!" They are all laughing now, including Shep.

"Okay, well, he has to go now!" I singsong at them while shoving them back to the house. "Say bye! Take your candy in!"

"Okay. Bye-bye, Step," Sally says as she follows after the other two, who are still giggling. Shep's about to say something to me when Sally turns back. "Step, ness time bring gum bears."

"Yes, ma'am."

"They're compulsive liars, all of them," I blurt when they shut the front door. "We're in family therapy over it." That sends Shep into a fit of laughter. Deep, big laughs that shake his whole beautiful face. I love it, even if I have died a thousand deaths in the last three minutes.

"Is that right?"

"Uh-huh. My mother's distraught. Sally especially, to start lying so young." More laughs. Just as I start to feel better, he looks me in the eye.

"Pink hearts?"

I roll my eyes and let my shoulders slump. I look away as I come clean. "That sign was up before, Shep. I'm over you now." He studies me, still smiling. I go on. "Seriously, I know we're just friends. I know we're not ever gonna be, you know, like that."

He reaches out his hand to me, and I hold my breath. I freeze as he tucks a stray strand of my wavy, frizzy locks behind my ear.

"Not yet, Bambi. Not yet." I remain frozen as he gets in his truck, still smiling like he's won the lottery, and drives away.

I rush inside and rip down the Shep sign, screaming a howl of frustration.

Not yet?

I don't know what he means when he keeps saying that, but I know one thing: I am not sitting around pining anymore, just waiting to be picked by a guy. I avoid Shep the rest of the semester.

CHAPTER 5

16 YEARS AGO
TULSA, OKLAHOMA

I feel different this year. Older and wiser. Not just because I kissed two different boys over the summer. The kisses were not especially thrilling, but they were interesting. The second kiss even turned into my first makeout session, and Josh Houston touched my boob over my shirt. It was all right, but we immediately stopped and both of us freaked out. I mean, we were at church camp. We both went to the altar that night and repented. I haven't talked to Josh since.

I starred in a summer play at the civic center, I finally beat my mother at Scrabble, and I got really tan for the first time. It takes dedication to get a nice tan if you're naturally on the pasty side. And I did it. So I was excited for this. Ready.

But mostly this summer, I watched people. Girls at camp, boys at the pool, even my own sisters and my parents. People are fascinating.

I'm watching them now. I thought I'd burst into this party— my first high school pool party—ready to show off my slightly bigger chest and much darker skin to . . . no one in particular. Susan's graduated, I'm on my own, and I'm not a little freshman anymore.

But there he is.

I'm frozen, watching the backyard through the kitchen window.

It's no surprise he's surrounded. There are two other players with him and maybe, what, ten girls? Cute girls of all shapes and sizes, in various styles of sexy swimsuits. One tries to splash Shep, and he throws her in. She pretends to mind. Another does the same exact move, loving his attention as he picks her up and hurls her into the water.

Two girls are off to the side tanning. They are not blatantly throwing themselves at the guys, but their glances give away that they are hoping their indifference is noticed. Eventually it is, by some other dudes. I can see the girls are disappointed. They wanted Shep. Everyone does.

Shep is laughing and talking. He ribs the other guys, and I can tell he's making jokes. He's also drinking a beer, it looks like. I guess there aren't any parents here.

But mostly, he's flirting. This is next-level flirting. I can almost see teenage hormones floating around in the air above the pool water. Shep's green eyes bounce around from girl to girl, while every girl's eyes stay glued to him. I roll mine as I shake my head.

If I go out there right now, I'll end up taking my tank and shorts off. I know it. I'll want his attention. At the least, I'll try to fake indifference; at worst, I'll swim right up to Shep, try to flirt, fail, then get jealous and annoyed. Maybe even hurt. I don't want to be one of Shep's admirers. I don't particularly want to hurt today. I've had a summer without much hurt, and it's been nice enough.

Shep gets out of the pool and walks over to the drink table near the kitchen window. Two girls follow and start chatting him up. He loves it. He shines in the spotlight of all that attention. He doesn't need more.

Just as I've made up my mind, his eyes find mine through the glass. His eyebrows raise a smidge, and his smile widens. I can tell he's thinking of coming in to get me.

I turn around and leave.

——

It's the third week of school when I really see him up close for the first time this year. He's yelled at me in the halls and smirked at me up in the stands, but today he seems to be . . . waiting for me? Outside the choir room? With his brother?

He pushes himself up off the wall where he was leaning. "When you gonna get your own car, Bambi?" Buck stands too, mimicking Shep's every move. I bet Buck doesn't even realize he does it. But why wouldn't he? Who wouldn't want to be like Shep Riggs?

I try not to show how excited I am to talk to him. "That's not my name, Poteau."

"Need a ride?"

"Yeah . . . how'd you know I would be here?"

"Didn't." He gives me his full, stop-hearts-and-drop-panties smile. "Heard you singin' in there."

I smile wide right back at him.

"D'you have a good summer?" he asks as he opens the door out to the parking lot for me.

I nod. "Did you?"

He shrugs. "Football conditioning, mostly." Something sad passes over his face. It's quick, but I don't miss it. I also don't like it. So, teasing it is.

"You're slower this year."

He stops walking. "I'm sorry, what now?"

"You heard me. All those big muscles are too heavy, slowing you down." I start walking. Buck walks with me, smiling and saying not a word. Shep takes a few beats before he catches up. His smirk is back.

"I'm faster than I've *ever* been." I roll my eyes, and he goes on. "Must be paying awful close attention, though, huh, Bambi?"

My smile evaporates as we reach his truck. "I hate it when you call me that!"

"I know."

"Just like you know you *are* a few seconds slower this year and you better fix it if you want to take us all the way to state, bigshot." I jab the words at him. He makes me so mad!

Buck gets in the back seat, waiting for us to finish our tiff.

"Us, huh? You hear that, Buck? Sounds like a big-time football fan to me." Shep pauses his hand on the gear, staring at me with satisfaction.

"Ughhhh you are so annoying! I don't care about stupid football!"

"Oh no, you said *us*. You're invested. You gonna come to all the games then? You gonna cheer for me?"

"The last thing you need is more cheerleaders, Shep."

"I do get my fill." He wags his eyebrows at me.

"Gross."

He just laughs. "Come on, come and boo at me then."

"Maybe." I look away so I don't smile. He wants me at his games. He starts the truck and turns up Rascal Flatts. He turns it back down again.

"You wanna ride with us, you gotta sing along to the radio."

My head snaps back to him. "I didn't even ask for a ride!"

"Still you're in here now, and I'm 'fraid I'll have to throw you out if you don't follow the rules, so . . ." He stares at me while he turns the knob a fraction.

Of course, because he wants me to, I sing.

———

For weeks, almost every day, I've caught rides home from school with Shep and his little brother. We sing, we make fun of each other, we laugh so hard I snort. I bring them snacks, and Shep tells me what weird fantasy, thriller, and sci-fi books I should read next. Buck is quiet, eclipsed by his brother, just like the rest of us.

I don't flirt or linger with the beautiful wide receiver who's become my personal driver. I'm too grossed out by the throng of girls that follow him around the school. I've seen him give sexy eyes to various cheerleaders and pom dancers. I've heard he's dated a few of them over the summer and even more than one girl in the short time since school's started.

So, I'm Shep's friend. And he's mine.

A couple times, he's been quiet. It's unsettling. Life for Shep Riggs is nothing if not a fun, happy ride. When he's quiet, I'm quiet. If I asked him questions, he would just make a joke.

One day, he shows up at school with a black eye. He tells the whole school he fought with a player from our rival team at a late-night tussle at Sonic.

I am pretty sure I know the truth. When I climb into his truck, I don't look at him right away. "Fight at Sonic, huh?"

He doesn't answer. I know I'm right. He doesn't want to lie to me, but he doesn't want to tell me his dad roughs him up. I turn up the radio and sing loudly, obnoxiously, until he chuckles and joins in. I turn and whack Buck in the leg, and even he sings with us.

———

That Friday night, for the first time ever, he texts me. Shep texts me! It's late at night, which adds to the excitement. He's in his bed thinking about me. I open the message.

> You read-E for ME yet BAMB-E? lol
> Bam Bam
> Bambinooooo
> Shit, I should have called you a lil sheep
> Baaaaa
> Get it? Like sheep and shepherd?
> Like I watch over you?
> Would've been smartr
> I'm such a moron

I call him. He answers right away.

"Bambiiiiiiii."

I hear his voice on the phone but also, outside? I rush to my window. There he is. His truck is almost diagonal in our driveway, still running. He's stumbled out, his driver's-side door hanging open. I rush downstairs.

"Shep? Did you drive here?"

He burps. "Well, smarty pans. I'm here. And my trucksss here, so you do the . . . the . . ."

"The math?"

THINGS I WROTE ABOUT

"Yes! You're so smart. I wish I's as smarts you."

"You are smart, Shep. Quit acting like you're not. You need to go home."

His happy face falls.

"I can't go home like this," he whispers. "Like him. I can't. I can't!" His voice breaks on the last word. I see so much pain and shame and anger flash across his perfect face, I almost don't recognize him at all.

"Okay, then, come on."

I am not thinking clearly as I try to guide Shep into the entryway of my house. For one, he weighs ten thousand pounds. We stumble and fall, and he laughs as I shush him. I get him propped in the doorway before I run back out and turn off his truck, lock it, and come back inside. When I do, I find Shep facedown on the couch in my living room.

I cover him with a throw blanket and consider what to do next. I tuck a stray hair from his face, enjoying the fact that I get to touch him, to take care of him. Then I remember that I'm standing in my living room with an underage drunk boy.

I decide not to stay downstairs. Instead, I put a glass of water on the coffee table and a precautionary bucket near the couch and go to my room. I set an alarm for 5:00 A.M. so I can get said boy out of the house before my parents find him.

———

I tiptoe down the stairs. I did hit snooze a couple times, but the house is still silent. Which is why I almost jump out of my skin when I find my father in the kitchen. His eyes are about to fall right out of his head.

He whisper-yells at me, "Sadie Lynette. You better have a very good reason for why Shep Riggs is passed out on my couch smelling like a distillery!"

"He drove here last night, I let him in, that's all. He needed a place to sleep it off."

"Why didn't he sleep it off on his own couch?"

I shift my weight and stare at the floor, looking for the right words. "Did you see he has a black eye?"

"I heard. From some fight with a rival team?"

"No, Dad. Not from a rival team." I stare at my father until he nods in understanding.

There are rumors the next Monday morning that the police paid a visit to Shep's house about "the big fight at Sonic." I know the truth. Dad is friends with the sheriff, and I saw the look in his eyes over the weekend. But I don't have a chance to ask Shep about it during the day.

That afternoon, when we pull into my driveway after school, my father is waiting for us. He walks up to Shep's door as I'm climbing out. Shep rolls down his window, and I'm pretty sure I catch him swallow. Buck clears his throat and appears to shrink into the back seat.

My dad gives him a serious glare. "You boys like spaghetti?"

"Yessir."

"We've made too much, come in and join us." My dad starts to walk away from the truck. It wasn't an invitation; it was an order.

The boys obediently climb out of the truck and onto our front porch. As they reach the door, my dad covers the open doorway with his arm. Buck looks down while Shep looks my father in the eye. Dad is a bit taller and has a lot of weight on Shep, even if it's not all muscle like it used to be back in his own football days.

"No drinking, no smoking, no going upstairs here, at all, ever. You got me, Riggs?"

"Yessir."

"I expect you for dinner often. My wife will be offended if she makes extra for you two and you don't show. You don't want to offend my beautiful wife, do you?"

"No, sir."

Dad lowers his arm and then stops them again. "I mean it, do not go upstairs. If the downstairs bathrooms are full, you hold it. The girls are in there doing God knows what—you *still* hold it. You leave or you hold it till you explode and die. *Death* is better for you than going upstairs in my house, you understand me?"

Shep nods. My dad makes a point of catching Buck's eyes too, and Buck also nods. They all look so awkward. I'm not sure how the boys feel about it until Dad finally drops his arm. Shep shuffles behind, and as Buck walks up to the door, he smiles the biggest smile I've ever seen on his scrawny face.

My eyes fill with proud, bittersweet tears that I don't let fall.

KELSEY HUMPHREYS

CHAPTER 6

1 MONTH AGO
THE CARIBBEAN

Sam: Who's coming kayakiiiiiing

Sam: [Selfie]

Skye: I was trapped making small talk with an acquaintance for two hours last night. I have done my duty and I will not see any of you today. Sorry not sorry.

Susan: I have three children.

Sally: omw

Sam: YAS Thank you, Sal!

Sam: Sadie?

Sam: . . . Sadie????

Me: Um I'm sorry, were you all not there last night? My ass is still throbbing!

Sam: [Anxious emoji]

Sam: Please come anyway? [Puppy eyes emoji]

Skye: Oh I was there and I have been replaying it in my mind over and over. The clang, the awkward silence, your toast at the end. Glorious.

Me: [Middle finger emoji]

Susan: You have to put that in one of your books. It was hysterical.

Me: Ugh! Why can't I be the introvert this time?

Skye: That position has been filled.

Susan: And if anyone gets to take her place for a day, again, I have three boys [Raising hand emoji]

Sam: Please, I'm worried no one is going to come do the excursions I planned!

Me: Fine

I wait as long as possible before heading to the beach. Once I get close, past the lawn chairs and flanked by gorgeous ocean and perfect palms, I spot him. He hasn't seen me yet, so I pause and give myself a moment. The group is milling about getting ready for instruction, as if on a happy vacation.

I guess they are. It's just me who's dying by the minute. I can't look away. Damn his bright blond hair. If only it had turned a muddy brown with age, or maybe gray. If only he'd let himself go. If only a lot of things.

Time to get that grip you keep letting go of, girl!

"You all right, gorgeous?" a buttery voice says from behind me.

"Benedict!" I smile at Emerson's younger brother. He has the same hot Henry Cavill vibes as Emerson, but where his brother comes off as cold and closed, Benedict is warm and open. A little too warm and open, even.

"Again, it's Ben, please," he purrs in his lovely British accent.

"But Benedict is so much more fun to say. *Benedict!*"

He tilts his head. "Have you been drinking?"

I groan through my smile. "I wish."

"It's almost noon on holiday, I can go grab you something?" His big blue eyes are sincere.

I shake my head. "I'm okay, thanks."

I start walking past the stacked beach chairs and equipment huts along the beach toward where our group is gathered. Benedict matches my slow pace as I watch the staff pull all the kayaks out onto the sand. After a few steps, he clears his throat. "It's all right if you're not . . . not okay. Emerson filled me in a bit."

"Ah." I look away.

Ben and I have hung out with our engaged siblings a few times, but it's still awkward. I wouldn't call him a close friend. I also wouldn't call him uninterested. He's tried to flirt with me, but I've shut him down each time.

"It's a right shame. I wanted to shoot my shot this week, but I don't suppose you'll want to muck about with a *third* grooms-man, yeah?"

I startle at his honesty. "No, um, I don't think I do . . . charming as he may be."

"That one's a twat, though, really." Benedict shoves his firm jaw toward Shep in the distance. "Wanker didn't even help you up last night—just stood there."

I smile. As much as I want to pile on, I should keep things civil. "He's . . . just Shep."

"Want to try to rile him up a bit?" Ben offers his elbow to me like an olden-time escort.

I feel a sparkle in my eye to match my friend's. "Always."

"Oh, good. Cocky bastard has been riding my nerves. Now laugh like I'm positively hilarious," he mutters into my ear as we get close to the group. I do as instructed, easily. Because it is fun-ny. Billionaire playboy Benedict Clark wants to help me make football's Shep Riggs jealous. And it doesn't feel that out of the norm for me. What a weird life.

I feel Shep's eyes on us as we approach. So I glance at him with a small, polite nod. This isn't high school. He knows I can sense him watching, just like I know he physically registers my hand tucked through another man's arm, even though he won't look down at it. It's just how we are.

The instructor interrupts my thoughts.

"Hello, everyone! I am Rocko. It's very important that while you're on the island, you please stay in the areas marked as public beaches, please. We have alligators, jellyfish, stingrays, and sharks—we don't want anyone to get eaten!" he jokes, and we all chuckle. "I will be your guide today in front and Marta at the back of the group. We will go along the coast into the cove and turn and come back. Please do not go outside of the cove, again, please, nobody die. I don't want to get fired." He smiles, and we all laugh again. He's good.

"You can leave all your belongings here at the hut and then pick a kayak. Please only one person per kayak, as two people will make you sink and again, die. No dying. I very much enjoy this job! Please, thank you!"

As Rocko walks toward the edge of the beach, everyone begins to ditch their shirts and cover-ups. I mean, I think everyone does. I only see one shirt come off, and I'm grateful I chose my oversize, extra-dark sunglasses today.

Because holy unfair crap on a hot tight cracker.

Shep Riggs is every bit as fit as he was when we . . . when he was still playing ball. How can he still look twenty-three? No. He looks better than twenty-three. *Lord, is this some sort of punishment? I'm calling uncle down here!*

He is bulky and hot and tan. He still has tan lines, like he always did. He's a man's man. His tan isn't from a booth or a bed, like some of the Hollywood types I've been with.

He's stocky, thick. He's not "lean perfection" like most of the men in my books. My male main characters are written with swimmers' bodies, or runners' builds, because that's what my readers like. Most of my readers would say Shep is too much.

They're wrong.

Very wrong.

I fight the urge to shake my head clear. Instead, my reflex is to subtly tense one hand, just barely. I slip out of my shorts as I gather my wits. I keep my loose, long-sleeve, dry-fit swim shirt on. I do not want to be perused by anyone present, or the rays of the sun.

I didn't know until I was around celebrities myself, all their secrets. One of which is that in person, up close, many of them are albino white. Translucent white. They stay young-looking because at eighteen, when they make it big, their agents keep them out of the sun for the rest of their lives. Hence my layers of sunscreen, long-sleeve shirt, and massive sun hat. I have a tan, of course, but from a professional airbrush artist.

I don't think Shep noticed me ogle him, but he's being plenty obvious about his own ogling. But not of me. Which is totally, absolutely fine. He eyes Janie, who honestly is ogle-worthy. Her dark skin holds the kinds of perfectly proportioned curves I thought about buying after my second film deal. Maybe I should have.

I watch Shep approach her with his signature swagger. He extends a hand. "Hi, I don't think we've met. I'm Shep."

Janie looks him over and opens her mouth. She closes it. She opens it again. "No."

She walks away.

!

What! I fight the urge to laugh. *Way to go, Janie! New bestie! I love you!* I make a mental note to tell Skye all about this later. She's Skye's best friend, not mine. She and I aren't even close! I know Sam and Skye have probably told her the extent of what little they know, but I couldn't have asked for a better reaction.

Shep isn't fazed. His smile remains intact as he walks behind her. The thought of all that she knows about him, about us, quickly kills my smile. I watch everyone walk to the shore, Emerson smiling at Sam, and Janie, Kat and Sally grouping up. No Dennis today, thankfully. *I appreciate that, Lord, but I'd have rather you made Shep turn fat, if I'm being honest.*

"C'mon, Sade, quit watching us like a creepo!" Sam calls from the water. I laugh and hustle to the water's edge. This portion of the resort's beach is on a peninsula, so all I can see is the bright turquoise sea in every direction. Shep is a ways down the perfect white sand, pushing his orange kayak in. He glances in my direction, so I slide up beside Ben.

"Here, let me," Ben says almost loudly, as he pushes a boat in and holds it steady for me.

"Oh, thanks." I smile up at him. He looks amazing too, now that I take the time to notice. Like a character I would write myself, he's tall, lean, chiseled. Light brown hair and striking blue eyes like Emerson. He's not doing anything for me, though. As if anyone in the entire universe could distract me from the blond wall of muscle currently sneaking looks in my direction. Not even Dennis could, if he were here. Still, I'm glad he's not. *So awkward.*

We all get settled into our tiny boats and start to move through the brilliant, shallow water. The kayak is easy enough to maneuver, and I enjoy the exertion. The coastline becomes lush and untouched as we move around the edge of the peninsula to a different section of island. Marta, just behind Ben and me, plays island music from a little Bluetooth speaker on her boat, and a breeze floats over the shallow water.

It's lovely.

We're led off the main coastline into the cove we were told about, and I can't help but gasp. It's like going back in time.

We're no longer at a beach—we're in a jungle. The tall palms have been taken over by thick brush and swinging vines. I've never seen anything like it outside of a movie screen. I should definitely write something set here. It's giving me lagoon vibes, maybe a modern shipwreck scenario? I don't realize that I've stopped rowing.

Sally, way ahead of me, breaks apart my little moment.

"Ugh, I'm not waiting for all you old fogies! Rocko and I are outta here!"

"Who you calling fogies?" Shep yells back from just ahead of my kayak. He and Ben are right in front of me. Both of them must've slowed their pace on my account. Or maybe they're also lost in admiration. The way they both begin to speed up again, eyeing each other, makes me doubt that.

I speed up too, but I also watch the testosterone on display.

"That all you got, Prince Ben?" Shep says, starting to pull away.

Ben laughs. "Hell, man, not everything is a competition."

Shep stops rowing quite a way from Ben, clearly the winner, and twists his boat. His smirk is ridiculous. "Aw, don't feel bad, Benny Boy. I'm a professional."

"Oh, do a lot of rowing as a lawyer, Shep?" I ask. It slips out before I can help it.

And I stepped right into it, because his smile widens as he straightens up his posture and flexes. He actually flexes like a teen taking a selfie. Only Shep.

"No, but does it look like I have a plain ole desk job?"

I let him have it. He wants me to get embarrassed, to fake indifference, to react in some big way. So I don't. I give him a genuine, friendly smile—not sexual, just honest. I raise my brows and shake my head. "No, you most definitely do not."

For a second, he falters. Anyone else wouldn't have caught it. But I'm me and he's Shep, and I can see that by complimenting him, I've taken the wind from his sails. He wants me to be tied up in knots. I'm not anymore. Not visibly, anyway.

Ha! I win this round!

The thought leaves me as quickly as it arrives, because in the next breath, Marta's speaker blares out a country song. I don't even recognize the tune. I just hear a male voice drawl a word, and a guitar note bends.

It doesn't matter the singer or the track. My heart literally hurts for a beat. It takes control to keep from touching my sternum. I don't listen to country music for this reason.

Sometimes a breakup steals an artist or a song, maybe a few albums. When Shep broke me, I lost an entire genre.

Shep's bright expression returns. "Well, feel free to enjoy the view." He twists his kayak back and begins to move away. Did he see my chest heave? Did my face fall at the sound of the music? Did I react?

It's all right if I did. It is. It's fine to remember the pain, it's fine for him to know I still feel pangs of grief. Grief sticks with us. I know he knows that. As long as he doesn't think I am still in love with him, everything is fine. I'm fine.

So fine that when the song changes to "Cruise" by Florida Georgia Line, I sing along. Shep is quite a bit ahead of me now, but he stops rowing. For a few seconds, at the sound of my voice over the water, every beautiful tendon in his back pulls taut.

I don't stop singing the song, but it hurts. I'm a masochist. Because it kills me to sing and it kills me again that he reacts to my singing. Is he hurting too? Shocked? Angry again, and if so, why? Why the hell is he still so angry?

I just want it all to stop aching already. It's been almost ten years. Ten. Damn. Years.

"You have a lovely voice, Sadie." Ben gawks at me. I totally forgot he was kayaking by my side.

"Oh, thanks."

"If the little writing thing you're trying doesn't pan out, you should definitely give singing a go," he jokes.

I laugh hard, letting out some of my trapped emotion. "I'll keep that in mind."

I don't sing anymore during the excursion.

Maybe the pain is over. Maybe that was the worst of it for the week—swelling choruses that brought me to tears again and again behind my sunglasses. I haven't been this weepy since living with Lorelei for those few horrible months. Maybe Shep isn't mad at all.

The look of pure vitriol he gives me when I climb out of my kayak begs to differ.

Game *not* over.

KELSEY HUMPHREYS

CHAPTER 7

Shep is a constant at our house now. Buck is around too, but not as often. The boys eat all our food, stink up our living room, and fill our TV with sports. My sisters don't love it. I do.

As does my dad. I think he feels like he won the lottery. He and Shep talk football so much I wonder how they don't tire of it. Dad gives Shep advice and surprisingly, the superstar receiver listens and asks questions. It's the only time I see him serious. I listen, watch, and learn as much as I can.

It's amazing how interesting a sport becomes if you fall in love with a player. I care about football now. I care a lot.

I think my mother also likes having the boys around. She mothers them, in her own way. One day she turned to Shep and said, "Your brother's clothes have gotten too small. Give him more of yours." She handed him a big bag. "You take these."

Shep's mask faded for a moment. He hesitated but finally just said, "Yes, ma'am."

She also chimes in about football. She explains the statistical odds and the records of Shep's plays as well as other receivers like him. Shep and Buck love peppering her with questions. She knows a million data points. My mother, the logical, serious, renowned surgeon, cares about football. She fell in love with a player too.

She turns to me one night after the boys leave and looks me in the eye.

"Shep reminds me so much of your father."

"Oh yeah?" I ask her nervously, trying not to display any feelings.

"And you remind me of me."

"I do? You're joking." I almost snort at the idea. My mother left for college early and finished her undergrad degree in three years, then blew through med school. She is an actual genius.

Meanwhile, I'm thinking of becoming a theater major.

"You know I don't really joke," she deadpans at me. She's being funny in her own quirky way.

I am probably the closest to my mother, even if I'm the emotional one of the family. Susan and Sam are more like Dad, outgoing, bubbly. They're emotional but in a sunny way. A way that bounces back quickly.

Skye and I are emotional in a more serious way. Skye is withdrawn, thoughtful. I am the most volatile. Passionate. Sally is still little but notably smarter than she should be for a four-year-old. She'll probably end up being the most like Mom.

"I am serious, Sadie. Yes, you're a bit too emotional, and of course you're much *much* better with people than I am. But you are brilliant and you watch, you study. I did that too. Maybe you should be a psychologist."

"Huh." I could be a psychologist. Maybe I should. I think a psychologist might tell my mother there's no such thing as *too emotional.* She pulls me back to our conversation with his name.

"And Shep, he is a good-looking boy, isn't he?"

I refuse to make eye contact with her. "Yeah, I guess."

"He is. I see how you look at him. And he looks at you too."

My eyes snap to hers. I'm taken aback. I thought I had been shutting down my feelings pretty well since I ripped down that stupid sign in my room. When things get crazy in my brain, I put my thoughts on paper. I hope no one ever reads that hot-mess express bound by a metal spiral I keep under my pillow. But I guess my looks have been giving me away? Also, did she just say he looks at me too? I start to smile.

"But wait, Sadie. You're young, but you love so big, my girl. You feel things so strongly. You're so serious, like me. And he . . . he's just a boy." She puts a hand on mine across the kitchen island. "Hold on to your big love and see if he's worth it. He has football right now. He has friends and parties and probably many girls. Wait until Shep Riggs becomes a man."

She gives my hand a squeeze and leaves me alone with a million thoughts.

———

The spring fills me with dread. Shep is leaving soon. He's achieved one of his lifelong dreams. Division I football. He's decided to play for the Sooners, down in Norman. It's only about two hours from here, but it'll feel like an eternity away. I'm grateful he didn't choose Alabama, because one, yuck. Everyone who isn't an Alabama fan has to hate Alabama with their entire being. It's a rule in flyover country. And two, he'd be even farther away.

But I don't think the physical distance even matters. He's going to be long gone.

And with every week, we've gotten closer. He's my best friend, and I know I'm his. He's come to all my shows at school and at the civic center. He's run lines with me, listened to me sing auditions in his truck. He's helped me watch my little sisters, always bringing gummy bears for Sally, and even letting Samantha paint his nails like it's his favorite pastime.

We sing karaoke and watch Susan's latest '90s movie obsession. He has even caught me doodling in my journal. At the time, I was writing greeting card ideas. I read him a couple, and he said I could write a whole line of cards someday.

I watch tape with him, quiz him on stats, and listen to his theories about plays and strategy. I watch sports movies and even read a few athlete biographies he recommended. I sing him songs and make him laugh and really go anywhere and do anything he wants me to.

I know that I'm too attached to him. On the days that he hangs out with me, I'm ecstatic. On the days we don't see each other, I'm depressed. I feel like my existence is wrapped up in him and his thoughts and feelings. Does he, please God, love me underneath our friendship? Does he dream about me? What's he doing, and who is he doing it with, on the nights I don't hear from him?

The only times he pulls away are the nights I know he's sad and angry because of things we don't discuss. He skips dinner at our house on those nights or eats quickly and leaves early. I know he goes off to party. I always hear rumors the following week. Drunk Shep this and Horny Shep that. When he drinks, he drinks too much. One day, I tell him so.

"You treat your body like a temple until there's alcohol around." His smirk fades, but he doesn't reply. So I push him. "Does it do any good? Do you feel any better?"

"I don't feel anything. That's the point." He's curt. It's unusual, and it stings. But I soften, knowing he must really be hurting to be so raw with me.

"I'm sorry, Shep, I know he—"

"Don't do that." His whole face tightens, darkens. "Don't you pity me like I'm the first punk kid from nowhere whose dad jerks him around. Big deal. You're right, I do drink too much. And it's got nothing to do with him. That's on me, just me!" He actually yells at me.

"Well, then quit it, you idiot!" I yell right back.

"Fine!"

"Fine!" I hop out of his truck, slamming the door. He doesn't stay for dinner.

That night, I get a text.

Shep: You're my best friend, Bambi.
Me: Please stop calling me that.
Shep: Never.

———

The next few weeks feel . . . tense. I catch Shep staring at me, just smiling like he knows something I don't. He's ecstatic about OU, but he's beyond senioritis. He doesn't care about classes or graduation. Maybe all that is making him lose his mind a little bit.

He must be losing it, because I'm looking down at the gym floor and suddenly he's in the middle of it. During a wrestling state finals assembly that he has absolutely nothing to do with. He sits on a chair one of his skirt-clad harem bring over to him. A mike stand appears . . . what the heck?

Then someone brings out a guitar?

What is happening!

Shep strums the guitar, but the amp isn't plugged in. He makes a duh gesture and then plugs it in and strums again. There is a terrible screeching feedback sound for a minute. Everyone laughs, but Shep doesn't care at all.

"Y'all shut up, it took me forever to learn this," he says, talking into the mike but looking down at the guitar in his hands. I am so confused, wondering if this is a football stunt? A senior prank? Why didn't he tell me about it?

"K, now I only know the chorus and I'm not very good, but I'll have Tug and Biggie flatten anyone who laughs at me." Someone laughs. "Guys, that kid right there!" He points into the crowd, and Shep's giant linebacker friends, who are actually total softies under all that muscle, play along convincingly enough that the whole gym dies down. The entire school population watches.

And Shep sings.

Shep Riggs plays clumsy chords and sings the chorus to "She's Everything" by Brad Paisley. He's got an okay voice and he's always been able to carry a tune. The key is how confident he is. He could sing every note wrong, and no one would care. When he ends the final chord, he looks right at me.

"So, Sadie, you gonna go to prom with me?"

The gym erupts.

I can't hear a thought. Annie and the other girls around me are shoving me, screaming. I'm smiling and shaking my head at how hard everyone else is swooning. You'd think he just asked all the mat maids to go with him the way they're literally back-flipping all around the gym.

"Say yes, Sadie Lyn!" he yells over the crowd.

"That's not my name, you redneck," I call back, high on the thrill of it all.

"That sounded like a yes to me. That sound like a yes to y'all?" he asks his adoring fans. The gym erupts again. He stares at me, and finally I nod.

He runs to me, climbing over rows and rows of people. Really just being a total jerk, stepping on people's stuff like nothing matters. But he's so happy and fun to watch, no one minds. Including me. He picks me up in a bear hug and then hoists me up onto his shoulder, like I'm a trophy he's carrying. I'd be embarrassed except his hands hold me so tight, I really don't care who's looking or what they think.

It's basically the best moment of my life.

———

"Shep Riggs, are you *nervous* right now?" I tease as we move through my living room to take photos with our prom group in the backyard. He tugs at the classic black bowtie around his neck. He looks even more amazing in a tuxedo than I imagined. And I spent an embarrassing amount of time imagining this night.

I chose a silky, sparkly, dark purple gown that hugs my figure. I have my hair in a low updo with a few wisps of hair around my face. I chose black shoes and a clutch and a pin for the side of my hair. He has a purple pocket square my mom found for him.

We look perfect together.

"You'd be nervous too if you just got that lecture from your daddy. I think he's gonna kill me at the end of the night no matter what. I might not even dance with you."

"You better, I could've gone with Josh, you know. He was going to ask. He has a crush on me."

Shep stops us and peers down at me. He looks almost serious. "You got a crush on him?"

My head rears back in surprise. He's genuinely asking me. "No."

"Good. I don't want to have to beat up some little junior on my prom night."

I giggle. "Um, he's taller than you, Shep."

He squints his eyes at me. "He's a dry spaghetti noodle, Sadie. I could snap him in half with my pinky."

I just laugh as he moves us out into the yard. For the first time, Shep holds my hand. Fingers linked and everything. Like a couple. My palm tingles. So does my heart.

We eat, we take pictures, we laugh. He dances crazy with the football players. We dance some fast dances together. A million girls try to dance around him and with him, but he shrugs them off. He doesn't try to do any bumping and grinding with me. I wouldn't want to. I mean, I do want to. I want to feel him behind me like that. I want to feel him everywhere. But not here, with half the school.

For the slow songs, he usually pulls me to the side for a drink or cake or to talk. I try not to obsess about it. I fail. Why won't he slow dance with me?

Toward the end of the night, the Brad Paisley song, our Brad Paisley song, comes on. Finally, at last, he leads me to the dance floor. He puts his hands on my waist, and I die. I'm dying. I'm going to die right here, right now.

"You're so pretty, Sade," he says, shortening my name like he does when it's just us. When we're talking about football or music, or arguing about something silly. It makes the tingles start again in my chest. I smile and I'm about to say thank you, and then I hear him curse under his breath. He suddenly breaks our hold. He takes my hand and leads me out of the ballroom of the event space the school rented.

I'm crushed. We danced for maybe ten seconds. I would pout, except confusion takes over. He walks me past the lobby, all the way out to the parking lot. Then he keeps walking, straight through the lot, to the front entrance of the event center. There's a little fountain in the middle of a circle drive, and he walks us right up to it.

He turns to me.

"Sorry," he pants.

My breath is ragged too. "What's wrong?"

His smirk returns. "Nothing's wrong, Sade. I just wasn't about to have our first kiss on the dance floor in front of everybody."

My eyebrows fly up into my updo. "Our what?"

He takes my face in his hands and gives me the smile he knows I can't refuse. "You heard me." He leans in slowly and whispers, "Finally." My eyes close, and he tilts my head with his hands. His lips are everything I thought they'd be. Firm yet soft. He's gentle, but his hands shake. He pushes my mouth open with his tongue, and I moan.

Shep Riggs is kissing me!

My whole body dissolves. His tongue is the only thing keeping me alive. It pushes and pulls. He sucks and groans and then pulls away.

"I waited, Sade, I held off as long as I could. Be with me, Bambi. Be mine." He kisses me again before I can answer. Something about the way he says the words dampens the sparks I'm feeling.

Why did he hold off? What has he been waiting for? I don't understand.

And *waiting* seems rather generous, since just a month ago I overheard a drill team girl discussing how her mouth had been intimate with parts of him that I've only ever dreamed about. A month ago, I died in that stall, hearing her brag.

I squeeze my eyes shut, blocking out that girl's voice. And my mother's warnings. He feels my resistance. He pulls away and looks me in the eyes with his brows knit together.

"What?" His grip on my face tightens slightly, but I start to shake it away. "Why are you shaking your head, Sadie?"

"No, Shep."

He waits, then realizes I'm saying no to him. No to being his. He takes a step back, angry. Shocked.

"No? What are you talking about! Seriously?" He looks up at the stars.

My voice is thin, but it comes out. "C'mon, Shep, think about it. You're leaving for summer training in just a few weeks."

He looks back at me, his eyes blaring. "Yeah, so?"

"So, you're going to be playing division one football, Shep! This is your dream, this is it. Your shot at the NFL, everything you want."

"And?"

"And what, you're gonna spend the few spare minutes you have, which will be, like, none, driving two hours to see your little high school girlfriend?"

He doesn't argue with me, and that's when I know I'm right.

"You gonna skip the team parties? Ignore the cheerleaders and sorority girls who follow you everywhere? To come back home all the time?"

He looks down, and his shoulders deflate. Fresh anger sparks in him, though, and he straightens and turns to me. "Yes, Sadie. Yes, I will."

"No, Shep, you won't." His lips form a flat line as he inhales. I don't care if he's angry, or if I shouldn't put my heart on the line. I have to say this. "Shep, I know it's crazy, but I want you for real. I want you forever. If we get together, that's it for me, you're it."

He rushes to put his hands on my waist. "You're it for me too, Sade. This *is* it, this *is* for real."

Tears gather on the edges of my vision, but I force myself to keep talking. "We both know I'll wait for you. I'll be sitting, waiting, hoping, and pining away and . . . and you'll break my heart, Shep."

"I won't! I won't, Sadie. I could never hurt you. You're . . ." He takes my face in his hand again as his voice breaks. "You're my person, Sade. You're my best friend."

"I know, Shep, but this time, *you're* not ready for *me*."

He sucks in a deep, rough breath. But he doesn't argue anymore. It kills me. It kills me that I'm right. I cry, and he holds me. I hear him sniff. He strokes my back and grips me tight. Eventually, he takes me home and hugs me hard again at the door.

I know I did the smart thing. I know I just saved myself years of being strung along. Years of limbo, years of heartache.

I just underestimate how many years.

CHAPTER 8

15.5 YEARS AGO
TULSA, OKLAHOMA

SHEP

Damn it! I punch the steering wheel of my piece-of-shit truck. *Do not cry, you punk-ass little bitch. Do not!*

Tears well anyway, so I growl in frustration and turn up the radio. I really do not want to go home. I hate it there. Course, I would hate anywhere right now.

This is not how any of this was supposed to go. I punch the steering wheel again, making the horn honk for a second.

I did everything right.

I waited until I could be serious, could be ready. I waited until prom, to make it special. I even took every ounce of strength in my body and waited until her song came on so it would be romantic and all that girly crap.

I held off until we were older, until her dad could see I was a man, a worthy man. I got a full ride to OU for shit's sake! I kept my grades up. I kept an eye on my brother. I kept an eye on her.

All day every day for four years, and now what? Now I go back to, what, being her friend? Her buddy?

I'm gonna be sick.

I see you, boy, hanging out with that fancy family. You think you'll ever be good for one of the mighty Jon Canton's pretty girls? You think because you can throw a ball around you're one of them?

I let the thoughts play through. Normally, I block his words out, but why fight it? Turns out he was right all along anyway.

You're nothing special. You're a project. A cute little sideshow for them to watch on Friday nights. You need to get your head out of the damned clouds, Shep. A princess doesn't get together with the gutter trash, son. Get it through your dumbass head.

I feel a sting like he's in the truck with me. He always hits me whenever he talks about my dumb head. And I am dumb. A tear escapes, and I hate myself that I let it fall. Thank God I'm getting out of here soon.

I had football and Sadie. That was it.

I guess one out of two ain't bad.

———

13.5 YEARS AGO
NORMAN, OKLAHOMA

I've heard lots of possible questions for God when we get to heaven. Right now, one I'm itching to ask is how, from the busy sidelines, with my helmet on, in a packed stadium with 88,000 people, do my eyes always find her? Did He do that to me? Is it the Holy Ghost? Is it a sign?

Whatever it is, it's annoying. Pisses me off something fierce. There were thousands and thousands of girls out there today, many of 'em with their eyes locked on me, and still all I could see was her.

And now, I'm looking for her like a damn puppy! *Get it together, Shep!*

I slow my steps as I make my way out of the back stadium doors. There's a gaggle of cheerleaders and fans waiting, so I make sure to greet every single one. The little boys in my jerseys are my favorite. I pick them up, rough them around, take selfies. Once I gave a kid in a wheelchair my actual team shirt off my back. It felt better than Christmas.

The Cantons are used to it, though, waiting on me. They hang back, smiling and watching like . . . well, like I'm family. I know better, though, deep down.

Still, I like saying hello. Today, Mr. Canton waits with his wife, the doc, and it looks like Sam and Skye came today. Skye must've hated it. And of course next to them, looking like God molded her just for me, is Sadie.

"Great game, Shep!" Jon says as I approach.

"That was your highest catch to date, the one in the fourth quarter. Did you know that?" Dr. Canton says with a grin.

"I didn't, ma'am. Guess that's somethin'," I say as Mr. Canton shakes my hand with a grip that reminds me he could probably still keep up with me in a fight. Maybe even win, if I'm having an off day.

"Can we take you to eat?" he asks.

"Ugh nooooo, let's go home already!" Skye groans. Samantha is jabbering on her phone, and Sadie just laughs at the two of them.

"No thanks, sir. You don't have to offer every time." I mean it. They don't have to keep doing this. I'm not sure why they do.

I watch Sadie's dad straighten and take a step back, seeming genuinely disappointed. "All right then. We'll see you in two weeks. Hell of a show, son." He gives Sadie a knowing look. "We'll let you know what restaurant your mother chooses."

Then it's just me and those bright teal eyes that look at me like they still love me. I take a deep breath.

"Let's hear it, then." I smile down at her, trying to stay relaxed as we walk along the concrete pathway under the stadium.

"Well, I mean, you're supposed to run *inside* that white line," Sadie finally says.

I laugh. "Motherf— You know that's literally only the second time I've stepped out of bounds in my college career!"

"*Literally*—oooo that's a big word. Four syllables, you okay?"

"Why do you wait in line just to bust my balls, girl?"

"Somebody has to, bigfoot! You're off your game." Her grin when she teases me makes my chest throb.

"Is that so? Kinda like how that final song was pitchy at your recital last week?" I jab back, and savor every second of the blush rushing up to her cheeks. She falters for a second. I actually make her speechless!

"Oh, like you would know if I was. How do you even know what pitchy means?" She huffs out the words, but I can tell I struck a nerve.

Not wanting to actually hurt her feelings, I confess. "I googled it."

Her spark returns. "You did?"

"Took me down a reeeal weird YouTube rabbit hole. I think I lost some of my hearing."

"Serves you right, googling stuff just to tease me." We walk in happy silence for a minute or so before she looks back at me. "I'm still super proud of you, footloose." She laughs and shoves a shoulder into me. That tiny bit of contact between us kills me. I'm angry again, just like that.

"Welp, I gotta meet up with the guys," I say, my tone sounding colder than I meant. She doesn't seem bothered by the change at all. She's just fine, as she says all right and gives me a lame-ass side hug and walks away. I fear for a moment that this is going to be my whole life—watching Sadie Canton walk away from me.

I shake it off and text my dudes. Enough moping. We won the game, and I had a few epic catches. It's time to friggin' party!

----

12 YEARS AGO
NORMAN, OKLAHOMA

Is that . . . Sadie?

"Hey, I'll catch up with you guys," I say to my teammates.

I almost missed her. We don't often run into each other on campus. She's on a bench under a naked tree. The day is gray and bitterly cold. She's so bundled up I can barely see her face, but I recognized her bright pink scarf. Plus, I just sensed her, was drawn to her, like always. Because God hates me.

"Sadie?"

She looks up at me, and as soon as she sees me, tears she was holding back break free. Seeing them streak her cheeks, I immediately see red. Sadie Canton gets upset, often, but never, *never* does she let herself cry. I squat down in front of her on the sidewalk. She looks so small under all her layers.

"Who am I fuckin' up, Sadie? I want a name."

She shakes her head and cries harder. I turn back to my friends and holler, "Q, Tug, get back here. Looks like we gotta go flatten somebody." I hear them hoot with glee and start running to where I crouch.

"No! No, it's not like that." She sniffs.

"It's the off season—we're just dying to pummel someone." I swallow and ball my fists. "Was it a guy?" The idea of anyone touching her makes my vision blur again, but I force the words out. "Just tell me who he is, right now."

"Shep, there's no one to flatten. No one hurt me."

I let out a sigh. "False alarm, boys," I yell to Q and Tug just as they get close. Their utter disappointment would be funny if I wasn't so worried about the girl in front of me. I sit on the bench next to her and wrap my arms around her tight. "What happened then?"

"It's stupid," she says between calming breaths.

"If you're crying about it, it's not stupid, Sade." I squeeze her shoulders.

"I just flubbed an audition, the first of many. I can't believe I'm crying over it."

"What else?" I push her for the truth.

She sucks in a shaky little breath. I hate the sound of it. "I didn't expect to get the lead or anything, but I didn't even get a part, and Marty, my professor, he was . . . ruthless."

"Welp, that's a name of a someone. I'm not above breaking a teacher's face." I grunt, meaning it. "Where can I find this Marty?"

"No, don't. He was right. He was mean, but he was right."

"Mean teacher. Even better." I pull away again, imagining the asshole's face in my head.

She puts a small, gloved hand on mine on her shoulder. "Shep, no, just . . . just stay with me?"

Stay with you? Always. Anytime. All the time. For the rest of time. I think a million painful thoughts, but I don't let any words out. Instead, I nod. Her hand leaves mine, but she puts her little beanie-clad head on my shoulder. I rack my brain about how I can help.

"Was it your uh, vibrato? No, falsetto. No head voice? Chest voice?"

She lets out a small laugh, and my chest puffs out. If anyone can make this girl feel better, it's me. She looks up and grins through her tears. "More googling?"

"Lil' bit."

"You're something else, Shep Riggs."

"And you're the best singer I've ever heard. And the best actress. Marty is an idiot. And a dead man walking if he makes you cry again."

"Right." She chuffs.

"I'm serious."

"Thanks, Shep. You're a good friend."

Any air left in my chest leaves me.

Friend.

I pull away. "You good now, Sadie Lyn?"

"Yeah, Poteau, I'm good."

"Good. I better go catch up with the guys."

I leave her, and it still hurts. Bad. I need something, someone to distract me. I know it won't last, won't heal me, but it helps, if only for a few hours. I tell Q to rally the troops and get a plan going. Girls, beer, games, the team. I keep hustling in the opposite direction of the tree and the bench and the girl, leaving my whole damn heart behind.

CHAPTER 9

11.5 YEARS AGO
NORMAN, OKLAHOMA

SADIE

I'm making too much of this. It's going to be nothing, just like the other times over the last four years, when I thought Shep would come back to me and then he didn't. He's just Shep, my childhood friend, my buddy. Why can't my heart—and shaking body—understand what my brain knows to be true?

He hasn't called me Bambi since that night, his senior prom.

I never knew how much I'd miss that.

Hasn't held my hand.

Our hugs have lingered, but he always pulls away first, giving me a polite, just-friends smile.

I've been at all his home games since he started playing, after his "red shirt" freshman year when he didn't play so he could play as a freshman in his second year. He's seen me in all my shows, sitting next to my parents, beaming with pride.

We text all the time, and he even calls sometimes after a really great win or terrible loss. Or if he's just bored. Or if he's had a run-in with his dad—I think. He doesn't say, but his tone is different. Sometimes I can tell he's been drinking, but normally he avoids me when he's partying.

Still, nothing.

This is like two years ago, over Christmas break. Shep and Buck were with us for a few meals, as always. I walked them out, as always. We joked, Shep even flirted, though lightly. I'd seen him flirt with girls, and we'd never reached that level. I convinced myself that was just fine by me.

But that night after Buck was already in the truck, Shep got back out. He walked me back to the door, citing the cold. At the threshold, he cleared his throat.

"Buck asked me something."

"Huh?"

He was still smiling, still carefree Shep, but he froze. It was like all the air was sucked off my porch.

"Buck. He asked me if you were mine." He dropped his smile. "Why would he ask me that, Sade?"

I was truly shocked. I had never been anything but distantly nice to Buck. We hadn't had a single moment of tension or affection that I could remember. Nothing. He was, well, like a little brother.

"I don't know!" I squeaked. Then, foolishly, I got hopeful.

Maybe Shep was finally done with college groupies and getting wasted every chance he got. Susan told tales. Shep Riggs was a man among men in high school, but at OU, he was a god. He played football, messed around with girls, and when they had off time, he drank. A lot.

That hardness in Shep, it festered after he left home. I imagine his father doesn't enjoy his son's success. I know he's at all the games, in the locker room, in Shep's head. I know that at home,

Buck still had us. I wasn't sure if Shep had anyone in Norman. Hopefully his teammates?

Whatever support he had, maybe it wasn't enough. He still needed to escape. Often.

We never saw him drunk, never openly discussed it, but we all knew. My dad hinted with lectures about character and honor. My mother rattled off how alcohol and dehydration affect athletes. He politely nodded and then, according to Susan, ignored their suggestions.

I'd thought, that cold night under the dim porch lights, maybe it was our time, finally.

"Maybe he asked because he knows I was your, um . . . I mean, he knows we went to prom."

Shep straightened and smiled.

"True. I'm sure he was just messin' with me."

"Wh-What'd you tell him?"

"Said you were too good for his scrawny ass, then hit him in the nuts. Obviously." Then without a hug or a lingering glance, he backed down the steps. "Merry Christmas, Sade." Then he was gone. My journal got an earful that night.

The next time my foolish heart went wild like it is now was that stupid, horrible party. Once I got here to campus, I heard plenty of Shep Riggs stories. Legends of threesomes and so many shots that everyone else got sick but him. I don't see Shep much around campus. As a theater major, I don't exactly move in the same circles as the football stars.

We text, though, especially after games. I always tease him about his very few, very tiny mistakes, knowing everyone else around him is probably worshipping at his feet. I tell him I'm proud of him too, every week. Just in case no one else in his life says it.

But as much as we're still friends, there is a large part of Shep's life that I'm not a part of. I went to join in one night, at Susan's invitation. She and Adam said I had to come, since it was a celebration of the team's conference win.

To know Shep parties and to see it, up close, are two separate things. I almost wish I'd never progressed from one to the other. At the same time, Shep drinking was Shep supersized. He was even more relaxed, funnier, louder, cockier. I enjoyed the buzz around the edges of my brain that night. I kind of "got it."

But the girls.

Cleat chasers, Jersey girls, cheerleaders, and water girls— they were all over him, all the time. I didn't want to see that. I'm not sure if he wanted me there, either. He cheered when I came in and made a big show of his best friend joining the party.

But then he was whisked away by a teammate, and it wasn't until late in the night that I heard the guitar. I was surprised that he was still playing. He'd actually gotten better. It was surreal, seeing him on the couch in the middle of the apartment, strumming.

"Sing something, Shep!" one girl called out.

"Nah, I'll play something, though. Holler when you know what it is."

His chords were messy, but it didn't take me long at all. He didn't even get to the chorus.

"'What Hurts the Most,'" I said, not loudly. "Rascal Flatts."

He looked up at me, and his eyes were hooded, dark. He was hurting. He looked at me while he played, staring. Everyone else in the crowded space disappeared. It was just him and me.

I couldn't breathe. The song is about almost being together but never quite getting there. Walking away even though you loved the person. He picked it on purpose, I was sure. I just wasn't sure what he meant by it. Was he still hurt, still missing me? Even though he never showed it? Did I walk away from him, or did he walk away from me?

But then he blinked. "Yep." He stopped strumming as soon as the word was out, after popping the P on the end.

"Aw, don't stop, Shep, you're so good," one little blond-haired wisp of a girl said sweetly. I'd seen her around him before. She was shy for a cheerleader. I was pretty sure she wasn't his girl-friend. Very few of the players made time for a relationship. Their lives consisted of football, the end, full stop. But that girl, she was persistent.

"Had to stop, honey, 'cause it's time for some shots!" He yelled the word *shots* like a stadium announcer, grabbed the pouty blonde, and threw her over his shoulder, then bolted to the kitchen.

I never saw him again the rest of the night.

I sigh.

Whatever this is—him coming to my apartment to talk to me now—is going to be the same. I've dated other guys; he didn't mind. I've flirted with his teammates in front of him, for curios-ity's sake, and he didn't like it, but he didn't say anything. Those guys never called me again, but everyone knew we were child-hood friends.

He's a friend. That's all this is.

"Hey, Sade," he says at the door. "Walk with me?"

"Of course." I hop out into the tree-lined street. It's a beauti-ful crisp evening on a pristine college campus street, like we're walking through a postcard. But my bulky, beautiful friend looks tired and his smile doesn't fill his face like it should. We walk for a while before I can't help it. "Shep, what is it?"

We've reached a little neighborhood park down from the house I'm renting with Annie. He sighs and sits down on a bench. I sit next to him, waiting, watching.

"I'm not going to the NFL, Sadie." His voice is so rough I think he might be crying, but his eyes are empty. Red and angry, but empty.

"What do you mean, not going?"

"All the agents, managers, coaches . . . they say I don't have the numbers. Not for my height and build."

"Bullshit!" I spit. His head jerks up at my unusual outburst. "People said that crap about division one ball, and look at you, you're the best in the country!"

He smiles a sad smile. "I could try arena football, and even then, it's a maybe. But the flat truth of it is, I'm just . . ." He swallows, hard. "I'm not good enough." He breathes deeply, and I am frozen, irate, and sad. "Just like he always said."

"So, play arena football then," I blurt, trying not to cry. I try to find something good to cling to.

"I don't want that peewee shit."

"So coach. Players listen to you, they love you." He gives me a half shrug, but I can't give up. "Or go into TV, you know all the stats like the back of your hand . . . even if you clearly have a face for radio." I nudge him, and he smiles a bit wider at my obvious joke. He only gets more manly and handsome every year. He's the flipping eighth wonder of the world in flesh and bone.

"Those TV jobs go to ex-pro players, not college kids. Maybe if I could get a real agent."

"Shep, you can do anything, you'll figure it out. We'll figure it out. This isn't the end of you and football."

He inhales a shaky breath. I said the wrong thing, or maybe the right thing.

"It is, though. This year, this is it for me. What do I do, Sade?" His eyes fill with tears for the first time in the seven years I've known him. I grab his massive arm.

THINGS I WROTE ABOUT

"You play the crap out of the rest of the season. You've got no reason to hold back. Break every damn record, get every award. You go have the season of your life, Shep Riggs." I point my shaking index finger into his chest. "That's what you do."

He sniffs and nods. He puts his hand on mine, and every part of me freezes, except my heart, which is arresting. I consider climbing into his lap and holding him, kissing him like I still dream of, all the freaking time.

His phone interrupts us. He has to check it, just in case it's football related. The screen lights up with the blond girl's face. He dismisses her call and shoves his phone back in his pocket.

"Who is that girl?"

He sighs. "That's Mary Ann."

I try to keep my voice light. "She's always around. Are you, is she your girlfriend?"

"No, but . . ." A hint of his cocky grin is back. "She's in love with me."

I groan. "Shep, don't be gross."

His voice gets quiet. "I'm serious, I think she is. But I don't—"

"You don't have time for a girlfriend."

He shrugs.

I push, twisting the knife in my own heart. "She's pretty. Seems sweet. You'd have adorable little bleach-blond-haired babies."

He chuckles at that, and I die a little bit. He's not arguing with me, not saying he doesn't love her, not saying I'm being ridiculous. He just sits here. I decide to go back to safer topics.

"Anywaaay, listen. You're more than football. Whatever you decide to do next, Shep, you'll be great at it. You'll be the best." A scowl passes over his face, a hint of the hardness he hides. "I mean it, you will." He gets angrier, which I don't understand at all.

"I'm not the best at shit. Just like he always said, and just like you—" He cuts himself off.

"Just like I what, Shep?" He stares at the ground, and I grow sick inside. "Shep? Just like I what? You know, you *know* I am your biggest fan. I have always been your biggest fan!"

"I didn't want you to be a fan, Sadie, I wanted you to be mine!" He yells it at me, pulling away on the bench so he can stretch his knees out. He puts his elbows on them and thrusts his head into his hands. After a second, I process what he's said.

"What . . . what are you saying?"

"I'm saying . . ." His voice is low and angry. "That I tried to do the right thing, tried to grow up. I waited until I thought we were older, until we could really be together, be serious, be in a real relationship, and you said I wasn't good enough!"

"That's not what—"

"And then I was so angry, so hurt that you didn't think we could do it, didn't think *I* could do it, that I went and proved you right! Every time I got sucked off by some random, every time I got wasted and every morning after. I heard my asshole dad in my head and then—" His voice cracks, and I move closer to him, but he flinches. "Then I saw you, standing there by that fountain, looking like my dream come true, telling me my worst nightmare. That I wasn't man enough to do long distance. To stay true to you. I wasn't strong enough, smart enough, serious enough." He stands up. "Damn it!"

"Shep, I . . ." Tears fall down my face. *What the hell do I even say right now? What have I done?*

He waves a hand. "Don't, just forget about it."

"No! That is not what I meant! I was just scared, and I didn't want to hold you back! I didn't want to get in the way of your big dreams and then get hurt. I . . . I just didn't want to get hurt."

"Yeah, well, guess *you* didn't," he grumbles, still not looking at me.

"What?" I stand up too. "What! Are you serious? I hurt every day! Every day for four freaking years! I'm hurting right now, and I'll hurt the next day and the next day and the next!"

"Why?" he grunts out, speaking to his shoes.

"Because I still love you and you know it!"

He freezes at hearing the words out loud. He holds his breath, and I hold mine. Until he closes his eyes and shakes his head with a big exhale. "I can't do this right now." He starts to walk away, and I gasp.

"Seriously? That's it? I tell you I love you, and you just walk away?"

"I can't do this now, Sadie! I'm angry, so angry. I've been serious about two things in my life, football and you. And I lost both. Now I have to figure out what I'm going to do with my future, somehow give my all to the team when my head is a damn mess. It's too much. I need time, I need to think, I need to figure it all out." He starts to walk away again. I let him go.

"All right," I say softly, in total shock.

He stops and barely turns his head. His voice is scratchy. "You're my best friend, Sadie Lyn." He waits, and I know what he needs me to say.

"That's not my name, redneck."

He smiles enough that I can see it in his cheeks, even though he's not facing me.

Then he walks away.

CHAPTER 10

1 MONTH AGO
THE CARIBBEAN

Sam: Sadie? Are you dead?

Sam: Has anyone seen her all day?

Skye: She's been hiding.

Susan: Leave her alone, this situation has got to be awkward even if she's fine.

Skye: She's not fine. How could anyone be fine with this weirdness?

Sally: I can understand why not. All three of you have hot men, but Shep Riggs is . . . uh, I mean wow. [Fire emoji] [Fire emoji]

Skye: Guess Sal likes 'em thicc

Susan: Skye! Must you send texts about our sisters and sex that will scar us for the rest of our lives?!

Skye: I must

Sam: LOL

Sally: I'm 22, guys, not 12. [Shrug emoji] [Laughing emoji]

Sam: ANYWAY!

Sam: Sadie, please check in with us!

Sam: I'm worried about you!

Me: I'm fine, though also scarred for life now

Me: Just found a quiet spot to do some writing

I snort to myself. Yeah, *writing.*

There has been grunting, sighing, staring off into space, and shaking my head at the sky. All part of the creative process, I guess. Except I'm not even brainstorming my newest series, I'm just reliving yesterday.

I can't unsee Shep's glorious back going as hard as the oar in his hand when my singing reached him. I keep looking into those bright green eyes, filled with rage. So much, well, hatred.

That's what it looks like. My soulmate, the man who gave me the best year of my life, hates me now? After what *he* did? I just don't get it.

I also keep flashing back to the moment on the beach when he pulled off his shirt. Sally's not wrong. The man is fire. I've got to stop this. I need to exercise, journal more, something. These circling thoughts about what if, why, how, if only—I'm going to drive myself insane.

Add to that mix that I keep getting sweaty and bothered like I'm twenty-one all over again! Luckily, it's cooler and overcast today. Even more peaceful than yesterday. I let myself doze off. It's not even an hour later when my phone starts exploding.

Janie: Ladies, I'm going to need you all to meet me! Main cabana ASAP.
Sam: J?
Sam: What's up?
Sam: Is it an emergency!?!?!
Janie: Urgent but not an emergency.
Skye: omw
Sally: Me too
Kat: One sec
Susan: I also need a sec
Sam: I need to know what's going on!!!!

Janie: No secs. Drop what you're doing. And . . . I'm not exact-
ly sure, but I know you're going to want to see it.
Me: Even me?
Janie: Especially you.

Color me intrigued. I make good time getting to the large cabana. The girls are huddled, waiting under the thatched roof, as
I'm the last to arrive. It's all the bridesmaids—Susan, Skye, Sally,
Kat, myself, and Janie, and the bride, clearly all coming from different activities. I don't think I was the only one woken up from
a nap for this. It better be good.

"So?" I yawn as they see me approach.

"Yeah, so?" Sam practically yells to Janie.

"Follow me." Janie has mischief written all over her face. We
follow obediently, although Sam keeps pestering her for more
information. Janie just laughs, unmoved. She leads past the
pools and a couple recreational buildings and stops at a corner.
We can hear the men's voices, so we start to whisper, asking her
a million questions. She simply motions with her hand for us to
follow the path around the building's side and see for ourselves.

Sam squeals. Sally laughs. Susan mutters an "Oh my."

Skye calls back to Janie, "Why didn't you tell us to grab some
popcorn and some drinks, Janie?"

I finally get up to Skye's side and see the spectacle and—

Oh.

My.

Is.

Right.

The men are chopping wood in various stages of undress. But
Shep.

Shep?!

What the hell is happening right now?

He's dressed exactly like at least ten scenes from my various books. Boots. Jeans. Plaid shirt with sleeves rolled, hanging open, sweaty chest exposed. *Chopping wood in the tropics in the heat of the day.* It's absurd. It makes no sense. He should be shirtless in board shorts and flip-flops.

It's . . .

He's . . .

Damn.

He's a fantasy come to life. I can't deny it. And *crap!* I'm not wearing my floppy hat or big glasses. My mouth is hanging open and my eyes are wide and my chest is jumping up and down as I gasp for oxygen.

I recover, but it's too late. He doesn't look at me, but his cocky smile lights up the whole resort. He knows.

All the guys look pretty amazing. Emerson, Matthew, and Adam, my brothers-in-law, are fit and solid. Emerson's brothers are both tall and built, though Byron, Ben's twin, has a dad bod creeping in at his middle. Dennis still looks great, tall and lean but not soft. Nothing about him was ever soft. This is the first I'm seeing him, though really I don't see him at all. He isn't looking at me. Ben is the only one looking at me, and as sexy as he is, I don't want to look back. I want to disappear. I also want to walk up and lick the sweat trickling down Shep's bulging chest.

WHAT?!

Sadie!

I have to escape, quickly. The men laugh and tease us about pulling up chairs to watch. Shep is positively beaming.

"Can I get an actual greeting now, Janie?" he teases.

"I'll greet you, honey. All I need is some sweet tea and something to sit on, and I'm fixin' to just camp out for this little show," Kat says in her accent that's much thicker than any of ours.

"I like the way you think, Kat. Sweet tea would be perfect." Shep gives her a lingering look, then adds, "I read somewhere that chicks love a man in plaid."

Read somewhere.

The bastard is making fun of my books. He's still not looking at me, and I sure as hell can't look back at him. One glance, and I'm thinking about sweat-licking. I watch Janie, but she just shakes her head at him. Kat has moved from staring at Shep to ogling Ben.

"Turn around and chop in the other direction, Mr. Clark," Samantha calls to Emerson. He does what she asks with a small smile. "Forget about your billions, I'm only marrying you for that ass!"

"Angel," Emerson pleads under his breath, but he's too late. The guys all pile on about his butt, cooing like a group of schoolgirls.

When the laughter settles, Skye stakes her own claim. "Matthew, for the first time today, I do not want to be alone. How about we—" Before she can finish her sentence, Matthew has dropped his axe and picked her up. She wails as he throws her over his shoulder.

"Yeahhh, uh, this is pretty awkward for me, so I'm gonna go," Sally says. She's over a decade younger than the men, and three of them are her brothers-in-law, so I get it.

I clear my throat. "I'll join you." I turn to follow her.

Susan clears her throat, way more awkward than usual, and decides to join us. "We'll leave you to it." Adam is blushing and hasn't said a thing. They are being weird, for sure. Noting that for later.

I don't have time to dwell on the note, though, because I need to flee. I feel the need to save some face with the blond bodybuilder in the middle, so I call back with a smile, "I will say, this scene is definitely going in a future book, so thank you for that, boys!" I laugh, hoping I pull off sounding like a sane, happy, normal woman. Sally, Susan, and I get the hell outta dodge.

———

This is what I needed. It's past the posted spa hours, the stars are out, bugs are singing, and no one else is anywhere near this Jacuzzi. The amount of bubbles is perfect, and the water is scorching. I can feel some of the tension leaving my lower back. And my bruises from the first night are feeling soothed too. I should do this every night.

I lie my head back on the concrete and try to quiet my thoughts.

"Still a night owl, I see."

Great.

Shep slides into the oversize hot tub, looking just as delicious as he did earlier, and yesterday, and always. I'm relieved when he chooses the spot across from me, easily ten feet away.

He continues: "You feeling tense?"

I roll my eyes with a small smile, refusing to be messed with. "Not really."

"Oh? You'd think seeing one ex at a wedding would be bad enough, but two . . . yikes."

I keep my voice friendly but concerned. Maybe he is struggling too. "Is it? Bad enough? Seeing me, Shep?"

"Can't see much of anything right now." His voice is low even though his smile is the same. He looks at the water below my chin. I'm fully submerged. He can't even see the top swell of my boobs. And I'm definitely not raising up or getting out now, even if it's hot.

Guess this is how I die, overheating in a Jacuzzi. *Fantastic.*

I shake my head. "Nothing you haven't seen before, anyway."

His eyes change, and his smile fades. I know that look. My entire body floods with a million sensations and memories and . . . desires.

"Never did get tired of looking, though." One side of his mouth raises, and he takes a step toward me.

"Shep. What are you doing?"

He keeps moving toward me and trying to shift toward the steps, his grin growing. "What you want me to do."

"I do not!"

"Don't try to deny it. I saw your jaw hangin' slack at the wood pile today, Sadie." He's relaxed enough for his accent to reappear. I'm not sure if that's a good or bad sign for me.

"So what? You're an attractive guy, we have a history, it's a normal reaction!" I struggle to move while keeping myself submerged. I'm nothing if not stubborn, though, so I'm not raising up until I'm at the stairs.

"Oh, so you sayin' you had the same reaction to Dennis then?"

"Yes, I did!"

"Bull."

"Shep, I'm not doing this with you."

"Doing what?"

I push myself as far into the wall as I can go. I motion between us. "Whatever this is, us, talking, fighting, flirting." I scoff. "Definitely not anything else beyond that. It's over, Shep, just let me be."

He squints down at me, still inching closer. "No."

"Ugh! You're impossible." I decide to cave, needing to get away before he reaches me but . . . what the . . . my bikini bottoms are caught? "Oh shit." I start to panic.

"Are you actually scared of me?" He looks amused but also confused, seeing my terror.

"No. Shep, my bottoms, they're caught."

I watch as he fills with absolute glee. "I'm sorry, come again?"

"The string of my bottoms! It got sucked into the thing!"

He cocks his head and furrows his brow. "Whatever do you mean?"

"The sucky inny thingy! It's sucked in the tie, of my bottoms!" My voice gives away how distraught I am. Though we both know it's less about the bikini or even drowning, and more about the fact that I'm trapped near him.

"So . . ." He is right up to me now, almost touching me. Even though we're both submerged in the water, I can feel him, our connection. If he touches me, I don't know what will happen. "What I'm hearing is that you're stuck here, with me."

He does exactly what I would've wanted, what I would've written, what I would've urged a star to do on-screen while watching a movie. What I might not live through.

He pulls out of the water enough to cage me in with his arms.

We're not touching, but we're panting like we might as well be. He's still smiling, though, loving my misery. I tug and tug, but the stupid little string will not come free.

"Are you going to help me?" I ask him, knowing the answer before he laughs.

"Not a chance in hell."

"Shep! Stop it, it's not funny! I'm gonna drown!"

He laughs again. "You want to get up, just take them off and get up. What's stopping you?"

"Motherf—" I stop myself as his eyebrows raise. He's still laughing. "At least go get me one of those towels!" I motion over his shoulder to the cart.

"Nope."

I growl in frustration. "Ughhh! I thought we were past this! I thought we were going to be friends!"

"Never agreed to that." He stops laughing and glares at me. He moves into me just barely. I can feel his hard chest through my bikini top when I breathe in. His breath catches. My breath leaves completely. I'm light-headed. I'm lost.

His eyes tell me he is too. Angry or not, I know he wants me. He may not want to want me anymore, just like I wish I didn't still want him. Oh, I wish.

But we're drawn to each other. It's electric. Electric and submerged in water . . . yeah, we're both going to fry in here. It terrifies me. He pushes in even more. He's squatting down in the water, his face so close I can feel his breath.

I will not live through this.

"Let me go, Shep," I say softly.

His face twists into a scowl in a blink. "You want to go, Paramour, go." It's the use of the stupid nickname that seals the deal. He's too bitter now, too mean. We can't move on or change into friends, or acquaintances. We certainly can't go back. We're irreparable. I just have to get away. I straighten my back and flatten my lips into a hard line.

"Fine, I will." I let the bottoms shrug off me and stand. He doesn't break eye contact with me as my torso pushes out of the water. I'm in a neon teal string bikini, and I know I look pretty good. At least, I better. I paid for double the personal training sessions for the last four months, knowing this moment was coming.

He starts to smile again as he moves his arm for me. He is loving that I'm about to have to bare all from the waist down. Thank goodness I trained for this like a pathetic little girl, still hung up on her crush. I have pushed myself to the max during cardio, I've eaten clean, I've chugged water, and glory hallelujah for the squats. So many squats.

So I don't look at him. I hold my head up high and I get ready to walk right out of the hot tub like I'm not dying inside. I don't rush. His view is only going to be my backside, thankfully. But as I'm about to lift out of the water, the door to the spa opens and in walks . . . a gaggle of little old ladies. Isn't it like midnight? What the . . . ?

Oh no.

"Crap! No! Damn it!" I whisper.

"What's the matter, honey? Nothing those gals haven't seen before," Shep says.

"That's Ann Wartzer. She's our biggest buyer in Europe, and Dad says she's thinking of pulling out or cutting back."

"Nice story." Shep looks to her and back to me, unmoved.

"Shep, I cannot do this! She's like the Queen of England! Her butlers have butlers! She wears gloves to lunch! I cannot strut my strip in front of Ann Wartzer!"

I see something pass over his face, but he recovers quickly.

"Maybe she'll want to come in for a landing."

"Shep!"

"She could be into women, we don't know. It's ageist and biased of us to assume—"

"Shep!" I cut him off. "For the love of my dad and Emerson and every *other* freaking Canton *except* for me, help!" I say. Finally, his features soften. In a flash, his shorts are off.

"Put these on."

I do as he says and then watch, in both glee and horror, as Shep thrusts out of the water completely naked. *Do not look down, do not look down.*

"Uh, sorry, ladies, you may want to stick with the pool to-night," he calls to the women as he walks over and grabs a towel to wrap around himself.

I sneak one quick look at his naked cheeks before the towel covers him. His ass is still a marvel. A beefy, hard, chiseled work of art. It takes significant effort not to bite my bottom lip. I quick-ly step out of the water, eager to get out of this entire situation. His bottoms are too big, but I've pulled the string tight enough that they're not falling down. Even so, it's totally obvious the shorts don't belong to me.

"Sorry, she just couldn't keep her hands off me," he tells Mrs. Wartzer and her posse as he throws an arm around my shoulder to walk me out.

"Pff, you wish," I mutter to him before I can help it. "It's not what it looks like! That ship sailed years ago!" I try to explain, but Shep has moved us past the women who are frozen in place. The expressions on their faces range from understandable shock to amusement and even desire, which is also understandable. They're female, they're alive, and he's Shep Riggs.

As soon as we get through the door, I shove him off me.

"Ugh." I take a breath to rein in the thousands of emotions coursing through me. "Thank you, I guess. That was, well, better than the alternative. So. Yeah." I turn to go in a hurry, but with my spine straight and my chin up. Then I hear him behind me.

"Hey." His voice is like acid. "All the work you've had done, it's workin' for you."

I freeze. My heart plummets into the floor. *All the work I've had done?* That's what he chooses to say to me in this moment when I am shaken and was almost literally laid bare and at his mercy? Even if I had had plastic surgery—which would be *fine* because it's *my* body to do with whatever I feel is best—the way he said it, the disgust, the venom.

He simply wants to hurt me. Who is this man? I don't know him anymore. My eyes fill with tears. I turn my head halfway.

"Good night, Shep." My voice is calm until cracking on his name. I turn to go, and I'm not deliberate or proud this time. I move fast because I might actually start to sob, and he'll know it.

He mumbles something, and it sounds like he's picking up pace to follow after me, so I literally run and hide around a corner.

I'm hiding from Shep in a utility closet.

How, how did we get here?

CHAPTER 11

I'm going to cry. I'm going to cry happy, sad, proud, overwhelming tears . . . about football. Not football, really. I know that, as I stand here in the cold, waiting. The parking lot outside the hotel is crammed with people, even though it's frigid. I don't mind the weather or the crowd, which I have found annoying in years past.

I've never been more proud of Shep, and that's saying something. The last few months, he's been more focused than I've ever seen him. Some say he carried the team to the National Championship, and I absolutely agree. There's been no partying, no wallowing, no raging against his fate. He's stepped up.

I don't know how he'll be feeling tonight. I told him I'd be waiting. Crowds always gather to cheer for the team when they get off the charter buses, so it's not unusual for me to be here. But tonight is unusual.

It was his last game, ever. The National Championship game. And the team lost.

But Shep Riggs was a menace on that field. He broke all his own records, a school record, and even an NCAA record. He defied gravity when he jumped to catch each pass, which he did flawlessly. He ran along the sideline like a dancer, never flinching. He was sure, solid, and perfect. Absolutely perfect.

My eyes burn again as the buses pull in. The crowd is going nuts. They played a great game, and they deserve the support. They were just plain outmatched this year.

I watch the bus doors, looking for a shock of bright blond hair in the parking lot lights. I always hang back, off to the side, so Shep can mingle with his admirers. There are the usual cheerleaders, kids, parents, and families; sometimes my dad or sisters are here. Tonight, it's just me, though, and I expect him to take his time shaking hands and waving at fans before he makes his way over to my spot.

But he doesn't. He looks at me right away and walks past everyone else. Even the kids. He doesn't even look at the group of shirtless guys chanting his name. He just stalks toward me, a sneaky smile on his face. He did what I told him to: he played the season of his life.

His eyes are wet, I think, and noticing that does me in. The whole world falls away. It's just us, him and me. We haven't talked about us, not since that day at the park. We went back to normal, texting and joking. But I know he's been different, and he knows I love him. He knows I want him.

And he's looking at me like he feels it all too. Like I'm his destination. Like he's at the end of his race, and I'm the finish line.

But it's me who runs.

I take off like a rocket, and his smile gets even bigger. He throws down his gym bag and opens his arms for me, as if we've done this before. We haven't. But when I leap into him, my whole body wrapping him like a glove, it's the most natural thing in the world.

He holds my legs around his waist, and we both tremble. He buries his head in my neck and breathes. I'm pretty sure he's trying not to cry. I pull back and hold his beautiful face in my hands.

"I'm so freaking proud of you."

He squeezes me as he looks up into my eyes. "Yeah?"

"Yeah."

"That all?" His voice is shaking.

"No." My heart explodes with bright, blinding hope.

He smiles so big it hurts me to look down at him. I can barely hear him. "What else?"

"I love you, Shep Riggs."

He swallows. "Be with me, Bambi. Right now. Tonight. Kiss me and make this the best day of my life." I sob as my mouth meets his. His lips are as soft and as smooth as I remember. His body is a furnace, hard all around me. He smells like soap and sweat and his same shampoo. I kiss him a few times, hard, never letting go of his face.

He pulls away before our tongues can meet. I forgot we're surrounded by people. Cheering people. I'm sure more than one of them has their phone out. So he just sets me down and then locks our fingers together as he gets his bag.

He drives my rental car to my hotel, which is just a few blocks over from where the team is staying. I ramble on and on about all his plays; he laughs and nods. Or argues. Or agrees. We just talk together about it all, and I gush over him without holding anything back. I'm also nervous, and the talking helps. So I keep up with the rambling, all the way to my room.

"Annie?" he asks when we're heading in.

"She drove back to Norman after the game."

"Good," he says, and for the first time, Shep's sexy eyes, which I've only seen from a distance, in theory, are staring at me, in reality.

"Yeah, she—" He smashes into me before I can think. He moans right away, opening me up to him. His tongue takes over my mouth, and I don't protest. I've kissed before. I've even kissed Shep before, but not like this.

This is desperation. This is need. This is pain, over all the years we spent not doing this. I think, maybe, this kiss is love.

He picks me up again, wrapping me around him just like at the parking lot. I whimper as he walks us to the bed and plops down. I'm straddling him and holding his face, but he's in control. He pulls away just long enough to pull off his team polo. I quickly pull off my shirt too. I begin to attack him again, but he pushes me back.

"Wait a minute, wait. Let me see you." His voice is garbled. He just looks at me, my neck, my chest. I can't breathe. He brings his head down and kisses me right in the middle of my chest, on the flat smooth bone. Then he moves, kissing all over every inch that's not covered by my bra.

I need more.

I reach around and take my bra off while he watches me. He shudders as he inhales. My light brown hair is frizzy and unruly around me, so I push it behind my shoulders with a hand, giving him an unobstructed view. He looks . . . amazed?

Emboldened, I decide to keep going. I get up and take off everything else too, watching him as I do it. It's not slow or sexy. It's just me with him, just . . . us.

I walk back in between his legs and stand before him in just a little black thong. He runs his shaking hands up my thighs, squeezing and rubbing.

He kisses my sternum again. "You're so perfect, Sadie," he says quietly.

"Yeah?" My voice is puny as I try to mimic him.

He looks up at me. "Yeah."

"Is that all?"

He smiles knowingly. "Nope."

My eyes sting, and I'm terrified, but I say the words. "What else?"

"What else is, I'm in love with you," he says, and I hold back a sob. He picks me up and, in a quick turn, has me underneath him on the bed. "Still." He shifts us up farther on the bed. "And for forever, Sade. For real." He kisses me before I can cry out. His tongue loves mine, slowly and firmly. Without questions.

He wriggles out of his jeans and grabs a small square from his pocket. He sets it next to us on the bed and then kisses me again as he moves me, pulling off my panties. I'm vibrating with feelings, one of them fear.

"Shep." He stops and meets my eyes. "I, um, I waited for you."

It takes a second for him to grasp what I mean. He settles beside me, dropping his weight onto his side in a wave of what I'm guessing is shock. Or maybe relief. "Wow," he mutters with a big smile.

But he looks back down at me, and I'm not smiling. My face is tight with nerves and regret and embarrassment. He moves his free hand to hold my face. He traces his thumb lightly back and forth on my cheek.

"It's not like you think, Sade. I've only actually *been* with a few girls."

"What? How!"

He shrugs and tries not to look pleased with himself. "Lotta times they were happy to, uh, do other things."

"Ugh, Shep!" I try to whack at his chest.

He stills my hand and leans down to kiss my nose. "I promise, I've never wanted anyone the way I want you. I don't *see* anyone else but you, don't think about anybody else. Definitely not right now. Maybe not ever."

My heart swoons, but I'm still so nervous. "But I just . . . I don't know what to do."

"You don't need to do anything." He runs the tip of his nose along my own. He whispers with his lips brushing over mine. "Trust me, Bambi, I'll take care of you."

And he does.

He does things with his fingers and his hands that other boys have only ever attempted. I shatter into happy little pieces faster than I expected. After I recover, he kisses me harder, faster, as I hear the foil unwrapping.

He readies himself and looks me in the eyes.

"Take a deep breath for me, Bambi." I do, and he eases us together. I cry out at the sensation and grip onto him. He doesn't move, other than to link our hands together. "Open your eyes, Sadie Lyn." I obey. He smiles at me in that way of his. Like there's no one else in the world but us. Right now, there isn't. "I'm going to start moving now, okay?"

I smile as I exhale. "Okay."

It is more than okay.

It is amazing.

It is amazing three times that night.

CHAPTER 12

11 YEARS AGO
TULSA, OKLAHOMA

"What in the world are you doing here at five A.M. over a long weekend, Shep?" I mumble out my parents' front door. We decided to come home and chill with my family for the few days off. I guess we have different definitions of chill, because here he stands, looking fresh and even excited, in his long-sleeve running shirt and pants.

"C'mon, Bambi, I told you, the couple who trains together, stays together."

I yawn and whisper, "That's not a real saying."

"It is, and it's true. Now let's get going."

"Train for what?"

"For life, dummy. We want to be healthy forever, running circles around our grandkids."

Our grandkids?! Okay, maybe I can take up running.

"Dummy? That's what you're going with to get me to agree to this torture?"

"It won't be torture." He is jumping and stretching on the porch in front of me.

"I will make it torture. I'll be super slow and whine the whole time and make poorly *paced* jokes like another *run* bites the dust."

"I'll live."

"You really want to run with me?"

"I want to do everything with you, Sade."

All right, that's it. I'm a runner now.

I open the door fully to let him in. The cold air follows him into the house, causing me to shiver. It also makes the touch of Shep's hands on my waist feel like palm-size space heaters.

"Sadie Lyn. Are you wearing nothing but my old football shirt right now?" His grip tightens.

"I was asleep." I shrug. He looks around the entryway, mutters some choice words under his breath, and then hoists me up into his arms. I wrap my arms around his neck and watch his face change from playful to hungry.

I am somewhat aware that we are in my childhood home with my sisters and mother and, most importantly, father sleeping just up the stairs. But the need in Shep's eyes and the way his mouth ticks up just a bit on one side makes me eagerly wrap my legs around his middle.

Within one second, we are smashed in the entryway coat closet. I'm pushed up against the fabrics, leaving him with barely enough room to stand between me and the closed door. Shep flips the light on in time to move a knuckle over one of the thumbtack-like points my body has created in his thin vintage tee.

"The coat closet? Is my boyfriend some kind of sex maniac?"

"Only since you."

"I don't think you can see me and not get me naked." I giggle as he pulls off my shirt with one hand, holding me firm under my thighs with the other. I wonder if we'll always be this way, if this is even normal. The man cannot keep his hands off me these last few weeks together, no matter where we are or what we're doing.

He starts kissing my neck and mutters, "I held myself back for years. Now, I'm not wasting a single opportunity." He pushes himself against me as he lifts me in his arms to give his mouth better access to my chest. I thrust against him, prompting him to flip us around.

I'm up against the door now, allowing Shep to get one hand free. He pulls down his pants and underwear to just below his knees. We both moan as his hand comes back to me. He hooks it into my boy shorts, then slowly, slowly moves his fingers down the crease of my thigh to my center.

"You ready for me, Sade?"

"Always." I can barely say it before he shoves my underwear to the side and moves into me in one strong thrust. I let out a moan.

"Shhh, Bambi." He smiles and puts his hand over my mouth. We both stay silent, just holding each other's eyes in the dim closet, listening to the brush of the fabrics against Shep's back. It may be the hottest sex anyone's ever had in the whole freaking state, the whole country. It's also the quickest Shep has ever come undone.

———

"You really think I can do this?" Shep shifts his backpack on his shoulders in front of the table. My stuff is sprawled all over the dining room in mine and Annie's apartment, but she doesn't mind. Neither does Shep, even though he doesn't technically live here. My parents would die.

No, he has his own place. We set it up over the summer, but it's just not as homey as my house. Plus, after years of being around his teammates constantly, I don't think he likes being alone. So he stays over a lot, like he did last night, before today, the big day. I get up from my twisted position in the wooden chair.

"You can do everything, Shep."

He grabs my waist and tucks me into him as I get close. His voice is low and buttery in that way that I love. "Got something I'd like to do right now."

"No! You have your first class! And I need to finish this."

"Sade, it's already done, quit fussin' with it." He leans in and kisses me. "Fuss with me instead."

"Shep! I'm serious. You have to go."

"All right." He smiles. "But I'm serious too. That screenplay is smart and funny as hell. Don't change anything else."

"You really think so?"

"Did I just say so or not?"

I huff. "I'm just nervous to write things people will actually read. My mom actually read it last night."

Shep shifts back from me, genuinely surprised. "The doc read your movie script?"

"She did. Dr. Sandra Canton said my little short film about five crazy sisters was, quote, *exceptional*." My smile tightens. "She also said she's so glad I've found something worthwhile to do while I spend my life auditioning. She says I should contribute to society by writing all my observations about humans into deep, emotional memoirs."

"I love your mama, but she's not quite right in the head."

I laugh. "Not quite right? She's Einstein!"

He kisses my forehead. "My point exactly. Have you seen that guy's hair? The dude was unhinged. You can write *and* be a famous actress. Doesn't have to be one or the other."

"And you can be the best damn sports agent in the world—*after* you finish law school, which means you have to actually go to your classes, which start today. Now git!"

"You know it makes me hot when you talk country to me, Bambi."

"GO!" We laugh as he kisses me again, with a firm grab of my butt, before leaving. It's crazy to see him less than completely confident about something. I feel the flutters of nerves for him too.

He really can do anything he wants—if he can quiet the demons in his head. Demons that have only gotten louder since he lost football. I didn't realize how much of a release the game was for him. It was an escape for him, just like acting and writing are for me. Without it, there's only one other escape he seems to find. Doesn't seem to matter what kind of bottle it is—beer, tequila, whiskey—he looks for answers inside.

I can help him through this, though. It's just a season. He's grieving the loss of football, of his past dreams, and I can hold him up as long as he needs. I just hope I'm enough support.

———

I didn't really know what to expect for my first birthday with Shep as his girlfriend. It wasn't this. It wasn't having to keep myself from weeping happy tears into a small flat gift box.

"I love it, Shep, I love it! Will you put it on?" He gets up from where he sits across from me at my small dining table. He takes the delicate silver chain out of the box and moves behind me to put it around my neck. It's a simple, small charm of a deer that fits perfectly on my chest. It's the sweetest gift I've ever gotten.

Shep clears his throat. "I know it's not big or expensive, but I happen to be saving up for . . . other things."

"Yeah?" I ask him.

He smiles at our familiar line of questioning. "Yeah." He moves to sit back in his chair. I follow him and climb into his lap.

"Like what?"

"Well, this girl I love, she wants to go to New York and become a superstar. And I'm all for it."

"Oh, you are?" I smile down at him.

"Yep. I just have to ace law school, pass the bar, then I'm going to take her out there and take some players with us. Get them set up with the Patriots, Jets, Giants, probably some endorsement deals. Then I'll get her a penthouse apartment in whatever the cool, artsy part of New York is so she's close to all the auditions and whatnot. We'll have a driver and a doorman, just like the movies, the whole works."

I chuckle. "Whatnot, huh. Is that all?"

He looks serious for a second. "Is that enough?"

I turn serious too. "More than enough, Shep. More than enough." Then I scoot down onto my knees and thank him for my gift in a way that makes him think it's *his* birthday.

———

"Bambi!" Shep yells to me. "Dammit you're hot." I'm in a simple white tee and tight jeans, but he tends to look at me like I'm naked no matter what I wear.

He slurs his words a bit as he rushes up to me. I smile brightly, though. I want to make a good impression on all his new law school friends. It's weird to be at a party that feels like a college party when everyone is older. I guess they're all still in school, though.

"Sounds like you started without me, Poteau." The nickname lets him know he's in trouble.

"Just a little bit, honey, I'm just letting off some steam." The use of the term *honey* makes me want to vomit. He only slips into this mode when he's been drinking. *Honey* is the term he used for any and all girls before me. Not me. He turns and yells to the crowd, "Blowin' off some steam after we all aced all our finals!" The whole apartment, packed full, cheers and hollers. I smile and relax my shoulders.

Shep grabs my hand, and I give it a squeeze, then look up at him with a smile. "Beer, please."

"Hell yes!" He runs off to the kitchen, I assume, looking ecstatic. He loves when I loosen up with him. One beer later, I'm already feeling a bit fuzzy when I see Shep has been stopped on his way back to me. He's talking to Tiny Blondie, who has her little hand on his big arm. He's not shrugging her off.

By the time he makes his way back to me, I'm livid.

"Here you go."

"What the hell is she doing here, Shep?"

He follows my laser beam gaze across the room. "Mary Ann? She's in my classes."

"*She followed you to law school?*" I can hear how shrill I sound, but I can't shrink back. I'm too angry.

"Don't be jealous, Bambi. She's studying family law, I think. Can't remember."

My mouth falls open. "But she's been in your classes, all semester long?"

He loves seeing me jealous. "Not all of them, honey, just some."

"Ugh, Shep, let's just go. You're going to get drunk and flirty with her, and every other female here, and then we'll fight."

He sighs and closes his eyes. "Don't ride me on this, Sadie, please, let's just have fun tonight." I hate that I'm hindering him, dimming his light—even if his glow is artificially lit via alcohol right now. It still makes me feel like a party crusher.

"Okay, Shep."

He yells and picks me up, taking me to the backyard where corn hole and Ping-Pong and other games are set up. I never get drunk, because that's Shep's job, apparently. I stop drinking after a while in order to get us home. Shep . . . does his best. He still makes jokes and smiles a little too freely with the girls who try to flirt with him, even as he shuts them down. For the most part, he keeps me tucked into his side all night long, even as he yells and takes shots and makes a fool of himself.

In the morning light, as always, we make things right.

"Thanks for taking care of me last night," he says to the top of my head. We are tangled up together but know better than to get anywhere near each other's morning-after breath.

"I cannot believe Mary Ann followed you to law school."

He gives me a reassuring squeeze. "C'mon, Sade, she didn't follow me."

"She did, and she'd follow you anywhere. The way she watches you, she'd walk right off a cliff after you."

"I'm too busy watching you to notice her watching me. You know I'm yours."

"She'd listen to whatever you say, let you do whatever you wanted. Wouldn't push you. You guys would never fight. She's actually perfect for you. She'd be so easy."

"Quit it. I don't want easy. I've only ever wanted you, Bambi."

"Pff, that girl is more doe-eyed than I ever was."

He chuckles around me. "Now that's the truth."

"Hey!" I push at him, but he holds me in place.

"I didn't call you that because you were doe-eyed, not after the first time. I called you that because it made you react and I liked it. I liked that I made you mad."

I can't help but scoff. "You still make me mad."

"Don't I know it." He shifts and starts kissing down my body through my clothes. He hooks his fingers into my PJ shorts and looks up at me, hot as ever. "Hopefully I make you feel some other things too, now, though."

I give him a side-eye. "Sometimes."

"Challenge accepted, Bambi."

———

"What is it, you're being weird," Skye says, watching me get ready in my old bathroom in our parents' house.

I close the bathroom door and look at her. "I think Shep might propose this week."

Her eyes explode. "Really?!"

"Maybe? I mean, he told me he was saving up, and I know he has money saved up from that endorsement deal."

Skye snorts. "You say that like he's the face of Adidas. He's in commercials for a local heating and air company!"

"Hey, it paid really well! And he looks amazing in those commercials. I bet women all over Tulsa are breaking their heaters hoping he'll show up." That earns me a chuckle. "Anyway, I thought he would over Christmas, but then he didn't. Now that we're home this week for spring break, I just have a feeling."

"He seemed kinda pissed last night at dinner. Did you guys fight?"

I sigh. "Well, he gets quiet whenever we come home. He has to stay with his dad, and Buck's not home right now, so . . . he wants to be out every night, partying, really doing anything to get away."

She just nods in understanding.

"Anyway, we're going out to meet up with some of his old football friends tonight, so I'm sure that will cheer him up. But! We're going to dinner first. A nice dinner, just the two of us. I just wouldn't be surprised if tonight's the night, you know?"

"Man, you engaged and Susan pregnant. Crazy."

"Totally."

I put on one more coat of mascara before making my way downstairs. I expect Shep to be waiting for me.

Me: Are you on your way?
Shep: I'm already at Tug's house, come meet us here?
Me: OK

I shrug off my disappointment. He needs this time with his buddies. Even if we don't get to go to dinner, we can still have a fun night. Maybe he'll propose tomorrow. I hurry to meet up with him. I arrive to a lot of cars and people. I guess the party has been going for a while.

"Shep?" I call as I enter Tug's house. It's a cute, new little rental home he shares with another friend. I don't know the roommate, or many of the faces here, but Shep does. Football connections.

"Sssssssadie Lyn in the flesh. Mmmm good-lookin' flesh too."

I cannot believe the state he's in. "Shep. It's only seven thirty, how long have you been here? What have you had?"

He lets out a heavy sigh. "The ole ball and chain, y'all, swingin' right into my nuts, soon as she gets here." I stand shocked for a moment. I can tell his dad set him off earlier. That's the only way he'd be so bitter and so drunk already.

"C'mon, Shep, let's go. You've had more than enough fun already."

"Hellllll no. We just getting' started, right, y'all?" The crowd hoots and hollers. It's always Shep leading a group in a cheer that I'm not a part of. I'm tired. But I'm also not letting him drink himself sick.

I walk over and hug him and then talk softly. "What about food, Shep, have you guys eaten?"

His eyes go wild like a kid. "Holy pig-shittin' balls, I'm hungry."

I can't help but smile. "I'll order pizzas."

"You take such good care of me." He tries to kiss my neck, but I push him back to make eye contact.

"No more drinking until the pizza comes, okay?"

"K." He sways on his feet. I sit him down on the couch and leave the room to order pizza. When I return, I see that he's listened to me, not drinking, and attempting to play some video game on the TV. I'm not sure he can even see the screen at this point.

The pizza arrives, and Shep puts away what seems like a million slices. As do all the other ex-football guys around me. At my insistence, he drinks water. I can see some clarity returning.

Apparently too much clarity.

"All right, had my pizza, time for some shots!" he says to the whole kitchen, who applauds the idea.

"Shep, no, it's getting late. Let's get you home."

"Sadie. I ate your pizza, I drank your water, now I want to let loose with Tug, who I see like once a year. Give me a damn break!"

"Fine, you want to drink yourself sick, be my guest. I'm leaving."

"Sade, don't be like this."

I sigh and lift a shoulder. "I'll see you in the morning, like always."

"Don't do that bullshit, Sadie," he hisses.

"Excuse me?"

"Quit talking down to me like that! It's just some drinks with friends for shit's sake! Cut me some damn slack!"

I raise my hands in what looks like surrender but also means I'm done. I can't keep trying to save someone who doesn't want saving. "You want slack, Shep? You got it." I storm out of the kitchen, and each step through the house becomes more painful as I realize he's not calling after me.

———

When I open my eyes the next morning, my first thought is Shep. I think about his angry face, about my storming out last night, about how he is this morning. I'm worried. That feeling is quickly trampled by alarm.

I realize it's so early it's still dark out, and I've been woken up by shouting.

No, not shouting—screaming. Wailing. Someone is wailing.

Dread and nausea fill me to the brim as I rush out of my room and down the steps. My younger sisters fall in step beside me. We stop on the stairs when we see him. Our father, Jonny Canton, our supersized hero, joy and drive and pride wrapped inside a man, is on his knees on the floor.

"No, no, no," he pleads.

There is a police officer I recognize, a family friend, standing in the open doorway, holding back tears of his own.

THINGS I WROTE ABOUT

My father's screams fill the whole house. "Sandy! My Sandy-girl, no! Oh God, no, why, no, Sandy . . ."

Skye screams too. Sally starts to cry. Samantha throws up all over the stairs.

I freeze in shock.

It is the worst day of my life.

Of all our lives.

CHAPTER 13

10 YEARS AGO
TULSA, OKLAHOMA

Shep rushes in. I think it's afternoon. He doesn't say anything, he just gathers me in his arms and takes me upstairs to my old room. He sits on the floor, cradling me. Tears fall down his face, but he remains still and calm while I sob.

He kisses my head, strokes my hair, and tells me to let it out. I hadn't realized I was holding back. I cry harder, louder. I vomit. He takes us into the shower and holds me there on the floor. He keeps telling me to let it all go, that he has me, that he's not going anywhere.

"My dad—"

"Shhhhh, Bambi, it's all right. Your grandparents are here. Your uncle's here. I'm here. Adam. Buck just got here too."

He dresses me, he gets me water, he has me eat crackers. He takes me downstairs and sits with me and my sisters. He runs to get things we need. He puts me to bed. When I wake up, he's still sleeping on my floor with the door open, as if my dad or grandpa would care about propriety right now. But the open door, Shep cold on the carpet, it wrecks me, because it's what my mother would've insisted on. He knows that.

After a couple days, maybe three, Susan begins to function again. There's a funeral to plan, and Dad is not in a position to do anything. I can almost visibly see the weight of our entire family landing on her shoulders. I need to help.

I start helping her and our grandparents make decisions about things we think our mom would have wanted. It's . . . heartbreaking. She had everything she always wanted.

She had Dad.

She had us.

She had an unbelievable surgery career.

She had a couple quirky doctor friends just as introverted and logical as herself.

And some asshole ended it all.

She always ran very early in the mornings, and a few mornings ago, it was dark and misty and a drunk driver simply took her out at a crosswalk. One minute she was here, running to oldies and loving her life, the next she was gone.

The driver, some young guy we don't know, Jason something, drunk and high, survived. This makes me so angry I get light-headed. Jason is here. He gets to grow old, to laugh, to read, to work, to live. And my mother doesn't.

Then I feel ashamed at those thoughts. So I try not to think about it at all. Instead, I focus on helping Susan with the program, the flowers, the music, and a million other things. I obsess over it, over things I can actually do, any actions I can take.

Susan sees our entire existence right now as boxes to be checked. She needs that, so I talk her through her lists, adding and changing and volunteering. I help Adam help her, which is what he needs right now. I have a good guess at what everyone needs. I make sure Skye is left alone. I make sure Samantha has a friend over. I make sure Sally has books to read, puzzles to solve, and the mothering from our grandmother. I know my dad has his dad and he has us.

And I have Shep.

Shep, while also seeming hollow and lost, does all that I ask and what I don't ask for. He asks if I'm all right before he disappears one evening. I assume he's going to let off steam in the only way he seems to know how. I don't blame him, but I also don't know how he can stomach the idea of alcohol when alcohol just killed my mother. I don't ask. He needs to cope in his own way.

A couple days later, the largest church in Tulsa is filled to its rafters with black. It overflows, with people watching the service on screens in the fellowship hall. It's beautiful and it's horrible. Hundreds of patients, hundreds of friends of the family, hundreds of admirers who only know us from afar. It's overwhelming. Skye and Sally duck out after the service, and I can't help but think Mom would've wanted to do that too.

I help Susan and Sam greet, thank, and, weirdly, comfort people who are trying to comfort us. Shep is nearby every minute. He keeps his eyes locked on me, my sisters, and my dad. He hurts too, as does Buck. My mom was the only mother figure they've had in their lives.

Time, somehow, keeps going on. We are all a mess. None of us are eating well or sleeping well. We don't say much. We worry about my dad. We mourn, I guess.

Shep goes back to Norman before I do. All my teachers have given me an extended spring break. There are manuscripts to turn in, tests to take, and a senior recital I'm supposed to sing in. I don't know if I can do it.

Still, I head down to Norman anyway. Skye does too, but she's a sophomore, still living in the sorority house, so we don't go together. We both want the alone time during the drive anyway.

Shep meets me at my place, coffee and chocolate in hand. He smiles, but I can't smile back, and he understands. That night we have the saddest, slowest sex we've ever had. We both needed it, the connection and the release, but it was hard and strange. Shep is different since Mom died. Of course, I am too.

———

TWO MONTHS LATER

Shep is still different. I am too, but something is off. With us. Or with life? It's been two months since I lost Mom, and still the world is only gray. I am supposed to walk at graduation soon, and even that seems bland and unexciting. Nothing is interesting. To me.

Shep is different in that regard. I think it had been two full weeks back in Norman when Shep finally asked me to go out with him to a friend's house. I couldn't do it. For weeks he was disappointed, but he understood. He understood the next few times. But I didn't.

I still don't, as I watch him get ready to meet his buddies, yet again. I restart the conversation we keep having.

"Shep," I start, grabbing his arm on his way out for the evening.

"Don't, Sade. Just let me go."

"You can't keep going like this. If you're not partying, you're planning the next party. I mean, what about your dreams and goals—you're willing to just drink them all away?"

"My dreams and goals are fine. My grades are good, we're completely on track, you're gonna graduate, then I'll graduate, we'll go to New York. Me letting off steam tonight doesn't change any of that, Sadie."

"And when we get to New York? Are you going to go out with the guys every night there too? Leave me alone in some apartment in a new city by myself?"

"No, I won't. You'll be with me. You can be with me now if—"

"I can't! Because my mother died, Shep. Died because of *a drunk*." He tenses, and I realize how that sounded. "You're not a drunk, Shep. That's not what I meant, I just . . ."

"Sure sounded like that's what you meant." He yanks his arm out of my grip and storms out of my apartment. My heart fractures when the door slams, but I don't cry. I haven't cried since the day she was taken from us. I don't want anyone worrying about me and my crazy emotions. I think all my tears are finally gone.

A couple hours later, I feel terrible. Just because he parties hard when he parties doesn't mean Shep is a drunk. He may have the start of a problem, but he has plenty of nights when he's home with me on the couch watching something stupid and drinking nothing but water.

I know what he heard, which is "you are your father." I went too far and I need to talk to him. He needs to apologize to me too, and we need to find a new normal. But we'll find it. We have to. I don't want to lose him too.

I head to his friend Mark's place, hoping I've got the right address. Looks like I do by the number of cars in the driveway. I make my way in, unsure. I only know a few of Shep's law friends, one of which is freaking Mary Ann, who I wish would transfer or find herself a boyfriend.

It doesn't look like she's here tonight, but plenty of other girls are. Some are undergrads, some look a little older. All of them look interested in Shep, who's telling some story on the couch. Everyone is laughing, but his words are slurring badly. I wait for him to finish his thoughts before I move into his line of sight.

"There she is! My girl. Everybody, move!" he calls out as if people are in his way when really he just can't stand very well.

"Time to go, big guy." I pull him to the entryway before he snaps to reality.

"Wait, seriously, you came just to make me leave?" He's actually angry.

Now I'm angry too. "I came just to talk to you, but you are wasted. Let's go, now."

"Hell no, I need this. I'm not leaving, Sadie. I'll see you tomorrow."

I huff in disgust. "You don't need this. You need to sleep. C'mon."

He huffs right back, his words slurring. "I do need this! I know you're sad, Sade, I know, but I'm sad too. Everybody copes in different ways, and this is what I need, to let go and relax a little bit! Maybe you should try it for once."

I take a deep breath, feeling rage building to the point of no return. "What you need, Shep, is to talk to someone about your dad. And your mom. And my mom. You need to deal with your shit! You need to grow up! You're better than this!"

Something in him snaps as he yanks his arm away. He stumbles forward a bit in a drunken, angry haze. "No, I'm not! You're always pushing me, always push, push, push! How about you just let me be me, Sadie, ever think of that? How about you just take me as I am? Not always trying to change me? This is it!" He gestures his arms wide and then points to himself. "This is me! This is as good as it gets, honey, and you know what?" He deflates, and his voice calms. "I can't do this anymore."

I straighten my back and swallow. "What?"

"I'm not built for this, Sadie. I wish I was. I tried but I'm not enough, I'll never be enough! Your grieving, your pushing. Your hopes and dreams for you, for us—it's just too heavy. I can't do it."

"Shep. What are you saying right now?" I try to find his eyes, but he doesn't look at me or answer me. "Are you seriously breaking up with me because things are *too heavy?* My mom is *dead!*" He only sighs, refusing to look at me. "Shep, if you're seriously . . . if you . . ."

Shock at his words subsides, and sadness and rage start to build up. I tremble as I find the words, finally. "If I walk out this door without you tonight, that's it. I can't keep doing this with you. I need you right now, even if it's heavy and hard and painful. If you can't stick with me through this, then I guess you're right, it's not enough."

I wait.

He doesn't look up.

I turn, but he doesn't move.

I grab the door handle, and a sob shakes through me. I don't hear anything behind me.

I walk through the door and pull it slowly behind me, seeing that he's still looking down at the ground. His face and eyes are red and swollen. But he doesn't say a thing.

He lets me leave.

———

I haven't talked to Shep in two days.

It has been an eternity.

It's been hell.

It's been quiet too, giving me time to think. I don't think I'm too hard on him, per se, but I think in that moment, I did the wrong thing. Pushing an ultimatum on him when he was drunk, expecting either of us to make good decisions in the heat of the moment, that was idiotic. I know better. Sorrow has shredded me down, so I'm constantly hanging by one last thread, and that night, the thread snapped. His strength is fraying too, I know it.

He hasn't called or texted or come by, but I did basically say he wasn't good enough for me. Again, all his worst fears, straight from the mouth of the one who is supposed to love him the most, support him the most. I kicked him while he was down. I hope he'll forgive me.

It's a Saturday night, so I'm pretty sure he'll be back at Mark's house near campus. I pull up slowly and realize I'm wrong. Hm. If they're not all hanging at Mark's house, maybe they're at Shep's place?

They are.

This is fine. I'll just text him to come out.

He doesn't respond to my text. I don't want to call. I decide to just go in to ask to talk to him. I'll use my key, slip in, see his happy face as he rushes toward me. Hopefully he'll tell everyone to go home so we can kiss and make up. I miss his kisses so much you'd think they were fresh air. Like I haven't been breathing enough oxygen for the last two days.

I let myself in and hear the usual sounds—a TV with sports on, ice clinking, someone yelling about some game they've got going. I take a deep breath to steady myself. The air in here smells like him, like home. I walk into the living room with a small smile, ready to find him.

I do find him.

With Mary Ann.

She's breezing in from the kitchen, where Mark and a couple guys are pouring shots, it sounds like. She has red cups in her hands, one of which she gives to Shep on the couch. As always, she's looking down at him like he's a saint, or an angel, or maybe God himself. I bet he feels a thousand feet tall under that stare, just like I always worried about.

She sits down next to him, but honestly she's almost on top of his lap at this point. He doesn't move away from where their thighs touch. I walk slowly into the room, in shock but unable to simply turn and leave. She says something and laughs, touching his arm. It's intimate, like she's touched his arms that way a hundred times.

I've been gone three days; maybe she has.

His green eyes are cloudy from alcohol, a look I know well now. He looks cold and detached when he registers me in the room. He doesn't move from her. Doesn't pull his arm out of her grip.

It's all totally foreign, like I can't quite comprehend what I'm seeing.

I'm frozen, staring at my nightmare, mouth hanging, eyes wide. I'm like an actual deer in a set of headlights. The realization makes me sicker, if that was even possible, so I quickly turn to leave. I am not going to throw up in front of all of them. It's only a few steps to get out of the hellhole, but I hear him curse and say my name. I slam the door and double over, trying to catch my breath.

I hear him calling after me, about to open the door, so I force myself to keep moving. As I run to my car, I work his key off my keyring.

"Sadie, I—"

I open my car door and scream at him before ducking in. "Shep, I never, ever, *ever* want to see you again." I throw the key onto the driveway. I hear it clink on the concrete before I slam my door and start the car. Shep doesn't run after me as I put the car in reverse. He doesn't run into the street.

I pull away, looking back for any sign of him following me. I don't find one. Just like two days ago, he lets me leave.

This is really it. I shake and pant, but I don't cry. I pull over to vomit. Twice.

I keep driving until I see the familiar lights of my parents' porch. I am stabbed with fresh grief at the view—Mom's morning glory flowers framing the steps. The worn bench where she used to sit and put on her shoes for her runs. I suck in air and use all the oxygen to push the thoughts away.

I barely register going up the stairs to my room, closing the door, and crawling into my bed. I try not to relive the moments in his living room, but they're also all I can think about. I didn't see him kiss her or touch her.

I could be wrong about them.

Except he isn't here. He didn't rush after me. He hasn't called or texted to explain himself. *I'm not wrong.* He did exactly what I always told him to do. He found someone easier to be with. Easier to love, to support.

Early the next morning, I find myself downstairs, hearing myself tell Dad I need to go. I can't walk at graduation. I can't be in Norman anymore. I can't be at home either.

I don't cry. I don't eat. I don't sleep. I start packing, and my family understands.

We are still not okay. How could we be? Each of us has broken down in our own ways over the past couple months. Skye continues to process her feelings alone. She dyed her hair black. Samantha clings to her many friends, rarely home and never alone. Sally and Dad support each other, and Susan supports them. Adam supports her. And I . . . I want to get away. Now.

I don't tell the family about Shep other than that I broke up with him. Dad doesn't pry. He puts me on a flight and gives me a job in the Canton Cards New York office. He tells me we'll sort out my final grades and get my diploma shipped. Whatever I need.

I'm not sure what I need.

I take my journal and some clothes, but I leave my sheet music. I leave all my pictures and mementos and even my phone. I'll get a new number when I land.

Twenty-four hours later, I feel myself start to come back into my body. Some of the haze clears, as if I've been asleep for days. I feel the tiniest bit better. Just as I planned, just like I always dreamed, I start my new life in New York City.

CHAPTER 15

10 YEARS AGO
MANHATTAN, NEW YORK

A throat clears awkwardly behind me, startling me from my work. I don't love assisting the sales team with their pitches and presentations, but I don't hate it, either. It's something to do. I turn to face the eyes I can feel on my back.

"How are you doing, Sadie?" Margaret's eyes are warm with concern, even though her demeanor is stiff and bordering on cold. She is the office manager and nothing if not professional.

I try to perk up but fail. "Fine, thanks."

"The boxes from your father are still in receiving, as they have been for three weeks now."

"Oh, yeah, sorry I'll, um—"

"I have arranged for them to be sent to your apartment." I feel some of the tension release in my shoulders as she continues. "I've also sent some meals—already made and refrigerated or frozen—and groceries, and arranged for a laundry service for you." She doesn't look down from my eyes to my person, which I know has looked better. A lot better.

"Oh, Margaret, thank you. You didn't have to do all that." My eyes burn, so I sit up straighter and raise my voice a tiny bit. "Really, you don't have to take care of me."

"Someone does, dear. Besides, I've been assuring your father that you're eating and sleeping, and that he doesn't need to come out here and drag you back to Oklahoma."

"You have?" I stare up at the kind blue eyes resting in a pretty, if a bit severe, face. Her grayish white hair is in its signature coif above her pearl earrings that match the short strand around her neck.

She nods once. "And I know you do not want to make a liar of me. So go home, eat, shower, maybe unpack some of your things. If you plan on staying?"

"I do," I say quickly. I cannot go back to Oklahoma any time soon under these circumstances. I just can't. I lean down to grab my purse, and when I look back up, I have to do a double take at the sight.

"I understand you two know each other?" Margaret says with a slight gesture toward Emerson, who stands beside her like an uncomfortable human fence post. I nod at the same time he does, but the gesture hurts my brain.

I have avoided him for a reason. He and Shep are friends. Or at least were friends. Good friends. Emerson ended up as a tutor to some of the football players during his time at OU. He's a tall, mute genius who somehow became best friends with brooding Adam and crazy Shep. Susan's doing, most likely. He went home to England after graduating, though, so I'm not sure when last he saw any of them. As I understand it, he recently moved back stateside and joined the Canton Cards accounting team.

"He's going to see you home, show you the city, introduce you to his friends." Emerson coughs at the word, and Margaret gives him the most searing side-eye I've ever seen. I almost smile. I bet Emerson has exactly two friends in New York, if that.

"Oh, he really doesn't have to—"

"He's thrilled to do it, aren't you, Mr. Clark?"

"Happy to, Mrs. Wayne," he says quietly.

I smile at that. I actually smile.

"Ah, she has teeth! See? Better already." She puts a bony, manicured hand on my shoulder. "You bear a lonely burden in an even lonelier city, Sadie. Let us bolster you up." I can barely blink before she composes her face, removes her hand, and shoots a stern look at myself and Emerson before slipping out of my cubicle.

"How is that woman not the CEO of something?"

Emerson's mouth hitches up slightly on one side. "Indeed."

"You really don't have to do this, Emerson."

He clears his throat and gestures for me to join him in the walkway. We wind through the few rows of gray cubicles. It's a small, somewhat dumpy office, but it's a start for us, for Canton Cards, here in New York. Emerson looks at me for half a second before looking away.

"I actually am happy to help however I can." His throat looks so tight I'm worried one of the stringy tendon things might snap, spurting blood everywhere like a bad slasher movie. Gross.

"Uh-huh, you look like you're filled with glee over it." He sighs when I look up at him. "Relax, dude, we both know you don't have any friends."

He smiles a small smile at my teasing as he pushes the elevator button for us. "I have three, actually."

"What! Three friends! So much conversation and eye contact! How do you even bear it!"

"We text, obviously," he deadpans. I manage to smile again. The second smile today. Maybe Margaret was right to barge into my life and start making demands. I don't say anything else until we reach the sidewalk outside of the building.

"I don't need you to walk me home. I enjoy the wandering."

"You sure?" His relief is palpable. This poor guy. I can see how he and Shep worked. Shep talked and teased, and Emerson stood there. I bet it was Shep's life mission to get him to laugh.

I bet he succeeded.

My heart slices open painfully in my chest.

"I need the walks. Alone," I manage to say.

Emerson makes a strange sound and then looks me in the eye. "I'm so sorry for the . . . unfathomable loss. She was . . ."

He can't find the words. I can't either.

"She was," I whisper. "She really was."

He straightens his tie with a shaky hand. "Fridays we meet for happy hour at a ghastly pub a ways downtown. Will you spare me Mrs. Wayne's wrath and join me tomorrow?"

"Sure."

"Brilliant. Until then." He bows like he's from an entirely different era, and then flees from our conversation like only a totally spent introvert can.

I start my journey back to my new studio apartment, trying to take different streets. In my first month here, I've become obsessed with mapping the city and learning its quirks. I've found the most crowded areas, and the most deserted, at various times of day. I've enjoyed quaint lesser-known green spaces, impressive street performers, and so many amazing cafés and restaurants.

Lately, I never have an appetite, but I file them all away. It's something to think about, something to escape into, this new concrete universe of mine. I love the different energy from one section of Manhattan to another. The city is a people-watcher's paradise. On the weekends, I venture to different boroughs, hitting hotspots listed on any and all New York–related blogs and Instagram accounts.

Margaret was right in her guess that I don't really eat or sleep. I don't cry, either. I haven't been able to write. I don't know enough people or playhouses to start auditioning yet. So, I walk. I try to be productive at the office, then I escape into the city as much as possible.

When the weather is bad, I binge some shows. I can't handle anything happy, romantic, or realistic, so there have been a lot of sci-fi thrillers and action-packed war movies. Which explains why, when I do sleep, I have insanely weird dreams.

Eventually, I make it to my apartment. It's a tiny studio unit, but it's in a safe part of midtown Manhattan, with a rent to rival Dad's whole mortgage back home, I bet. He says it's a company apartment, but I wouldn't be surprised if he got it knowing I wanted to move here someday. I wouldn't be surprised if my mother put together a spreadsheet and a graph before they decided this spot was the right one for me. And now I can't text her all about it.

I turn my attention to the boxes to distract myself. I unpack one box of clothes before inspecting my fridge, curious. My eyebrows shoot up when I find not foil packages and restaurant boxes but actual porcelain dishes. The dishes have little handwritten labels on them. My jaw drops when I realize said dishes contain none other than casseroles. Casseroles!

Me: Dad, where is Margaret from?
Dad: Arkansas.
Dad: Used to work for the Waltons.
Dad: Why?
Me: Wow, I always thought she was from around here, but clearly not.
Dad: How'd you figure it out? I've never heard an accent.

Me: The woman made me casseroles.
Dad: That's a true heartlander right there.
Me: I'm surprised there's not a gallon of sweet tea in here too.
Dad: Why's she making you meals? You okay, sweetheart?
Me: Yeah. Okay. You okay?
Dad: I'm okay.

We can't expect or hope for better than okay. Not anytime soon. Still, I do feel a hint of hope in the back of my consciousness. Tomorrow I'm going to my first New York City happy hour. Suddenly I could eat. I pull out the dish marked CORNBREAD CHICKEN BAKE and mumble to myself, "Mrs. Wayne, you sneaky little southern sweetheart."

———

I find myself feeling almost excited when Emerson arrives at my cubicle. I chose a flouncy dress under a light suit jacket for today and heels to replace my flats. I'm actually doing the whole day-to-night wardrobe transition I've only ever read about in magazines. So city girl of me. *Peak Sadie.*

Sadness pierces me in my empty stomach as soon as the phrase, one of my mother's favorites, enters my mind. What I wouldn't give to text her a photo of my ensemble, to chuckle at her carefully-thought-out reply. How I wish I could hear her drone on about a surgery or explain a recent discovery from a book she'd just read.

"Shall we?" Emerson says softly, making me realize I was frozen. Sometimes grief does that, it arrests you, suddenly. Between my mom and Shep, I freeze up all the time. It's like my internal software is faulty. Grief is a glitch in my inner matrix.

"Yeah." I smile at him, though I'm not sure it puts him at ease. I'm not sure Emerson Clark is ever at ease. Still, I'm grateful.

We walk in almost total silence for a few blocks. It's comfortable silence, at least. I hear and smell the pub before we reach the wooden doors.

"Don't hold this against me or my kinsmen," Emerson mutters as he opens the door for me.

"What? Did you just say *kinsmen*?" But before I can tease him, I see what he means. This little place isn't a cute English pub. It's a weird, jam-packed rectangle that's *trying* to be a cute English pub. It's so over the top, with the flags and crests and an actual life-size knight statue in the corner, I can't help but smile.

"Ah, there he is. Come be social for an hour, you twat!" an excited Idris Elba doppelgänger yells at us from the bar, causing Emerson to curse under his breath. "And who's this with you?"

"Warren, try to be bearable, will you? This is Sadie Canton. Sadie, this is Warren Eaton."

"Canton, like your boss? Oh, this is bloody brilliant!" Warren says as I reach the group.

Emerson sighs. "And that's Jessica."

"Cheers," Jessica says with a bright smile and a wave. She is petite with gorgeous bright red hair and sparkling blue eyes. They make an interesting, quirky but very attractive group. The accents don't hurt.

"Hello, Sadie," a deep, buttery British voice says from my other side. I turn to see Tall, Dark, and Handsome, personified. He doesn't smile as he extends his hand. He kind of looks like he wants to eat me. I'm not sure how I feel about his intensity. "I'm Dennis."

———

I feel great about it, I've decided. It's been an hour, and Warren, Jessica, and I have made a lot of small talk. Warren, a real estate broker, makes me laugh; Jessica, an event planner, is open and friendly. They've all known each other since childhood, where together they attended what I'm sure is a crazy fancy and unbelievably expensive school.

Dennis, a CFO for a fancy tech company, is quiet but extremely interested. In me. He stares at me without reservation. It's unnerving but not unpleasant. After one drink, Emerson announces he's had all the friendly banter he can stand.

"Sadie, would you like to split a cab?"

Before I can answer, Dennis leans closer to me. "No, Sadie. Stay."

"All right," I concede. "Thanks, Emerson. I'll see you Monday."

"You'll see her home?" he asks Dennis.

"Of course."

Emerson turns to me, uneasy about the arrangement. "Just text that you make it back to your flat, yeah?"

I nod, then continue chatting with Jessica and Warren for another round until they leave as well. Then it's just me and the enigma staring me down.

Dennis is attractive, obviously. But more than that, he's alluring. Mysterious. Serious. Intriguing. Like he's a rich truffle I want to try, even though I'm pretty sure I'm not a truffle kind of gal.

"I know a few actors here, working in the city. I can introduce you."

"Really? That would be great," I say, trying to look more excited than I feel.

"Come to a show with me next weekend." He leans in, not leaving me space to refuse.

"Oh, uh, like, you don't mean, like a date?" I stumble all over myself. He's older than me by maybe five or six years? And so serious. I don't think he's smiled one time tonight. But shit, he's hot. Also, I don't think he had more than one drink, which I noted and appreciated somewhere in the back of my psyche.

"Yes, I do mean. Let me take you on a date."

"Okay." I give him a small smile, and for the first time in hours, he gives me one too.

He joins me in another drink before he walks me to the subway. I'm nervous and buzzed and grateful for someone to walk with. After taking my phone and inputting his number, he commands me to text him that I make it home okay.

As we pause on the platform, he leans in and I die a little bit.

He towers over me, too tall. He smells sophisticated, like a very clean man who spends his time in the woods. The smell is nice, but not quite right. Right for what, I don't know.

I just know I'm not ready for this.

My lips aren't ready for Dennis. For anyone. My lips still feel like they belong to Shep. I feel sick at the realization, especially when Shep's lips are probably locked with Mary Ann's.

I'm overthinking things, though, as always. Because Dennis is a gentleman. He gives me a soft kiss on the cheek and then a wave after I'm secure in my seat on the subway.

The sick feeling of almost kissing another man sticks with me until I get home. I rush to the kitchen for a water. I only ate a few fries at the bar, so my thoughts slush around in my head.

I can't believe I agreed to go on a date! I'm not ready to date! I'm not ready to . . . anything! What am I even doing in New York without Shep? How am I living without him?

How am I living without Mom?

How am I living without my sisters?

Am I living at all?

My head twirls as my eyes sting. I am nauseated, angry, sad, hurt, confused. A breakdown looms, I can feel it in the hairs on the back of my neck. I put a hand there and stare up, spotting a bottle of wine at the top of my fridge I'd forgotten about.

I don't want to feel all this shit anymore. I don't want to feel.

I grab the bottle, unscrew the screw top—*classy, Sade!*—and chug straight from the neck. I put on an Adam Sandler movie and chug a bit more. All the heavy feelings lift a little bit. I laugh, I lie down on my tiny couch, and finally, blissfully, my mind goes blank.

CHAPTER 15

10 YEARS AGO
MANHATTAN, NEW YORK

"Dennis! You said 'a show.' I thought you meant like a little off-off-broadway play! This is crazy." I squirm in his town car next to him in the back seat, because there's definitely a driver. The man is gorgeous, mysterious, British, and, apparently, filthy rich. I knew Emerson was loaded, and it makes sense his friends are too, but there's loaded and then there's, well, this. *Emmy Boy, I owe ya one!*

"This is a show," Dennis says, clearly pleased with himself even though he's barely smiling.

"This is *the* show. *Spider-Man* on Broadway has been all anyone has talked about for like a year. How did you get tick— Wait, do you really know some actors in this?!" I squeak. The car comes to a stop outside the theater doors, lit up under a dazzling marquee and rows of big old-fashioned round bulbs, just like you'd imagine Broadway theater doors should be.

"I do. Come, let's get a drink before the overture." He climbs out of the car and extends a hand to me. I take it, reeling over the fact that he knows what the overture is. I'm also glad, as I look up at him in his posh navy plaid suit, that I decided to take a risk on the dressier side with my black dress and heels.

I think I feel Dennis's penetrating stare on my cheek throughout some of the show, and I know I feel it afterward as I marvel backstage. As if prime center seats weren't enough to dazzle me, we get to waltz through the security checkpoint at the side door. The packed hallways behind the stage are buzzing from post-show energy, and I am absorbing it all like a happy sponge.

Eventually, we arrive at a group of cast members. Dennis pulls aside a guy I recognize from the ensemble. "Hayden, this is my friend Sadie. She's also an actor, new in town."

"Hi! Nice to meet you!" he says in a yummy accent to match that of both Emerson and Dennis. He is short and boy-next-door attractive, and he looks like he can really move. He must be able to really sing too, to make it to Broadway.

"You too, the show was just incredible," I gush, trying to keep my cool but losing it completely.

"Really, you guys enjoyed it then?"

"Very well done, mate. Never seen a show like this before," Dennis says warmly.

"Yeah, the effects were amazing, the whole cast was incredible. I'm reeling!" I say, and Hayden smiles wide.

"Sadie is insanely talented, but she could use a guide. Could we take you for coffee next week?" Dennis asks his friend.

"Take me for coffee—what am I, an investment banker? Meet us for drinks tonight at eleven thirty. Pink Lady's down the street."

"Oh, I don't want to impose," I start.

"No imposition when Denny here's buying." Hayden laughs, slapping my date in the chest.

Dennis nods and grins. "Sadie, myself, and my wallet will see you then."

I laugh a small, genuinely surprised chuckle at his joke, and the sound makes him look at me with . . . well, whatever it is, it's too much. I look away.

"I hope Canyon is okay between now and drinks?" Dennis asks me as we wait for his car to arrive.

"Canyon?"

"It's a steakhouse, is that all right? I took a guess and made the reservation based on Emerson's musings about Oklahoma." He looks genuinely concerned about his choice for dinner. He could've taken me to Steak 'n Shake in the park, and I would've been impressed. With the fact that he planned a date, with his having made reservations, with the way he takes control . . . with him.

"There are vegetarians in Oklahoma, you know. I've heard even Texas has—" I gasp for effect and whisper the last word, "Vegans."

"You're putting me on," he says.

"I am. Steak sounds perfect." I smile up at his face above mine. It's a genuine expression, and that unnerves me. Am I ready to smile at another man? I don't think I am, but I don't want to think at all.

I spend our dinner distracting myself from my own thoughts and feelings by peppering him with questions. His answers are open and honest, if not very animated. He is not holding back or uncomfortable; he's just serious. He's serious in a way that only drinks two glasses of wine, watches the time closely, and orders what I need, like water, napkins, dessert, and a to-go container, before I think to need it.

I'm pretty sure I could get used to it.

"There they are!" Hayden says as we enter what turns out to be a burlesque bar just after 11:30. "Let's get this night started now that my dear friend Mr. Moneybags is here!" We laugh, and I feel a thrill at the idea of our night *starting* after 11:00 P.M. How very New York City!

Hayden introduces me to a gaggle of actors, some from his show, some from other shows, and all very standoffish. At least they were before the drinks started flowing. Now Dennis is their absolute favorite person, and they are showering me with promises about guidance, wisdom, and connections. They also shower me with shots. We talk about music, shows, auditioning, acting, singing—it's electrifying. They are living my dream, and being so close to them makes me feel close to my own goals.

Hayden keeps asking for another round, and I keep joining in. Dennis keeps a hand on my back and a water nearby. He orders appetizers and desserts and catches me when I almost fall out of my stool laughing at one of Hayden's jokes. Dennis is a steadying anchor behind me, a pillar I can lean against, sometimes literally.

"Let's get you home, darling," Dennis eventually says to me before turning to the bartender. "Another water over here, please, and the bill."

"The bill for all of us, Dennyboy!" Hayden adds before launching into a serenade with an altered version of "Danny Boy." Dennis nods and sighs in a way that sounds like an eye roll. Hayden pulls him away to tell a story to a group at another table, but I can't follow. My ass is stuck to the stool. How did that happen?

The bartender, a striking woman with deep brown eyes and even deeper brown skin, sporting a million ear piercings and effortlessly cool long dreadlocks, pushes a water toward me but doesn't let me take it from her hand.

"If they don't come through on all their liquid promises your boyfriend bought, I'm part of a reading group that meets here for lunch on Tuesdays and Thursdays. Come by if you want."

"Oh, thanks, but he's not my boyfffriend. And I'm Sssssadie," I tell her.

She laughs before nodding. "You're wasted is what you are. I'm Tash." She turns as Dennis joins us to sign the tab. "This is for her, not you," she says as she scribbles on the receipt.

Dennis walks me out to the curb just as his car pulls up.

"As much as I want to escort you home, I need to see to Hayden. He took two different pills . . . that I counted."

I feel my eyes grow wide. I can't believe I missed that. That's unlike me. I realize that I wasn't studying everyone in front of me, because I was actually participating in what was happening around me. And it was fun.

"Ed will get you home, and then you'll text me, okay, darling?" Dennis says. He's bossy, but surprisingly, I don't hate it.

"Okay." I'm about to duck into the car, but Dennis pulls me close to kiss me on the forehead. Then he covers my head and tucks me into the car like I'm a porcelain doll. I thank him for a great night and then relax into the plush leather seat of Ed's car. Ed, the driver of the town car taking me home from a bar where I hang out with a bunch of actors until 2:00 A.M.! I giggle as I watch the city blur by.

———

I wake up with a headache and a blackhole in my memory where getting into my apartment, changing clothes, and going to bed should be. *Yikes.* I search for my phone and almost drop it when I see it's past noon. I also see a conversation with Dennis that I don't remember.

Dennis: Did you make it home?
Dennis: Sadie?
Me: Yes I did!
Dennis: Good. I would hate to have to murder Ed.

Me: You can't murder Eddie, he's the sweetest. He helped me get my giant key in the teeny tiny keyhole.
Dennis: Did he help you with anything else?
Me: No, just that pesky key.
Dennis: Okay.
Dennis: I hate that I wasn't able to walk you to your door like a proper date. Come with me to an event next weekend.
Me: An event?
Dennis: Yes, an overpriced fundraiser.
Me: Like a flashy, expensive dinner with ball gowns and tuxedos?
Dennis: And drinks and dancing.
Me: Do you dance, Oh Denny Boy?
Dennis: On occasion.
Me: I'm not sure I can imagine you cutting a rug.
Dennis: Then I suppose you'll have to come with me to see for yourself?
Me: I suppose I will.
Dennis: Fantastic. I'll forward you the information tomorrow.
Dennis: Good night, Sadie.
Me: Good night!

A gala. My first Manhattan gala! I've been to many fundraising dinners with my family, even some impressive galas. But never in New York City. Not on my own, not with a date. A totally gorgeous, successful British date! I feel happy for a second, and then I feel bad for feeling happy. How can I be happy about anything that I can't share with my mom?

I notice another text notification, so I tap it, hoping for another distraction from the pain shooting through me.

Me: This is Sadie! It was great to meet you.
Tash: You too. Come hang out Tuesday!
Me: What do I need to bring?

Tash: Whatever you're working on, lines to run, an audition
piece, a manuscript, lyrics, whatever!
Me: What time?
Tash: Elevenish

I feel a thrill again. While Hayden was a riot, I don't feel like
I could text him, and definitely not to get together and work on
material. Tash's invitation feels like a soothing balm on my bat-
tered soul.

I have a new friend.

———

I make myself wait until 11:30 before walking up to Pink Lady's, which, from the street, looks dirty, odd, and a little sad in
the light of day. Inside, though, the atmosphere is cheery. All the
lights are on, and the magenta shades to the front windows are
open. Music is playing, and a group of people are debating something loudly in the center of the dining space. I project confidence as I approach, then internally relax a smidge when I spot
Tash on the other side of the dinner-theater space.

"Oklahoma! You made it!" She smiles brightly. She's even
more striking in the bright light. She's about my height, 5'5" or
so, but leaner and much more toned. I smile, but she must catch
my apprehension. "You don't remember that nickname, do you?
I learned most of your life story Saturday night."

I wince. "Really?"

She laughs loudly. "No, not really. Just a tiny bit. Moneybags
wanted you to share a lot more, but Hayden and his crew kept interrupting. Anyway!" She speaks up so the small groups around
the whole venue can hear. "This is Sadie, just moved here from

Oklahoma. And she is . . ." She does a drumroll on the wooden table she's standing at. "An actor!"

The whole place cheers.

"A singer!"

"Heys!" ring out.

"Dancer?" Tash asks me. I give her the hand wag that everyone understands to mean so-so. "Okay, so probably a killer dancer too. What else?"

"Writer, I guess?" Everyone cheers again.

"Songs or scripts?"

"Screenplays." A few people cheer.

"YouTuber?"

"Nope."

"Influencer?"

"Nope."

"Life coach or personal trainer?"

"Definitely not."

"Oh, thank God." She sighs. Someone yells a string of profanity at her from the side of the room that houses the long old-timey bar. She flips them the bird in response.

"Stand-up comedy? Poetry, fashion line, painting, sculptor, crochet?"

I laugh a little. "Crochet?"

"I'm just listing all the various versions of crazy you'll find among this gaggle of losers. To the Pink Ladies!" She raises a glass of what looks like soda. The place cheers again, and everyone goes back to what they were doing.

I shake the shock off my face as Tash walks to meet me.

"Don't get too excited. The name means nothing—half of these people would stab you in the eye to steal your spot in an audition line, and all of us are broke as a joke."

"So." I shrug. "Just a regular bunch of artists, then."

She throws back her head with a cackle. "One thousand per-cent. Welcome to New York!"

KELSEY HUMPHREYS

CHAPTER 16

ONE MONTH AGO
THE CARIBBEAN

SHEP

Today, I've got to do better. To be better. I keep reverting to the bitter, broken man I don't want to be anymore. This is harder than I was expecting. But then again, I'm not very bright, am I?

Her in that skimpy bikini . . . hot damn.

Hot. Damn!

I *hate* that she still gets to me. Especially when I don't seem to get to her anymore. Why would I? She made quick work of moving on, and she sure as hell kept moving. Thank the Lord above I haven't had to see Dennis much, or things could get ugly.

Hell, things are already ugly. Just the way she looked, relaxed in the water by herself. Her face looked so open, unguarded, young . . . until she saw me. Then it was shields up, weapons drawn.

My blood rushes when I remember her totally at my mercy last night. I was so close I could've reached out and felt her lips, touched her skin. I could've grabbed her, held her. Not that any of that is a good idea, but it was what I wanted in the moment. Nothing emotional, just a way to let our chemistry out of our systems.

It's still there, that heat. Somehow. It's completely unbelievable and almost unbearable. I'm pulled to her like a comet heading down to earth. But obviously I'm gonna burn up on entry after the way she pulled away from me with such disgust.

The moment she shoved me away, all the old anger just bubbled right up to the surface.

This woman ruined my life.

I'm sure she would say I ruined hers too. But she doesn't even know the truth of it. Maybe we could have recovered. I used to think we could have. But she was just gone. Vanished across the country like she wasn't leaving anyone important behind.

She was everything, and she made it clear she thinks I'm nothing, over and over again.

I want to scream at her.

I also want to hear her scream. Or moan or cry or anything. Any kind of reaction at all. She's gotten even better at acting with age. Writer, my ass. She should have a wall of Oscars and whatever all those other stupid TV awards are. Her mask is impenetrable. But it didn't used to be impenetrable for me.

I sigh as I slip my room key into my pocket and grab my phone.

I don't want to be her enemy, though. I love Adam, Emerson, her dad, her whole stupidly perfect family. I don't want to start a war with her right before this wedding. Well, I want to. Because I'm still a big competitive child, I guess. And possessive of someone who's no longer mine.

I hate seeing Emerson's tool-bag brother sniffing around like she's gonna give him the time of day. I wanted to flip over his kayak and yell, "She's not pickin' up what you're puttin' down, dummy, quit embarrassing yourself!" I barely kept my mouth shut.

He's Emerson's brother, and Clarky, as I call Emerson, much to his dismay, is one of my best friends. The Cantons are like family to me too. I can be civil and make it through this tropical hell for a week. I can be Sadie's *friend*.

My stomach curls up into a tight ball.

Nope.

Not gonna be her friend.

But I also shouldn't be cruel. Last night, I finally got a reaction, and it was after insulting her appearance. Could I be a bigger dick? Especially when she looks beyond beautiful. She looks like some kind of unattainable angel. But also downright edible at the same time. A woman in her prime. Better than when we were kids, somehow.

I shake the thoughts from my mind as I adjust myself in my shorts. No one is around me in the hallway leading to whatever silly activity Sammy is making all of us do. Emerson said to keep our traps shut and make his girl happy, and we all agreed.

But dread fills me up and makes me slow blink as I reach the lobby. Fury follows right behind it when I spot her laughing casually with Janie. Just giggling away like this isn't the worst week of her life. Like it's not painful to be around each other and to celebrate other people who've figured out all this love and commitment shit. She and I are clearly incapable, with each other, sure, but with anyone else too.

Tiny shorts display her long tanned legs. A light, silky tank top hangs over her perky chest. Her toned arms adjust an OU cap on her head. Her hair is in a messy low ponytail.

She looks like a kid again. She looks like the Sadie of my memories. The happy ones.

Like maybe she could still, should still, be mine.

171

Get a grip, dickhead. You hate her, and she hates you.

I use all my control to pull my eyes off her and spot Dennis across the lobby, watching her closely. He looks like a man scorned. Like they are the ones at war. Like he's the one who makes this week hard for her. Like she could or should still be *his.*

Oh. I let out a grunt at the idea. Absolutely not. No way.

He doesn't have a friggin' hint of a clue how wrong he is. Crap, my balled fists are shaking just watching all this from afar. I'm seeing red again, and it's not even midday.

How the hell am I gonna keep my mouth shut and play nice?

"Okaaay guuuuuys!" Samantha singsongs at us. It's a good thing we have the whole resort to ourselves with the volume level on this girl. We all laugh, since Sammy is either literally or figuratively a little sister to almost all of us.

I look at my buddy. Emerson has an arm locked possessively around her waist, and he's looking down at her like she's his one and only source of happiness. And for the grump that he is, that actually might be true. But it kills me a bit to see him this way. I want to be happy for him, but man, I want what they have, and I know it's not in the cards for me. Not anymore.

I sense with my whole being the moment Sadie ducks out of the lobby to a restroom down the hall. I'm irritated by this. How can our souls still feel like they're attached when they've both been ripped to shreds? What's even left of my heart at this point?

Just being near her sparks fresh pangs of grief and loss. Hearing her voice float across the water. Seeing her smile, watching her laugh. It's . . . heartbreaking. That's what this week is. A smashing of the few pieces still rattling in my chest. And it's all Sadie's fault, so why, for the love of all things holy, am I still sensing her every move? Must just be the chemistry, the unending attraction.

"Today we've got a moped tour around the island!" Samantha explains. "Rocko and Marta are going to lead us the long way to a beautiful beach for lunch all the way on the other side, and then straight back. The mopeds are lined up out front for us. Let's roll!"

I'm already one of the last in the group as it files out of the door, so I hang back, feeling Sadie's presence somewhere behind me. I don't turn to greet her, but I'm not sure I could walk any slower. *Really subtle, Shep. Wow.*

Sure enough, she and I, a reluctant Janie, and stupid, smirking Benedict CumberTwat are the last ones to the mopeds. Rocko hands each person a geeky little helmet and watches as everyone pulls away in one long procession. Ben and Janie take off, with Ben looking back repeatedly and obviously. Sadie takes a minute to get situated because she has to take off her hat.

I start my moped's engine, and just as I'm about to gun it away from the siren next to me, I hear her scooter stall. The engine emits a loud clanking noise and a rush of smoke. That thing ain't startin' up today.

"Oh no, miss. I'm so sorry. That one keeps giving me so much trouble, miss, so much trouble."

"Oh, okay, do you have any more mopeds?" Sadie replies to Rocko.

"No, miss, so sorry."

I watch as her beautiful face falls. *Don't do it, Shep. Don't do it.*

Rocko looks to me and then back to Sadie.

"Uh, can I ride with you?" she asks him.

"No, miss, I am not allowed. My apologies, m-miss," he stutters, still glancing between us.

Don't do it . . . don't . . .

"She can ride with me." *WHAT!* I hear myself do it. Smiling a wide, mean, sonofabitch smile.

She huffs a laugh at us. "Uh, you know what, I can just skip today."

"No, no, miss, you don't want to miss today, very pretty ride. It is a favorite. You should get on with one of your friends, please, miss."

"What's wrong, Sadie, you saying you can't handle a quick scooter ride with a *friend?*" I sneer.

Holy hot sauce on brisket, I'm like those people who take selfies with rabid wild animals. I'm poking the shit out of this bear, and there's no doubt it's going to bite my head off. And enjoy chomping down on my bones, judging by the way she's staring at me.

She sighs in resignation, and every cell in my system starts to buzz, preparing for her nearness.

"I guess that's fine." She moves toward my moped. Immediately I feel two distinct desires. I want her hands holding tight around me. And I want to get moving, take a tight turn, and throw her off the moped and into a ditch. No, not a ditch, a ravine. A deep one, with sharp rocks and alligators at the bottom and—

She's touching me. I am frozen. She's trying to lean back, to create distance. But this is a small scooter, a fact I both love and hate right now, and so her front is up against my back. My brain is . . . my heart . . . my . . .

"Uh, Shep?" This time I can hear she's sporting the shit-eating grin. "We gonna get moving or what?"

"Oh, honey, you're gonna regret that." I peel off as fast as this little machine will go. I'm thrilled at the garbled terrified version of my name that escapes her. She grabs onto my sides for half a second before realizing what she's doing. She quickly lets go of me and grabs onto the seat instead.

This is going to be fun.

I zoom past everyone else in our group, weaving in and out and around the mopeds in sharp, jerky movements. People honk, Sadie screams. Still, her hands aren't back on me yet.

Rocko is suddenly beside us. "Sir, please slow down! My job, sir!"

"No can do, Rocko, you better lead the way before I take us all off a cliff!" I shout.

"Shep! What is wrong with you!" Sadie yells at me, her body coming closer so she can yell into my ear.

"Just your general nearness, sweetheart! Makes me erratic!"

"Well, youaaaahhhh!" she screeches, as I twist the steering to purposely hit a pothole the size of a small country. Her body is flailing around and still, she won't grab onto me. Stubborn woman.

"Seriously, for Pete's sake, just let me ride with someone else!"

"Who's Pete?" I bark back. "Another fiancé?"

"Really? *Who's Pete?* And a fiancé joke? Soooo original. Just as smart as I remember!"

"'Bout as smart as pissing off your driver!" I call back to her, slowing down so I can swerve around Emerson's scooter and speed off again.

"Shep, slow down! I'm gonna fall off!"

"That's kinda the idea!" I've slowed down again just to zoom once more, and the threat does it. She wraps around me so tight my breath actually hitches. A bit tighter, and her grip might even hurt. She's grown strong, I'll give her that.

"If I'm going, you're going with me, asshole!"

"We'll see!" I threaten again. Her arms tighten on me, and I hate how much I love it. I love that she's bothered and scared and calling me names. I can hear the smile in her voice. She's having fun, thanks to me. Serious Sadie, letting go. And holding on.

I feel every adjustment she makes of her skinny arms around my frame in the tightening crotch of my shorts. Hell, I feel her touch in my toes. In my damn earlobes. She still holds all of me in her hands. The thought terrifies me. It enrages me again and makes me slow the bike and miss a giant bump in the road.

I straighten up and yell, "Okay, Rocco, I guess I'll let you keep your job, buddy."

"Thank goodness," Sadie mutters as she removes her arms. But I hear it, she's disappointed.

And I hate how happy that makes me. I want to zoom off again. I want to pull over and make her talk to me. Make her listen. Make her react and explode, preferably underneath me.

But I seriously cannot do any of that.

Because I don't think I can survive this girl again.

CHAPTER 17

10 YEARS AGO
MANHATTAN, NEW YORK

SADIE

I sway a little on my new, black sky-high heels. I never wore platform heels with Shep because it made me seem taller than him. *Crap, why am I thinking about him!* Dennis still towers over me tonight, with inches to spare.

I want to glance over at him as he talks to a man almost as glamorous as he is. They stand in tailored tuxedos, drinking amber liquid from sparkling tumblers. It's like a scene from a movie. The other guy makes jokes and laughs, but Dennis just smiles politely.

I don't look, though, because I know I'll find his dark irises on me. The most serious, heavy pair of eyes I've ever encountered. Every time they've overwhelmed me, I've gulped down my drink. I guess I've been overwhelmed a lot tonight.

Still, I've had so much fun. I've met some fascinating people. So many in this room seem to want to impress Dennis, and I've enjoyed learning about him, laughing along to their stories, and feeling like a New York woman. Not girl—woman.

Dennis has shown me off proudly tonight, introducing me to anyone and everyone. There was a red carpet and a photo booth, and he stood patiently beside me, smiling and posing and letting me ham it up. His hand has been on the small of my back, he's kissed the side of my head. But the way he watches me . . . I should probably switch to water.

"I think we've made enough of an appearance," Dennis says softly in my ear. On our way out of the glitzy ballroom, he hands me a water from somewhere. I see a spread of tiny dessert plates that look like individual works of art, and he insists I try as many as I want. Then we're through the door, and I'm tucked into the car, feeling somewhat detached from my body.

With water and dessert in my system, I sober up the tiniest bit on the drive home. Still, the late night and mixture of liquors have me feeling less than stellar. Dennis's hand holding mine is not helping matters. My hand is not ready to be held. I roll down the window so I can breathe.

"You all right, Sadie?" My fingers are squeezed. I look over at my date and nod but don't answer. I focus on breathing and drink more of the bottled water his car had stocked in the back console.

When we arrive at my building, Dennis helps me out of the car and then steadies me on my shoes that are far more cute than they are stable. Or maybe they're plenty stable and I'm just tanked.

"Easy." Dennis chuckles. "Looks like I have been doing a piss-poor job of taking care of you."

"Actually, you're doing a great job."

"Am I?"

I nod, thinking. "I don't let loose very often. It's been forever since I could just, you know, let go."

"What about your wild oats? You didn't let go in college?"

"Not really." I look from the street down to my hand that he's holding again. I think about how celebrating or letting off steam felt for me over the last year. "Someone had to stay grounded, be the serious one. That was always me."

"I've been told I am *too* serious," Dennis says quietly, causing me to glance up at his expression. He raises an eyebrow.

"You? I'm shocked." I chuckle.

"Maybe I am serious enough for the both of us." He says the words as if they're a question.

I shake my head, feeling a little embarrassed at just how drunk I got on our sophisticated date. On a night that feels like the start of my new, weird, totally different life. "I'm sorry. Sorry I got carried away. Hayden last weekend, me tonight. I know how it is. It's not exactly fun to be the one who has to take care of everyone else."

"I quite enjoyed taking care of you." His voice is low, and his face comes closer to mine. I close my eyes reflexively, feeling fuzzy and confused and all twisted up. "Sadie." It's almost a growl, and my eyes pop open.

"Hm?"

"Let go again, right now." I feel the sound of his voice in my core, and I do. I quit thinking completely as he smashes his mouth on mine, pushing my lips open and taking everything he wants from me. The kiss is fast and sloppy and foreign and almost erotic. There is something about it that feels wrong in my mind, maybe my heart, but apparently, not in my body. I collapse into it. I collapse into Dennis. And, gentleman that he is, he catches me.

———

"Dennis DeLane? *That's* your boyfriend? How am I just now hearing about this?" Carly squeaks. Her voice is tiny like the rest of her. She's got a soft, innocent air about her that actually reminded me of Mary Ann at first. Except she has long fire-red locks and cusses like a sailor when she's frustrated. She makes me laugh.

"Invite Moneybags for lunch—maybe he'll buy us all pizzas," Tash adds, without looking up from her script.

"Um, yes please! I would die!" Carly grows so loud the rest of the place glances over at her, except for the guy at the piano. I look around the smoky club, lit up in all its dirty, dusty light-of-day glory. The quirky place seems homey to me now, even if the smell in here is awful.

"Definitely not," I say to both of them. "I didn't mention it because he's not my boyfriend, and this is *not* his scene."

"No, his scene is probably penthouses and Bentleys and helicopters and oh, does he have a private elevator to his place?"

"I actually don't know. It's a fancy building, but I've never been up."

"Wait." Tash's eyes pop up, wide. "You've been dating Hot McRichPants for weeks—actually, has it been a couple *months*?—and you haven't been to his apartment?"

I shrug and avoid eye contact. "We're taking it slow. He's a gentleman."

"I'll bet he is. My panties are burning just thinking about his suits and his town cars and his driver." Carly sighs, and Tash snorts at her. "Is that what your play is about? A simple Oklahoma girl comes to the city and an older Manhattan man makes a woman out of her?"

"No!" I choke on a laugh. "It's about fated childhood sweethearts," I mumble. "Or, it was. I am beyond writer's block at this point."

"Becaaaause *lame and boring!* They say write what you know, and right now you know the feel of a billionaire's hands on you. Billionaire with a B! I'm so jealous I could spit in your drink." I do a double take at my fiery friend. "I won't! I won't! I'm just saying I *could*."

"You know, you've been coming here for a while now, but you don't audition. You run lines with me, you harmonize with her." Tash points her chin at Carly. "You sit and stare at that binder. Why don't you let us read it, give you some notes?"

I squirm in the sticky corner booth that's become our regular spot at Pink Lady's. We're an odd little threesome, but Carly is from Utah and only a year older than me. Tash, from Pennsylvania and a year older than Carly, thinks we're both "adorable."

I pick at the corner of the binder where the plastic is coming apart. "Eh, it's not ready for readers."

"Duh. We help you get it ready. Gimme," Carly says, hands outstretched. I hesitate, but she grabs it from me. I don't fight her. Tash is right. Both of them have become good friends in a short amount of time, and I've been happy to help them, support their creation. Maybe it's time I get back to my own creating.

I want to, I do, but I can't pick up my pen and finish the piece. It's not the story of me and Shep, exactly, but it's close. I added a bit more drama and made the personalities more extreme. But now it's just too painful to even look at.

Everything is still painful. Much of the time just existing is still excruciating, if I pause long enough to be honest with myself.

That explains why I don't pause. I focus hard at work, trying to push Canton Cards to be better than ever. I owe it to Dad. I miss him, but I don't call. It's hard to hear his voice, which is no longer the same. Grief can change even our vocal cords, it turns out.

Maybe that's why I don't really sing anymore. Mom loved my voice. So did Shep.

I know a lot more about auditioning, but I keep putting it off. Instead, I've continued to obsess about the city. I'm not alone in my wandering anymore, though. Dennis joins me for my walks. He has spent his time here in cars, ballrooms, and skyscrapers, so some of what we explore is new to him too. It's been nice.

We eat posh dinners and go dancing and party at clubs. Or I party, and Hayden joins me with his long-time boyfriend. Tash has come along a couple times. Dennis dotes on all of us, smiling and watching me.

I'm not proud of how many late nights I can't remember, but I'm also not going to shame myself over it. I'm young! This is New York City! And I'm chasing my muse, as Carly says. I just can't seem to find it.

Most days I'm hungover and tired, which is another reason I am not regularly auditioning. I make sure I'm not too tired to perform well at my job. Margaret has stopped fussing over me. Emerson has stopped his obligatory check-ins. I'm not sure how he feels about me with Dennis, but I don't really care what he thinks. This is my new life. What people back home think of it or of me is really none of my business.

That means I'm okay, I think. On my nights in and alone, because Dennis is working late, I read with a bottle of wine. The wine and the words together drown out my own thoughts. I've always read, devouring any and all kinds of novels. Lately, I've escaped into thrillers and fantasy, not able to stomach the romance books I used to love. I do miss those tidy, happy endings.

"Sadie? If it's that big of a deal, just say so." Carly frowns at me, holding the binder back in my direction.

"Sorry, no, uh, what?"

"You zoned out again, Oklahoma. Late night last night?" Tash chuckles.

I shake myself back to reality. I smile at Carly sitting across from me. "It's fine, you guys are right. It's time for some feedback."

"And, while I'm reading this, you start writing about Dennis DeLane so I can read that!"

I roll my eyes at her. "Are you always going to say his first and last name like that?"

"Yes, and you should too. In bed." Carly moans dramatically. "Yes, yes, yes, and write it all out for me, in detail. The smuttier the better. Ugh, I need to get laid."

"Girl, same," Tash says. We laugh, but the subject makes me uncomfortable. I haven't ever thought of it as getting laid. I've only ever made love with my best friend. I've only ever thought of sex as the joining of soulmates, as something special. Holy, even.

I scoff at myself. Men certainly don't view sex that way. Shep didn't. I bet he was with Mary Ann on every surface of his apartment before my plane landed in New York. The thought wrecks me with nausea. I need to walk this off.

"I'm going to head back. I've taken a long lunch as it is."

"Uh, does it matter if your name is on the door?" Carly cocks an eyebrow.

"That actually makes it matter more. See you guys tomorrow," I say, almost running out into open air filled with fast-walking strangers. I suck in a breath and put my headphones in my ears.

Will this happen the rest of my life? My chest constricting, my thoughts spiraling. Her legs in Shep's lap. The dead, vacant look in his eyes. Driving all the way home to a house that felt wrong and cold and empty without my mother inside. Getting on a plane and leaving my sister's sad faces behind. Checking my new phone for calls and texts, hoping he hunted down my number. Waiting for apologies that never came.

Shep is gone.

My mother is gone.

I just need to walk.

I just need to make it a few more hours, and then I'll drag Emerson to a happy hour or meet Dennis for an early dinner, cocktails included. I can already feel the buzz. Things will be a little easier, lighter, better.

Maybe we'll try karaoke. Maybe I need to try to sing. Maybe I need to try to write.

And, I think with a burst of one thousand emotions, maybe I need to try to *get laid.*

———

I can. I can do this with Dennis. He's kind, gentle, protective. He's taken care of me all night. He's taken care of me for almost two months. He follows me around the city, takes me to classy events and dinners. He has sent me flowers, chocolate, champagne, and five-course meals from Michelin restaurants that don't even offer takeout.

Like always, he's prepared to leave me at my doorstep with nothing but a searing kiss. We've made out a lot, and he's grasped at me over and under my clothes. But not everywhere. He always feels me tense up, and, good man that he is, he leaves. But not tonight.

He pulls back from me, breaking our embrace. "Good night, darling girl."

I grab his arms. "Stay with me?"

"Sadie, you've been drinking quite a bit, sweetheart. I don't want to—"

"I want to." I cut him off. It's now, while I am feeling braver and lighter and looser, or maybe never. He's been patient. I need to get this over with. I need to move on.

I turn and lead him in by the hand. He's seen my place before. We've made out on my couch. But tonight feels different. We make it to my bedroom, and all the loose, fuzzy feelings start to evaporate. My hands shake as I start unbuttoning his shirt.

He clasps his hands over mine.

"Sadie, darling, what do you want?"

"I want . . . I want to let go. With you," I whisper, looking at my hands on his bare chest.

"Do you trust me?" he purrs, his accent wafting around me, mixing with his expensive cologne. I nod.

"Sadie." His voice changes. His eyes darken, and his posture grows taller. He wants control, and I'm happy to give it to him. "Take off your clothes. Now."

———

My eyes flutter open despite their dry, sticky lids. I didn't wash off my makeup after . . .

Holy crap!

The night comes back to me in a rush. I look over, and there he sleeps, dark and still and taking up all the space in the room. I inhale deeply through my nose. I swallow, but my mouth is a desert. I slowly grab my phone and creep out of my room.

My brain throbs in my head. My thoughts scramble. I feel the overwhelming need to talk to my sister. Tash and Carly wouldn't understand. Hayden and I aren't close enough, and I don't need him spilling my secrets to Dennis.

I need Susan.

Me: Sooooo I did it. Like did IT! With Dennis. Last night.

She doesn't respond, which is odd, especially since it's late in the day on a Saturday. She normally texts me back right away.

Me: I was nervous and tipsy, and it was weird and a little sad, but also it was pretty freaking hot. He bossed me around the whole time, totally overpowering me, but in a good way. I couldn't really think, which I think was what I needed.

Me: He was gentle. It's not like he tied me up or anything weird . . . though I could see him doing that . . . more like he took care of me and my thoughts and my worries by just telling me what to do every step of the way. Like a teacher. A hot billionaire sex teacher!

Me: Okay, that last sentence was a test. You must be asleep or in a movie theater. If you don't write back soon, I'll assume you've been kidnapped by aliens and alert the authorities.

I get my coffee pot going and pull out ingredients for omelets. Finally, my phone buzzes. But it's not Susan.

Adam: The baby is coming early!
Adam: Susan is asking for you. Can you get on the next flight out?
Me: Yes. Omw

Dennis walks into the kitchen in just his slacks, which hang low on his waist. He's barefoot, and his hair is disheveled. After last night, he's gone from objectively gorgeous to scorching, blinding hot. But I can't think about that right now, and he sees it on my face. "Sadie? What is it?"

"My sister went into early labor. I need to find the next flight home." I'm already scrolling through options on my phone.

"Don't book a flight. My family has a jet." He wraps his long arms around me and kisses my head as he pulls his phone out of his pants pocket. He starts barking orders to someone before telling me to get in the shower. Once again, he takes charge of me. It's exactly what I need.

CHAPTER 18

10 YEARS AGO
TULSA, OKLAHOMA

I don't have the mental capacity to fully appreciate the private jet that takes me home. My mind is full of worry for Susan and the baby. I'm excited to see my dad and sisters, whom I've missed. I just wish I didn't have to do it in Oklahoma, where Shep and Mary Ann happen to live.

Are they together? Will I see Shep? Surely not. Adam wouldn't invite him to the birth, would he? I mean, they're best friends, so maybe? They don't know he ripped my heart out and crushed it under his boot. I didn't tell them. Maybe I should have.

I also wish I wasn't headed to the hospital.

The hospital used to be special and exciting. It was where Mom was. It was her happy place, and she was always ecstatic to see us visiting. She beamed at us, her white coat stretched wide as she'd lean down and open her arms for a hug.

My eyes burn as the plane lands. Within minutes, we're on our way, since Uncle Robert was waiting for me right off the runway of the small airport. He explains, with a tight throat, that Susan isn't at the hospital. Apparently in the last few months, she decided to give birth at a women's center instead. I sigh, and he nods in understanding. We will all be avoiding the hospital from now on, for as long as we can.

It feels similar, though, I realize as I rush in the door. Same smells, sounds, same beige and gray and bright, terrible lighting. I see my family waiting, everyone huddled together, looking nervous. Skye sees me first, exhaling as she stands, and takes her earbuds out of her ears. Sally feels her get up and is so scared she looks even younger than thirteen.

"Sade!" Samantha almost yells, then everyone is up and we're all hugging.

"Sweetheart!" Dad says, his voice unsteady. Unlike Sally, he looks much older. Thinner. Sadder. I grip his shoulders hard and will the tears away from their ducts. As always, they obey. But I think I am the only one with dry eyes.

"I texted Adam you're here," Skye says, and then adds softly, "but don't think we're not going to pester you about the new guy and his private jet."

"Yeah, a jet? Is he your boyfriend now? What's his name, Don, Susan said? No, David?" Sam wonders loudly while my dad shifts his weight and looks away. He loved Shep. Actually, *loves*, present tense. I start to feel the loss all over again.

Luckily, Adam bursts through a set of double doors to save me. I exhale a grateful, shaky breath. I am not ready to solidify whatever Dennis and I have by discussing it with the Canton Committee of Opinions. I'm also not ready to think about what the arrival of Dennis means in relation to the departure of Shep from my life.

"Sadie, thank goodness. They say it's almost time to push, but she . . . she's terrified. I've never seen her like this." He loses the words as I hug him. I stand tall and think about my sister as he pulls me through the doors with him.

Susan is used to her ordered lists and color-coordinated spreadsheets. She's not easily upset or bothered—she's pretty even-keeled. Nothing about birth is even-keeled, though. But I remember her telling us she was pregnant and she was excited, calm, ready for the next phase of her life. And then I realize. Mom was supposed to be here. Mom was going to guide her through this.

"Sade! You got here so fast! Adam said Dennis has a jet?" Susan says. I smile. Of course she's thinking about logistics.

"I'm just in time it sounds like!" I rush over and hug her. She's shaking. I pull back and look into her eyes. "Suze, what would she say?"

"Wha-What?"

"Tell me what Mom would say, if she was here." I squeeze her shoulders, and she starts to cry. Adam begins to huff, but I shoot him a look that shuts him right up. I know what I'm doing. I know my big sister. "Come on, let's make a list of all the things she'd say."

"Uh, okay, um, she'd say this is a routine procedure?"

"Yes!" I smile. "Women have been doing this since the beginning of time with and without medical assistance! What else?"

"Trust the professionaaaaaals," she says, a contraction taking over the word. She's almost smiling, though, remembering how Mom would say that about everything. Not only did she say that to us when she was treating us as her own patients, but Dad didn't have time to be handy and sometimes made things around the house worse. She'd yell at him to trust the guy—the one sent to fix the washer or set up the internet. She even said it about our teachers and later our college professionals.

"Breathe, baby," Adam says to her as Susan grips his hand on one side and mine on the other.

"Holy cow, you're going to break me!" I screech.

"Uh, seriously? Who's the one with the vagina currently splitting open?!" She cries out again, and her body shakes.

"Right! Back to Mom. What else, Suze?"

"Trust God's design, your—"

"Your body knows what it's doing," I finish for her. "Yes! Her big period speech. Remember when Samantha got her period and was sure she was dying?" She nods and then crunches some ice chips Adam offers.

She gives me a new worried look. "How are they doing out there, Sadie, being back in a waiting room, a medical . . . after . . . without . . ."

"Hey. We're all fine. Everyone is totally fine and just worried about you and this baby. Dad's got the whole church praying, Samantha is blowing up Facebook, Skye's got Sally, we're good. Of course you're worried about all of us. What would Mom say about this behavior?"

She smiles and closes her eyes. "Peak Susan."

"Exactly." I watch as some of the worry finally leaves her. Adam catches my eye and mouths *Thank you.* I nod. Susan's nurse and doctor are back, and the room reaches a fever pitch because it's time for her to push. I keep coaching Susan through it using all of Mom's words and phrases that I can remember.

Soon my nephew is on my sister's chest, crying and, from what they can tell so far, totally fine, even if a bit early. I decide to duck out to give them a moment. Also, I need to recover because childbirth is disturbing. Beautiful, glorious, but . . . I'm disturbed.

I pause in the hall. My family doesn't need to know I'm disturbed. Or that the real reason Susan lost it wasn't as much labor as it was laboring without Mom. They need comfort. I prepare myself and then burst through the double doors. "It's a boy!"

My family erupts with cheering. There are tears too, some painful, some bitter, but at least right now there are some that are sweet too.

———

"We need to stop here. Suze said she wanted us to bring her some horrible junk food," I say to Sam as we pull into a grocery store between the house and the women's center.

"Sweet or salty? Snacks or candy?" Sam asks as we head in.

"All of the above." I smile, and she does too. Susan is doing well, but apparently there can be a steep learning curve when it comes to breastfeeding. We're all taking turns swinging by to let her nap, dropping off things from home, running errands. Buying mounds of unhealthy crap is a relatively fun assignment. "You want to take salty, and I'll take sweet?"

"Aw, can't we shop together? I've missed you so muuuch!" she singsongs at me.

"I guess," I say, pretending to be grumpy about it. I've missed her too.

We grab an obnoxious amount of dips, chips, crackers, and cookies, then head to the very far side of the store on a quest for the candy aisle that's usually by the pharmacy. Samantha starts deliberating over types of fruity hard candies, while I hunt for Susan's favorite chocolate-covered almonds. I don't find them with the candy. Maybe they're with the bulk stuff? I turn the corner to go that direction and—

Shep.

Shep and Mary Ann.

Together.

They're looking at a kiosk of frozen stuff a few aisles away, so I don't think they've seen me. As if Mary Ann could see anything when she's so busy staring up at Shep like he's the Lord here to rapture us. I can't, I just can't believe this!

I drop to the floor like some sort of ninja, if ninjas are ever completely terrified and green with nausea. I doubt it, as I try to suck in any oxygen I can find. This store is suddenly toxic!

Why, why, why did I come home?

I have to admit the truth to myself. I thought, I hoped that maybe Mary Ann was a fling. A way to hurt me in return for hurting him. A final tryst before Shep would get his life together. Quit the partying, give up the booze, and ask me to marry him.

I thought there was a chance that the one time I called home weeks ago, that that conversation—which led to me throwing my Bambi necklace into the corner of my closet so hard the clasp broke—had just been a bad dream. I was holding out that he'd come to congratulate Susan as an excuse to talk to me. Ask me to take him back. Ask to come out and finish school in New York, or beg me to come home. At the very least, in my mind, he would show up to tell me that he had ended things with *her*.

But here they are. Months later. Shopping together. And not just a quick errand to Target—they have a cart of food. They're getting groceries as a unit.

I waddle along in my squatting position like kids do in the shallow end of a swimming pool. It's not exactly easy to do on land. Am I going to fall down? *In front of Mary Ann!?*

No. I. Am. Not! I clinch my core and vow to start working out. Finally, I feel like I'm in the clear enough around the corner. I pop up and sprint to my sister.

"Sade, look, new tropical flavooooors!" Sam is singsonging again.

"Shhhh!" I whisper.

"What?"

"Sam, we have to go, now." I sneak a peek over my shoulder.

"But the snacks?"

"Shhhh! And forget the snacks!"

"Why are you shushing me? What is it, what's going on?!" Samantha grows giddy over the fact that there's drama unfolding and she gets to be a part of it.

"Samantha. For once in your life, I am begging you to be quiet." I sense him before I hear him. Shep's low, smooth drawl says something. Something funny. Mary Ann laughs. They're growing closer.

"Really. Let's go." I try to grab the package of Starburst out of Samantha's hands.

"Not until you spill it!" she says, pulling back on the bag.

"Sam!"

"Sadie! Let me in! What's going on!" In our frenzied state, we are really doing this, standing in the middle of the aisle, playing tug-of-war with a supersized bag of fruity chews. We're idiots. And Mary Ann just laughed again, closer!

I set my sights on the weird little patient room next to the pharmacy. The door is open, lights are off, no one around. I drop my grip on the candy bag and run. But as I let go of Sam, I barely register that she's still pulling with all her strength.

As I hit the little room, I sneak a look over my shoulder, just in time to see Shep and Mary Ann turn the corner and join me in watching Samantha fall—no, fly—into a huge kiosk display in the center of the walkway. Of off-brand maxi pads. Not tampons or liners, but a massive display of Heavy Flow Super Pads.

And she's down.

All the way, flat on her ass, covered in boxes of pads.

"Sammy?" I gasp the tiniest bit at the sight of him talking to her, like he has a million times before. I see him walking into our kitchen, stealing one of my mom's undercooked cookies. I see him throwing popcorn at Skye's head until she takes her headphones off. I see him sitting on top of me because I refused to move over on the couch. Because I had to be near him.

I don't think my gasp was audible just then, but I duck behind the door in a split second. He didn't see. She didn't see. I'm still pulled tight as a spring, though, waiting.

"Uh, hey, Shep, long time no see! Long time, long time, dude!" Samantha is yelling. She's gone into Samantha's Panic Mode, which is considerably louder and faster than her default setting.

"You all right?" he asks, and I hear her shuffling to get up.

"Yep, yep, yep, just a little slip on the, uh, floor. There's a slippery patch of concrete there. Everywhere, really, the whole store—you gotta watch out, it's a hazard. They should post signs, big signs that say BEWARE! SLIPPING , you know? What if I was a little old lady, I could've broken a hip and died, Shep! Died!"

"Uh-huh?" I can hear the laugh in his voice as he watches her disintegrate into what I'm sure are crazy hand motions to go with her crazed string-of-consciousness babbling.

"Anyway, got what I needed, just a few pads. Well, guess I have more than a few now, huh? Ha ha ha. Sometimes you need the big guns for the red dragon, you know? No, of course you wouldn't, Shep. But like, here comes Aunt Flow and girls gotta go, am I right? Hi, I'm Samantha. Do you have a heavy crimson tide too? Because these things are the Cadillacs of pads right here. More like diapers. They've got you covered front to back and every which way. Ride that cotton pony, girl! Yep, yep, yep! Here you go!"

"Oh, um, I . . ." Mary Ann is no doubt staring at multiple boxes of pads that have been shoved into her hands. In this moment, I could not be more grateful for my sister. I'm so proud of how she just goes off about periods without a hint of shame. If I weren't scared out of my mind, I'd be inspired. And talk about ride or die.

She's riding a wave of awkward and dying a slow, painful death out there. For me.

"Do you, uh, need help, Sam?" Shep asks quietly. He knows something is up.

"Nope, just these shark week supplies and snacks for Susan. She had her baby, did you know? Oh, right, of course you knew. You brought Adam his bag. Anyway, I'm good, great, fine. Thanks for asking. I'll find an employee to help me with the mess, then I'm back to the hospital! Easy-breezy lemon-squeezy! Ha, more like tomato-squeezy, I guess!"

"You sure?"

"Never been more sure of anything in my life! Got pads, will travel! Just going to go find someone who works here. Where's the intercom thing, right?" Sam laughs and then, as if she isn't loud enough, yells, "ALERT, ALERT, CLEAN UP IN THE PERIOD AISLE!" She laughs some more and then, finally, she must walk away.

"Is she on drugs?" I hear Mary Ann whisper.

"Nah, that's just Sam being Sam." He's chuckling, but I hear Shep's hesitation. I think he's looking this way.

Does he know I'm here? Does he sense me? Does he hope I'm here?

Wait, if he saw Adam, surely he knows I'm in town?

He knows I'm in town.

And he didn't text or call. Didn't come by.

It's really over.

For good.

I keep myself frozen solid and my breathing soft. They still aren't gone.

"Shep? C'mon, babe, I'm sure someone will come help her."

Babe?!

Okay. I'm okay. A couple more seconds of pushing away these tears that are building. Then that's it. People break up and move on all the time. Not worth my big messy feelings. *Come on, Sadie, chin up!*

"Yeah. All right." His once-soothing voice is now like gritty sandpaper on my tired soul. They leave, but I stay rooted behind the door until Samantha finally appears beside me.

"I think it's all clear," she whispers. *Now* she whispers.

"I owe you one."

"Ohhhhh, it's more than one. I have one million questions, and you're going to answer all of them, starting with why you dumped Shep, skimming over who that beeyatch was, and ending somewhere around who your new boyfriend is and how does he have his own plane?!"

"Okay." I smile at her. "Let's get out of here first, and you can give me the third degree in the car."

"Is there something past that?" she mutters as we start helping a grumpy teen male employee pick up box after box of feminine hygiene products. "Because it's gonna be more like fifth degree. Tenth degree! Twentieth degree, Sadie!" I nod and give her a quick hug as we both laugh out our nerves.

When her questions start, I steer my answers away from Shep and toward Dennis. It's not hard. Dennis is new and exciting. He's older and richer and he's just so, well, *New York.*

As I tell her about how he has taken me under his wing and guided me into my new life, Dennis sounds pretty amazing. He's texted me a million times since I left yesterday. He offered to come, but we both knew it wouldn't be the right time for him to meet my family, even if we were at that stage of our relationship, which we aren't.

He's kind and handsome and he's there, just waiting for me. We arrive at the hospital, and I pull out my phone one last time before getting out of the car. I see another message from him.

I decide right then that I am not spending another second thinking about my past. Even if it hurts to move forward. Even if I'm not quite ready, I can't go back. I have to move on.

Dennis: What can I do? Tell me what you need.
Me: I just need you.
Dennis: Then come home, sweetheart.

Home. My home is New York. And my future is Dennis.

Me: Omw

CHAPTER 19

"Damn, the way that man looks at you, mm mm mm," Carly almost moans into her drink. We watch Dennis listen to Hayden as he entertains his gaggle of friends with a story. They're at the other side of the bar, but once every couple of minutes, Dennis looks over at me.

"She's not wrong," Tash says from behind the bar.

"I know, I know, I'm the luckiest bitch alive," I mutter to them before sucking another large sip of chardonnay.

"But, like, really, though." Carly doesn't look at me as she talks. "You move from wheat fields to the big city, fall for one of the most eligible bachelors in the world, who for some reason loves you back."

"Rude!"

She continues, ignoring me. "He helps you heal from the loss of your sweet mama, encourages your art, even introduces you to your new besties. It's amazing."

"What art?" Tash snorts.

"Hey! I've been auditioning!"

"Forget auditioning. Forget all of us and just write. Your screenplay is so amazing, I hate you even more than I did before, Sade. I neeeeed you to finish it! I'm desperate for the end of the story, that's how good your writing is."

"Thanks, Carly, but I think I'm giving up on that one." I sigh. Since I caved and let them read the manuscript months ago, they have both pleaded with me to finish a hundred times. But working on it feels like digging through the past. I'm done with that.

"Does that mean you have a new one I can read?"

I laugh. "Nope, still blocked."

"You know . . ." Tash takes my empty glass and pours me another. She clears her throat. "If you don't like the ending you had envisioned for it, just change the story. Write a new ending. I think you're too worried about sticking with what the characters need or how it should play out, or how it would unfold in real life. Write what you wish could happen."

"Uh, what? That's the definition of fiction. Are you drinking on the job, Tash?" Carly asks, not understanding the Obi-Wan vibes Tash is suddenly giving off.

Carly doesn't know my whole story, but Tash does. I actually sensed grief in her first, a terrible past she was trying to leave behind. I pushed Tash to share her story with me, and, surprising both of us, I let my walls down too. She lost her brother a few years ago. I didn't go into heavy details and I didn't cry or complain. It was more like a laying out of facts. Still, Tash gets it, she gets me. So I know she's not talking about my script at all.

"Yeah, Tash, that's what fiction is." I echo Carly but give Tash a look that secretly says *I hear you.* I add, "You know what helps with writer's block? More alcohol!" My friend and everyone around us cheer in agreement.

I move the conversation from my projects to everyone else's. We chat for a few more rounds about all our failed auditions and stalled projects. It's another fun evening out in my favorite city.

Dennis slides an arm around me from behind and leans into my ear. "I'm ready to take you home." He pauses and lowers his voice further. "Are you ready to be taken?"

Holy hell in a handbasket.

I mumble something and wobble my way out of Pink Lady's. I don't remember much after that other than cool sheets, hot commands, and restless sleep.

I wake up to an empty room. Dennis has left a note that he has to go into the office for a few hours but will bring back a big Sunday brunch spread. I work my way through my routine of Advil, water, coffee, and toast. I feel badly enough to recognize I can't drink tonight, or I'll still feel crappy for work Monday morning. *Dang it.* I can't seem to stop overdoing it.

Anyway. It's fine, we'll have a cozy night in. Dennis and I do have those—they're just not my favorite. I don't dwell on why that is.

I sit at the table next to the windows and take in Dennis's amazing view. I still can't believe I'm here, even if I'm not exactly living my original dream. He Who Must Not Be Named isn't here, but also, I'm not auditioning much. I don't take dance classes or voice lessons. I'm not writing . . .

Write what you wish could happen.

I replay Tash's words in my mind. Then I hear Carly.

You move from wheat fields to the big city, fall for one of the most eligible bachelors in the world . . . he helps you heal . . .

Dennis and I aren't in love; we're in, well, hot, tipsy sex. And I'm far from healed. I still don't even talk to my dad or my sisters. I have cut off basically everyone from home because it all still hurts too much. Carly's words aren't true. But wouldn't it be amazing if they were?

Write what you wish could happen.

I can't see it as a movie or a musical, but I can see the story play out as a romance novel. I know the format, the pacing. I've read a hundred books this year—surely I can *write* one? A sweeping story about a serious older man, a lost girl, a glamorous city, and a heart that heals?

I grab my laptop from my work bag in the entryway and settle back at the kitchen table overlooking Manhattan. I pour another cup of coffee. I stretch and take a deep breath.

And I write.

———

MONTHS LATER

"I don't want to use my last name, I told her that." I growl at my phone. Unbelievably, I have another offer to publish my book. My agent Barb, an acquaintance of Dennis, has been a godsend the last few months. What a freaking whirlwind.

Once I started, the words wouldn't stop. I could feel what the reader wanted, the tropes, the plot twists. I wrote myself and Dennis into a real-life book. It wasn't easy, but it was simple. And it was a thrill.

I couldn't believe I was writing five thousand words a day. Well, on the days when my head was clear. I often started my writing sessions with a headache from the night before. I wrote before work, during lunch, and all day on Saturdays and Sundays. Some mornings I had to delete entire paragraphs of wine-soaked drivel I'd tried to write after a night out. But once I got into the groove, I forced myself to stay home and write for at least a couple nights in a row.

The writing *is* an escape, so I didn't feel that desperate need to check out as often. I was sort of checked out already. And man, did those dry days pay off.

I'll never forget Dennis's face. I paced through his apartment all day, biting my cuticles and bringing him food and drinks as he read the book from start to finish. He reads even more than I do, but mostly nonfiction. His face grew red in parts, and I think he may have teared up a couple times. I tried to tell him, and my friends, that it was only loosely based on us, but apparently the emotions on the page seem too real.

The grief is real. The wandering. The sex scenes are very real, the realest part. Plus, I don't want to admit that behind the hopeful, swooning chapters, I'm still broken. So, let them think whatever.

Dennis closed the pile of loose pages and smiled as I bounced around the living room waiting for him to speak. "It's not my usual genre, obviously, but I didn't want to put it down, darling. I think it's . . . beautiful."

I squealed and climbed him like a tree. I squealed again when he flipped me over onto the rug like a rag doll. Clearly, he was moved.

His confidence inspired me to share about the story in a few online book clubs. I showed it to Tash, who showed it to a few people she trusted. Soon, the entire artsy, bookish population of New York City was buzzing about my book. It spread like wildfire through the concrete jungle, and then beyond.

"Sweetheart, you already have your pick of deals with your pen name. She's just a genius, getting you more money and a better marketing plan," Dennis argues across his kitchen table where we've been, him reading, me checking emails. "The Canton name is gold in the middle of the country. Use it."

"But people will just assume my dad got my book published."

"People are morons, darling. Your writing needs to be in people's hands. Let it get there, let it go."

I smirk at him, because he's right. And he's using my own words about needing to let go against me. And he's gorgeous. "You just want everyone to read about Don McClure, the sex tutor."

"Why would I, when you insist he isn't really me and Shea isn't really you?" He stands and moves around to my side of the table. He leans down so his dark, heavy eyes are level with my own. "Come, time for a lesson."

"It's not uuuuussss!" Before we can finish our discussion, I'm thrown over his shoulder as he stalks to his bedroom.

————

This might be the best night of my life. No, it is. It is the best night of my life. I feel warm and sparkly as I look across the table. Dennis, Emerson, Hayden, Barb, Carly, Tash, and my new publicist Gwyn are all buzzing with excitement. I've signed the papers and I have a release date, an editor, a cover designer, and even a few fans from the online forums that begged to be on my street team.

I am an author.

I am an artist who is getting paid for her work! Creative work from my crazy brain! Words I made up from nothing, and people are actually going to pay to read them. I squeeze my fists with glee. And anxiety. But that's nothing a little more champagne won't fix. Okay, a lot more.

I look up at the stars above us. Dennis got us the best table at a rooftop restaurant that's been booked solid for months. People around us are eyeing our swanky group, at the best table, clearly celebrating. Women give Dennis double and triple takes. Gwyn and Barb go on and on about all the best sellers I'm going to write.

How is this my life?

And how is Mom not here to see it? I finally did it, I made something. I wrote over one hundred thousand words, and *the experts*, as she'd call them, editors, publishers, early reviewers, they think it's good. It's not a deep memoir, and my muse didn't quite take me where I thought I wanted to go. And I had to go alone. I shake my head, close my eyes, and take a deep breath. I'm not alone, and I'm right where I'm meant to be. Right?

I can't think about it because I'm pulled back from my fuzzy thoughts by a hand on my knee.

"Darling."

Dennis is down on one knee in front of me. *Holy motherfffff—*

"A few weeks ago, you were lamenting about your last name, how it followed you around and hung over you like a shadow. Well, I think I can offer you a solution, sweetheart." He pulls out a box and opens it to reveal the biggest oval diamond I've ever seen. It's on a plain thin band. It's definitely an antique, probably an heirloom. It's blinding. "DeLane is arguably a very strong surname, darling, and it'd be my honor if you'd take it. Marry me, Sadie. Make me the happiest man in New York and say yes."

"Y-Yes. Yes!"

I hear the word come out of my mouth, and I feel like I'm watching myself cry and shake, as if I'm a bystander across the patio. Everything is twinkly and romantic, and he's so earnest and stunning. I don't love that he didn't actually ask me, but rather told me what to do. Just like the first time he said I love you, he told me, say you love me too.

But that's so very Dennis of him. That's what I've said I wanted, isn't it? To fly free, knowing he would tether me? He would guide me? I've followed his strong, serious lead. I've done as he's instructed, for almost a year now.

Okay, sometimes his intensity makes me itchy, especially when we're home and sober and quiet. Sometimes his domineering is less sexy than it is manipulative. Both of us use sex as a way to avoid opening up. But the sex is pretty amazing. And we have time to open up, to meet each other's families, to fall in love and really become a team. Loads of time.

His eyes are misty as he lifts me up and spins me. His laugh is jarring, since I'm not used to hearing it. I do hear our friends, cheering and clinking their glasses. Dennis takes my head in his hands and kisses me over and over.

I can do it. I can smile and sigh and continue to let him lead me. I can be his. I'm going to become Sadie DeLane. That sounds fine. That sounds pretty, even. I'm doing it. I'm marrying someone other than S— I mean! I *want* to do this.

Dennis loves me, and I . . . I'm going to marry him.

CHAPTER 20

"Thanks for saving me today."

"Saving you from Shep or from Dennis?" Sally asks me as we return to our room. I yawn, and she does too. We're stuffed from our beach picnic, tired from the sun, and windblown from our moped ride back. It was fun letting her be the driver, since we're ten years apart.

"Both," I say.

She nods slowly, her brilliant brain working. "Shep looks at you like he wants to spank you." I choke on my water. Did not see that assessment coming. "Sorry," she adds quietly.

"It's fine, I love when you blurt out your observations like that. It reminds me of Mom."

"Yeah?" My little sister's voice sounds sad, but her eyes light up the whole beachy cottage.

"Totally. She wouldn't have sensed my reaction and said sorry, though. She would've just plowed on with her analysis. Still, you're so much like her."

She blinks rapidly, so I offer her a reprieve. "And Dennis? Please, continue dissecting my train wreck of a life."

"Well, Dennis, he looks at you like he could actually kill you. Is he dangerous?"

I laugh. "No! Dennis would never hurt me, or anyone."

"He comes from crazy money, though. Maybe he's in organized crime?"

"You mean, the mob?"

"Mob, Mafia, Bratva—what's his cultural heritage?"

"You read too much, Sal."

"Maybe." She shrugs, still thinking aloud. "I can picture you with Shep. I think I even remember that vaguely. Or at least I remember pictures and video. But I can't see you engaged to the mobster."

"Again, not in the mob. And what makes you say that?" I ask her as I place my water, jewelry, hat, and sunglasses on the side table.

"I mean, I don't think I've heard him talk or seen him smile one time."

"Well, I imagine he is less than excited about being here this week."

"You're laughing and smiling, and this week has got to be much worse for you." I see the moment her mind makes some sort of connection. "Wait! He's the grump, you're the sunshine! He's the enemy turned lover! You two were the basis for all your opposites-attract stories, weren't you?"

"Eh." I cock my head, remembering. "That's not fair to him. He's serious but not really a grump—definitely not a villain. He always went out and had a good time, enjoyed himself, he was affectionate, and he was even a pretty good communicator."

"But?" she prompts, waiting. "What happened?"

My body sags, remembering. I exhale the truth. "I just couldn't marry him."

"And then —"

"Sal," I yawn her name, cutting off the rest of this painful conversation. "My body clock says it's nap thirty. We can talk more later, okay?"

"Lame, but okay."

I head to my room and change into my buttery soft pajama set. What are vacations for if not afternoon naps? I'm just not sure I'll actually be able to sleep. My eyes are droopy from the wind and sun, but my body is buzzing almost as badly as my brain.

I flop myself onto the bed.

Stupid Shep and his stupid scooter.

Did he want me to put my arms around him? Why would he, if he still loathes me so much? Does he still loathe me, or is it an act? Or maybe all I'm feeling is residual sexual tension, not emotion. Or did he just really want to terrify me? Hurt me? And again, the million-dollar question, where does this guy get the frickin' nerve?

He checked out when I needed him most. He didn't technically cheat, but he didn't waste any time running straight into Mary Ann's arms. The most painful rebound option, which he knew. He betrayed us, our love, our whole life of friendship. And since that betrayal, he has barely said one civil word to me. A decade of snide digs and comments under his breath. Not to mention what happened in New York!

I shouldn't have let him goad me onto that moped. It was too much, touching his rock-hard torso. Feeling the heat of him, sinking into his broad back like I used to do when I'd sneak in for a hug. A spot that used to be so comforting. So was his smell. Breathing in his scent killed me. Getting up close and personal with his smooth, tanned neck.

I always had a thing for his neck. He even let me trim his thick, wavy, blond model-esque hair when we were together. Or attempt to. The haircuts always ended with me on the tiles underneath him.

I don't understand this connection. Shouldn't it be gone by now? Or at least faded? Shouldn't it have weakened to a warm, distant memory, like my connection with Dennis has? Not that the two connections were even close to the same.

Dennis may have been hot in the bedroom, but Shep Riggs has always burned me up from the inside out. He consumed me fully from the age of fourteen. And I guess I'm still on fire, even though I should be a pile of forgotten ashes at this point.

Anyway, why am I thinking about this? He hates me, and I can't even endure a simple conversation with him. I guess there is one obvious cause of my frustration. I get up and head to my suitcase. I brought some tools to take care of this problem, at least.

I grab my newest fully charged favorite, settling down into the sheets. I relax into the sensations. I try to clear my mind. I try to envision nothing and no one, just the physical reactions. But then I'm back on that cold, smooth bathroom floor, writhing and almost crushed under the hot bulky weight covering me. In zero seconds flat, I explode. And, surprisingly, I fall into a deep, peaceful sleep. Rest I desperately need in order to face the night ahead.

———

"Who convinced you to set foot on a boat again?" Skye asks Samantha as we walk across the bridge to board a huge, sleek yacht.

"Look at this thing—it's like an aircraft carrier. Not a sailboat. It'll be fine, right, Em?" Sam looks adoringly up at Emerson. I can't believe he allows that syrupy nickname. Of course, she could call him Sir Hairy Monster Balls, and he wouldn't care. He mutters a "Yes, Angel" into her hair as he kisses her head. They're so sweet and in love, I kind of want to jump overboard.

"Plus," my sister says excitedly, "it has a state-of-the-art dance club, better than anything the island could offer. It's gonna be so fun!"

A chorus of fake cheers, groans, and a couple actual woo-hoos echo around us. We're almost all old enough to forego tradition-al bachelor and bachelorette parties, but I don't love the idea of a joint night out, and I know I'm not the only one. I can think of two handsome, successful, painfully bitter men who do not want this, either.

I take a deep breath. The two of them, and myself, can suck it right up. This is for Samantha, and really for the whole family. All the guests have been invited to join in tonight, though Sam was smart enough to start the thing at 9:00 P.M. and call it a dance party. I don't think I'll have to worry about seeing Mrs. Wartzer here tonight.

I do have to see Shep, though. And hell, he looks amazing. It's an unexpected look on him: black dress shoes, black jeans, and a black button-up untucked and unbuttoned at the top. He looks very much the polished lawyer turned sport broadcaster tonight.

I don't want to think about what he sees if he looks at me right now. Not after his comments. I chose a tight teal tank dress that shows off my figure and my eyes. One thing about them, the actual irises, they don't get fat or wrinkle or droop. Thank the good Lord for that.

Wait, am I really praying about the attractiveness of my eyeballs? Sorry, God! This night is going to be torture. Especially since everyone else will be drinking, Shep included. I've been able to avoid that for the most part this week so far. This is a dance party, though, and no one dances for longer than a couple songs when they're stone-cold sober. I'll just find a corner spot and get my creeper on, as my sisters would say.

The ship is beautiful, and the club space is as impressive as Sam said. I find a pub stool off in the shadows on the side of the bar and ask the bartender to keep club sodas with lime coming my way. I still need a drink of some sort in my hand. This is a fact that bugs me, but it's still true.

I indulge my sister in a few girls-only numbers like "Single Ladies" and a few too many Meghan Trainor songs. Mostly, I happily watch everyone get tipsy. I'm surprised to see Dennis out on the dance floor, and not at all surprised to see Shep out there. Dennis has a scotch in his hand, and Shep has a beer in his, and both sights make me uneasy. I look away.

I try not to think about the fact that Shep hasn't said a word to me since the scooter ride. It's like he flipped a switch in himself and went from angry at me to unable to even see me. I thought he'd ask me to dance or make side-eyes at me across the room. Nope. I'm invisible over here on this stool. Invisible can be good, I guess.

Unable to watch the buzzed dancing anymore, I study the bartenders, a cute young guy and girl who move around each other as if they're dancing practiced choreography. I start writing a romantic backstory for them. They hate each other, but both got assigned to this job and now they're forced to work every night in a six-foot space. They met while working odd tropical jobs, both on the run. But! She doesn't know he's her childhood friend who's done everything to find her and save her from her villain. He got out of their poor town and became a billionaire, just undercover here to find her. But she's not like he remembered. *Perfection.*

When I'm handed what seems like my thousandth club soda, I have to explain what I'm doing because the guy behind the counter looks concerned. I guess I have been staring. And scribbling furiously on a bar napkin. Eh, celebrities are expected to be weird, and writers even more so.

"Fancy a spin with me, gorgeous?" Ben says, suddenly right next to me. He senses my hesitation and adds, "Just one harmless dance between friends is all."

"All right, Benedict, just one," I concede, not wanting to be rude. I keep turning him down, and he keeps coming back for more. The least I can do is a dance. He's been taking shots with the guys, and it shows. Still, I'm sure he'll be a gentleman, so I follow him out into the pulsing sweaty crowd.

We sway easily to Dua Lipa's latest hit, and it's actually fun. Ben is tall and firm behind me, moving and laughing. He keeps his touch light, but he definitely looks at me like I'm the sexiest thing he's ever seen. I don't mind it one bit. Even better if a certain someone who no longer likes what he sees were to see Ben seeing me this way.

Shep's eyes aren't on me, though, I notice. Janie finally gave in, and he is enjoying every second of his dance with her. I don't think she'd sleep with him under normal circumstances, but this is a wedding in paradise. This week has drunken-hook-up-meet-cute-relationship-spark-starter written all throughout it. I need to start a napkin for that, but with the jungle angle I had going earlier.

The thought of them starting their own story hits disappointment into my joints with every beat of the bass notes in this song. I can't believe it. I'm still affected by Shep with someone else. Affected in big, breath-stealing, tear-gathering ways. Still! Ugh!

I wish more sober friends had warned me about this. Getting clean is a real bitch. You have to face all the feelings you were hiding from. Sobering up doesn't solve everything in life. It solves most things, I truly believe that. It's why I donate so much to rehab centers and speak at closed AA events.

But sobriety also forces you to fix the parts of you that you were pretending weren't damaged. Addiction almost broke me, but it was my own brokenness beforehand that drove me into addiction. It's a terrible chicken-egg mess that's difficult to untangle.

One very long, ever-present string in my knot of feelings is Shep Riggs. Loving him, losing him, missing him, never making up with him. That string feels as if it's closing in on my windpipe right now. I give Ben's hand a squeeze and shout that I need some air.

I weave through the crowd to the side doors that lead out to the deck. I keep moving along the boat's side deck until I come to a dead end near the front of the ship. I grip the railing and breathe. When I close my eyes, I can taste the margarita I wish I was downing at this moment. I know that's what my sisters were having, though none of them drink that much. I start to remember the buzzy feeling that would enter my mind and whisk my thoughts away.

No.

I open my eyes and say the word out loud.

"No. It's not worth it." One drink would turn into twenty, until my younger sisters are worried and holding my hair back as I hurl into a toilet. Not. Worth. It. Every breath of the warm humid air is fortifying. I focus on how grateful I am for my family, this occasion, and the fact that I'm even alive to participate. How I never ended up in the hospital is a miracle to me.

I stay rooted in my spot watching the mood over the water. It's not long before the boat is pulling into the resort's small marina. I make my way back to the club. Skye is by my side the second I enter the room.

"You good?" she asks, peering into me like she's trying to scan a read out of my very thoughts. I look back, letting her see the clarity I feel. I nod. I look away from her in time to see Shep glaring at me for the first time. I can't read his expression, but, shocker of all shockers, it's not a positive one. Our brief stare-down is interrupted by my sister claiming we need a bridal party photo out on the bow of the boat.

We take sloppy group pics while the rest of the guests load into shuttles. We file down toward our own shuttles, one for the groom and his guys and one for Sam and her bridesmaids. I hear Matthew tell Skye only a few more minutes until she can be alone on their balcony, at the same time I hear Emerson tell Samantha that he'll miss her during the drive. I also hear Shep say something cocky to Janie that I can't make out. Will they meet up? Will she go to his villa and creep back into ours at six in the morning? Can I live through that?

I've already sent up some vain requests. I wonder how bad it would be to beg God for a tsunami to make it all stop. Probably pretty bad.

We joke and sing on the short ride back, then spill out of our vehicles into the breezeway in front of the resort. The guys are laughing loudly, clearly having consumed more alcohol than their female counterparts. I think even Emerson is drunk. We all wobble into the lobby together. Well, *I* walk; everyone else seems to wobble. My married sisters peel off with their husbands.

"Can I walk you to your villa?" Ben asks me, magically materializing at my side again.

"Oh, yes, bloody hell, man, take your swing at the wench even though you're gonna miss," Dennis mutters from behind us. He clearly said the words much louder than he meant to.

"What did you just say?" Shep growls beside him. Sally grabs my hand, offering support I didn't know I desperately needed.

"Piss off, Shep. You know as well as I do." Dennis shrugs off Shep's hand on his arm and turns to Ben, who is frozen in shock beside me, Sally, and Janie. "Listen, mate, maybe you'll get lucky and she'll bite her little lip and lie to your face too. I mean, I'll give her that, she's a seductive little b—"

Before Dennis can finish the insult, Shep's fist is uppercutting into his jaw.

"Try and say something else about her, you bitter little piece of shit!" Shep yells in his face.

"Why would you defend that—" Again, Dennis can't finish his thought. This time, Shep sweeps a foot and grabs him by the collar at the same moment. He smashes his taller body down into the marble lobby floor like he's a rag doll.

Shep keeps screaming at Dennis. "That what, asshole? Go on, finish your sentence, *please* do it. I've waited a decade to beat the hell out of you, you—" Shep's voice trails off, but he lands another heavy blow in Dennis's face before Adam and Emerson pull Shep away. Benedict and Byron have moved in to intervene as well.

Adam turns and glares back at me as he untangles himself from the scuffle. "What did you do, Sadie?" he barks at me. I can tell he regrets the words as soon as they're out of his mouth, but it's too late. I am finally at max capacity, and with nothing else to do, my body decides on exorcism. I projectile the entire night's worth of food and club soda all over the pristine white floor.

"Adam!" Susan scolds as she and Sam rush to my side.

"Crap, I'm sorry," Adam mutters, but I can barely hear it over Dennis yelling that Emerson needs to let him go and Shep trying to lock eyes with me.

"Sade? Are you okay? Sadie?" Shep cries.

"Shut it, all of you! Shut up and clean up!" Susan says behind her as she turns my body away. "Come on, sweetie, we've got you. Sally, text Skye and have her meet us at your villa. Sam, order some crackers and ice. Sade, Sadie? Sade, you need to breathe."

I realize as she says it that I am sobbing. And not breathing very well. Everything is tight, my arms, my chest, even my fingers. Is this a panic attack?

"Breathe, iiiiiin and out," Susan repeats, soothing me. I breathe with her and feel some of the tension loosen. She doesn't look at me when we reach my door. "I think it's time you finally told us what all happened, exactly."

"Yep, looks like it's Sadie's turn," Samantha says from behind us.

"Turn for what?" Sally asks.

"Another freaking sistervention," Susan mutters, sounding like she's as wary of the idea as I am.

CHAPTER 21

8 YEARS AGO
MANHATTAN, NEW YORK

"Ca-arl, LaTashaaaaaaa!" I yell as I burst into the Pink Lady's doors. I spot my friends in our corner, as always. The other groups around us have changed over the last two years, but we've remained, probably because Tash still works here a few nights a week. Instead of heading to my usual seat, I go to the fridges under the bar. I grab two bottles of champagne and three flutes.

"What are we celebrating?" Carly side-eyes me when I plunk down in the booth.

"You guys aren't gonna believe this!" I squeak.

"Uh, have you been doing some pre-partying, Sade?" Tash jokes. Her smile is a bit too tight for my liking. She needs to let me live up this moment. Of course, she's about to realize that.

"I didn't want to say anything until it was official, and it's taken months and I thought it wasn't going to actually happen because, really? But it is, I can't believe it."

"What! Spit it out!" Carly says, more irritated than I expected. Maybe she just bombed an audition. I calm myself. It's not like me to let my emotions go wild.

"Sorry. Okay. As of this morning, *Don of a New Day* is officially being turned into a movie!"

"What! Sadie! Amazing!" Tash shouts as she jumps up to hug me.

"Wow, I can't believe it." Carly's voice is flat, but then she catches herself. "Sorry, rough morning, and I mean, the wins just keep coming for you, don't they? How can we get some of your voodoo mojo to rub off on us?"

"Shut up, hoe." Tash turns and looks down at her, where she sits frozen in the booth. "It's not voodoo—it's talent. And she's worked her ass off! Be happy for our friend!"

Carly shakes off her weird emotions and jumps up. "You're right. My bestie is making a movie! Weeeee!"

We jump up and down and squeal and hug together. Carly's fake smile bothers me, though. She gets bitchier by the day, and I think it's just at me. Tash always diffuses the tension, but it was Tash who warned me how competitive and fake this town can be. I almost feel like Pink Lady's isn't a safe space anymore.

The thought makes me miss my sisters, and I realize I should probably call my family to tell them the news. It's been months. In fact, I think the last time I reached out was to tell them that Dennis and I broke off the engagement.

Ugh. Letting him go was the right thing to do, but I do miss him. He was a good friend for a year, and he was my connection to everything in this city. He's still connected, and I'm, well, just here. He still goes to all the splashy events, with models and actresses. I mostly write in my pajamas. I still work a couple days a week at the company, I still wander the streets, and of course I go out. I'm young and single in New York! On the nights I can't find someone to go out, I order in, drink wine, and read by the window in my chic new apartment.

These are the best years of my life, right here, right now. I have Tash, and I have friends at the office. I still see Hayden sometimes. I'm not alone. But right now, it feels a little lonely.

Wait, who cares if I'm lonely? My book is becoming a movie! And with the contract I signed earlier, I just became low-key rich! I need to shake off all these mopey feelings and celebrate.

"Forget this champagne. We need shots!" I yell. Carly and a few Pink Ladies cheer. Tash doesn't cheer, but she does walk over with me and help get the glasses out. It's going to be a great night!

———

"I need to tell you something you don't want to hear," Tash says as she tames a flyaway hair on the top of my head.

"Um, pass?" I feel my face twist up.

"You need to have a dry night tonight, Sade."

"Pff, what? It's a party!" I wave her off and move to my dresser mirror in order to apply some lipstick.

"An industry party. Your publishers will be there, your producers, the director, actors, writers. It's a big night."

"A big night for *my* movie, and you're telling me I can't toast to my own film?" I glare at her in the reflection.

"Sade. I know you like to party, but you've been getting sloppier and sloppier. My boss even said he wasn't sure you should keep coming in during my shifts."

"Kurt said that?" I whisper, suddenly sick with something heavy and sticky. It coats me completely, suffocating my airway.

Shame. I'm so ashamed. I've done a lot of stupid things, but now I'm embarrassing my friend at work?!

"I told him you were going through some stuff, which is true, but it's also been true since I met you years ago. Tonight is important, yes, but you need to rein it in. I'm, like, genuinely worried, Sade."

"Okay, okay. You don't need to worry. It is a big night, you're right. I'll just do the toast and that's it." I can't look her in the eye, but I make out that she nods behind me. I'll just have one drink at the party, and then I can really celebrate afterward. I can do better, and I will.

We grab our purses and head down to the street. In the taxi ride over, I try to brace myself and pep myself up at the same time. Tonight is a celebration of so much hard work. Not only did I finish my novel, but Barb got me an amazing publishing deal. Plus, Gwyn whipped up a media frenzy that resulted in movie offers.

The studio worked with me to make the script amazing, the casting perfect, and the buzz totally off the charts. Dad is ecstatic for what this is doing for the Canton name outside of the cards and gifts arena. I'm actually happy about having lines from the book turned into a sweet, gorgeous greeting card line. It's a symbiotic relationship between all the various media. It's almost unsettling how perfect everything has been.

Except, of course, it's mostly lies. Dennis is not Don, and I'm not Shea. I haven't recovered from my grief, I don't think, and I definitely don't have my heart put back together. I probably should, by now, but I still feel broken. It's so much easier not to feel at all, to escape through writing in another world, living through fictional pages of my favorite authors, or going out and turning my brain off completely.

Even though *Don of a New Day* wasn't based on a true story, I've let Gwyn spin it as if that's the case. Breaking off the engagement with Dennis almost tanked the movie deal. Luckily, by then, fans of the book, now series, were already rabid. While I worked hard and wrote my little ass off, I know this was part luck and part timing and part, well, Dennis.

He won't be here tonight. He can't be around me. I don't blame him. I didn't mean to lead him on, but that's what I did. Not that he was all-in on our relationship, either. I never once saw Dennis let go. He may have loved me in a way, but the man never fought with me. He never got frustrated or upset. Even when I broke things off, he was freaking polite about it. I think we both stuck around longer than we should have because our relationship became a media circus, and we didn't want to provide the final jaw-dropping act. But we did, with our "amicable separation."

It's for the best, but it'll be a little weird without him here tonight. Even if I haven't seen him in a long time, he was a big part of this story. The party is to announce the release date and premiere the various trailers. There's a short commercial version, a long trailer for movie theaters, and an even longer trailer for YouTube.

"You good?" Tash's voice interrupts the silence in the cab as we pull up to the small theater that the studio rented out.

"Yep, I'm good. Let's do this." We both nod and get out of the car. As instructed, we head into the back entrance to avoid paparazzi. The studio wants control over every aspect of what breaks when—the live stream, the behind-the-scenes photos, all of it. Surprisingly, I've been fine with giving them all that control. This is my first book, so I'm just happy to be here, honestly.

Gwyn greets us and parades me around to everyone in attendance. There are real movie stars here, and producers who are multimillionaires, if not billionaires. Even their staffers are powerful, connected people. I can't help but think, "Uh, one of these is not like the other." Tash trails us and tells me I'm crushing it, keeping me loaded up on Diet Coke and tiny appetizers.

Finally, we are told to take our seats for the big moment. The lights fade, and our director says a few words to much applause. Then we watch the first trailer. It's bouncy and fun and gorgeous, with snappy scenes of the couple and quick looks at New York. The actors are incredible, and the cinematography is flawless. I like it—it's a great rom-com commercial.

The longer trailer, for movies, shows more of the grit of our main female character. We see a tiny bit more of the grief she has to work through, and her insecurities as she arrives in New York. There are a few shots of the Oklahoma plains that cause a physical ache I didn't expect. But it's perfect, I like it, and I think moviegoers will too.

The director gets up again and explains the importance of this long trailer for YouTube and other social media sites. Everyone cheers again, and we all lean in a bit in our seats, ready to see more of the movie come to life. This one starts with the same upbeat feel but quickly changes to be more serious. There is much more emphasis on the pain of loss and the angsty romance.

It's not what's on the screen that's moving me, though. One thing I've had zero control over is the soundtrack for the movie, and the trailers. Music supervisors make those decisions, based on the feel they want, the energy, and also which artists are hot at the time.

I guess right now, this song, that plays almost all the way through in this long version, is hot right now. I vaguely remember Gwyn talking about it. It's called "If The World Was Ending," by a newish artist, JP Saxe. It doesn't even fit the story, really, but the vibe works. And it's beautiful.

There's only one problem.

If today was the end of the world, and everything was crumbling around me, there's only one person I'd need next to me, one person I'd cross the country to see one last time, one person I'd call and beg to forget our past and just come hold my hand.

I can't breathe. I clutch the armrests of the seat and focus on breathing. Tash gives me a concerned look. I think I'm going to throw up, but I hold it in until the end of the trailer, which lasts an eternity longer, four maybe five more minutes.

As soon as the screen goes black and people start clapping, I stand. I hobble apologetically over people to get out of my row, then run out into the lobby. Gwyn, Barb, and Tash are right on my heels.

"What is it?" Tash asks.

"Uh, I don't know, maybe the shrimp? I need to go," I manage to get out.

"I'll grab a water!" Gwyn says nervously before running to the concession stand.

"Yeah, you look like you're about to go on as Elphaba." Tash's reference is lost on Barb for a second, then she remembers the green witch from *Wicked*. "If you need to go, let's go."

"Uhhh no." Barb cuts Tash off. "You're contractually obligated to stay for the live streams, you have a Q&A, and we need to post to your stories. There's the cake cutting, a photo booth, and JP Saxe is going to perform just for us."

I cannot live through that song again.

"I can't, I'm going to be sick."

"Then go be sick in the bathroom and then come back out. I'll get a makeup artist in there to fix"—she motions over my entire torso—"this."

"Waterrroh!" Gwyn reappears. "Oh wow, yeah, you look even worse now."

"Forget water, I need alcohol. Now," I say. She yells something affirmative as she runs away again.

"Babe, I thought we talked about this," Tash mutters, giving me wide eyes.

"There's only, like, an hour left?" I ask Barb.

"Maybe hour and a half."

"I won't get drunk in an hour, Tash. I need some liquid courage."

"Courage for what?" she whispers. I just shake my head and start to head for the restroom. I down a white wine Gwyn shoves into my hand, then another. The stabbing around my being lessens somewhat.

But the song. The damn song is everywhere. JP performs it, then the trailer is playing somewhere around us at all times. Tash stalks me like a hovering mother the rest of the night and gets us in a cab the second Barb says I have fulfilled my requirements.

"You want to tell me what the hell is going on with you?" Tash puts a hand on my arm in the back of the cab.

I shake my head. "I just want to go home."

I meant *my apartment* when the words left my mouth. But I think Tash sees in my eyes, at the same moment the ache returns in my chest. Home. Home was him. Home was awkward calls with my mom. Home was joking around with Susan and Adam and Dad and Shep, all together, talking football and teasing one of my younger sisters.

Home is gone.

And I am finally feeling just how much I miss it.

Tash tries to come up, but I refuse.

I get into my little space and grab one of my wine bottles off the little rack on the counter. I pour a glass and then move to the couch. I open up my laptop on the coffee table. Buzzed and exhausted, I pull up that song.

The lyrics wash over me again and again, tsunamis of heartbreak. Shep and I didn't work out, couldn't work out. It turns out he needed someone who wouldn't push him so much, someone less driven, less intense. Maybe less selfish. I needed . . . I need . . . well, I don't know what or who I need now.

I needed him to be stable and solid so I could fall apart. I wanted him to tell me he'd step up and be the man he could be. I wanted him to chase goals with me, to make plans and run after them. I wanted him here. Now I'm in New York and becoming successful and he's not next to me.

He would've teased me about the actress playing my part, he would've made fun of the cheesiest lines, then he would've earnestly taken it all back later that night, inside me, around me, under me, over me. Would have. Should have. Maybe even could have.

But is not, will not, cannot.

For the first time in the three years since I've been in New York, I weep.

Sobs wreck my malnourished frame. Snot runs down my face, and mascara ends up trailing all the way down into the high neckline of my dress. I actually think of him, Mom, home. I remember it all. I yell and rock in place. I pick up my I Love NY ceramic tile coaster and throw it at the wall. It smashes into dust, and I can relate.

I start to feel like I'll throw up, but I just drink. This is too massive a feeling to live with. I can't carry it anymore.

CHAPTER 22

7 YEARS AGO
TULSA, OKLAHOMA

I was doing all right until I walked through the doors. Seeing the vast farmland from the airplane window, landing in the familiar, tiny airport, even driving around town didn't affect me too much. I'd tried to mentally prepare for the sights and sounds, but it's the smell.

The second I rushed into the emergency room entrance, the smell of the hospital, Mom's hospital, assaulted me, almost violently. I had to blink away immediate tears. My footsteps slowed too as I walked up to the check-in desk.

I can handle this. I lift my chin and put my shoulders back instinctually. This will be hard, but it's only for a few hours, right? I'll laugh with my family, and then surely we'll party it up this evening. My being home is an excuse for a nice dinner or a get-together at the house. I can bring in catering and the best wines the local liquor store offers. I just have to make it until, like, six. It's almost lunch time now, I got this. And I brought a couple little miracle pills. I'll pop one real fast to perk me up for the family. It's understandable, since this is an actual crisis. I can't be dragging around when my dad needs me.

"Jon Canton?" I ask the man in scrubs seated by the computer. He offers a polite smile while still at his computer, a smile that I think says, *Another one for Doc Canton's husband*. Then he looks up, and his eyes go wide. I guess my large sunglasses aren't doing me the favors I thought they would.

"Uh, he's not in the ER anymore, miss. Um, just go out that set of doors, then down the corridor until you reach the front elevators and then go up to the cardiac waiting room, level four."

"Thank you," I say, already moving in that direction.

It's taking effort not to run, but Susan said he's going to be fine. It wasn't exactly a minor heart attack, but they're pretty sure he's in the clear. It was the *pretty sure* that got me on a plane. I started booking a flight on my phone before we'd even hung up. I packed and boarded and got all the way here in a half-awake, wholly-hungover state.

As I walk through the corridor, I notice people noticing me. Of course the whole place must be abuzz to have Dad here, so I wonder if the staff expected me. I decide to pop into the hospital gift shop for a bottle of water and hopefully a hat I can pull down low on my face.

The gift shop is almost the exact same as I remember it. Mom brought us in here from time to time to get better candy and snacks than they have in the waiting rooms. We also bought gifts for a few of her patients in here, I think. The thought makes me smile.

Something that is new, however, and makes that smile stop dead in its path across my skin is a whole rack of my books. It's a display case with both of my books and a write-up about me, Dad, Mom, the Canton family, and the movie that just came out. It even has the release date for book three. It looks . . . impressive.

A weird sensation creeps over me as I read the promotional words about how *romantic* and *imaginative* I am. This is why I avoid my own marketing efforts. It's too smarmy.

It was Gwyn who came up with *Sadie loves love, and America loves her for it.* Do I love love? Pff. If I do, I'm pretty sure the feeling is unrequited. I know I say the line in every interview about my books and my boyfriend at the time, "I can't help falling in love—I do it over and over again!" But in reality, I study my readers and what's trending. I study the classics, the basics, and all the rules I should break to make a hit story like the first book. I know what my readers want, and I simply give it to them.

But no one wants to hear that. So I don't admit it. I just live out the lies Gwyn crafts for me.

My face is the only thing bigger than the name Canton on the display banner at the top. There's a big focus on Oklahoma, and my guess is Dad and Gwyn worked fast with my publisher to put these up all over. I can just see myself and my books right next to the hot-dog-warming stations at convenience stores all over the state. Lovely.

The insanity doesn't end with the book, though. Oh no, there are also a few tabloids at checkout. I guess I could have predicted this. It's just that there are so many of them. I actually reach out my hand, with the impulse to buy them all, stuff them under my hoodie, and run out the front door. Then I realize right now it looks like I'm about to read an article about myself. I quickly tuck my hand back in my pocket. I can't stifle my groan at the headlines.

STAR ROMANCE WRITER SADIE CANTON SNAGS SWOONY
SINGER LIAM MYERS

WORLD'S MOST ROMANTIC COUPLE SPOTTED RING SHOPPING

THERE ARE NO WORDS! TROUBLE IN PARADISE FOR IT COUPLE "SADIAM"

Sadiam?! If they're going to print blatant lies about us—we weren't ring shopping, and there's no trouble in paradise—couldn't we at least have a cool couple name? And how in the world is any of this newsworthy, especially half a country away? Damn, this is already a lot and I haven't even made it up to Dad's room yet.

Five more hours, it's fine.

I plop my new hat on, receiving a wink from the clerk behind the register, and head to the elevators. Fatigue descends during the ascent. I feel clammy and gross, and my headache is returning too. Still, it doesn't matter. None of it matters, because I need to see my dad.

And then there he is. Looking older and smaller and altogether wrong in a hospital gown in a bed. He's too gray and too still. At least he's yammering to my sister a mile a minute, that's comforting.

"Sweetheart!" He stops mid-sentence when he sees me.

"Dad!" I choke it out and throw myself onto his chest. "Oh! Sorry!" I say as I realize I probably shouldn't thump my whole body weight onto his weakened heart.

"Oh, hush, I'm fine." He grips me back with more strength than I was expecting. I'm grateful to feel it.

"Fine my butt, Dad. It was a major cardiac event!" Susan scoffs.

"You didn't need to come all the way home, Sade. I'll be out of the hospital tomorrow," Dad says as he lets me go.

I turn to hug Susan and Sam, then Sally and Skye join in. There's a lot of greeting, squeezing, laughing, and sniffing, the latter of which comes from the stoic man in the hospital bed.

Well, crap. That's enough to make anybody weepy. *Just a few more hours.*

Susan talks me through Dad's heart episode, treatment, and course of action. He hems and haws through the whole ordeal like he's immortal and we're all idiots. Then there is a long, loaded pause with sideways glances, where all of us admit silently that, unfortunately, we know firsthand how parents aren't immortal. And looking around at the tired hazel and blueish-teal sets of eyes, I'm not sure we could've survived it again. I know I couldn't have.

"Hey!" Samantha almost yells, wanting to redirect us. "Why did I have to find out from my dental hygienist that you're dating *the* Liam Myers?!"

"Yeah, what the heck is that about, Sade? Why didn't you tell us?" Skye pinches her eyes at me.

"He's, like, famous," Sally says quietly.

"Well, so is Sadie now! So freaking cool!"

"Sam, hun, we're all right here," Susan whispers, making a settle-down motion with her hands. "Dad, you need to rest. We'll just step out in the hall."

"Uh-huh, girl talk, I get it." He pretends to be upset but yawns as he says it. I give him a quick kiss on the head before my sisters usher me out into the hall for a serious inquisition.

"Famous boyfriend! Spill!" Sam starts.

"He is *super* famous, so I think it's *super* weird you wouldn't have at least sent us a text." Skye remains skeptical.

"I'm sorry." I exhale in defeat. "Life got really weird really fast. What do you want to know?"

"Oh man, everything! I want to know it all! Is he as hot in person as he is online? Does he sing to you all the time? Do you really write his songs?"

"You're not really living together?" Susan asks, which is more of a statement.

"Not *officially*," Skye murmurs. Sally giggles uncomfortably.

I laugh a deep, gooey laugh that bubbles up from a sisters-shaped hole in my very identity. "All right, let me see." I tap my finger to my mouth to add the kind of dramatics that my younger sister lives for. "Yes, he is every bit as hot in person. He doesn't sing to me, but he will sing as he writes and sometimes in the nearby vicinity."

"Like in the apartment you guys are totally *not* sharing?" Skye raises a brow.

"At both of our separate apartments." I bump Skye with my hip and keep going. "I do not write his songs, and he doesn't help me with my books. We do sit and write side by side, though."

"Omagah love iiiiiiiit!" Samantha squeals.

"How did you two meet?" Sally pipes in.

"Yeah, and are you really ring shopping?" Susan whispers the question as if it's sacred.

"We met at a party because my agent Barb is friends with his manager. And no, we were totally not ring shopping. But we have *talked* about ring shopping."

"WHAT!" Samantha has turned her default volume setting up multiple notches now.

Skye rolls her eyes at Sam before putting them back on me. "Let's discuss these parties, because you two are all over the internet."

"Eh, it's not as fancy as it seems. The guys in his band are always inviting people over, or Tash and I go out with actor friends and he comes along. Gwyn sometimes arranges invitations to actual fancy parties for SAG or the Academy or whatever, but those are not the norm."

"SAG, or the academy, I'm so Hollywood I can't even handle it," Samantha says in some posh accent that is made to make fun of me, but ends up sounding like an old lady from Minnesota.

"You are the absolute worst at accents!"

"Facts." Sally agrees with me.

"Plus, Hollywood is the other coast, Sam. So, what's he like?" Skye poses the question in a way that feels more serious than the rest of our conversation.

"He's a creative genius, of course, very loving and supportive. He gets my work, gets my process, which is amazing. He is also a lot of fun. If we aren't writing, we really are out and about doing things all over the city. I love it."

"Do you love *him*?"

I pause at Skye's question, offended that she seems to question not just my relationship but my life in New York, my work, my whole new self. "Yeah, I really do," I say, and I try to sound convincing.

I care a lot about Liam. It's only been a few months, and he's a crazy whirlwind of a person, but I meant what I said. He is loving and supportive. And he gets that I want to let loose and chase my muse. He is the one who showed me how to put together the right mix of smoothies, electrolytes, and pills to cure a hangover every time.

I love his art, I love all the time we spend together, I love how he loves me. I especially love the idea of our future together, making art side by side, on the road, all over the world. I think I do love him.

After more questioning, answering, sighing, and laughing together, my sisters decide to head back to the house to rest. Skye hugs me again and then leans back and studies me, searching my eyes for something. I'm not sure what she's looking for, and I'm uncomfortable, because whatever she finds, I don't think she'll like it. Luckily, she lets me go.

I take a shift sitting by Dad's side. After a couple hours, he wakes up, which wakes me up. I guess I fell asleep in the chair. He asks me a million questions about the books and the movies. He tells me how well my line of cards is doing and begs me to ditch my existing publisher after this series ends.

Canton Cards already publishes a few coffee table books, and he wants me to build out that whole arm of our business. As exciting as it sounds, I don't know if I can handle that pressure. I'm only twenty-six, and, though I don't say it out loud, there are some days I'm barely getting out of bed. *Shit, I don't want to think about that right now!* It's time to go arrange that dinner party.

I give Dad another hug and confirm one more time with my Uncle Robert that he's on his way. I put my hat back on but leave off the sunglasses. Wearing sunglasses indoors is just too much. I get in the elevator and make the slow trek down, asking Sam how close she is to picking me up. The doors open, and I walk out, looking down at the location Sam shared with me.

"Wow, look who decided to show up."

My head snaps up at the voice that sounds familiar but strange. Oh, it was his voice, after all. It's changed over the last four years, but not much. His accent has faded, and maybe his register is deeper. Mostly, though, it's his tone that's changed.

I just stand there frozen, shocked to see him. He's in scuffed brown boots, jeans, and an untucked white button-up. His hair is cut a lot shorter than his signature wavy locks that used to flop over his face. Now it's spiked and gelled up more straight. With this new cut, nothing hides his rugged beauty, complete with those green eyes that could surely start traffic. He stands casually with his hands in his pockets, like we run into each other all the time.

I know I look disheveled and tired. My makeup is smudgy, and my hair is oily under this hat since I left in a hurry this morning. I'm sure my eyes are bloodshot and bagged enough to hold a week's worth of terrible sleep.

"Shep?"

"Still my name." He is squinting down at me as if angry. *What the heck?*

"What, uh, what are you doing here?"

"Coming to check on your daddy, obviously." I don't have a chance to ask before he continues. "Truly did not figure that I might run into you, though."

"Excuse me?"

"You heard me. Didn't think you'd be here."

"What the hell are you talking about? My dad is in the hospital! Of course I'm here!"

He lets out an airy, bitter grunt. "You think this is the first rough spot he's gone through? Think this one is even the worst of them in four years? A few months ago, your own damn father asked me how you were doing. *Like I would be talking to you!*"

Shep might as well have punched me in the throat. I can barely whisper, "He did?"

He steps into my space, clouding me with his scent and his . . . Shepness, crowding me until I'm up against the wall by the elevators. We don't touch, and his hands remain in his jeans, but my body buzzes all the same. Having him close, it's like my cells know and react to each of his, whether I want them to or not.

"Let me guess, they didn't grieve the right way. Maybe they don't say the right things about your books or shower you with enough compliments. Now nobody in the universe is good enough for *the* Sadie Canton, huh?"

"Some people are, just not you," I spit back at him. Where the hell does he get off?! My answer was particularly mean, but he's not fazed.

"Uh-huh. Sure. But I think there's leaving, and then there's running, and seems like only one of those would mean you never pick up the phone and call your pops or ever text to check in on your little sisters." He looks me up and down quickly, with obvious disdain and adds, "So the question is, Sadie, what exactly are you running from?"

The elevator dings at that moment, and he leans back and takes a few steps to get on it, as if I'm not even standing here. As if he didn't just chew me up and spit me out in the middle of this bright, sanitized lobby. My hands tremble as I pull my hat farther down on my head. I vaguely registered texts coming through as Shep was dressing me down. Samantha must be here. I start to walk to the main entry doors.

Shep still talks to my dad? And my dad asked about me? Why would Dad do that when we talk all the time? Between the line of cards and the press ops and his publishing goals, he calls regularly. I don't always answer, but we email and text a decent amount too.

And how the hell does Shep know if I'm texting my sisters? Is he still close with Susan? Surely not, that'd be too weird, wouldn't it? Or maybe it's only weird for me? Maybe everyone else is still living their lives with Shep like he didn't smash my heart and crush our future. After I loved him for seven years straight.

No. There's no way they're all still close. He and Dad must keep in touch about football, play golf together, go to the club. Man's manly man stuff. That's got to be all it is.

"Ready to go home, Sade?"

"Nope."

Sam's face falls. "Oh, then where are we going?"

"The liquor store," I say flatly.

"Oh, are we having a party?"

I chuckle, wondering exactly what drunk Sam is like, since I missed her twenty-first birthday. I missed a lot of things. Shep's not wrong, and I hate it.

I smile wide and crank up her bubblegum-pop radio station. "Damn straight we are."

"Sadie's home! Woo-hoooooooo!"

I can't ever go home again, not really. I know that. But I can do better with my family. I can check in more, FaceTime, invite my sisters out to New York. I have a whole new fabulous world to show them. There's so much fun to be had, and not just for me, but for all of us. Starting with tonight.

CHAPTER 23

6 YEARS AGO
MANHATTAN, NEW YORK

Me: Look at the lewk
Me: [Photo]
Sam: ERMAGER LOVE!
Susan: Stunning but still professional
Skye: I picked the shoes.
Sally: [Fire emoji] What is this for again?
Me: They asked me to be a panelist at a big Writers Guild event.
Susan: What's your panel about?
Me: Bridging the gap between novels and screenplays.
Sally: Cool
Sam: Skye, I can't believe you're not going with!
Sam: Well, I can believe it. But won't there be a ton of celebrities there?
Me: You mean other than me? 12
Sam: Yes, other than you, SUPERSTAR! [Star eyes emoji]
Me: She's in her happy place!

I snap a photo of Skye reading on our little couch and send it off. I smile and tuck my phone into my snazzy suit pants.

"You sure you don't want to change your mind?" I ask her.

She gives me a *no duh* expression and then says, "Don't forget to put that thing on silent, or Sam will blow you up all night long."

"Good call." I put my phone on silent right then when I'm thinking of it, smiling. Since the rude awakening that was Dad in the hospital a year ago, my sisters and I text almost constantly. Skye moved in over the summer, ready to take the art scene here by storm, and Sam says she wants to join us here too.

As rude as he was with the delivery, Shep's message was one I needed to hear. I talk to my dad more often, and we all FaceTime about once a week. It's not always easy, but things with my family are a lot better.

Skye is only cramping my style a little bit so far. She never wants to go out, but that has worked well. If she did join me, she would only get on my case about how I let off steam. For the most part, I write while she paints during the day, then I meet up with friends in the evening and get home after she's asleep. I call out a goodbye to her at the entry table before putting my ID, lipstick, credit cards, and a small foil pill packet into my chic little clutch.

I end up not needing any little mood-enhancing friends. The caliber of writers in this room is energizing enough. I only have a few sips of the champagne before the event starts, wanting to keep my mind sharp for the panel.

I sit down backstage in the greenroom reserved for speakers and panelists. To my right, I notice a very stunning, sophisticated, and maybe familiar woman. She's typing furiously on her phone, so I decide not to intrude.

"Is this your first panel?" she asks with a thick accent. It's mostly British but laced with something else—German or something.

"Yes, is it that obvious?" I chuckle nervously.

"It is, but I love it. There's still some hope in your eyes." She can see I'm startled by her jaded words. "Sorry, love, I've been in this game too long. Don't listen to me. Lorelai Kent." She extends a hand to me, and I take it. As I do, a gaggle of volunteers passes us, eyeing her like she's Beyonce.

"Sadie Canton, nice to meet you . . . ?" I don't mean to ask it, but my eyes follow her adoring fans as they move toward a back door.

"As a writer, I go by Lori," she says flatly, and then a whoosh of realization hits me, as if someone just turned on the air-conditioning. I break out in goose bumps and force myself not to freak out.

"Wow, forget 'been in the game a while.' You *are* the game! My best friend Tash is obsessed with mafia romance. She has every single one of your books, each edition, special covers, the works. You're like the J. K. Rowling of romantic thrillers!" I can feel myself starting to Sam Out a little bit, as my family would say.

"That's a bit weird, but I'll take it, I guess. Thank you."

"Sorry, I'm just realizing I've been around a lot of actors and directors and all that, but this is my first time being in a room with so many authors."

"Ah," she says, looking out to where the stage is. We can hear the audience noise growing beyond the curtain. "Well, we're all just as cutthroat as the other lot, don't let them fool you. I had a million author friends until I became successful. Now I have none."

"That doesn't surprise me," I say, following her gaze. "My best friend, well, I thought she was a pretty good friend at least, actually stole an entire story from me and signed her first publishing deal with it."

"One like your current city series?"

"Um, okay, dying a little bit that you know about my books." I smile before continuing. "But no, worse. It was a much more autobiographical story about young love. I shared it with her when I first moved to New York. Turns out she made copies, and I guess just waited until she was too jealous to hold off any longer."

"Is she here? What's her name? And why don't you just have her blacklisted? You have plenty of pull in this town," she says, totally matter-of-fact. As if it's crazy that I haven't ruined Carly's career already. I lift a brow at her. "It's no small thing what she did, darling—she's a hack and a thief. Really, you almost have a moral obligation to out her to anyone and everyone in the industry."

"That's what Barb said, my agent. But after her book came out—*my* book—she grew a massive social media following fast, and I wouldn't be surprised if she ordered her whole army to flood all my titles on review sites with one- and two-star ratings."

"Been there, lived that."

"What? Really?"

"Yes, and it was so pitifully obvious that it backfired." Lorelai waves her hand like being demolished online is nothing. "Don't you have your own army?"

"My army shows up at the box office and the bookstore, not the comments section."

"Well." She levels me with a mischievous grin. "My army will show up anywhere. Should I let them have a go?"

I laugh. This chick is something else. Her vibe is so effortlessly cool and confident, I wonder if she is, in fact, part of a family crime syndicate in real life.

I shake my head. "No, but thank you. At least not yet. I have a feeling she's more of a flash-meet-pan situation, and I'm in this for the long haul. Can you imagine trying to write a series based off someone else's work? She won't make it. I'll simply outlast her."

"Brilliant. You really do have that homelander charm I heard about. Where's it you're from again, Montana?"

"I think you mean heartlander." I chuckle, trying not to pester her with questions about how she heard of me, from whom, when, and everything that's been said. "And Oklahoma. It'd be like if Montana had an ugly half sister. It's flatter and windier and . . . beige."

"Beige? Like taupe?"

"Whatever color you'd use to describe wheat—we got a lotta that."

"Darling, in this moment, I'm struggling to believe you made The Times list."

A loud laugh escapes me. "You're right. I'll come up with some better adjectives. Anyway, the ugly terrain doesn't matter. The people are great."

"So I see." She dips her chin at me. I think she's near my age, maybe five or six years older, at the most, but she is definitely an old soul. "And do you miss it?"

"Definitely not."

She laughs loudly this time. "Now there's a feeling I can relate too. I love love *love* home—Austria, that is—but to go back? I should think not!"

"Oh, looks like we're being summoned. I'm nervous!" I admit.

"Just be honest, don't let other panelists speak over you, myself included, and then we'll go for drinks, yeah?"

I exhale some nerves and nod at her.

She adds in a loud whisper as we enter stage left, "Blast it, guess I've got to change my number to one now."

"What?"

"Author friends."

I smile as she walks away with a wink, ever so fabulous. My jaw drops slightly, in shock of the night I've had already, and the event hasn't even started yet. Lorelai and I meet up with Liam and the guys and a very shocked, starstruck Tash. It's funny to see my hard-as-nails bestie turning to goo. Not only that, but Lorelai actually blushed when she met my *Rolling Stones* cover boyfriend.

We're all around celebrities all the time; yet, we've all got a shortlist of people that we would still fangirl over. If Kristin Chenoweth ever appears within a mile radius of me at any point, in New York or Oklahoma or otherwise, I will combust. Dead.

Lorelai drinks a couple fruity cocktails before calling it a night. I try to convince her to move to our next destination with us, but she says she has to be fresh to get seven or eight thousand words in the next day. My mind cannot compute writing that fast.

Tash begs off too, as she often does. Lorelai promises to text both of us for a brunch date this week. I get up to hug them goodbye and feel the multiple rum and Cokes I've had rush to my head. I laugh and then follow my handsome boyfriend out into the glimmering New York City night. I am not sure where we go next, who's with us, or how exactly I get home, but I know tonight has been a blast.

———

I had heard Emerson and Dennis whine about how hangovers get worse the older we get, but I honestly felt immune. Until today. I've had my disgusting smoothie, a greasy breakfast, and my combination of pills that would normally have me up and at 'em by now. Espresso. I need good, strong coffee.

Skye is looking at subleasing a studio space she wants me to see, so I can venture through the city, sip my brown life juice, and listen to some tunes. Maybe inspiration will strike as I do it. I'm severely behind where I should be on my latest novel. For the first time ever, I think Barb is concerned. She stopped by just to "say hi." Agents do not just say hi, she and I both know this.

I grab my venti coffee that I'm pretty sure could thin paint, and start walking. I don't put my tunes on just yet, since I'm fighting the start of a headache. I decide to take the busy routes through midtown today, hoping the hordes of faces might inspire characters or emotions or . . . anything for this dadgum story. I wonder what America would think if they knew their lover of love was completely over all of it. Pull the curtain, roll the credits.

Tash and Skye are both convinced I never really loved Liam. They say my face didn't light up when we were together, and I wasn't crushed when we broke up. I'm not sure if they are right. I am sure, however, that being cheated on very publicly by your famous fiancé sucks balls. Big blue hairy ones.

Gross, Sadie.

The whole thing went from bad to worse when he assumed we'd stay together. He couldn't imagine that I'd actually leave him for being unfaithful. He said a million mean things that all basically meant I wasn't good enough for him anyway. I threw all his worst reviews back in his face. I think. We were both pretty far gone at the time.

All things considered, I feel like I should get a year or so off from writing happy endings. Gwyn laughed at the idea and started sending me on dates with New York's most eligible bachelors. It's been a media circus, with Gywn in the center practically dancing with a Hula-Hoop while balancing a beach ball on her ecstatic face.

I look for love around me, but I'm not finding it today. Instead, I pass blank face after blank face. *Maybe I should work on a zombie thriller.* Skye would dig it. I start to imagine some of the passersby as secret zombies waiting to attack. I start to smile, but I'm stopped short.

The hairs on the back of my neck tingle. Only one person in the world gives me this sensation. I search left and right, and then I almost fall over.

Up, he's up on the giant screens that the networks have playing on the outsides of their buildings. So he's not on the street. He's in one of the nearby studios. Shep is on national television.

Shep is on national television?!

I'm behind on the captions, but under his stupid smokin' hot face they have his name and his NCAA wide receiver award title. But they're talking about a few guys who I know are his clients. As much as I have tried to block him out of my life, I still hear about him from Dad.

My father is one of those who thinks he's being subtle while bucking and stomping and breaking all the tea in the whole China shop. I move the conversation along when he mentions Shep went to a *singles* event at church or came by to eat because he *didn't have anywhere else to go.* I don't ask the follow-up questions or even comment. Dad is trying to play matchmaker, but he's a few excruciating years too late. I knew Shep was killing it as an agent, but . . . national television.

Wow.

I'm actually surprised it took him this long, now that I see him in the studio. His charcoal-gray suit is perfection, and whoever told him to go with that green tie deserves a raise. His eyes look otherworldly. And he has had work done on his teeth, not that they needed it. It's like he went from supermodel to alien life-form, in a good way. Beam me the hell up . . .

"Wake up, lady, you're spilling everywhere!" a man yells at me in a thick New York accent. Oh, yes, my leg is hot and wet. Wow, I've spilled coffee down my pants and the sidewalk. Will I ever not be caught in the beam of attention that's commanded by him?

"Sorry!" I say absently to the guy who is long gone by now. I shift my focus from the screens behind the glass to my reflection looking back at me. Oily hair, oversize glasses, sweats that are swallowing me whole, beyond fashionably baggy.

What a scrawny, tired, rumpled, coffee-coated mess. Lorelai is right: I have two settings, either full Hollywood or total hobo, there is no in between. Shep's segment is over, and now, I realize as my esophagus feels like it's being pinched, he is in my city. I could run into him around any corner.

I make a beeline to Skye's studio space, faster than I've ever walked in my life. He may already be on a plane back to Okla-homa, but if there's even a chance he is out seeing the touristy spots, I sure as hell am staying away from them. I am not run-ning into him at all, but especially not while in hobo mode.

CHAPTER 24

6 YEARS AGO
MANHATTAN, NEW YORK

Skye: LOL get a load of our superstar this morning LOL

Skye: [Photo]

Me: It's coffee, not urine.

Me: And I'm never relaxing around you again! I knew you were sneaking a pic!

Sally: Thanks for the clarification.

Sam: Is this a lewk, homeless chic?

Skye: OMG I'm going to send that and this photo to Gwyn, see if she can spin it

Me: Gwyn will chew you up, spit you out, and give the remains to Barb's chihuahua, so I wouldn't.

Skye: [Grin emoji]

Susan: What happened???

Skye: Think gummy bears, football, and crazy orgasms (I'm guessing).

Sally: That is a very odd grouping.

Susan: Wait, y'all saw Shep?

Sam: Shep Riggs?!! Orgasms?!! Are you back together!?

Me: NO!

Me: Skye, keep in mind that I'm like the only person you know in New York at this moment.

Me: I saw him on a Jumbotron while walking and spilled my coffee.

Susan: Oh that's right, he was going to be on Game Day this morning I think!

Skye: He was on all right.

Me: Skye, do you need to take an ice bath or something?

Sam: I pulled it up, he is SO HOT!

Sam: Not handsome

Sam: Not gorgeous

Sam: Hot Hot Hot!

Skye: Is he hot, Sam?

Sam: At least 90 in the shade [Sun emoji]

Sally: Link?

Sam: [Link]

Susan: Adam and Dad are beside themselves. Game Day is a big deal!

Me: It's a massive deal. And he did look amazing.

Sam: So?

Sam: No lingering feelings?

Sam: I mean, look at that hair!

Sally: Oh, I am looking.

Me: No, but I'm happy for him.

I see Susan's text bubble pop up and go away a few times. I wonder if she's actually in a separate text thread with him, Adam, and Dad right now. It wouldn't shock me. As far as my sisters know, over four years ago, I broke up with him because of his drinking, then left town.

So what if she is talking to him? So what if they're besties? It doesn't matter. He'll always be on the outskirts of my life through Adam and Dad, and I have to accept that. I have accepted that. He did look amazing, and I am happy for him. I hope he feels the rush that I do, finally reaching some of the goals we used to talk about.

I also want him to trip on a subway grate and smash his face up a little bit. Nothing permanent. Just enough to keep him off TV and out of Manhattan. This city is my place, my escape, my new life. There's not enough space for both of us here.

———

"Hold on, let me take a pic of both of you from the back! Our sisters want to get the whole vibe," Skye says, holding up her phone. "Tash, you really do know your way around a curling iron."

"Thank you very much," she says with a bow.

"Very smart, aren't we?" Lorelai puts an arm around my waist and faces the door, allowing Skye to get the shot. "But let's get on, or else Barb and the rest will be full up our asses."

"Not to mention your actual date," Tash teases me. I groan while all three of them laugh at my suffering. Tonight, I'll be on a second date with Sean, a very handsome, very boring actor. Gwyn says the public loves us together, so I'm grateful he's nice, at least. He knows accompanying each other tonight is for publicity and nothing more. I've had worse company.

Even so, I'm totally jealous that Lorelai gets to walk the red carpet on her own and mingle without having to keep an arm looped through anyone else's. Tonight is a big charity event put on by multiple guilds, meaning it will be a total celebrity pony show for the press. I'm sure the actors and musicians will be mostly B- and C-listers, if I got invited. I'm not even an A-minus on the screenwriting lists, but Lorelai is. I still can't believe that in just a few months she's become as good a friend as Tash.

Lorelai and I say goodbye and turn to go. Tash shoots me a look that says *keep your shit together tonight.* She would lecture me about counting my drinks if my little sister wasn't standing next to her. A little sister who doesn't miss the strange glare. I flip the bird with a giggle on my way out the door.

We share a quick ride over to the library, where Sean is supposed to be waiting in his car. When we pull up, he steps out, meeting me at the exact right time. His kiss on the cheek is effortless, and he does a good job of, well, his actual job: *acting* like we're on a real date. I'm not too shabby at the charade myself.

There's a red carpet set up in the center of the library's grand front steps, with journalists and photographers on one side yelling questions. Lorelai agreed to go first, taking some of the heat off us. If her career continues with each hit title and subsequent movie, I have zero doubt she'll join the very tight ranks of the world's female billionaires. What's a little greeting card heiress from Oklahoma after that?

According to the clamor across from us, she's not nothing. Wow. I guess Gwyn is incredible at her job. Sean and I can't keep up with the questions, so we just smile, wave, and pose. I don't miss some of the jabs about two failed engagements. I think one asshole even said Sean was a dead man walking. What does that even mean? I'm a vampire now?

"Wankers," Lorelai says over her shoulder so I can hear. Sean decides to ride the frenzy and lean in for a loving kiss on the cheek. I let him, and give him an Oscar-worthy gaze in return.

And we're off. We're through the library doors, headed to shake hands and be seen. We bid on some auction items, comment on some displays, eat tiny appetizers, and drink large champagnes. I mean, they're regular size, but I go ahead and drink two at a time. How else do I get through a night of *loving love* and *writing America's happiest endings*?

Kill me dead.

I turn, and almost drop the flute in my hand. I expected every moment I've endured so far, but I did not expect to see her. It's a shock of red hair I notice first. Then I notice her brilliant green gown. She looks incredible. She always had a lush hourglass figure, if petite, but she must have sky-high heels on right now.

I squeeze Sean's arm in an attempt to pull us very quickly, very far away from her line of sight. But I'm too late.

"Sadie! Babe! You're here too!" She takes a tiny step toward us.

Here too? Here TOO? Oh, this bitch better watch herself . . .

Lorelai appears beside me as if my murderous thoughts called her like a bat signal. Maybe she'll write that into her next thriller: a logo of a creepy axe in a woman's head, projected on the ceiling of a gala. Before I can answer, or move to, maybe, slap her across her face, she carries on. "Sean Boren! In the flesh! You two look amazing together. Love that for you."

Sean fumbles a bit because I've most likely cut off all the blood flow in the right side of his body. "You look amazing yourself, Miss . . . ?"

"Atlas, Carly Atlas, or at least that's my pen name. Oh, and here's my date, let me introduce you!"

Hairs on my neck, stinging in my gut, pain in my chest.

Out from a table behind her where he was writing a bid, now standing beside her. Her dress matches his eyes exactly. Maybe I should've picked up on that. He's in a standard tux but tailored so well, it makes it seem like tuxes were invented just for him. Sean should just strip down and let the idea go—no one can wear a suit now. But as always, Shep knows this. He also knew, his grin tells me, that I'd be here.

"Shep Riggs, nice to meet you, man," the God of Tuxes says to my date. Then he turns to me with a dip of his chin. "Sadie."

At the sound of his name, Lorelai chokes on her champagne, because she knows enough to know: shit's about to go down.

"Oh." Carly barely pretends, with a bat of her huge fake lashes. "Do you two know each other?"

"This bloody bitch . . ." Lorelai mutters, mentally pushing up sleeves she's not wearing and sliding on a set of brass knuckles.

"And who is your stunning friend?" Shep extends a hand to Lorelai, eyeing us sheepishly. As if he didn't plan this. As if he didn't come with the person who stole my story, *our story*, from me and sold it as her own.

"Someone who knows better than to shake either of your hands." Lorelai looks at both Shep and Carly with open disgust, then she pulls obviously at my arm. "Excuse us, but Sadie, darling, you're needed at the producer's table."

I hear Shep huff in disbelief as we walk away. I'm sure he's not used to being openly snubbed. His date makes a noise too. The burn by my new best friend is not lost on my old one. Carly is not a producer because she can't secure a movie deal. Because she can't write a sequel. Because she's a weak, thieving, jealous hag.

I've really tried to work out of my insecurities and evolve past berating other women, for any reason. I really have, but she is vile. I knew she was jealous of my wealthy mostly happy family, my writing skills, and my relationship with Dennis. She could not fathom that I would break off an engagement with someone she deemed me unworthy of. She must be terribly unhappy to have such horrible ideas about where one's worth comes from.

Not only that, but she's living a lie. I know better than most how much that will slowly kill you from the inside out. *Enough about her,* I think with a slow blink.

Lorelai hands me another champagne. "So he's the one, huh?" she asks me quietly after sending Sean to find more hors d'oeuvres.

"The one?"

"The one who shattered you."

"I . . . I mean, you know he hurt me, but I'm fine. I'm not shattered."

"Do you even remember how you got home last night, love? Or Wednesday night? Or Monday?"

I am blindsided. Lorelai's never even seen me drunk or high, I don't think. She's never told me to straighten up or given me a warning look, either. Have she and Tash been talking? That doesn't seem like Tash.

"You're letting yourself stay broken on the floor right now, I know, because I have been there. And I know it'll have to be you who decides to get up and start reassembling your pieces. When you get to that point, I'll help." She looks away as she adds, "Until then, I won't lecture you with wasted breath. You're smart enough to know you can't carry on this way forever. And neither can your art."

Well, I was not freaking prepared for all this! What the actual hell! My nemesis, the ex-love of my life, my new best friend, a mini intervention—what happened to a boring night with a boring date?!

I suck in a disjointed breath and take a step back. I need to take about fifty steps back. I also need some little helpers from my purse. My buzz is not anywhere near strong enough to compete with this disaster of an evening.

"I'm going to get some air."

"Want me to come?"

"No!" She isn't surprised. "Sorry, no, I need a second to just . . . I need a minute."

"Of course, darling, go. I'll keep Sean entertained."

Staying on what's turned into the A-list side of the event, I weave toward an exit. I've never scanned a crowd more. If I see even a hint of any shade of green at this point, I might just drop to the floor and army crawl out of here. Air. I need air. I exit out into a side hallway that's mostly deserted, but it's not enough. I've got to get outdoors.

I turn a corner and spot an exit to the outside. I pick up my pace. But I don't make it. A hand grabs my arm to stop me.

The hand turns me, then, of course, all I can see is green.

CHAPTER 25

6 YEARS AGO
MANHATTAN, NEW YORK

"Shep? Wh-What are you doing?"

"Following you, against my better judgment," he grunts out.

His anger sets me off.

"But what are you even doing here?"

"I was invited, but let me guess," he almost growls, "you don't think I belong." He tugs me out of the middle of the walkway. "Think you own Manhattan, honey? Did you think I'd never make it here, couldn't get here without you?"

I can't even process that he's here, in front of me, throwing these words at me like knives. I realize his ever-present companion, alcohol, is not currently in his hand. "How much have you been drinking, Shep?"

"Not half as much as you, by the looks of it. You're a mess, girl."

"So why are you talking to me!"

"You think you can just run to the other side of the room? Avoid me?"

"Yes, and I don't know why you wouldn't avoid me too. Clearly you have a type—wispy little four-foot worshippers at your feet, and I ain't that, Poteau."

He cocks his head. "And you? That your type now—tall, dark, rich, and boring as hell?"

"Better that than—"

"That your boyfriend in there? Are you together?"

My mouth drops open in shock for a beat before I can answer. "None of your business! Seriously, what are you doing here, Shep?"

"I live here. I met a gal, she asked me to be her date to a party. Turns out it's a writer party. Thought I might get to see the famous hometown celebrity in the flesh, and here you are."

"Fine." I gesture my arms wide. "You've seen me. Now let me get back to my date."

He moves into my path, blocking my escape. "Is he the next Mr. Sadie Canton? You in love with that pretty boy?"

I ball my fists to keep from putting my hands on his chest to shove him. "How dare you show up here, with her, and have the balls to ask me anything!"

He freezes, looking confused. "What's your deal with Carly?"

The sound of her name on his lips is all wrong.

"Go ask her, asshole! I'm done talking to you."

I move again to go, but instead of letting me pass, he grabs my arms and shifts me back further, so I'm up against the wall. It's cold and smooth against my back, and the hall light is blocked by Shep, putting me in shadows. I feel both terrified and thrilled. He drops his hold on me but lifts an arm to block me from the few staffers scurrying around down the hall.

"Answer the question, Sadie."

I feel woozy, and my voice comes out thin. "What? Let me go."

"Are. You. With. Him?"

"If I was—" I can't finish the words because Shep is on me. He keeps one hand on the wall, but he smothers me with his frame. He grabs me, pulling me into him around the waist with his other arm. He doesn't hesitate for even half a second before his lips take over my own. He opens me up and takes what he wants from my mouth, and when he groans, I melt into the kiss, despite myself.

His kiss is angry, sad, broken. But at the same time, it's home. My body instantly heats from the inside out, and my left hand fists his shirt. He moves his hand lower to grip me and pushes a leg in between mine. I whimper, and it triggers something in him. Just as fast, he pulls his mouth from mine.

"That's why I came here. To remind you what you left behind." His face twists, and he starts to release his hold on me. "And you know what? It's not all that, after all. Guess I'd built it up in my mind all these years. That I let the great Sadie Canton get away. But doesn't look like you're doing too great now." He backs away a couple more steps, keeping those green beacons trained on me. I sag against the wall, unable to hold myself up, hold any of it up anymore. He huffs and turns to leave me.

"I get it now," I call after him. He stops, but he doesn't turn. "I wake up in the morning and count the hours until I can escape. I plan my life around it. With backups too. I keep bottles in every room and pills in every purse." I push myself off the wall and make for the bathroom I spotted at the far end of the passageway. I can barely slur out the last words I'll say to Shep Riggs. "I didn't understand before. I do now."

SHEP

Shit, no no no no. Not Bambi. What have I done?

I never felt that way, the way she just described. I partied because I was a coward. I can get carried away after I get started, which is why I stick to a two-drink max now. I learned the hardest way possible that it's not worth it. But to plan your day around your next drink, to wake up with escape on your mind, that was never me. I've known players that way. One of them lost his wife and kid in a messy divorce. The other lost his life.

Damn it!

I hardly hear the nonsense out of my date's mouth the rest of the night. I don't know if Carly sought me out or seized the opportunity when we met, but there's a whole story between her and Sadie that I don't know. I don't have time to figure it out right now, though. I just watch Sadie like I'm special ops and my only objective is getting her home in one piece.

Sadie's friend, Lori something, already left her alone here. The C-lister date she came with is working on his own high. Carly would be too if I hadn't cut her off. Hell, do any of these people think about how they'll get home? How do they function the next day? We're not twenty-one anymore.

I study Sadie, but I don't think she notices. She's still a stellar actress. She's chatting with suits and hugging models and laughing like I didn't just rip her heart out and spit on it. Hell, maybe I didn't. Maybe her heart forgot all about me the moment she left Oklahoma.

But she kissed me back. She leaned into me like my chest holds an empty indentation in the shape of her body, just waiting to be filled. She made soft sounds I haven't heard in so long, and I'm not certain my ears didn't bleed.

Because it hurt.

It hurt like hell to feel her in my arms and then remember . . . everything. So much I need to tell her, to explain. But not tonight. Maybe not ever. I had to pull away. I didn't have to open my stupid mouth.

I didn't mean to take it so far. The woman just makes me insane. She's still my kryptonite, even if she's too thin and too tired. The light's left her eyes, and that's probably the most terrifying thing of all.

I want to look away. I want to leave. I'm still so angry with her it's hard to even be in the same room, but I'm not letting her overdose or get taken advantage of.

The party is fizzling out, but Sadie stays close to the bar. Her intake is increasing as she loses herself. She probably also knows everyone around her is too far gone to notice how wasted she actually is.

She's sneaky, which is another sign that she's really addicted. I had to get close to see the truth of it, and even then, I wouldn't have connected the dots if she hadn't given that slurred speech before heading to the bathroom. What else she took in the bathroom, God only knows.

The library finally ushers everyone out. I pace us so I'm within earshot of Sadie. I'm not sure she even notices me nearby—another bad sign. I hear her say she'll join a group at an afterparty at a club. I curse under my breath. Guess I'm going clubbing.

"Shep? Ready?" Carly blinks up at me, flopping those silly lashes like she's an innocent little dove. I ignore her and hail a cab. One pulls up, and she tries to take my hand to get into the car, but I pull away.

I give her an equally sticky smile as I tuck her into the cab's seat. "I don't know what stunt you're trying to pull, but I hope it fails miserably, and I also kind of hope I never see you again, Carly. Get home safe now." I slam the door and tap the top of the car just in time to see Sadie and her group—who decided to walk, which seems like a hazard to themselves and the city of New York—turn the corner.

I follow and I watch for an hour, getting more and more pissed. This girl is clearly trying to kill herself. She can hardly stand or keep her eyes open. Some guy walks up and tells her it's time to dance, and I can't take it anymore. He could carry her away, and she wouldn't protest.

So I carry her away, almost.

"Hey, Sade, time to go home," I say in her ear as I guide her out of the club. She mumbles some things, including my name. I know she won't remember this, though. I pull her phone out of her purse and get her to unlock it. I look at her recent texts. I think Skye lives here now, but I'm not sure. I see Lorelai, but since she bailed, I skip that thread. Tash seems to be her go-to.

I send a message as Sadie, to Tash, saying I went too far and I'm headed to her place. I say I need help, to throw up, eat some heavy food, water, and take a shower. She doesn't respond at first, so I blow her up, asking for the address and door code and anything else Sadie might need. Eventually, she replies with everything and some middle finger emojis. She also says, "I got you, Sade." I exhale. Thank God someone, somewhere, has her.

Now maybe, surely, I can let her go.

SADIE

Am I dead? I feel like I might be dead.

"No, surprisingly, you're still with us," Tash grumbles at me.

I said that out loud? And Tash is here?

I slowly open my eyes. I did not expect to find myself in her apartment. "I'm glad you're alive, and that you came here, but

I'm still mad about the sleep I lost, the meltdown I had that maybe I should take you to the ER, and *and* I burnt my finger making you grilled cheese last night."

"You made grilled cheese? How, um, how did I get here?"

"You texted me even though you were out of your mind, said you were scared, had gone too far, and needed help." She hands me a bottled water.

"I'm sorry," I say, hating the itchy morning-after sensation that's on me like a blanket. A thick weave of regret and embarrassment.

"Lor said Shep was there? With *Carly*?"

"Yep."

"Do you know why? Are they together? How?"

"Nope."

"This town." She sighs and looks at the ceiling. "I really worry it might kill you, Sade. Dennis, Carly, Liam, and now frickin' football golden boy? We need a new island."

"What about just a beach?"

"Huh?"

"Lorelai is thinking of moving to LA so she's not traveling back and forth to the studios as much."

Tash gasps, still a bit of a groupie of Lori's even after all this time. "She is?"

"Let's go with her."

"You think she'd live with us?"

I laugh, then wince at my throbbing ... well, everything. Even my nail beds are pulsing. "Not a chance."

"Neighbors?"

"If I can afford a place for us near her, I'll make it happen." I can see Tash getting excited at the idea. And I want to flee this floating slab of concrete like I never have before. But the idea kills me too. "Tash, could we really leave? I mean, we love New York."

She cocks her head. "Yeah, but I don't think she loves us back. I'm still a bartender with three credits to my name, and you're being actively haunted by all the ghosts you got. This city needs to get her shit together, then we'll come back."

"Then we'll come back."

She grabs her phone. "Texting Lor now! Hollywood better brace itself."

CHAPTER 26

ONE MONTH AGO
THE CARIBBEAN

I feel so awful when the light hits my eyelids that I am captured by terror. Did I slip? Have I relapsed? Am I hungover?

No. I remember now. Not hungover, more like wrung out. Empty of all nutrients, tears, thoughts, feelings. I haven't thrown up like that in years. And I cried, hard. In front of everyone. I groan at the memory, not just of me but everything. The bitterness in Dennis's eyes, the rage in Shep's face. How quickly he rushed to my defense.

"Water. Aspirin. Coffee." I hear Skye close by, but I'm not ready to open my eyes yet.

"We know you're awa-aaaake!" Sam manages to singsong a yell while whispering.

Sally snickers. "Awake may be generous."

I sit up slowly, without opening my eyes. A hand grabs mine, shoves some painkillers in one and a cool glass of water in the other. When the water hits my lips, I decide to face the music. The music is four gorgeous, similar, fresh faces staring warily at me. Skye is next to me on the bed, Sam sits at our feet, Sally sits on an ottoman she's pulled over, and Susan hovers.

"You think you can handle a plain bagel?" Susan turns from me to a tray behind her. "Or maybe toast? I ordered a variety of all the carbs y'all never eat."

"You hardly eat them, either," Sally reminds her.

"Skye mentioned coffee?" I croak.

"You shouldn't load your sensitive stomach with that right off the bat. Have half a bagel."

I smile as my sisters take turns teasing Susan about her attempts to parent me. They squabble back and forth as she cuts the bagel, butters it, plops it on a plate, and shoves it in my face. I take a few bites, then on cue, Skye hands me a steaming mug.

"Okay, you're awake now. Let's freaking go."

"Skye, why do you sound like we're about to take off on some epic journey?"

"Aren't we?" She raises a happy eyebrow at me.

"Oooo love this for us!" Sam squeaks. "Sadie the storyteller *finally* telling us her own story."

"Guys, you've been in my life, you know it all." I shrug.

There's a short beat before all four of my sisters explode, talking at once.

"Psh! Ha!"

"What!"

"You literally forbid talking about it."

"Good one! You tell us nothing!"

"We haven't been able to so much as whisper all four of their names! For years!"

"Unbelievable."

"Sometimes I call you the Vault."

"You think we're dumb-dumbs."

"Give me a freaking break."

"Fess up, biyatch!"

"We're not letting you off that easy!"

The excitement dies down enough for Sam to talk over all of us. "Here's the dill, we're in a pickle." We all groan.

"She's ridiculous but right." Skye sits up. "Because I want to go paint by the beach, Emerson wants Sam back at their villa, but we've made a pact. None of us are leaving this room until you've spilled your guts—metaphorical this time—so where would you like to start?"

"Ugh. Was this just as jarring when we sistervened on you two?" I look between Skye and Sam.

"Yes," they say in unison. We all laugh.

"I feel like it might be easier for you to ask questions than for me to try to rattle off my whole life story."

"Okay, why couldn't you marry Dennis?" Sally starts.

"Forget Dennis! Why did you dump Shep Riggs?!" Sam yells.

I take a few gulps of water, nod, and take a huge sip of coffee.

"That's maybe a good start. I didn't actually dump Shep." I close my eyes and talk quickly. "We fought, right after Mom died. He said everything was too heavy for him. Which was a cop-out. I told him to quit partying or lose me forever, and he let me walk out the door." I reopen my eyes but don't look at their faces. "I know, an ultimatum was probably the worst thing I could've done at the time, but a couple days later, I went to ask him to forgive me, and he—" I swallow. "He was with Mary Ann already. She was practically in his lap. The girl who'd been following him around for years, just waiting for her moment. He'd always said there was nothing between them, and maybe there wasn't, but she was an easy place to land, and he crashed down in a hurry."

"No," Susan whispers, as a few missing puzzle pieces fall into place. I know she was a huge part of their life as a couple, Shep and Mary Ann. I'm sure in this moment she feels pretty terrible, which is why I didn't want to tell her. It's ancient history now. And even today, I can't stomach thinking about Mary Ann.

"Yeah, but it just showed we couldn't take it. He and I weren't strong enough. And I guess in the end, they weren't either, but I really don't want to talk about them. So. I left his place and drove straight to Dad, then got on a plane and started a new life."

"With Dennis?" Skye asks, unsure.

I sigh. "Dennis was one of my first new friends in the city. He was the opposite of Shep in every way, right when I needed that. He was serious, grounded, safe. I do think I loved him, but I was so lost in grief and depression, who knows. I just knew I couldn't marry him. Not in that state."

"And then there was Liam," Sam says to the sky in a breathy voice.

"Uhhh, he's single if you want to call this whole thing off, weirdo." I kick my foot into her butt through the comforter.

"No, sorry, he cheated on you. We totally hate him. And he's no Emerson, that's for sure. But the two of you together were so dreamy. Like a living music video fairy tale or something."

"Heavy on the 'or something.'" Skye takes a turn kicking her.

"Did you love Liam?" Susan asks, finally taking a seat next to Sam on the bed.

I throw my head back against the headboard, hating where this is headed. "No, I didn't. Like Sam just said, I loved the idea of us, traveling the world, making art, and partying, honestly."

Skye sucks in a breath. "About that, have we reached the party girl Sadie chapter of the story yet, because I have some questions."

"Wait, first I want to ask about the others!" Sam almost jumps off the bed.

"The short answer to your questions, Sam, is no. I didn't love any of them. Half of the relationships you heard about weren't even real. We just let the press foam at the mouth. America's Paramour? The girl is a sham." They can hear the shame in my voice, the exhaustion. I think they're a little shocked and a little hurt. I really have kept a lot of myself from them. I decide to get to the deep stuff.

"Skye, let's go there. Four years ago, I had a run-in with the press when I was with Bryce."

"Fiancé number three?" Sally finally chimes in.

"Well, that's just it. I was drunk and high out of my mind, and the press was there to witness it. It was early on in the night, totally embarrassing. In a panic, I yelled, 'Guess what, guys! We're engaged!' And then grabbed Bryce's face. That was the happy kissing photo plastered everywhere the next morning. No mention of me having a drug issue. Problem solved. Except for poor Bryce, who had just started dating me. He thought I was insane, and I guess at the time I kinda was. I made sure our fake relationship and breakup all worked out for his career."

"You sure did. That man is everywhere now. All from starring as your small-town bad boy." Susan's voice is proud, which gives me strength to go on.

"That, uh, that was a low point for me. Tash had already moved out, tired of my shit. Lorelai had been distant, Barb had dropped me, and Gwyn was livid about the fake announcement. I was only texting you guys and Dad, never calling, because I was either wasted or hungover and I knew you'd know something was up. Especially you, Skye."

Sally's face twists when she clears her throat. "How did you keep writing through . . . all of that?"

"I limped through, writing a few hours at a time here and there. And I was pounding espresso and uppers and B_{12} shots, just to get those few hours in."

Skye's voice is soft, thoughtful. "Until four years ago, then you started cranking out books."

"Right. I went to Lorelai, and she locked me in her house for ninety days."

"My Lorelai? The mafia romance genius?!" Sally gapes.

"Freaking A! Between Skye's obsession with Loya and your love of Lorelai's books, I'm really starting to get a complex here!"

"I'm your number one fan." Sam raises her hand, but Skye interjects.

"I *knew* it! I knew you weren't traveling for the movie!" Skye whacks me with her arm. "The whole thing was filmed in freaking Burbank! I just couldn't figure out where you were."

"That was thanks to Gwyn, who would've personally photoshopped my body into stock photos of Uzbekistan if I'd asked, because she was so glad I was finally getting help."

Whack!

Susan slaps my shoulder.

"You went through all that *alone*? For years, without telling us? What the hell is wrong with you!" She cries, literally, with tears streaming down her cheeks. She also looks away immediately, a weird expression of guilt crossing over her brow.

"Ow! Anyone else want to whack me?"

"Yes," they all say in unison.

"Seriously, why?" Susan puts a hand on my leg.

"My therapist would say that, because I felt so many emotions so strongly, so erratically, I believed I was a burden. I believed I should keep things bottled and hidden, a habit I'm still working through. But looking back, I mean, we were all grieving, Suze, and I think each of us tried to just, you know, not make it worse for anyone else." Everyone is sniffing now, myself included. "And a lot of it is just good old-fashioned shame. I, Sadie Canton, America's whatever the hell, one of Dad's precious girls, and more important, your sister, coworker, and friend . . . I'm an addict."

"No, I don't think so." Susan shakes her head. "You just liked to get crazy, needed a release."

"I love you, and I understand that I hid this from you, but don't do that," I say, offering the same words I had to give some of my friends. "I was very high functioning at times, and secretive, so you need to believe me when I say I am an addict. All those big feelings? I never learned how to feel them, and I got hooked on escaping them altogether." I suck in a deep, cool breath. "I realize I turned to the very thing that ruined my life. The black ick that took Mom's life and stole my first love, I jumped into it. And I drowned. I almost let it ruin my life twice. I've done a lot of therapy and self-work, and I am okay with this now, with the truth . . . even if it's hard to face." My eyes sting, seeing the shock and disappointment in my older sister.

"Hey." Skye catches my eyes with her big hazel set, also wet on the edges. "Addiction is a disease. Some people are born with it, and to varying degrees. All I hear is that you're a fighter and a freaking champion."

"FACTS!" Samantha sobs through a proud smile.

I nod and take a few more deep breaths. We sit for a moment sniffing, reflecting. Sally perks up first, anxious to finish the open loop in her mind that is my life's journey.

She rattles everything off on her fingers. "K, Shep, New York, three fiancés, go to Los Angeles, quasi-rehab, start writing like a freak, more movie deals, and then why the move to Dallas?"

"No big revelation there. LA is a party scene, and while I loved the artists there, there were a lot of fake, untrustworthy people around me. It just didn't feel like the best idea for my mental health. I knew New York wasn't the right option, and I missed home. Downtown Dallas was a good fit."

"So . . ." Sally looks from the wall, where I'm guessing she makes mental notes as we talk, to my face. "Is this the first time you've seen Shep in nine years?"

"Ohhhh no. He's bounced all over like I'm his own personal pinball machine," I grumble. After another half a bagel, I tell them, in the vivid detail Samantha demands, about the pharmacy, the hospital, and finally the charity gala. They all lose their minds when I explain the truth behind Carly Atlas. They vaguely remember her one-hit-wonder book years ago. I feel like the twists and turns of my journey have worked Susan into an anxious knot.

"That rat bastard, showing up with her! I had no idea. I'm going to rip him a new one till kingdom come, Sadie, I promise you."

I laugh. "No, Susan, don't. Because *he* hates *me* now, and I just can't deal with any more of his crap."

"He didn't seem to hate you when he rushed to your defense last night." Sally raises her brows.

Skye starts to climb out of bed, adding, "Maybe he just really wanted to throat punch Dennis!"

"Either way, let's just focus on pulling off a wonderful, romantic, punching-and-vomiting-free end of the week for Sam."

"Honestly? I'm here for the drama," Sam admits with a mouth full of toast. We all cackle wildly at her refreshing honesty. "For real! This is the stuff of telenovelas! We're, like, living out one of your books, Sade!"

"More like a whole series," Skye says as she shoves a bite of something into her mouth. I can visibly see her social battery draining the longer we all talk.

"So that was it? The benefit in New York—that was the last time you saw him?"

"Nope, unfortunately, that was *not* the last time."

CHAPTER 27

3 YEARS AGO
TULSA, OKLAHOMA

"Why's it always like this?" I hear his drawl come from somewhere to the right of where I'm frozen. I'm hunched over on the curb of the country club driveway in what I thought was an inconspicuous spot. I was trying to pump myself up to go in, which is just another quick life lesson. I'm collecting those now. This one is a reminder that you should start before you're ready, because you'll never feel truly ready. Instead, I stalled.

Ugh.

I'm facing this spectacle sober, which is still a relatively new way of living for me, so I'd purposefully waited over an hour past the start time. I was going to text my sisters and slip in the back, avoiding anyone and everyone. Or one, specifically. Even if I'd convinced myself he wouldn't be in town for this. Why would a hotshot football agent, now a New Yorker, come home for a little local light show?

Well, it's not little.

The Canton Family Christmas Wonderland is eclipsed each year only by our Fourth of July Celebration. Both are almost legendary. Grandpa started the latter, and Dad began the former. Both of them live for these events, even more so than Sooner football. We didn't even cancel them the year we lost Mom. Even though the sparks and lights twinkled all wrong without her. *It's for the community,* Dad claimed.

"Why's it always us on the outside?" He fakes a chuckle, but we both know it's not funny. "It's like you and I can't ever actually get inside to where the party is."

I don't turn my head, but soon he's in front of me.

"I think it's actually always *me* who's on the outside. You could always just . . . walk on by."

"Not sure I could, unfortunately for me." His answering voice has the sour, prickly tone I heard at the charity benefit.

I still haven't looked up at him as I half laugh, "Want to give it a try?"

"Nah." He moves closer and, to my shock, sits next to me on the cement. "Never could pass up rubbernecking a good train wreck."

I sigh. "Are you trying to impress me with your use of metaphors?"

"Ha! Stopped trying to impress you about, what, thirteen years ago. It'd just be pearls before swine, as my gramma would say."

"First I'm a train wreck, then I'm a pig?" I actually turn to face him.

When will I learn? When he sat down, his scent alone was almost enough to get my eyes misting, and now I'm totally trapped in his gaze. As always, one look and I'm caught up in all of him. The thick shock of blond hair that reflects the parking lot lights. The firm jaw that's become more chiseled as he's aged. The smooth brow above my brilliant green undoing.

"My nutritionist said bacon doesn't agree with me, so it checks."

"Well, I've never liked pearls and nothing that valuable ever comes out of your mouth—certainly not anything wise."

"You really want to go round and round with me?" The acidic edge seems to be leaving his words the longer we talk.

"We're already going." I gesture between us.

"I argue as my job. You get that, right?"

"Eh, I heard something about you being a hotshot lawyer, but you look like the same ole hillbilly to me."

His face lights up. "Hotshot, huh?"

"Don't be gross."

"Gross, still? Talk about same ole—thought you were a master wordsmith?"

"Find us a Scrabble board!"

Shep laughs, hard. It sounds like home. "That's got to be the nerdiest thing a woman's ever said to me." I join him in his snickering until his voice grows downright soft when he adds, "I always was a sucker for a pretty nerd."

For a second, all the earth's molecules still. The Oklahoma wind stops its bellowing. Both of us have a slight smile on our faces. It's as if we're teenagers again, ribbing each other over nonsense just so we could keep the conversation going.

Shep clears his throat. "I didn't know about you and Carly knowing each other."

And the moment's over.

I shake my head, not wanting to remember. "It doesn't matter."

"It does. She pulled one over on me. After, I looked her up and put the pieces together. She stole your story . . . our story."

I just nod.

He goes on. "She knew who I was and she probably figured I would want to see you." I huff an affirmative sound. "She was right."

"Welp, you got to see me, all right," I spit at him, remembering how he cornered me in the hall and then fled.

He shifts his body toward me. "You look good. You look better."

"Thank you?" I say, sounding more shrill and hurt than I want.

"You look beautiful?"

"You asking me?"

"Holy crap, woman. You look like the Sadie I know and not the shell of her? You look like a dream? Take the win, I'm trying to give you a compliment!"

"Well, try harder, *guy*, because no woman in her right mind wants to be told." I make my voice sound as low, slow, and dumb as I can. "Uh, you look better."

"Surprise, surprise." Shep takes a piece of grass he'd picked up from between us and throws it into the wind. "Doesn't matter what it is I'm doing, I'm not doin' it right."

"Sounds like a you problem, Shep."

He flashes the cocky smile that always shows up before he gets inappropriate. "I bet I could find a few women inside that country club who'll swear up and down I'm *not* the problem."

"Few? I hear it's a lot more than a few."

"And every single one wanted seconds."

"Ugh, now who's the pig?" I stand, suddenly irate. "Go find them then. Good luck to you."

"Wait!" Shep stands and grabs my hand. "Dammit, I miss fighting with you." We both exhale at the same time, and I feel his gloved thumb move ever so slightly over my own. He looks down at our hands, and I almost don't hear him plead with me. "Don't go in yet."

"What?" I ask, and my voice snaps his gaze up to my face.

He squeezes my hand and speaks up. "Stay out here, keep talking with me."

"It's freezing."

"I'll give you my coat."

"They'll look for me."

"You can text them." He lets go of my fingers and moves his hands to my jaw. I feel the clutch of his fingers on either side of my head like he's not wearing gloves at all. Almost like we're both stripped down naked in this moment. "What else you got?"

I let myself lean into his hands, closing my eyes. "You'll be mean to me."

"And you'll be ugly to me."

"Shep, we can't keep doing this."

"We also can't seem to stop." I feel the heat of him near my lips, so my eyes fling open.

Wait, how did we get to this? Five minutes ago, I was trying to hide! Just a few short years ago, he did this exact thing—pulled me in, kissed me senseless, then left me in a sagging heap against the wall.

I can't. I can't do this with him. Everything feels raw, and Shep Riggs is the salt. I have to stay sober. I have to stay whole. I have to stay away from him.

"Sade," he whispers as he leans in. I can already smell spearmint and sense his soft lips near mine.

I blurt a half truth. "I'm engaged."

Shep goes rigid. "What?"

"I'm engaged," I repeat. It's a lie, except it's a truth I'm living out with Bryce in the press right now. We agreed to keep up the crazy charade of our engagement until he's secured more roles, and I've silenced any whispers about drugs or rehab.

Shep drops his hands and pulls away. It hurts all over again to lose his warmth. "Shep, I—"

"No. Don't you even bother!" he shouts, with his back to me. "You had it right the first time. When the *hell* will I learn my lesson to just pass right on by? Motherf—" He cuts himself off, noticing cars pulling in and out of the parking lot.

It's very possible we're being watched or recorded. All the more reason I was right not to let him kiss me. He growls with frustration before hitting an open palm to a No Parking sign as hard as he can. He rushes back at me with a crazed look in his eyes. They're the darkest I've ever seen them.

"My turn to say it, now, though I know he won't answer my prayer: I hope to God I somehow, someway, get the blessing of never having to see you again."

He stalks off into the parking lot without looking back. A deep hum of a sports car starts and zooms away. I manage to sit back down on the icy curb even though I'm shivering badly. Fighting my instinct to be alone, stay alone, and fight all these wretched feelings alone, I call Lorelei. She talks to me until I can breathe again.

CHAPTER 28

ONE MONTH AGO
THE CARIBBEAN

"So." I shrug to my sisters, still enraptured around me on the bed. "Now I put on a smile and go face my nemesis and my ex-fiancé at your luau!" I raise my coffee cup to Sam.

"I would like to make it clear that I am very mad at you for keeping so much from us for so long," she starts. "But I am also very, very proud of you, and feeling very, very badly about all the drinking this week."

"I wouldn't've come for the whole week if I couldn't handle it, Sam."

"Speaking of the luau, we only have just over an hour now to get ready. I think we better mosey," Susan suggests.

"Wait, now that I realize how truly horrible this is for Sade, I feel like she needs some mantra time."

"No, Sam," Skye moans.

"Oh yes! It's my wedding week, so you have to do what I say, and I say we're doing it! To the bathroom!"

Skye holds firm. "I refuse to participate in this madness."

"Fine then," Sam throws down. "I'm coming to your villa to get ready with you. I'll just stick to your side like glue the whole night!"

Skye growls at a glowing, victorious Sam as she gets out of the bed she'd just climbed back into. I'm reluctantly doing the same on the opposite side. We file into the island-chic white-on-white bathroom with a huge, modern, glowing mirror. I feel like it's taunting me.

I look at Susan in the reflection and scold her. "This is your fault, you realize."

"Hey! I showed y'all tons of nineties movies, I didn't know she'd cling to this one for dear life."

"This is the weirdest thing we do in our family," Sally mutters.

"By a long shot," Skye agrees.

"It's not weird, it's motivating!" Sam screeches as she moves me front and center. She stands to my right, serious. As if we aren't a group of fools right now, losing our actual minds.

"C'mon, you know the words," she says.

"I see pride," I say with absolutely no enthusiasm.

"She's just gonna make us do it over and over if you don't get into it. You're a member of the Academy, Sade, give it to us!" Susan bosses at me. Skye has put her head in her hands. Sally is grinning in the back.

"I see pride!"

"There it is!" Sam cheers.

I let it rip. "I see power!"

Sam beams. "Louder!"

Skye hunches over. "I want to die."

I add in the accent to finish it out. "I see a badass mother, who don't take no crap off of nobody!"

"Now, all of you better say it, for Sadie, bitches!" Sam actually cups her hands around her mouth, as if we aren't crammed together into a tiny, tiled space.

As my sister prepares to call out the words, I see her in all her five-year-old glory, when for some reason, she watched the Jamaican bobsledding movie on repeat. She stood on the coffee table, to Mom's horror, and made us all participate. This happened so often, Skye has called her Bob since.

Sam begins, "Feel the rhythm!"

"You better only make me do this once, guys," Skye warns.

"Feel the rhyme!"

Susan, fully on board: "Loud and proud, Cantons!"

Sam raises her brows with her final call. "Get on up, it's Bobsled time!"

"Coooool Runnings!" we all bellow out, dissolving into the kind of laughter anyone would expect from this utter ridiculousness. Tears fall down my cheeks, and I let them run. I laugh hard and grip my sisters around me. I will always remember this moment, this tiny slice of time—with Susan relaxed, Skye's eyes sparkling, Sally laughing, Sam radiating joy, feeling truly open and present with all of them—as one of the happiest few minutes of my life.

One thing I have learned about myself in three years, I feel big, deep, gaping sadness and disappointment, sure. But I also feel epic, euphoric happiness. I get the highs with the lows. Numbing myself out from one meant I missed the other. I am so grateful in this minute to be fully awake, aware, and alive.

I hope I can hold on to this feeling for the long, uncomfortable minutes ahead this evening.

I take a hot shower filled with prayers, tears, and more mental pep talks—without any movie quotes. I get ready alongside

Sally and Janie, who had a considerable number of questions about what she'd just overheard in the bathroom.

The theme tonight is simply the luau, so I'm wearing a floral-print strappy wrap dress. It's got built-in lining in the cups so I don't have to wear a bra, which is a win, and it's totally comfortable while still looking dressy. I have a feeling I may need to stuff my face with comfort food this evening. My ensemble is prepared for such an occurrence.

Having learned my lesson, I ask them to stick with me on the walk over to the big grassy lawn where tents are set up for us. However, my attempt to avoid being cornered, it appears, has failed. In the elevator bay right before the exit doors to the party, there he waits. He's leaning against the wall in linen, looking like he just walked out of a Sperry's ad. He's confident and relaxed but noticeably sweaty.

So, maybe not so relaxed.

"Can I talk to you for a minute?" Shep asks me, eyeing Sally's tight grip on my arm. I love that my tiny, considerate, almost mousy baby sister is ready to beat his ass right now. She's like a pretty little hummingbird ready to take on a lion.

It's a weird mood.

"All right." I break the tension. "I'll see you out there, Sal," I add, nodding at her questioning glare. After a beat, I say, "Couldn't do this out there in the sunshine?"

"And ruin our outsiders streak? No way." He smirks. The elevators open, and a few guests file past, obviously eyeing us while thinking they're being chill. The ogling makes Shep chuckle. "Let's walk?" he asks, and I lift a shoulder. I don't want to try to talk in yet another vestibule.

He holds open the door for me, and I get a waft of his manly scent. I also feel the heat of him on my side as I pass through the door. I might be imagining it, but I think he holds his breath for me to walk by him. Instead of walking straight ahead to the tents, we go left toward the beach. Shep turns onto a wood plank walkway running along the edge of the resort where grass dissolves into sand.

"As always, you were right." He finally breaks the breezy silence. I look up at him. "This week isn't about us. But then I went and screwed that right up like a damn fool, turning last night into the Shep Show."

"Eh, people love a good train wreck," I say softly. He chuffs out breath and looks over at me, his eyes sparkling. I wonder if either of us has ever forgotten any words we've spoken to the other. I doubt it.

"Touché, Wordsmith." He stops walking. "So, I wanted to say I'm sorry and you're right—we should try to be friends."

"Good," I say too quickly, hating the way the last word left his lips. I don't know if I can be his friend. Again, I'm doubtful.

"Great," he says just as quickly, his voice rough. I am unsure of what to say or do. So is he, it seems. We stand there, not looking at each other, frozen in the weirdness. "Well, damn, this is already awkward."

I let out a giggle. "Very."

"Quick, make fun of me for something."

"Your outfit is dumb. Only a bride can pull off all-white linen."

"Try again, we both know I look amazing." He poses again, this time looking off into the distance like he's in that Sperry's commercial. He has got to be the only adult human who does this regularly. It forces me to really laugh. He drops the pose to say, "There we go, you laughing at me. That I can work with."

"It does feel right," I add, starting to walk back toward the party. He follows.

"As your *friend*," Shep restarts, clearly hating the word, "I'm sorry for making you lose your lunch last night. And dinner. And maybe everything you've eaten this entire week."

"I get it! It was gross! I don't forgive you!"

"You gotta. It's in the Bible."

"Bless your heart," I say with a southern drawl.

"Wow, no need to be so hateful," Shep jokes, putting a hand to his heart like the passive-aggressive southern phrase has wounded him.

"Why did you?" I ask as we near the sounds of the party.

He shrugs. "Nobody can be mean to you except me."

"Is that so?" I ask, batting my lashes.

"Turns out." He shakes his head as if he's in disbelief at his own feelings and actions.

"Well, that feeling is not mutual. I'll let anybody be mean to you, anybody and everybody," I say.

He laughs. "I guess that's okay."

"Actually, I might start requesting it. My sisters would love to tell you off. Maybe we could get them in a line and let them loose on ya."

"Bring it."

"And Dennis, I'll let Dennis take a swing."

"Fine, Sade." He stops and turns to face me, his smile boyish but his tone serious. "If that's what it takes to be your friend again, gather 'em round and let's do it."

I squint my eyes at him. "Maybe later."

"K."

"Also," I add as I start walking again, "don't be nice. It's weird."

"Here we go, can't do anything right," he mutters, but I can tell he doesn't mean it.

"Much better." I smile.

"Shall we?" He gestures toward the big tents when we reach the end of the path.

"You mean we're actually going to go in, to the festivities, together?" I pretend to be shocked. "Do you think we can handle it?"

He swallows and searches my eyes for all their secrets. "I think we should try."

A tsunami of feelings barrels into me without warning. Those lethal green rays, the earnestness in his features, the crack in his voice. What the hell is happening here? Why does he look like the Shep of a decade ago?

Do I want that? Can I even handle that? What about all we went through? We can't just slap a friendship Band-Aid over the stabs in my back, my brain, my soul.

He moves like he's going to extend his arm, but I know I cannot take it. Grabbing him and touching him, skin on skin, *no*. Not now. Not yet. *Not yet? No! Not ever.* So, I take my purse into my hands instead.

"Yes, let's try, but I teared up back there. Do I look okay?" I ask, finding a tissue in my little bag.

"You look breathtaking as fuck."

"Shep!" I gasp, immediately looking around for my father or uncle or our family pastor who is on the guest list.

Shep lets out a big laugh. "Sorry not sorry. One, it's the truth, and two, you were being weird all of a sudden. Come on, Hollywood, let's give them a show." He starts walking, hands in pockets, clearly no longer trying to escort me by the arm or hold me by the hand or touch me at all. And as I watch his perfect backside saunter away, instead of relieved, I'm . . . disappointed?! *Lord, it's me, calling uncle again.*

This is going to be such a long night.

———

"You're out of your mind!" Shep points at me with the cupcake he's about to shove into his mouth. "That campaign made Gator a rich man!"

"It was the dumbest Super Bowl commercial the world has ever seen."

"I wa' hystrrryclll," he insists, his mouth completely full of white cake and white frosting.

"Gator Aid, though?"

"He helped a little old lady learn how to FaceTime, all you could see was her forehead, he moved it down for her—it was adorable!"

"But 'for athletes, there's Gatorade. For everything else, there's Gator Aid.' That's the best they could come up with after spending that kind of obscene money?"

"You know what, it could've been the most clever, most amazing commercial in the world, and you'd still shit on it just because of me."

I tilt my head. "It's possible."

He smiles and mutters something under his breath before he's interrupted by an audio feedback sound from the speakers placed throughout the tent.

It's been this way with him all night. Ribbing, teasing, laughing. He hasn't been too mean, and I haven't been too sensitive. There's been no name-calling. There also hasn't been any flirting or touching. Not that I wasn't tempted. I almost touched his arm about fifty-five times. I almost looked at his lips about one thousand times. But I stopped myself.

I've been neutral. We've been . . . friends. It's been a nice night between friends.

Maybe I can do this with him, after all.

The screeching sound stops as a new song comes on the speakers, some very old song about London that does not match the pop music that was playing before it, or the tropical music playing before that.

"This is a weird playlist."

"Right? I bet all of them have some meaning. Sam and Emerson are both so sentimental."

"Saps," Shep jokes.

"Totally."

Shep's voice lowers. "Of course, maybe I shouldn't talk. I can roll with anything, but only as long as they don't play JP Saxe."

Then again, maybe not.

KELSEY HUMPHREYS

CHAPTER 29

ONE MONTH AGO
THE CARIBBEAN

My whole self snaps to attention. "W-What?"

"That trailer. For your movie. It played on repeat all day every day, no matter where I went. The whole town was so proud, I couldn't even take a piss in a restaurant bathroom without seeing your face, or your name, or hearing that damn song."

"Yeah, well, you got me back."

"Huh?" He shifts in his chair so his leg is against mine. The sensation of his warmth touching me through his thin pants is enough to dim the whole room out of sight. I also can't hear the clink of forks or the crazy song anymore. "What do you mean?"

"Your big mug was all over New York, and you know it."

He smiles in that cocky way I keep trying to hate. "The camera does love me."

"Oh, barf." I pull my leg away from his playfully.

"Again? Thought you had enough of that after last night."

"That was your fault!"

"I can't help it if my impressive display of raw manliness made your stomach flip."

"Impressive display of raw manliness?"

"Is that what you heard? Because what I said was an unfortunate slip into toxic masculinity."

I throw my head back and let go, and he laughs too, for the millionth time tonight. He really is the only person who can make me laugh this hard, this much. It's not just his humor but his delivery, the vulnerability in his eyes while his words are totally cocky. The way he can still make fun of himself while being the most confident guy in the room.

I was too distraught to think much about how hot his *display* was last night. Him coming to my defense, to literal blows. It felt like he cared. Actually, it felt like I was his. And I loved that. And that is not a good sign.

"I think I'm going to call it," I decide, suddenly overwhelmed. "I'm sure this is about to turn into a wild party, and I've had more than enough of those in my life."

Shep stands as I do. "Same."

I stammer. "O-Oh, you don't have to, um, you should stay." I don't want him to miss out on his fun because of me, like old times. He can do whatever he wants. Although, now that I'm thinking about it, he had iced tea all night. Plain sweet tea.

"I'm tired. Didn't sleep well last night."

"Oh."

We slip out of the party almost completely unnoticed. I manage to wave a goodbye at Samantha, who is obviously smiling and staring at Shep next to me. I try to tell her to cool it with my eyes, but she refuses to be cooled. Skye and Susan are both long gone, and Sally is distracted with our cousin. Kat is the wild Canton, much tamer after having Lucy.

It's a bit awkward this week, since we all know she's a fill-in for Nicole, Sam's previous best friend who was secretly trying to sabotage our family. We are close to Kat, though, and she's ecstatic to be involved. And on a vacation. Right now, it's clear tonight she has taken off the role of single mother and decided to resume her duties as the fun cousin. Currently, she appears to be refereeing a drinking game. *Oh, to have a young metabolism again . . . and a non-addictive personality.*

I start for the doors that lead back into the hotel, but Shep calls my name.

"Sadie, this way." He nods toward a path that leads inland, into shrubbery and trees.

"Are you dragging me off into the jungle to kill me, because they'll all know it was you."

"They'll think it was Dennis," he replies ahead of me.

"Damn. You're right. So, this is how I go, huh?"

"If I were going to kill you, I'd obviously go with poison in your coffee like true crime shows have taught me. Now, less talkin' more walkin'."

I follow him in silence for a few more minutes until he stops. We're still on a cement path, not far from the resort buildings. I'm confused what exactly has Shep stopping, but he turns to the side and pushes his chin out in the direction he wants me to look.

"For the inevitable jungle romance you're gonna write." He sounds a little sad? Angry? Irritated? I'm too stunned to pinpoint what I hear.

In a grove of fruit trees and swinging vines, an actual jungle, is a light show to rival Dad and Grandpa's. I've never seen so many lightning bugs condensed in one area. Not to mention they are huge! You can actually hear their lit abdomens blinking on and off.

"I've got to show this to—"

"Your dad. I told him."

"You did?"

"Your mama had a thing for bugs, right?"

"Right," I whisper. Mom loved bugs when she was a kid, but it became a whole thing with her and Dad. It went beyond bugs; there were turtles and flowers and a whole thing. I can't believe Shep remembers any of it. But then, I also can.

"Now look up."

"Wow." The stars are crazy beautiful here on this island. There isn't much city sky pollution, and the ocean swallows up so much light, the stars are a show on their own. At this spot, with the clearing around us and the bugs in front of us, it's extra magical. "Thanks, Shep. It's incredible," I say, after we've been standing in silence for a while.

He looks at me, and I can't read his eyes in the light, but I hear seriousness in his voice. "Sometimes it pays to walk the long way around."

Nope.

I'm not going to do this. I'm not going to ask if it's a metaphor. Or pile on with a line about how one could also get lost as hell out here. About how maybe it doesn't pay at all; it's just that you're so desperate to reach a happy end of the trail, it seems like you were meant to go the long way. I don't think I have it in me to spar with him right now.

"Can you point me in the direction of the villas?"

"Sure," he says, his voice back to its usual lightness. "C'mon."

We wind back through jungle, then shrubbery, and then manicured lawn surrounding the various buildings. We pass sheds and meeting halls, open cabanas, and smaller villa units. Finally, we get near to what looks like the row of huts that includes my home for the week. As we reach my villa, my nerves go berserk.

Is he going to try to hug me good night? Will he ask to come in? He seems like he might want to keep talking. Do I want that? If we open that can of worms, it will keep us up all night. We'll cry and yell and probably rip each other's hearts out for good, only to have to face each other for all the rehearsal stuff tomorrow.

No. I'll just say good night. As I'm about to lay down the law, we hear people laughing, a group of teenage boys, it sounds like. Shep grabs my hand and pulls me out of the walkway to the side of my building.

"Shep?"

"What about benefits?"

"What?"

"Friends with benefits." I blink in shock. He grabs my other hand in his and keeps talking. "Tell me you don't still—after ten damn years—don't still feel fireworks in your hands right now."

I can't respond yet. I'm just panting, in shock. And yes, my hands are exploding. Shep takes the silence and fills it with his body, pressing me further into the cold stucco wall behind my back. With our hands still linked, he presses his whole body into mine, moving his leg in between my own.

He leans his head in so close to my face, I can smell the sweet citrus and sugary tea that I know his mouth must taste like. My own mouth waters, and my lips part. I still can't quite speak. Because what do I want to say? Yes? No?

"Used to, I could just look at you and you'd fall apart for me. Do you remember?" He whispers the words along my cheek. "Do you remember how we felt? Do you miss it?" He breathes down my neck, taking in a deep breath of my hair and perfume and sweat.

Inhaling me snaps something in him, and his left hand shoots up to cradle my face so fast, I would've bumped my head into the concrete if he hadn't held my neck in place. His right moves up my arm to my shoulder.

"Tell me you can fight this between us. Tell me you want me to stop." He moves his hand to the base of my neck, where the triangle of my wrap dress starts. He hooks a finger underneath, and the graze of his knuckle kills me like it always has. He looks down at his hand caught in the fabric and licks his lips.

His eyes come back to mine. We're in a patch of moonlight between buildings, invisible to everyone else walking by on the path, but totally visible to each other. In the blue glow, he looks like a dream. "Tell me to stop, and I will."

"Shep," I whisper.

"All this tension between us, let's just let it go, get it out of our systems for good."

"Sh-Shep."

He watches me as he takes his finger under my dress and pulls slowly. I should say stop, I should shove him off me, but I'm transfixed. I'm hot and throbbing and blinded by need and want. And confusion too.

The lower his hand goes, the more the triangle of the wrap dress moves with it as he tucks the fabric away, exposing my left breast to the cold night air. He glances down for a second, but then his intense stare is right back on my face, watching. He moves his hand to the other side and slowly pushes that triangle of silk away too, until my entire chest is bare in the moonlight, hard in anticipation of whatever he'll do next.

Again, he only actually looks down for a flash. He keeps a hand on my jaw and studies my face. He looks for a reaction as he puts his hand flat on my sternum, hot and firm. I know he's feeling how erratic my pulse is. I can feel his is too, through his fingertips. He moves his flat palm down to cup me and lets out a sigh as he squeezes.

"Shep," I gasp his name.

"I'll stop, just say the word," he rasps out as he watches my reaction, then he pinches my left peak, hard. He groans before leaning down and attacking my chest with kisses. He's a storm all over my skin. Moaning, sucking, licking, biting, and cursing under his breath. I start to writhe under him, already ready to detonate, even though we haven't even kissed.

He pulls back and moves his hand to the hem of my dress above my knee. His hand is sure but slow as it moves up my thigh.

"Shep," I say again, unsure of what I even mean anymore.

"Say the word, honey."

Honey.

Honey?!

This asshole.

I am not, nor will I ever be, one of his honeys, and he knows it.

Suddenly out from under whatever crazy spell he's cast over me, I remember that I, too, possess hands. I take one and place it on his chest, eyeing him like he's eyed me. He looks so hot I could die, but I'm too angry to care. Let me die. I'll take a certain package with me as I go.

I slowly move my hand down his chest, right past his waist to the main event tenting out his pants. It's my turn to cup my hand over him, and he closes his eyes for a second, steadying himself.

"Stop," I say, quickly adding, "this is all just a bit too *heavy* for me."

"YES!" Shep yells as he pulls away.

"What?"

"Thank God!" he yells up at the sky, smiling, reeling. I am stunned as he shouts for joy and pulls on his hair. "Finally! Holy hell, woman, you—" I don't catch what else he growls as he grabs me and tosses me over his shoulder like a sack of flour. He stalks away from my villa, and I quickly try to cover my tits, which are still out in the breeze, just offering a little show to those teens if they're still nearby.

"Shep! What are you doing!"

"Taking you to my room, like I shoulda done when we got here!"

"Are you insane?"

"YES! You make me insane!"

"Put me down!"

"No!"

"Shep!"

He slows as we reach what I guess is his villa. "Still my name, though I liked how you were saying it a second ago much better."

I scream in frustration. I hit his back as he gets out his key at a door and starts taking us in. He's unmoved by my fists and slaps.

"Finally!" Shep starts laughing like a madman. In this moment, I am concerned for his mental health. *What the heck is happening here?*

He walks us through the door, slams it shut behind us with his foot, and then plops me down on the couch. I can feel my mouth fall open in shock. The living room of the villa is just like mine, with a couch set across from a small, lit fireplace, a rustic low coffee table, an end table, and kitchenette area. One wall is doors that lead to the patio, and the other side leads to the bedrooms.

"You almost had me—you even sang! Being my friend and taking everything I threw at you. I really thought it might actually be over," he pants, talking almost more to himself than to me.

"It is over!"

"No, Sadie." He says it with such conviction I lean back into the couch. "We will never be over. You know it, and I know it. We have been in the wrong time, the wrong place. We've been stupid and stubborn and scared, but not over."

"We hate each other!"

"Try again." He stands in front of the fire with his hands on his hips, daring me.

"We can't even be in the same room!"

"Correct. We're on track to ruin their wedding."

"We will kill each other in this villa."

"Worse ways to go. What else you got?"

"It's too late for this." I sigh, my voice weak.

"As you said, we can't even be in the same room. I don't think we have much to lose." He crosses to grab two water bottles from the minibar. He extends one to me as he looks me in the eye. "But we have a hell of a lot to gain, Sade. I know you remember. Like I do. We have been broken a long-ass time. Now we fix it. We fix us."

I stare up at him. He waits and watches with a vulnerability in his face that I haven't seen since we were together. He extends his arm a little more, looking down at the water bottle.

We're both already thirsty and tired. We're worked up and unsure. I know as soon as we start talking, we'll both grow furious. We'll cry. Shep will probably throw something. Because we'll have to relive the hurt.

I'll have to relive it. I'll have to feel my heart splinter apart again. There'll be nothing to dull the pangs of grief. I won't be able to take the edge off. This conversation will be all edges. Hell, even I might have to throw something.

I stare desperately into those green eyes I still see when I close my own. The eyes I find in my dreams and in moments of exceeding happiness or deep disappointment. Am I ready to get lost in them again? I look down at the water bottle that's shaking slightly.

With a trembling hand, I take it.

CHAPTER 30

ONE MONTH AGO
THE CARIBBEAN

SHEP

She takes the water bottle. I close my eyes with relief and then look up to the ceiling. *Thank you, Lord! Now I'm gonna need some serious help down here.*

"Did you just pray for us?"

"Yep."

"Me too. Old habits, I guess."

"Think He'll listen?" I ask. I smile at her, resulting in a stretched frown that says *it's not looking good.* I clear my throat, deciding to man the hell up. "I'll start." She takes a sip of water and waits.

Crap. This is a lot. I told myself I'd let her go. We were done. Too far gone. Too broken.

All of it was bullshit. Back when I said it three years ago in that parking lot and every moment I've tried to convince myself this week. One look at this girl, and I'm a goner, every time. No point in carrying on the lying anymore, to ourselves or each other. I take a deep breath, and it's shaky. My hands are vibrating too. I ball them into fists and decide to pace.

"First of all, I never cheated on you." She shuts her eyes tight. I can see emotions warring in her, but she hasn't settled on hatred yet, so I keep talking. "I didn't, Sade. And second, I'm sorry for being such an ass to you this week. And all the other times we've seen each other."

"Why . . ." She sniffs, upset already. "Why were you?"

"Because I was so mad. I'm still so mad at you! You left us!" I pull on my hair and grit my teeth but force myself to keep going. "Okay, we had a fight, a big one, sure, and Mary Ann was there when she shouldn't have been. But she and I weren't together. Which I went to tell you, but you had just cut me off, blocked my number, and went to New York alone. I couldn't believe you took our dream, our future, and just went without me! Like I was nothing. Like you weren't leaving anyone significant behind."

"Are you serious?"

"And then, and *then!*" I cut her off. "I wasn't actually with Mary Ann, but you sure as hell were with Dennis! You had a new man, a new life, within a month! I saw it all online, and that's when I think my heart really—"

"YOU MARRIED HER!" She stands and screams at me at the top of her lungs. It's so loud, laced with so much hurt, I almost fall backward. Time freezes for a moment, like the release of all her pain halted the whole dang universe.

She goes on, through huge tears that prompt my own. "You married her, Shep. How can you stand there and say you were mad at me for *anything*? You went straight to her arms, and then you made *her* Mrs. Riggs." She plops down in defeat. Her voice breaks when she says my name. I hate my name in this moment. I hate myself. I rush to her instinctively, kneeling before where she sits on the couch, and I try to touch her knee, but she violently pulls away.

I take a second to muster some strength.

"I wasn't really with her when you left. We hadn't, I mean, she'd barely kissed me at that point. I let her hang around because I was angry, and ashamed, honestly. But then I went after you. I drove up to Tulsa two days later, after I realized you had gone home. But when I got there, your dad told me you were already gone. He also—" I clear my throat. "Well, I should point out the obvious, that your daddy wasn't totally in his right mind. Nobody was then, but he really still wasn't, and you'd just left and I think that messed him up all over again."

She winces, so I hurry on. "Anyway, your dad said, mostly to himself, like he was thinking aloud, that if your mama was there, she'd know how to talk you down and keep you home. He rambled on, saying that your mama swore up and down how we shouldn't have gotten together yet, that we—that *I*—wasn't ready. That I wasn't a man yet, just like he hadn't been either, or something to that effect.

"Honestly, I only half heard the man. I was out of my mind trying to reach you, then I was so pissed that you'd left, really the only words that stuck out to me were *not man enough*. Again, that same message." I run a hand over my face, exhausted.

I know I need to keep going, though.

"You were all right about me, by the way, clearly. But it killed me to hear another person I love and respect say it. Shortly after, I saw you with Dennis, and there she was begging to be with me, so I let Mary Ann into my life. But . . ." I hate saying this part out loud. "It wasn't serious. I didn't want to marry her, Sadie. I . . . I had to, because she got pregnant."

Sade's head snaps up, and I quickly answer what I know she is asking. "She lost the baby. It was at thirteen weeks, right when we were about to tell everyone. It was . . . rough." My voice aches in my throat as I remember the room we'd already cleared out to be the nursery. We had buckets of soft yellow paint ready to go. Sadie leans in my direction, like she might touch my shoulder or say something. She doesn't, but it's something, at least. She's not recoiling anymore. I go on.

"I tried to do the right thing, to be a man and make it work, I did. We tried to stay together for a year or so after that, but we weren't in love in the first place. She was infatuated, sure, but we didn't have real love. Mary Ann admitted it to herself after the miscarriage.

"What happened, though, in my messed-up state, is, well . . ." I look away from her gorgeous blue-green eyes. "I blamed you. I blamed you for pushing me to her, even if I only ended up there to make you mad at first. It was all your crazy idea. Then I blamed you for leaving and getting with Dennis so fast that I decided to actually *be* with Mary Ann. I blamed you . . ." I let a tear fall but don't let the sobs break out. "For a marriage that I didn't want . . . and for the loss of a child that I did."

We sit in silence for a while, reeling. I'm still on the rug in front of her where she sits hugging her knees on the couch. She looks about sixteen sitting that way. Man, if only we could go back.

"I think I blamed you for my engagement to Dennis," she finally says in between sniffs. I get up and cross to the hall bathroom where I know there's a box of tissues. I come back and hand her the box and decide to sit on the couch. I don't sit too close, but I already feel better as she turns perpendicular on the couch in order to face me.

"Blamed me how?" I ask, since she seems to have clammed up.

"Well, I wasn't sure I wanted to marry him, either, but you were already married. So, just like you, I thought, why the hell not marry this nice, rich, hot British guy who adores me? I mean, there was nothing stopping me."

I choose to ignore the *nice, rich, hot* crap. "But something did stop you."

She nods. "I couldn't do it. And the hesitation showed me I didn't love him. Not fully. Which wasn't fair to him. I think I broke his heart a little bit."

"Ya think?" I scoff softly.

"So, that's it, all this time, you were mad just because I left?"

"Hell no," I say, feeling it all bubble up yet again. "You're kidding, right? Sadie, you write love stories! Beautiful, epic, swoony stories." She tilts her head at me, looking confused and annoyingly adorable.

"I heard you wrote this amazing romance, got a book deal and everything. I thought, 'Okay, surely this is it, she wrote about me, about us.'" I get up from my seat because I can't stay still as I relive it. "It was about pansy-ass dickwad Dennis!" I pace and keep thinking out loud. "Then the next one, I thought, 'Okay, *this* time.' But no. Every single dadgum time it was the same."

"You . . . you read my books?"

"Twenty novels, Sadie! You didn't write us, you didn't write *me*, once. High school sweetheart story? Not me. College second-chance romance? Not us. Even the football story you wrote—that guy wasn't me, either! I could spot over time, I'd think, 'Oh, this book is about Skye, this book is clearly Sam. This book is another version of Dennis.'" I swallow down some of my swelling emotions. "I only saw glimpses of you, to be honest, but there was never, never even a *whiff* of me. Each book my heart broke a little more."

"And you got angrier."

"Yeah." I pause, pulling up images in my mind. Because right after the books came the press coverage. "Then all the interviews you did, you were everywhere all the time and always *so in love* with someone who wasn't me. I mean, I know I got married, so I have no right. I shouldn't have been mad or still be standing here upset, but *three* engagements? Not to mention boyfriend after boyfriend, and I saw them all."

"Shep, why would you read all that crap, watch it all, why didn't you block me, block it all out?"

I flatten my mouth to a hard line and give her a glare. "Tell me you don't know who each of my clients are and haven't seen most of my TV segments."

She sniffs with a half smile. "Touché."

I cross back over and sit again. "See? We've got some kind of soul glue on us. We're stuck. And we're so stupid for trying to fight it all this time." Her smile fades. I try to recover.

"I stopped the partying when I thought I was going to be a dad. Now I stick to two beers when I'm out with the guys. I, uh, I'm not . . ."

"An alcoholic," she finishes for me.

"I was just lazy and scared and immature. I've had players and friends go through that, *fight* through that. Some won the battle." I hesitate. "Some didn't. I realized watching them that I'm lucky I didn't get my dad's genes." She raises her eyebrows with a nod and a polite smile that agree wholeheartedly about how lucky I am. "You want to tell me about it?"

She winces. "Do I have to?"

"Yeah."

"What?" She almost laughs at me. "You're supposed to say, 'Nah, whenever you're ready,' or something like that!"

"You're ready. And I want to know."

"What do you want to know?"

"Everything. Every single thing in the last decade, except if it has to do with Dennis or Pussy One or Pussy Two, as I call them."

"Wow," she snorts. "So mature."

"Pussy is a compliment, haven't you heard?"

"Oh man, my mother would *go off* in agreement with you."

"She did, she gave me the whole lecture. It scarred me for life." The memory makes Sadie smile, and I wish I could just press pause on this moment, give us a bubble to breathe in before we have to soldier on. I stay quiet and wait. Eventually, though, too eager to hear her whole story, I nudge her knee with mine.

"Um, obviously, I was grieving and depressed, and in a new city that was intimidating and crazy and lonely, so that could've been the catalyst. But also, I think that back before then, with you, I always had to keep myself in check to make sure you didn't drink yourself sick. I had to get us home. But when I found D—" She stops to avoid saying his name, which brings me an irrational amount of satisfaction. "When I found a new group of friends who would look out for me and let *me* be the crazy one, I really started to get drunk. Like actually out of my mind. No thoughts, no sadness, no loss, just the buzz and then the nothingness.

"Of course, that got worse and worse, drinking more and more to chase the same feeling. I would drink in private on my own when I got home from an event, or I'd only stay out and party with people who got as wasted as me. Then L— let's see, Pussy One, I think you said, he introduced me to Adderall and all the other uppers—yes, including cocaine sometimes later, which I started taking too." *Damn.* I am taken aback that she went through so much. Without me. She takes a deep breath, seeming so weary that I'm worried about what she'll say next.

"Then it was shame. Shame that I couldn't just quit. I would say, 'Tonight's my last night living like this!' Then I'd last two days, maybe three max, then give in. The old feelings, the grief and loss and anger *plus* the crippling shame on top—it was too much. So I'd go right back out. Then I thought, 'I'm so weak. I'm not worth it. I'm not worth the fight to get sober.'"

"What! You—" I lean forward and grab her calf, wanting to grab all of her but holding back.

She raises a hand and cuts me off, but she doesn't pull out of my grip. "I know that's not true now. I am trying to tell you how it went for me. The shame spiral was real. More shame led to more using, more alcohol, more pills, more aspirin and smoothies and morning IVs of fluids and B_{12}. It was all pretty insane. I think I would've ended up dead without Tash."

"And . . . Lori?"

"Lorelei. Yes, her too, but Tash knew me for longer, held my hair back a lot more, both literally and figuratively."

"And, uh, now?" I ask, not sure what to expect.

"Now, I am just over three years sober." She smiles a tentative but proud smile.

"Don't do that with me. You know better."

"What?"

"Don't hold back. You're being polite. You're pretending again like you have all week. Quit it. Tell me you're three years sober like you really want to say it."

She laughs and thinks about it. "Well, it turns out I'm kind of a badass."

"Hell yes, you are." Relief pulses through me, to see that she has at least some idea of how amazing she is.

"I mean, it was not easy, and I am ashamed of a lot of things. Not being an addict, but the choices I made, some of my actions, I made so many mistakes." She gives me a weird look. "One of which is that I lied to you."

"Okay?"

"The night of the Christmas Wonderland," she says, avoiding my eyes. "Bryce and I weren't actually engaged."

"What? I saw it everywhere."

"I know, but it was a publicity stunt. Well, more than that, it was me saving my ass. I got wasted in front of the paps, so to distract them, I announced a fake engagement with my brand-new boyfriend. We maintained it long enough for him to make bank and for me to get clean."

"So . . ." I look down and exhale some angry steam through my nostrils. "You're telling me we could've done this three years ago?"

"Shep, I'd been sober for, like, one minute. I wasn't ready, and you were so angry." I get up and try to pace it off. "See? You're still angry!" she cries at me.

"Well, this is all starting to feel a bit one-sided here, Sade. I mean, that night I would've done anything you asked. You could've told me the truth, told me you needed time. Plus, any time since then, any minute in the last three years, you could've come to me."

"Um, I'm sorry," she snipes sarcastically. "*You* said you hoped to *God* you'd never have to see me again!"

"Well, pretty sure He laughed in my face!"

"Well, pretty sure you deserved it for praying for something so stupid!"

"You're right!"

She starts to yell back at me but stops in surprise. We are both panting and standing with our hands on our hips, and I'm fighting a smile. I think she is too, though she's harder to read now than she used to be. And that bugs me. I need to know the truth.

"Why didn't you write about us, Sade?" I say so low it's almost a whisper.

She doesn't answer, so I lift my eyes up from the wood floors, where I've practically carved a rut from my wild pacing back and forth, to where she stands. She's in between the couch and the coffee table in her dress, and barefoot, looking small and cold in this big airy room. The big tears are back, marking black lines of mascara down her cheeks. I freeze, watching, no idea what she's gonna say.

"I couldn't," she finally manages to get out.

I take a step toward her without even thinking. "Why?"

"Because it was too painful to think about us, to think about you." She puts her head in her hands and lets out a cry that sounds like she's ripping in half. Her shoulders shake, so I take the last couple steps but don't let myself touch her yet. She still hasn't answered me.

"Why?" I whisper, getting my face so close to hers, I know she can feel my breath on the backs of her hands over her eyes.

"Because I still loved you."

"Yeah? That all?"

"Because I still love you!"

I pick her up before she can finish saying the words I needed to hear so badly that I had been holding my breath. We both let it all go. We weep, together. I wrap her limbs around me like I'm putting on a jacket backward. My favorite jacket. She fits perfectly, like she never left that spot. I sit on the couch with her in my lap, squeezing her so tight I have to calm myself mentally so I don't bruise her. I cradle her head, I kiss her hair, I rub her back and arms.

I know we have more to talk about.

I have more to tell her.

But now that she's home, in my arms where she's always belonged, I don't care what else is said, what else I learn, or how she reacts, or what else happens from now on.

I'm not letting her go again. No matter what.

CHAPTER 31

ONE MONTH AGO
THE CARIBBEAN

SADIE

What? Where? Am I dreaming?

Shep is carrying me, cradled in his arms, through his villa.

"Shep? Did I fall asleep?" I croak.

"We both did," he whispers. "My arm cramped up. Sorry to wake you."

"It's okay," I say, and then I realize he's laying me down in his bed. I immediately start to tense up.

"It's after three. Let's try to get some sleep," he says before walking around to the other side of the bed. He shrugs off his shirt and pants and crawls in in just his boxer briefs. I blink at the sight and realize my eyes are sticky and . . . I think I have snot crusted on my face. Wow.

"I need to wash my face. I probably look like a raccoon."

"Yeah, you do." He smirks.

"Well, you're all swollen like a puffer fish from all your girly weeping, so." I tilt my head and watch as his smile grows wide on his face.

"So ugly to me, all the time," he mutters softly.

"Speaking of ugly, can you put on a shirt?"

He laughs, knowing what I just said is absurd. "No."

I roll my eyes. "Okay, well, can I have one of your shirts?"

"Yeah, right there by the bathroom, help yourself." He points to his open suitcase that holds all his non-hanging items. It sits on a luggage rack by the closet near the bathroom. His room is just like mine, beige and the lightest of aquas, with a linen texture on the walls and way too much fluffy bedding on the bed. There are wall-to-wall windows and a sliding door on the other side of the bed, where Shep had placed me. A dresser is across from the bed on one wall, then on Shep's side of the bed is the door that leads into the bathroom.

I make quick work of washing the disaster zone known as my face. I also use the toilet and take a second to check out Shep's manly stuff on the counter. Cologne. Cuff links. Aftershave. Fancy electric toothbrush. A grooming kit with multiple razors.

More than one watch. Shep Riggs packed more than one watch for himself. Something about that thrills me.

I smell his cologne, a familiar scent he used once or twice when we were together. I think my mother actually bought it for him. I love it. I also take a long sniff of his shirt before putting it on. I take off my earrings and stacked bracelets and put them on the counter next to his things. Again, this small act has me almost giddy.

I need to sleep.

I take the hair tie I had tucked in with my bracelets and put my hair up in a top knot. I give myself one more glance in the mirror. I look puffy and exhausted. Good. Because I'm not going to do anything in that room other than sleep and maybe talk. We are not ready for anything else. I head back out to get into bed.

"So? What did you think?" he asks, putting his hands behind his head on the overstuffed pillow.

"What?" I play dumb as I get under the sheets, staying as close to my edge of the bed as I can without actually falling off.

"I know you snooped through all my stuff in there."

"Psh, like you're that interesting. Why aren't you sleeping, anyway?"

"Too excited."

I feel all the blood run from my face. I'm not ready! Except, I think all that blood went straight south on my body. Maybe parts of me are ready.

"Not for *that*, just . . . just you being around me."

I can't believe this is real. Shep saying, well, such a sweet Shep thing, in a bed, an arm's length from me. I turn onto my side to face him, and our eyes lock like two beams of electric current. This whole bed could go up in flames. How can I be so exhausted but so wired at the same time?

Shep shifts closer to me, turning onto his side with a sly smile. "I don't think I could fall asleep right now. I'll be too worried about you falling ass-backward right off that edge."

I close my eyes and shake my head, a little embarrassed.

"If I promise not to touch you, will you move in? One hard sniff or fart, and you're a goner."

"Shep!" I start to giggle, delirious.

"You could hit your head on that nightstand corner on your way down. You'll have to be choppered out of here to a hospital, and you'll ruin the whole wedding!"

"Fine, I'm moving!" I shift closer so our bent knees are almost touching.

"Now . . ." Shep yawns the word, then continues in a whisper, "I'm not going to attack *you* in your sleep, but if you want to maul *me*, let me just say all clear, yes, I consent, we're good to go. Locked and loaded."

"I am not going to maul you!" I whisper-yell at him.

He closes his eyes, grinning. "We'll see."

———

I come to, because I guess I actually did fall asleep, feeling warm and happy and safe. I inhale a mix of happy scents.

"What'd I tell you?" Shep's low voice rumbles below me.

Below me?!

Sure enough, I'm tangled around him like a sheet. I start to pull away, but he holds me in place. I groan, and he chuckles in triumph. I let myself relax.

"What time is it?" I wonder aloud.

"Late. They'll be hounding us for rehearsal stuff soon."

I sigh and let myself sink into him for the time we have. Snuggle, actually, that's what I'm doing, is snuggling my face into him. It's heaven.

"Pussy One," Shep says softly.

My eyes fly wide open. "What?"

"We skipped over him . . . D'you love him?" His voice sounds surprisingly sad and serious. He's scared of the answer.

"No. I loved partying with him. I also loved his talent, the way he—"

"I think I got it." He huffs under me. I look up at his face. He's staring up at the ceiling, looking lost.

"What about . . . were you serious with anyone else?" I ask, suddenly also afraid of answers.

"No one ever lasted more than a few months." He starts to slowly trace lines up and down my arm. A chill passes over me, erupting goose bumps all over. Instinctively, I move my legs into his, eager for his warmth.

Shep grits out, "Easy. Keep moving like that, and you'll start something I'm gonna have to finish."

"Sorry." I move my leg away. "I'm uh, we, I—"

"I'm not exactly ready for that myself?"

I pull back to look at his face. "You're not?"

"Oh, I am. Believe me. But I'd be lying if I said reading all your pornos didn't give me a bit of a complex."

"Pornos! My books are like PG-13 compared to the market! You should see what I have to edit out so I don't tarnish the precious Canton family values."

He looks down. "You edit parts out!?"

"Paragraphs." I smirk.

"Unbelievable. I have so many questions."

"Fire away."

He clears his throat. "For starters, why's every dude you write gotta be like six-five? You know the average man in the US is five-nine?"

"Pff, because that's what women want in their fantasies. *Average.*" I poke him. "And did you google that, Wolf?"

"I may have, Paramour."

"Ugh, I hate that nickname."

"So do I." He looks into my eyes and pushes a lock of hair out of my face. "I won't use it anymore." Shep looks away, as if our connection is too much. I understand the feeling. "So. In women's fantasies, every man is ripped and seven feet tall."

"I don't think size matters, pun intended, it's about feeling protected and cherished. My reader wants to feel like she's delicate and precious and her hero would go to war for her."

"Hm."

"Like, say, knocking a guy flat on his ass in the middle of a hotel lobby to defend his woman's honor." I see his lips turn up a little bit. "What else?"

"Why are they all so broody and quiet? You don't want a man to talk to you?"

"Eh, that's only at the start. We want the beast, but we want to tame him just enough so he only talks to us. Despite all our modern progress, we're still somewhat stuck up in our lofty Disney princess towers."

"All right, I guess I'm done talkin' then."

I chuckle. "You haven't even asked what you really want to ask yet."

He sighs, and his voice becomes gravelly. "Seems like there's suddenly a lot of talkin' when it comes to the, uh, dirty variety."

"You noticed that, huh?" I smile. "It's funny, a lot of women will clutch their pearls and say they don't like it, all the way to the checkout counter, book in hand. From what I've gathered, readers love when the man goes out of his mind with desire. He's not thinking clearly anymore. He's back to being that beast for her, and she's the most desirable thing on the planet."

Shep is stone-still next to me, and I make sure not to move either as I elaborate, hoping to comfort his worries. "It's not about making love in those scenes. They want that too, but there's time for that near the end. At first, though, the ladies love them some angry sex."

Shep clears his throat and starts to move. "I need to get out of this bed now."

I'm unsure of what to say as I watch him get up and go to his suitcase. I never in a million years expected him to be less than confident, overly confident even, about his powers in the bedroom. And they are powers. He was always like Superman, with X-ray vision to the inner workings of my body, and, as much as I hate to think about it, every other woman's body too. I'm amused but also concerned. I'm a little hot from the conversation but scared, because if he were to make a move right now, I don't think I could resist him.

"Got something for ya." He grins and throws a small plastic bundle my way.

Aaaand the mood is officially killed.

I can feel my cheeks start to burn looking at the small pack of maxi pads. "You saw me?"

"As if you could be within a mile radius of me and me not know it." I pull my hand over my hot face. "That was some kind of ninja move. You ducked down." Shep grunts as he mimics my escape that day. He's down in a complete squat, waddling along the side of the room. I can't help but cackle at him. "I still don't know how you moved so fast down in a squat like this!"

"Ughhh, so embarrassing!"

"Sadie Canton, before she was famous, waddling like a drunk penguin in the middle of the grocery store! Oh man." He stands, inhaling after laughing out the words. "I would've laughed if it wasn't so heartbreaking, you running from me."

"Poor Sam and the display. She was my hero that day."

"She really was," he says.

I look down at the package. "Wait just a second, you had these in your suitcase?" He looks away sheepishly. I jump up and wave them in his face. "You went to buy maxi pads just to travel across the world with them and embarrass your ex-girlfriend?"

"Not only that. I-I've been wearing platform dress shoes."

"No!" I squeal. "I knew you were taller! I thought I was imagining it!"

He shrugs. "Just trying to reach Book Boyfriend status."

"Football's Shep Riggs wore platforms in his shoes to impress me."

His small smile turns deadly when his lids lower a fraction. "You know what it does to me when you say my full name like that." He takes a second to glance down at my bare legs under his T-shirt.

My chest hard and heaving, I take a step back. I look down. "Shep, I . . . I'm still a mess. I don't know if I can be a partner right now. I mean, I can't really eat sugar, or else I will eat alllll the sugar. Like, there's no having one cookie, I'll eat the whole dozen. I drink a full pot of coffee. I find myself reading for eight hours straight or writing for even longer. I—" I stand up straight and say it plainly. "I am an addict, Shep. I just keep moving from one addiction to the other, even if they are much less destructive. I still have a lot of work to do."

"Could, hear me out, could you maybe switch to a sex addiction?"

"Shep!"

"I'm just teasing. Mostly."

I throw the wad of pads at his head. Of course he catches it without even looking. "That's not funny. That's a real addiction too. I am so much stronger now than I was, but I don't know if it's enough." I hesitate before the painful words have to find their way out. "It will be *heavy* sometimes, Shep."

He takes a step toward me. "I know I let you down. I know I crapped out when you needed me most. I'm so sorry, Sade." He sniffs. "But I'm a hell of a lot stronger than I was. I'm in therapy. Like actual therapy with the couch and all. My butt's in church every single Sunday like your mama would've wanted. I read a couple books a week again like I used to when we were kids. I eat like it's a science, and I take my job so seriously I'm downright boring. I'm all discipline and mental toughness now. That's my whole game. I keep an insane workout schedule."

"You don't say?" I point at his amazing upper body, hulking and on display before me.

"Looks like it may pale in comparison to yours, though." He looks at me from head to toe again. His gaze travels slowly back up to my eyes. He lowers his chin and puts his hands lightly on my upper arms. He looks me in the eye with such severity my breath stalls. "I'm a wall, Sade. Solid cement. I'm a damn fortress now." His voice catches. "Let me support you."

I collapse into his arms easily, willingly, happily. I am crying again, and so is he. He holds my head and strokes my hair. He squeezes me hard and rubs my back. I unfold my arms from in between us and reach around him, hugging him. He's so warm and hard. He does feel like a fortress. My fortress.

He kisses the top of my head with a sniff. I pull back to look up at him. He lets me go so he can put both hands under my head, using his thumbs to wipe the tears from under my eyes. I reach up and do the same, wiping a few tears from his scruff.

"You let yourself cry now?" he whispers with a quiet smile.

"Personal growth," I mumble.

"Look how evolved we are, crying like babies. I think that's a good sign."

"You do?"

"Uh-huh." He leans closer, nose to nose. "I'm tired of crying, though. We did some good making up. I reckon it's time for the kissing part." I lift my chin up with a tiny nod, suddenly desperate for him.

His lips touch mine just barely, warm and even fuller and softer than I remember. He gives me a few firm kisses before twisting my head and slowly opening me up with his tongue. We both let out a noise that's a cross between a moan and a whimper. This kiss takes me back to the fountain in the parking lot ten years ago. There is an underlying urgency, but it's eclipsed by almost awe. Reverent. That's what this moment is. It's a sad sweet, beautiful appreciation for what we had and lost. What we've been fortunate enough to find again.

Shep shifts his hands to wrap around me, locking me to him. I push up onto my toes to wrap my arms around his neck. His mouth moves faster, demands more from me. Remembering his body like I remember how to breathe, my hand reaches up into his hair involuntarily. He groans and quickly moves a hand to my ass, grabbing like he owns me. And in this moment, he does. All my senses are flooded with Shep. I need him and want him and love him. I am still in love with him.

He pauses, pulling away to look at me but not moving his large hands from their holds on me. "We gotta go."

"Huh?" I think I say. I can't be totally sure. He moves his hand up to more neutral territory and loosens his hold on me.

"I held them off as long as I could, but our phones are blowing up."

"Held . . . held who? What did you say?"

"I told Emerson you were with me and neither of us was showing up until the last possible second today."

"You're thinking about Emerson right now?" I squeak.

He laughs. "No, I'm thinking about all the things we don't have time for right now. The last thing I want is to be interrupted by my best friend or your gaggle of sisters."

Reality rushes into our little sanctuary. "Oh crap."

"What?"

"My sisters. If you told him, he told Sam, so there's got to be a nuclear meltdown worth of texts happening right now."

He gives me a squeeze. "They'll calm down."

"Um, have you met them?"

He laughs. "Yeah, you're gonna be in the hot seat for a while. Maybe the wedding will distract them?"

"I don't think an *actual* nuclear meltdown would distract them."

"Sorry. We don't have time to make an emergency game plan because we have to be at the beach for rehearsal like . . . ten minutes ago. Let's get dressed." He releases me with a quick kiss on the forehead.

"Get dressed? Shep, I'm in last night's dress! And, I, we—" My brain trips over everything that is suddenly happening. How much of this am I ready for? Have I even been thinking the past few hours? Are we back together? That's what I want, right?

I need to make sure he really wants it too. I mean, he didn't say he still loves me back. He didn't say he's still in love with me. We can't do this casually. We can't even try it back on for size. It'll kill us. This has to be a till-death-we're-in-this type of situation. And we can't even discuss it right now because I have to do the walk of shame across the resort! Meanwhile, he's humming while he puts on a shirt. He's humming!

"Shep. We cannot show up there together. You go ahead. I am going to hightail it to my place to change and try to fix my fluffy face and dodge the Spanish Inquisition happening in my messages. I'll see you when I see you!"

"Okay, Sade."

"Okay?"

He stands there in another linen shirt, khaki shorts, and flip-flops, looking ready to go. He gestures his hands up and down at himself. "Fortress. You tell me what you want or need, and that's what I'll do."

My mouth falls open. I can't really think coherent thoughts. Instead, I'm all feelings. Shock, awe, gratitude, frustration, and overwhelming relief. Like I had been gripping, grasping, trying to hold on to something for years, and finally, I can let go.

Shep extends a hand, which I take. He pulls me past him and into the bathroom. He kisses me on the head again and then ducks out and closes the door. I'm left with my dress and jewelry.

Right. Time to get dressed and face the music. The crazy, confused, determined tune of my four sisters and their one million questions.

CHAPTER 32

ONE MONTH AGO
THE CARIBBEAN

Sam: OMG
Sam: OMG
Sam: OMG
Sam: OMG
Sam: Def Con 5
Sam: Or is 1 more urgent than 5?!
Sam: Def Con 1
Sam: !!!!!!!
Skye: Good morning to you too, Samantha
Susan: What is it?!
Sally: [Yawn emoji] ???
Sam: Emerson got a text from Shep
Sam: That he and Sadie wouldn't be showing up today until the very last second.
Sam: HE AND SADIE AS A UNIT!
Susan: Are you sure?
Skye: Sade, care to release an official statement, here?
Sally: What Sam said: !!!
Sam: Susan, they left the luau together last night! What else could Shep mean?

Skye: Can you relay the exact message—what if you're Sam-
ming this up?
Sam: K it says, "Not coming to breakfast. Will show up just in
time for rehearsal. Sadie too."
Sam: !!!
Susan: Well I'll be.
Sally: I think Sam's reaction is appropriate in this case!
Skye: I have to agree
Sam: I told you! Def Con 5!
Sam: Weeeeeee this is so exciting!
Sam: Best week everrrrrrrrr!
Susan: Sadie???
Sam: Will the real Slim Sadie please stand up
Sally: Who?
Skye: She can't respond right now, because she's gettin'
boned [Eggplant emoji] [Explosion emoji]
Susan: Boned, really. [Eye roll emoji]
Sally: lol
Sam: Getting railed.
Sam: Nailed!
Sally: Banged!
Susan: Sometimes I wonder if I'm adopted with you lot.
Skye: WAIT. I've got it.
Skye: She's busy gettin' Rigged
Sam: LOL YASSSSSSSS
Sally: [Perfect emoji]
Susan: [Laughing emoji]

A chuckle escapes me as I hustle across the rows of villas until I reach my own. I almost reply *If only.*

Then the thought wakes me up from my tired, frazzled vulnerability hangover as I unlock the door to my little hut.

It's a good thing I didn't get, ahem, Rigged last night. It is. I'm
still just not sure about us. About being an us again.

This is all so much, so fast. I mean, I guess one could argue it hasn't been fast at all. It's been year after year of heartache. But two days ago, he was still giving me death glares and spitting insults my way. And Mary Ann. Pregnant.

I haven't even had time to process that. Not only did he look forward to being a dad, but he blamed me for the loss. Holy hell, that's heavy. And I am already carrying my sobriety and my career and a staff of people in our publishing division. It already feels like a lot.

But wow, Shep standing there asking to be my fortress. That was beyond my hopes and dreams. That was all my secret fantasies and lifelong prayers, materializing before my eyes. I head into the bathroom to wash my face. As I close my eyes and let the cool water soothe me, I envision his sweet eyes and firm jaw as he stood there.

I believe him. I believe he's strong enough to carry us through this. I think his thick shoulders can stand the heavy loads of baggage, not just mine, but ours. The heaps we'll have to sort through to come back together.

I just need to make sure that's what he wants, forever. No questions, no lingering doubts. We both have to be all in, no matter what. I quickly change into a casual sundress and grab my hat and glasses. I decide to send my sisters a preemptive text before I see them on the beach.

Me: No Rigging. At least not physically. We talked almost all night and morning. It was a lot. Good, but a lot. Omw now. Love you guys.

When I arrive at the beach where the ceremony will be held, the bridal party is just milling around. Ben chats with Dennis, who has a wicked shiner peeking out under his sunglasses. Sam said he told Emerson he plans to pull me aside and apologize as soon as he gets a chance. I'm betting he won't get one. Not if Shep has anything to say about it.

Looks like we didn't delay things too much. Sam and Emerson are discussing something with their coordinator while staff bustles around setting up decorative structures, chairs, and tables in the sand. I try to sneak my way into the group, but Skye can't pass up the opportunity to tease me and all my sisters pile on with knowing looks.

The guys talk among themselves, unaware of the way Shep eyes me. He looks at the tiny straps of my sundress like he's mentally edging them off my shoulders. His eyes go up and down my body slowly until he looks me in the eye and bites his lip. Then he winks at me. I feel the tiny gesture in my depths.

Yep. We need to talk as soon as possible so that we can get to not talking.

I lick my lips and look away, hoping he gets the silent message.

We run through the ceremony twice before being dismissed to clean up for the rehearsal dinner. I bolt out of there on a mission. Namely, Operation Avoid My Sisters and Shep and Any Conversation Whatsoever. I succeed, hitting the safety of my shower without being intercepted.

The theme tonight is, oddly, ice cream. We're all meant to wear specific pastel colors, and there will be a huge ice cream bar after the dinner. I'm sure there will be more dancing and partying and toasts. I feel a bit like an awkward teenager. Do I sit with Shep? Will we dance? Should I avoid him until we talk things out? Because if I don't avoid him, there's a very high probability of us sneaking away so I can get myself properly Rigged.

Sadie!

I shake my head, hoping some sanity will fall back into place. I'm not sneaking off to anywhere. This is Sam's rehearsal dinner. I need to support her, and for Sam, support means we all party alongside her until she can't keep her eyes open any longer. Or until Emerson can't take anymore and she decides to save him and shut the party down.

I'm just finishing my last coat of mascara when there's a knock on my bedroom door. I assume Sally wants to chat, so I brace myself. After a steadying breath, I open the door. And there stands a blond, cocky, khaki-clad dream. His shit-eating smirk, so pleased catching me off guard, falls completely when he looks down at me. His eyes grow wide and then deeply relaxed.

Sam said we all needed to wear shades of blush pink, so I'm in a long, slinky, silk cowl-neck dress that clings softly to my curves. If the fabric was a little thinner and the slit cut a little higher on my thigh, it could pass as lingerie. I have my hair in big glamorous waves pinned to one side.

"Shep? I'm up here," I say, teasing him. His eyes seem to have gotten trapped at the point where the slit begins on my leg.

"Hey," he barely says.

"Hi."

"Can I walk you to dinner?"

He still looks almost drunk with lust. I laugh. "I don't know, can you?"

He laughs too. "Honestly, I'm not sure now." He adjusts himself as his cheeks turn pink. "I'll give you a minute and wait outside."

"Yeah, why don't *you* give *me* a minute," I joke, loving how he has to force his eyes away. I hear him mutter some choice expletives under his breath as he leaves my doorway. I slip on my sandals and grab my clutch and join him.

Sally and Janie walk with us, which is probably for the best. At dinner, Shep sticks close and sits next to me and discreetly keeps his hand on my thigh. I separately give each of my gawking sisters the *please just be cool* glare, and they actually oblige.

Although I can tell Skye is physically pained in doing so, which makes Shep laugh. He misses nothing.

After dinner and dessert, I sit back and wait for an announcement about dancing. Instead, we are informed that in lieu of dancing, tonight there will be karaoke. Most of the crowd cheers. The Cantons love themselves some karaoke. Shep grabs my hand and squeezes.

I haven't sung for my family, not really, since we lost Mom. Not that tonight is some kind of performance, but the likelihood of me making it through tonight without being begged to sing, probably by the bride herself, is low.

A few of the young kids get us started, and it's adorable. While they sing, most of the adults start downing their liquid courage, should they be called upon to dazzle the crowd. A few distant cousins surprise us, then we're all floored by Aunt Lee's significant talent. Eventually, Sam decides it's time. All Canton sisters must join her on the stage. Shep squeezes my hand one more time in support. At first, it's just upbeat Taylor Swift and Meghan Trainor songs, which are no problem for us. Sam and I take the verses while the other three harmonize. We sound pretty good. Sam beams, Dad gets choked up.

Then it happens: Sam turns to me, pleading with her eyes.

"Pleeeeeeease will you sing it?" she asks. "We haven't heard you in so long."

"How about I just do 'Popular'?"

"It's not the same. Mom loved it so much. Please?" she begs. She wants to hear "Defying Gravity." Not only is the song a beast, which I haven't rehearsed or warmed up for, but it's emotional too. I sang it in high school, and again in college. Mom did love it. I hear Dad muttering encouragement, and all our family and friends who haven't called it a night yet stare on, hopeful. The song is a crowd-pleaser, if you can actually sing it. But in this moment, I'm not sure I can.

"Sammy, can I jump in line?" Suddenly Shep is on stage with us. Sam becomes even more giddy at the mere idea of Shep stepping in. The energy around us buzzes, as if the whole room collectively gasps, *Is Shep Riggs going to sing?!* The drama of this moment could very well be his wedding gift to her. Meanwhile, I almost collapse with relief. He catches my grateful eye as I walk away, and I see him, saving me, protecting me, supporting me.

I watch, curious what he'll sing.

He takes a microphone and adjusts it so he can sit on a stool. He leans in, and the room grows silent. In the quiet, Rocko bursts through. "Here, Mr. Shep! I found it!" He's sweating and holding a guitar.

"Ah! My man!" Shep takes the guitar from him and looks back at the audience. "Rocko went to track this down for me from a villa on the other side of the property, so everybody give him a big fat tip tonight." The crowd laughs, and Shep adds, "Listen, Rocko, this group right here is good for it, just between me and that table right there." He points at Emerson and his entire family. "You just became a rich man." This time the crowd erupts.

Shep goes on: "I have played this song probably a billion times in my life, but I've only sung it once, so y'all be nice." He strums the guitar a few times, adjusting one of the second microphones to pick up the guitar audio since there's no amp. He's so natural up there, as if he does this every single day. Once he's settled, he starts to really play.

Holy crap.

He wasn't exaggerating. He must practice all the time. He plays so well I am not paying attention to the actual tune, and then it hits me. His voice quivers slightly as he starts to sing. My song. "She's Everything" by Brad Paisley, but he's starting at the beginning, not the chorus. He even goes up into falsetto. Then laughs at himself as he does it. The crowd cheers like he's Brad himself.

I can't. I . . . I mean. It sounds even better fifteen years later. Fifteen years. I don't realize I'm crying until Skye hands me a napkin. I wonder if she knows. I was sixteen, and she was twelve, but even so.

Shep singing to me at school was the highlight of the whole year. The whole town. Susan comes up on my other side and squeezes my hand. I know she remembers.

But then there's a line, that says she—I?—is his unborn child's mother and his voice gives out. He skips a few words and keeps playing guitar. He comes back for the bridge, and on the line about when we're ninety, I can't handle it. I back up against the wall and then slip out into the lobby to hyperventilate.

After he sings one last chorus, he ends the song quickly and the room goes insane for him. He says something about taking donations for Rocko that I can't hear. I push myself up against the cold wall, squeezing my eyes shut, trying to find a calm that just won't come.

"Shit, I'm sorry," Shep whispers in my ear as he pulls me off the wall and into himself. I cry harder for a second in the safety of his arms. Soon his hold around me and his hand rubbing my back calm me down. Shep lets out a half laugh. "It was supposed to be romantic."

"It was," I screech into his chest.

"Tell that to my shirt," he mumbles, and I pull back to see yet another mascara tragedy happening down his front.

"Oh, sorry. I owe you *two* shirts now."

"Good thing you're wildly successful. I only wear fancy designer shirts now."

"Gross." I sniff, he laughs.

"Come on, looky-loos are looky-loo-in' at us." He glances down at my lips and starts backing up, leading me by hand. Before he turns to start walking, he adds in a deep tone I feel more than hear, "And I wanna look at you."

CHAPTER 33

ONE MONTH AGO
THE CARIBBEAN

Shep leads me to the villas, and then past them. We keep going to a far edge of the property that seems almost deserted as we get closer to the beachfront. After a quick jaunt through a patch of manicured shrubs is another villa. It's much newer than the big ones we're all staying in. It's like an adorable, coastal tiny house. Shep walks up onto the patio.

"Did you switch rooms?" I ask as he pulls out a key card.

"Mhm," he says, letting us in. It's gorgeous. It's just an A-frame over a box shape that is only big enough for a bed, bathroom, small closet, and even smaller counter area over a mini fridge. The colors are the same white on naturals, and there's no fire-place or kitchen or anything. And yet, it feels more glamorous. The bed is a natural wood canopy with sheer white fabric draped over the beams.

And the windows.

Three of the four walls are windows and glass doors that open onto the wraparound porch. The end of the bed is only a few feet from the doors that open directly onto the beach. The side windows look out into jungle. It's our own little paradise. After looking around the gorgeous space, my wide eyes land on Shep.

He steps to me and whispers with a grin, "You'll catch flies in there, girl." I snap my mouth shut and clamp down so I don't smile wide like a goof. "You like it?" I just nod, mouth still stuck. He puts his hands on my hips. "I figure I got a decade's worth of grand gesturing to do." Some reaction must pass over my face because he frowns. "What? What's going on in that wild brain of yours?"

"A lot!" I exhale. "The song, which, what, you're insanely good at guitar now?"

"Thank you?" he says, amused, but I carry on, gesturing at the room.

"Now this. Which is a dream, obviously, I love it. But we have so much to talk about still."

He takes a step around me to sit on the edge of the bed. "Lay it on me."

"Well," I start, and then stall out. My mind reels with everything we've talked about in the last twenty-four hours. It's a mess I can't quite sort through, but there's one main question that beats out all the rest. "Well, what are we doing? Are we getting back together?"

"Yes. Next question."

"Yes? Just like that?" I cross my arms and put my weight on one hip in disbelief.

"Just like . . . ?" He trails off, exasperated, and stands in front of me again. "Just like nothing! Listen, breaking up was a mess and getting back together will be a mess. We'll probably need to talk things out for a month straight. Which we will do. Together."

"That's it?" I say, hearing myself talk in such a high register I sound a little unhinged.

"What else do you need? Tell me." He talks lower and softer to balance me out. He puts his hands lightly on my waist, grounding me.

"I need you to reassure me that you won't bail when things get hard," I say.

He opens his mouth but stops himself, looks down for a second in thought, then back to me. "What I know now is that being without you is harder than all the hard things we'll face together." He squeezes his hands where they rest on my hips. "*You* won't run away either, right?"

His voice doesn't sound like he's actually worried about it. And really, he doesn't need to be. I've imagined a million times how different things would be, how the last decade would've gone, if I'd just stayed, talked to him, fought it out with him instead of fleeing to New York.

"Right," I say. I flex my hands and ball them into fists, resisting the urge to put my hands on his shoulders. "I'm not the same girl, you know. I used to think I couldn't, didn't, exist without you. I was totally codependent, and that's not me anymore."

"I can't wait to learn all the ways you're different." He rubs his thumbs over the silky fabric on my waist. "What else?"

"Well, Shep . . ." I let it out. "Uh, talk about one-sided here! You haven't said *you* still love *me,* haven't said you're still in love with me. The actual words. And when you say 'back together,' you better mean forever, done. Like this is it, for good. Because we can't do casual. We can't just date and see how—"

"Sadie." He moves his hands from my waist to my neck, holding my face. "I—" He stalls, and I go rigid. What if he says he can't love me like he did? Or is about to say he thinks we should just date and see what happens? Or—

"Hey." He smirks at me. "Quit imagining whatever you're imagining. I just don't have the words, is all. You write about love for a living—it's a lot of pressure!" I shake my head and open my mouth to comfort him, but he keeps going. "I guess I'll go with the classics." He takes a deep breath, and when his voice does come back out, it's like sandpaper through the air. "I love you, Sadie Lyn." My heart loses its rhythm completely at the sound of my quasi-nickname on his lips. I stare up at his green eyes and watch a tear escape one side. "I am still in love with you. I will be in love with you until I die." My own eyes begin to leak, yet again.

"Now that I have you in my hands, I am not letting go. You're stuck with me. For good this time." I let out a small sob, and he keeps going, his voice trembling badly. "I'm sorry I failed us. Forgive me. I've regretted it every day. I've missed you every minute for ten years, and now I'm begging you. I'll get on my knees. Sadie." His voice drops to a whisper. "Bambi." He pulls my face in closer to his. "I feel like I've just been lost and alone, wandering. Let me come home." The sobs he is holding back shake his whole body. "Let me come home."

I launch to my toes and kiss the word *home* from his mouth. Hard. I hold his face, and he moves one hand to wrap around me and tug me closer into him. He takes over our mouths, loving me with each firm stroke of his tongue. We aren't desperate or sad or searching, but rather locking back into place. He tilts my head and sucks on my bottom lip before taking my mouth again. He grunts, I moan, and his hand moves down, slowly sliding over my ass before gripping me hard.

I pull on his hair, becoming needy for more of him. He moves his other hand from my head and slides down to palm my breast. As he does, he pulls away.

"The fact that I could even carry on a conversation with you in this dress." He squeezes me. "Fortress."

I smile. "Uh-huh."

"Herculean strength," he mutters while his eyes turn into a deep forest green. He pulls back to run a hand from my knee up to where the slit stops. His other hand moves there so he can gather the fabric. He looks into my eyes and bites his lip as he starts to pull the dress up. I suck in a breath as a chill shakes through my body.

I help him lift the dress off completely and then stand still before him, in nothing but a stretchy lace thong. I start on his shirt as he watches, his eyes slowly covering every inch of me. His hands rest back on my waist.

"You're still the most stunning thing I've ever seen in my life. So beautiful."

I almost snort, feeling self-conscious. "That's not what the tabloids say. I'm an ad for wrinkle cream."

"Sade." He grunts. "You are even more beautiful now than before. Still so perfect it makes me angry."

"We're done being angry, Shep," I whisper as I unbuckle his belt.

He smiles and starts to move his hands all over me. "I am going to make love to you now, but there is angry sex in our future. Furious sex. Livid that I wasn't inside you every day all this time. Look at you! Fuck!"

His mouth is back on mine in a frenzy. He keeps kissing while he gets rid of the rest of his clothes. He picks me up and drops me on the bed, falling on top of me. Now we're desperate. His mouth moves to my neck, down to my chest, my stomach. He leans back to pull, and I lift so he can take my panties off. The second they are gone, he spreads me wide and holds me to him, kissing me hard at my center. I cry out and grip onto the sheets for dear life.

When I start to tremble, he replaces his mouth with one hand while reaching behind me to the nightstand with the other. In no time, he's opened the foil and sheathed himself. He puts his huge warm arms on either side of me, positioning himself.

"You ready for me, Bambi?" he whispers across my lips as he nudges into me.

"Always," I whisper back, opening wider and moving up to meet him.

"That all?" He looks into my eyes.

"I love you, Shep Riggs."

"I love you so much, Sadie." He collides all the way into me, all the way home. It steals my breath and stings my eyes and feels like heaven.

Thrust after thrust we cry and say we're sorry. We each say I forgive you, I missed you, I love you, a thousand times. It doesn't take long for Shep to reach his end, but he slows his movements and moves a hand down to where my body is most sensitive. He watches me and works me slowly, then faster and faster until I totally combust. He lets go at the exact same time, pushing us both into a white-hot oblivion that's unlike anything I've felt in my entire life.

He collapses on top of me, making me exhale. "Wow," I sigh.

"See?" he mumbles into my neck. "And we haven't been doing that all this time? Furious. I'm bending you over and spanking you next." He starts to move off me but gives me a glare. "And I'm going to talk so dirty to you." I laugh, and he smiles as he goes on. "I'm talking absolute filth. You better prepare yourself, girl. I'm definitely tying you up at some point. And choking. We're going to try all that crazy shit."

I let out a shocked laugh. "I can't wait."

He moves to the bathroom and calls back, "You're gonna have to give me a minute. I'm not twenty-two anymore!" I laugh harder as he mutters a slew of curses under his breath.

"I love you!" I singsong the words to him.

"Livid!" he jokes back.

THINGS I WROTE ABOUT

He comes back from the bathroom and jumps onto the bed like a five-year-old. His face looks young too, his eyes bigger and greener. He pulls me into him like a snuggly bear, with promises of another round momentarily. I wrap around him so fully, I'm almost lying on top of him more than I am the mattress. We whisper about all the little things we missed, things we remember, things we want to do again. Soon, like a couple of thirty-somethings who just wept their hearts out and had the best sex of their lives, we pass out cold.

CHAPTER 34

ONE MONTH AGO
THE CARIBBEAN

I put my hand up to the door of Samantha's villa and brace myself before knocking. Today is going to be a roller coaster, maybe even more so than last night. I give myself one more second in my bubble of absolute joy.

I remember Shep waking me with his tongue in the middle of the night and, as promised, spanking me with his hand this morning. We said all the words all over again, and we laughed almost as much as we cried. I know I'm puffy and pale from lack of sleep, but I could not care less. Still, it's time to get Sam's day started. I knock.

Skye flings the door open. "There you are, you saucy little minx!" A chorus of squeals and shrieks and sighs rings out from all my sisters.

"Sadiiieeeeeee!" Sam's voice rises above the rest. She throws down a hairbrush and bounds over to me, her hair half-brushed. She's adorable in her monogramed BRIDE robe. "Listen, whatever gift you were going to get me for the wedding, scrap it. Instead, I need you to tell us every single detail of last night."

"And the night before!" Susan adds.

"Sam," I sigh. I knew this was coming; still, it's so overwhelming.

"Hey, Kat, Janie, Emerson's mom and sister, and the little flower girls will all be here soon, so start talking and talk fast!"

Sally appears next to me in the doorway where I am frozen, hot coffee in hand. "Bless you," I say to her. Then I indulge my sisters. By the end, everyone is emotional.

"Fortress?! I mean, did you write that? Did you tell him to say that?" Sam wails.

"Nope," I sob back, snorting and pulling another tissue from the box Susan passed around.

"I'm so happy for you," Skye says. She is barely teary-eyed. We're similar in that way. Or we were. Now I guess I'm a weepy fool.

I'll never forget her wedding day, basically the one and only time I've seen her all blubbery. Matthew stood there glowing, tears streaming down his face but overall composed, while Skye could barely get through her vows. It was beautiful.

Today will be beautiful too. And hard. Because Mom isn't here.

"I knew that man had it in him. I just didn't know it'd take him so long," Susan says, sounding awed.

"Okay! Now we can focus on Samantha. Our little sunshine," I say, standing up and crossing to hug her. We dissolve into another round of sniffs and hugs. This carries on all day as more family and Sam's one million friends join us in the bridal villa.

I pull out my phone to check the time as the ceremony grows near.

Shep: Hurry up and come to the beach, I need to hold you.

I resist the urge to jump up and down like my fourteen-year-old self would have done.

Me: It's only been a couple hours!
Shep: A couple hours too long.
Shep: This is how it's gonna be, Bambi. Ten years we have to make up for. I'm a needy bastard now. Get out here!

I laugh and excuse myself a few minutes early, taking a load of bouquets and mini packs of tissues with me. All of which almost flies out of my arms when Shep attacks me from behind. I don't even reach the holding tent where the bridal party is supposed to wait. He kisses me senseless, then escorts me to the tent, mad that he doesn't get to walk down the aisle with me. Samantha made the four of us draw numbers, because she couldn't pick just one maid of honor. Peak Samantha.

The whole ceremony is breathtaking. The aqua beach and white sand is the perfect backdrop behind our dresses, all varying shades of pale yellow. Sam is a dream in a dramatic white silk gown that is an exaggerated mermaid cut, hugging her curves and then flaring out wide. She's dripping in yellow diamonds the size of small cars, a gift from Emerson to match her giant engagement ring.

She hits the aisle with Dad and sparkles like starlight, inside and out.

But Emerson.

He wrecks us all.

At the sight of his bride, Icy Robot Man turns purple, his mouth in a firm line, breathing deep and shaking, trying to hold in what must be massive sobs. His shoulders vibrate as a few tears line his cheeks. When Dad hands Samantha off, she reaches up to wipe his tears and nods up at him.

The comfort she offers him in that moment, it's the sweetest thing ever. Everyone gets sniffly, including Shep. I can feel him staring at me nonstop, and I can only look his way occasionally, or else I really will turn into a puddle of feelings.

Although, it appears everyone is a puddle. Even Skye is dabbing at her eyes. The groomsmen all look shaken up except for Adam, who looks pained. Maybe that's his default setting for holding in his feelings.

After the gorgeous ceremony, we take bridal party photos, during which Shep insists on standing behind me in a prom pose, even though that wasn't our official order. The coordinator and photographer seem irked by the change, but Samantha allows it happily. She also insists Shep join in some of the family photos, a move that makes Shep clam up, and Dad turn to me with a cocked eyebrow and a small smile that says *We'll be discussing this soon.*

The reception starts flawlessly, with Sam and Emerson dancing to their song, "In My Life" by the Beatles. There are a few more standard dances and then, of course, the band begins what must be listed on every wedding's must-have playlist.

"Come on, Bambi, redeem country music with me," Shep whispers in my ear and then kisses the side of my head. I take his hand and follow him to the dance floor. There we sway, misty-eyed, to Shania Twain's "From This Moment On" with Samantha gawking over at us, as if she planned the whole thing.

Shep stays glued to my side for the rest of the festivities. He keeps the club sodas coming and gets us extra portions of cake. He pulls my chair closer to his, needing to touch as much of me as possible at all times. I look over at him, looking like a vision in a light gray three-piece suit. He told me he was keeping the whole thing on, vest and tie included, until we could make proper use of it later. I'm not sure what that means, but I think he wants to boss me around. I'm ready to be bossed, that's for sure.

He catches me staring and winks. I shake my head a bit in disbelief. This has to be one of the happiest moments of my life.

SHEP

All right, it's time to do this. I hope this isn't a dick move, waiting until now. I can argue both sides, of course. Maybe I should have laid this on her before we recommitted to each other. Maybe I should have told her this the second we became "friends."

But I have a feeling waiting until after the ceremony was the right call. Plus, I meant what I said and I hope she did too. We're not running. We're not bailing. At least, she better not. I grab her hand and pull her up.

"Walk with me," I say. She's all smiles, lit up from within. She glows every bit as much as Samantha, even without the diamonds. Though, I'd be lying if I said today didn't make me want to buy Sadie a set of her own.

I lead her away from the party, toward the trees. We take off our shoes and walk a ways, through our own random sandy jungle path, through trees and bushes, winding near the beachfront, in happy silence. She leans into me, and I squeeze her and kiss the top of her head. Once we're far enough that we can barely hear the resort, I guide her to sit on a big bent palm tree that could almost be a bench. I take a step back.

She cocks her hand at me, and I just jump in. "Sade, there's something I need to tell you." Her face flashes with confusion and then anger.

"Shep, if you tell me you have a love child—"

"No."

"Or cancer or some other terminal disease—"

"No."

"So help me—"

"It's nothing like that. This isn't one of your crazy stories." I hold up a hand to stop her spinning mind. I look up and ask God for a little help.

"Jason Workman."

"Wh-What?" she whispers. I know she could never forget the name of the drunk driver who took her mama from us. I don't repeat it.

"He was at the party with me, Sade." I'm able to say this now without breaking down, but I'm not sure what her reaction will be. "I was awake. I was standing at the kitchen counter chugging water and I saw him stumble through from the living room. I wasn't sober, but I wasn't wasted, either, and he came to me and . . ." The shame rushes through me, but I push on. "He pointed at the counter and said, 'My keys.' And I . . . I handed that bastard his keys and watched him literally fall out the door. I was out of it and didn't even realize until I heard the news about your mom, and it rushed back. I even remembered that I had had the fleeting thought, Sade, I *thought it,* that I should probably stop him. Take the keys back. Tell him to wait. But you know what I did instead? I turned and fell onto the nearest couch and went to sleep."

She is shaking her head and sniffing, her brow twisted up. But she's not saying anything. I keep going.

"It wasn't holding you up that was so heavy for me, Sadie, it was the guilt and shame and so much self-hate I couldn't see straight. I couldn't be there for you because—" My voice cracks. "Because I basically killed your mama."

Sadie sits frozen, staring. I'm not sure how long time passes. There's just the noise of the bugs and the water lapping softly on the sand behind me. Without warning, she gets up and starts to walk, fast.

"Sade?" I stick to her side.

"I need to think!" she sobs out, almost running from me toward the beach.

"Okay."

"I can't, I don't, I—" She just shakes her head and makes a sound after that, still walking right toward the water. She comes to a stop suddenly and turns around. "And you couldn't just tell me!?"

"Just tell you? Tell you that I *helped* kill your mother? That I could've saved her, could've stopped him? I could barely think. I was a wreck. We all were. But on top of all that grief, I saw how much you were hurting. You two were so close, and it was all my fault! I could barely look at you."

"I know the feeling!" she screams, turning away from me. "If you could've just said something."

"When I came up to Tulsa, I was going to tell you, but you were gone. I wanted to explain and I ran into your daddy and he was a blubbering, crying mess and I decided it was too late. It was all too late."

"It was." She stomps off again, but I stick with her step for step.

"No, I was a coward. And *you* were a coward. And neither of us are cowards anymore."

"Leave me alone, Shep, I need some time."

"No."

"Ugh! I'm serious! Give me a minute." She takes off faster, toward the water. She rushes into the small waves, in her fancy dress, and I stick with her, wading deeper and ruining my suit.

"Take a minute, take however long. You wanna be mad, be mad, cry, scream, give me the silent treatment, I'll be right here." She grunts in frustration at the sky. "There's none of your stupid third-act breakups here. I'm not— OW!" Something burns up my leg just as Sadie cries out. I've been struck again. "Ow! Damn it!"

"Ahhh! Shep!" she screams, looking down, and I see them too. We're surrounded by jellyfish. Hundreds of them. This is bad. Very bad. I walk to Sadie and get one arm around her. I clench my mouth shut as she screams. I start to move my legs, but the pain is unbearable.

I manage to get out my phone and call Adam. My arm seizes up with pain as it goes to voicemail. I curse, focusing all my strength on holding up Sadie, who is going limp beside me. I think she's passing out from the pain. I push toward the beach slowly, step by step, in total agony. I let the screams out as I push through the water like it's cement. Stinging cement. I have to turn my face and throw up as Adam's phone rings again. He picks up.

"The beach, ambulance. Chopper. Jellyfish! Sadie! Sadie! Now!" That's all I can do as I collapse at the water's edge. I turn so Sadie falls on me, trying to keep my hold on her, but everything fades to black.

CHAPTER 35

THREE WEEKS AGO
MIAMI, FLORIDA

SADIE

Beeping. What is that awful beeping? I try to open my mouth to ask for someone, anyone, to shut it off. Because my head is throbbing. My words get caught in a dry tangle. My mouth is like sand. Terror grips me. What did I do last night? Where am I? Did I relapse? What do I remember?

The wedding.

Shep.

Shep!

The jellyfish.

Holy crap, I'm alive. Is Shep alive? He was carrying me!

"Sh—?" is all I can get out. I can't get my eyes to open.

My hand is squeezed by hot calloused fingers. *Shep.*

I'm relieved and my pulse slows, making the beep slow too. I focus all my energy on lifting my eyelids. I'm in a hospital room. A private room, not the ER. So, I've been here a while?

"You're all right, Bambi," Shep says, his voice hoarse and dry. I close my eyes and turn my head to my left where the sound came from. Everything hurts.

"There she is! Here, honey, have some water," a bubbly voice says. I open my mouth. Apparently, I can only handle one motion at a time. The water is heavenly. The beeping stops too. The combination gives me the boost I need to open my eyes again. I catch the nurse on her way out, saying she'll grab our doctor.

Shep looks terrible. Happy, but terrible. "You almost killed me." He smirks. I can't get my mouth to work. He keeps talking, slowly. "You almost killed you too. But we're okay now. You have it worse than me because I'm so beefy."

I exhale what would be a chuckle. It hurts. I glance at my hand, where an IV is fed into my veins. My eyes go wide, and Shep catches the tiny change.

"They know, Bambi. It's in your chart. Once you were stabilized, no narcotics. Susan's orders. That's why I look so great and can already make hilarious jokes and you can barely talk. Just rest. Just close your pretty eyes and rest, Bambi."

I do.

I don't know how long I'm out, but it feels like a very long time. It's Shep's voice that wakes me, sounding much better than the last time I heard it.

"Uh-huh . . . No, you can leave all that. I'll get the rest squared away next week or week after . . . Yeah, you have my Dallas address . . . Right. Thanks, man."

I open my eyes and make some kind of grunting sound. Shep, whose bed is now touching mine, grabs the water cup from his other side and puts the straw in my mouth. I take a few big gulps.

"You feeling any better?" he asks, and I am able to nod a tiny bit. Shep presses a call button on his bed. "I'll have them bring you some more ibuprofen now that you're awake."

"You—" I get out, but it's scratchy. I take another big sip of water. "You have a Dallas address?"

"Uh-huh." He's grinning at me like he's up to something.

"You live in New York."

He shakes his head. "I know you almost died, but try to keep up, Bambi. I live wherever you live now. We have a penthouse in Dallas. I haven't seen it, but I bet it's swanky." I frown and sigh and try to smile, but everything still aches.

I fall in and out of sleep. When I do wake, I just keep my eyes closed and think. Shep dropped a bomb on me before we almost died. I think through all that he said. All this time, all the heart-break, if I'd just stayed, if he'd just told me . . .

If only doesn't get us anywhere. I know that. I remember Shep's dead eyes, the brokenness in him. He carried all that shame and guilt, alone. I open my eyes, it's light out. I don't know how many days we've been in here, or even where we are. I look to the left, where his hand is gripping mine.

"Hey," he whispers at me.

"It wasn't your fault, Shep."

He reaches over and kisses my head. "I know that now, Bambi. Logically, I know. I'm just so sorry I didn't tell you what happened."

"I'm sorry I left."

"I know. We're all right. Everything is all right. Just get better, okay? I love you so much, Sade . . . And boy howdy, you love me so much you can hardly stand it." I am able to actually chuckle, so he leans into it. "You're a little obsessed with me. Honestly, it's kinda embarrassing. Get a hold of yourself, woman. Jeez." I squeeze his hand. He shifts over so he's almost on top of me, which lets him slip an arm under me and tuck my head onto his chest. "Rest now, we'll get out of here, then we're gonna go live our dream, Bambi. Okay?"

"Okay," I say before the doctor arrives to explain we both suffered minor cardiac events and are staying for a couple days to be monitored. We could have actually died, from the venom or from drowning when our bodies went into shock. Shep saved us.

The weight of everything exhausts me until I'm falling into another long, deep sleep. I dream of what our new life together will be like, knowing we're both going to do whatever it takes to make the dream a reality. I feel weak and shaky and not totally unafraid of what the future holds for us, but I know no matter what, Shep will be there, holding me.

CHAPTER 36

THE PRESENT
DALLAS, TEXAS

SHEP

I heard her alarm go off, so she's got to be wrapping up. I knock on her office door before I go in. I pause for a second, looking at her crazy hair up in a top knot, silhouetted by the windows her desk is pushed up against. My breath catches, as it tends to do now, randomly, at the littlest things. Little things that are big things. Because we get to do them together.

I pass the weird painting of a bobsled that Sam shipped to us. Skye painted it, and apparently it's some family ritual to tap it on the way out of the door for strength. Sadie acted like she'd been sent a priceless artifact. I asked about it in the sisters group text, and they only sent back a *Cool Runnings* meme.

These Canton women are something else.

I walk up behind my Canton, making sure my steps make noise so I don't scare her half to death. When Sadie gets in the zone, she *gets in the zone.* I put my hands on her shoulders and lean down to kiss her neck.

"I'm done, I'm done," she mutters, still typing. "Just this one. Last. Thought. Okay." She turns to face me, energized from an entire day of writing. I like to think it helps that she's finally writing our story, but she's probably always like this when she works. She stands up and melts into me. I love it when she does this. She pulls back. "K. What did you say we're doing tonight?"

"I didn't. I just told you to get fancy," I answer, loving the way she bounces a bit in my arms. Her eyes light up, and I can't get enough. I'd grand gesture the crap out of her every day just to put that flicker there.

This is a little more than a grand gesture. This is a giant freaking risk, is what this is. I hope I'm not an idiot. I mean, I'm not the brightest tool in the shed, my life has shown me. But I think this is a good move. A bold one, but a good one. It sure as hell is romantic.

I follow Sadie out into her apartment—our apartment for the last three weeks and for the immediate future—and watch her almost skip through the space. It's pretty and girly and sweet, just like her. She's said she's going to "man it up" for me, but I don't mind. After I watch her get all the way down the hall, I check in with the squad.

Me: We good?
Sam: YES!!!!!!
Sam: Locked and loaded, Shep! Can't wait! Hurry up!
Skye: Don't worry. We've got Sam under control, despite the exclamation points.
Me: Thanks
Emerson: Share your location with us so you don't have to text updates.
Me: Good call, Clarky
Me: [Shared Location]
Sam: Yes! Now I can obsessively track you!!

Sam: !!!!!

I chuckle and check and recheck all the pieces of my plan. My stomach flips all the way over. This might be insane. I guess I'm about to find out.

About thirty minutes later, as her sisters predicted, she comes out looking completely amazing.

"Will this do?" She bats her made-up eyelashes at me. She's in that tight teal number she wore at the beach. Her hair is in those big soft waves I love, and she's got on her Bambi necklace, which I still can't believe she kept polished and wrapped all this time, and the dangly diamond and aquamarine earrings I got her when we got out of the hospital.

They aren't big rocks like Emerson chose for Sam. I wanted something daintier for my Bambi, something romantic. I guessed, and I chose well. She loves them even more than I do. As I look at the little pins of light they reflect all around her face, I hope I'm guessing correctly about tonight too.

We head down to the building's valet where my Mustang GT 500 waits for us. I tuck her in and go around to the driver's side, sending up my hundredth quick prayer to the Good Lord about this whole scheme. We drive about thirty minutes, holding hands and singing to the music. Well, she sings. I told her she missed a lot of good country in ten years, and while she avoided the genre, I went for the masochist approach. I've wept and listed to Keith Anderson's "I Still Miss You" so many times, it's embarrassing. She asked for a happy country playlist. Obviously, what she wants, that I can give, she gets.

Anything for the girl who saw the man I am today, deep within me, before I did. For my biggest fan and closest friend. For the girl I broke, who broke me, who's putting me back together now, piece by piece. Anything and everything. Playlists, diamonds, and my personal favorite, all the "research" for her books. Most of all, we want time. Loads of time. Both of us have canceled everything over the last few weeks to just be. Well, and to recover from almost dying.

We finally pull into what sort of looks like an abandoned parking lot. Mentally, I check a couple boxes. Pulling around the side of a warehouse-type building, there's a lit fountain. I glance over at her, but she just looks confused. When I park close to the fountain, she smiles at me. It's a pretty good likeness of the one from prom.

I walk around and open her door, and she just grins. She doesn't know what's coming, but she seems to like the sentimentality so far. I lead her up to the pool's edge and turn to face her. Her eyes dart around, confused.

"There's no picnic. No, uh, string quartet or marching band." I take both her hands in mine and start to stammer. I'm not sure why I'm suddenly listing what her sisters had at their proposals. Nerves, I guess. A hell of a lot of nerves.

"Okay?" She gives me a timid smile.

"At a fountain just like this, about sixteen years ago, I asked you to be mine." She gasps a little bit, and I think it's the good kind. "I never should've taken no for an answer. I wasn't ready back then, you were right. But I think we would've made it. I think we would've figured it out." I drop to a knee, trying not to cry or hurl. "I'm ready now, Sade. And so are you. And it's only been a month, but we can figure it out. So, Sadie Lynette Canton, Bambi, will you be mine for good this time?" I pull out the ring box and open it.

"Shep!" She gasps again.

"Will you marry me?"

"Yes!" She starts to shake and cry. I stand and take out the rings. I hesitate before slipping them on.

Here goes nothing.

"There's just one thing, Sade." Her face falls for a second. "See, these on either side are wedding bands. And they're all three fused together." She lets out a small chuckle. Okay, so far so good. "And well, I love you, but your track record sucks." Now her brow is scrunching up. It's adorable. *Please say yes.* "I don't want to be engaged to you. I don't want to spend another minute of our lives where I'm not yours and you're not mine. So, well, I want you to marry me right now, tonight."

"Wh-What?" Her turn to stammer.

"I told you that you make me insane, and uh, I may have gone a little overboard on the not-taking-no-for-an-answer bit." She's half-smiling. Good! Yes! I point across the empty parking lot. "See, our closest friends and family are inside that building. For our wedding. In about—" I look at my watch. "Thirty minutes."

"You . . . you planned a wedding?"

I laugh. "Did not peg that as your first question. Your sisters planned it at my request. And Lorelei and Tash. It's just for us, and we can have a real wedding later, a huge party or a beach getaway or in a pretty church or whatever kind of wedding you want, Bambi. But our pastor from home is in there and a marriage license and, really, that's all I care about. That, and these rings never coming off your finger once I put them on. So? You still sayin' yes to me, Sadie Lyn?"

She blinks a few tears away, still smiling and shaking. She sniffs. "Yes, Poteau. Yes!"

"Yes! Thank God!" I exhale and laugh as I put the rings on her finger. They're blinding. A huge round diamond with an intricate diamond-studded band that looks like an antique. A matching dainty band flanks the engagement ring on either side. The jeweler called it modern but romantic, and that seemed perfect to me. "You like it?"

"I love it. I love love love it! I love you." She collapses into me, then she pulls away. "But you're insane! A wedding?! What, I-I mean, what am I going to find inside that building, Shep Riggs?"

"Let's go find out." I take her hand and put her back in the car. We drive to the front of the building. As soon as we pull up, a gaggle of Cantons spills out the front doors. The women are losing their minds, loudly. Emerson and Adam wait by the door, smiling. Sadie is pulled away as Sam squeals a lot of words about dresses and flowers and shoes.

"Don't let her leave the premises!" I yell, only half joking. Sadie looks back at me and gives me what I think anyone who knows me would call a Shep Riggs Wink.

SADIE

"I can't believe this." I can't. I'm standing in an event center bridal suite with my two best friends, my sisters, and a rack of designer wedding dresses.

"RIGHT!" Samantha squeals.

"Wait until you . . . well, just wait," Susan says, sounding wistful but sad too.

"How does one become your best friend, exactly?" Skye asks Lorelei while eyeing the dresses that my glamorous friend had brought in. No doubt she had some of them flown in from New York. They're gorgeous.

"Come, darling, we're on a time crunch," Lorelei says.

"How'd you get these giant ball gowns in here?" Tash asks, looking at each dress on the rack. They've all been kept, or repressed, to perfection.

"Money, of course," Lor says.

Sally looks at Lorelei a little starstruck. It reminds me of Tash in the old days.

"And you guys, the teal?" I ask.

"That was Shep's call. He said he wanted the accent color to be his favorite, which is your eye color."

"Awww!" Sam gushes.

I flip through the options, deciding on a simple yet romantic option. It's white fitted silk hugs my body but doesn't flare out into a full mermaid cut. The part I love, though, is the tiny floral lace detail. It's romantic but not too frilly. My sisters approve, which is good since I don't know what kind of ceremony I'm about to have, but they do. I didn't want to pick anything too simple or too dramatic for the setting. Although as Susan tacks up the front hem of the skirt, I realize I may wear this one again for the other ceremony, if we even have it. What more could I want besides me, Shep, and these people who are here?

After almost exactly thirty minutes, thanks to Emerson's meticulous timekeeping, I'm guessing, Dad comes in. He's already tearing up.

"Dad, don't start!" I say.

"This one's a bit different. He . . . you . . . I just, you all went through so much and I wish . . . well . . . I really think your mom is smiling up there tonight."

"Me too, Dad. Me too." I hug my purple-faced father, and we all dab our eyes, yet again, before heading out. My favorite women in all the world file out from the lobby, not into a big event hall but off the side doorway into a small, beautiful chapel space.

I can barely see the men in their classic black suits before the chapel doors close. Emerson, Adam, Matthew, Shep's brother Buck, and his buddy Tug are waiting on the right side of the chapel. There's a string quartet playing already, and I realize as they finish that it was a slow rendition of "Nothin' 'bout Love

Makes Sense." I smile and laugh a teary laugh at Shep's choice. The quartet changes to the wedding march, and Dad takes a small step toward the doors.

I feel myself go into a tiny bit of shock. This morning I was still having to explain to Shep some of the quirks of my building. He has shipments of his things that haven't even made it to Dallas yet. There are friends of his in New York I haven't met. And he hasn't even experienced Gwyn in all her glory. But then the doors open, and I see him.

His eyebrows shoot up, and his mouth hangs slack for a second. Then he's smiling so wide, so bright, he could power the sun. He beams so much at me. Love and gratitude and awe. And his own sneaky confidence, pulling all this off for us. For me. He somehow looks both seventeen and thirty-five at the same time. His blond hair falls over his firm brow just like I prefer it. Tears pool at the sides of his eyes but don't fall down his hard, beautiful jaw that has some scruff on it. Also my preference.

When I get to the end of the aisle, I notice that our people arch around us rather than stand on the stage or sit in the pews. The chapel beyond our little huddle is empty. Everyone we love is within almost an arm's reach. It's perfect.

Our childhood pastor makes a few opening jokes and quotes his usual Bible verses about love and commitment. Then he says it's time for our vows, and I expect to repeat the standard phrases. But he nods his head at my groom, and Shep clears his throat.

Shep looks at me. "I told him we'd want to do our own vows. Which, with you, Sade, is a lot of pressure," he explains, and our loved ones chuckle with me as he adjusts his stance, widening his feet and straightening his spine. "Well, I put some lines together. Some of these are maybe a bit cheesy, but in my defense, I didn't write them." I tilt my head, totally not knowing where he's going with this. I wait. He clears his throat and starts reciting.

"You are the whole world for me, an entire planet of life wrapped up in a single being, and I . . . well, I'm just happy to be within your orbit." He looks into my eyes, with mischief in his own. "There's affection, and then there's what we have, which is poetry, laughter, and anguish, loyalty, passion, and ecstasy, all wrapped up into a connection so strong it healed us, it healed me . . ."

My words.

These are my words from my books.

That he's memorized.

"I know I'll have to prove it to you, that I won't hurt you again, and I will. I'll be by your side proving it, every second of every day . . ." He goes on and recalls one excerpt from each book flawlessly. The last few passages are vows from wedding scenes in the books that had actual ceremonies in them. After the last vow, he adds his own. "Sadie, I vow all that and more, in richer, poorer, sickness, and health, before God and our friends. And that I will be—" He has to stop and gather himself. "That I will be a husband worth writing about, and that I will help you build an epic dream life that rivals anything and everything you can imagine, which is saying something!" I laugh through my tears, as does Shep, and everyone around us.

I stop and stare at the man in front of me. I think about what he needs to hear and what I want him to understand. I get an idea and then I just let the words out.

"Shep. My love for you is too . . . too vast to be put into pages. And it's . . . too complex to be contained in nicely placed vowels and consonants. I do, I do have a wild imagination, but I couldn't begin to dream up a better man for me."

Shep lets out a sob, and I have to take a deep breath to hold it together and keep going.

"Parts of you inspire every character I've ever created. Our love is the original blueprint from which all my stories start. All the things I wrote about, they pale in comparison to the guiding light that is the real thing—you and me, Shep. Our unending love for each other. I vow in sickness and health, richer or poorer, before God and our friends that I will strive to be the kind of wife that you, the best man I know, deserves."

I let myself cry after I get out the last word. Shep grabs me, snotty and covered in tears.

"Can I kiss her yet?"

The pastor laughs, also crying, and says as fast as he can "BythepowervestedinmeinthestateofTexasInowpronounceyoumanandwife!" Everyone laughs and cheers as Shep pulls my mouth to his.

"I love you so much, Sadie," he says with his forehead on mine.

"For real?" I ask softly.

"Forever."

EPILOGUE

MONTHS LATER
DALLAS, TEXAS

"Bambi! Bambino! Bam bam! Bamalamadingdong, we gotta roll like *now*!"

"Coming!" I call, grabbing the paper off the printer with a smile. His phone rings for the millionth time today. I take him in from across the living room of our sprawling house.

Well, really, it's more like a mansion.

Once we factored in square footage for the state-of-the-art gym spaces for Shep's clients, space for hosting family, my writing studio, and vocal studio, rooms for the children we hope to be conceiving soon, we were looking at palatial houses on acreage.

We're embracing it.

We're that couple with five garages and our own pond. Even I roll my eyes at us sometimes. But Shep loves every single inch of the place. We have a team of lawn-care professionals, yet he insisted on getting a riding lawn mower so he could cut his own lawns. Plural.

He's got one hand on his hip, standing with his feet spread like the boss that he is. "No, Cam, I told you, he's not doing that

365

campaign for less than three million. He's not a rookie anymore . . . No. Look at what I sent you again. All right." He spots me watching him and saunters over to me, eyeing me up and down in my red cocktail dress. "K . . . I'll see you at this thing in a little bit, right? . . . Uh-huh. Bye." He tucks his phone in his pocket and puts his hands on my waist. "How do you look so stunning in everything? I was desperate for you earlier in sweatpants, and I *have* to have you now in this dress. Let's skip tonight."

"Shep!" I squeal as he tries to get a hand under my skirt. "We can't skip our own press event."

"Haven't you heard? We're a power couple," he says into my neck. "We have people now. Have your people go, and I'll have my people go."

"The movie studios didn't just sign on for a movie based on the lives of our people. This is *our* story, and we have to go."

"Ughhhh!" He removes his mouth from where it was nibbling my collarbone.

"Hey, there's a problem with this release." I hand the papers to him.

"What?" He frowns. "I thought Gwyn coordinated with my guys at the office?"

"She did, but look here. I had to change this part. Read it back to me, please." I point and then dig in my purse.

"'The couple married in a secret ceremony with their friends and family in Dallas, Texas, months ago. The network has partnered with Canton Entertainment, a new production arm of Canton Publishing and Canton Cards, International, based out of Oklahoma. Sports power agent and ESPN commentator Shep Riggs is credited as a producer on the upcoming film with his new wife, New York Time's Bestselling Author Sadie R—'" He stops reading. He looks up at me and says softly, "This says Sadie Riggs."

I hand him my new ID, which I got without telling him. The man is all up in my business twenty-four-seven, so this surprise was not the easiest to pull off. Worth it, though, seeing the teary shock on his face right now.

He gingerly takes my license in his fingers and clears his throat. "I thought you said you'd never change your name."

I reach up to put a hand on the side of his gorgeous face. "I've written your name by mine in my journal since I was fourteen, Shep. It wasn't that I didn't want to change my name. I just couldn't bear to change my name to anything other than Riggs."

He sniffs. "What about your books?"

"My pen name will change to Sadie Canton-Riggs."

"I wouldn't have asked you to do this, Sade, but the fact that you did, I was already the happiest man alive and you just keep making me happier."

"I love you, Shep Riggs."

He sighs. "I love you, Sadie Riggs . . . holy crap, that's hot. Damn it! We have to go!"

I laugh, pulling him toward the garage. "Yes, we do, c'mon!"

"Seriously, what's the point of having people if not to free me up to get laid!" he whines, repeatedly, on our drive.

———

Dear reader, for over a decade, in every one of my interviews . . . I lied.

I get chills when I hear myself reading the line from my now-viral blog post in our teaser video. That post turned into a series of tell-all interviews, a screenplay idea, and now a major motion picture.

The entire family has joined us in downtown Dallas for the big announcement. We even invited Shep's dad, since he's sober now and trying to make amends. Tonight feels huge. It isn't just about our marriage or our love story becoming a movie. We're also unveiling the new arm of Canton International. Dad is beside himself. And tonight, after my little surprise earlier, so is Shep.

We are at a restored local movie theater built in the 1950s. We created a red carpet and a makeshift film set backdrop where we release our official statement and the short trailer. In the background of the trailer is the voice of none other than JP Saxe, who let me sing harmony with him on the track. He's here too, though I'm not up for singing live yet. He's been such a good sport, happy to be a part of our story even if he ripped our hearts and smashed them. Now he's part of putting them back together.

Shep and I take a million questions and photos and live stream on social media. Our mixed audience of sports fans and romance readers is a bit weird, but they're rabid for the movie already. Shep has his arm around me the whole night, whispering how proud and happy he is. It's a dream. Everything is perfect.

Until it isn't. Dean, the head of security for myself and Shep, and another guy I don't recognize start giving Shep, Dad, Matthew, and Emerson hand signals.

"Shep?"

"I'm sure it's nothing, but they want us back in the back," Shep explains, giving Dad a serious nod and taking me by the hand. We're led into a back storage area behind the theater space that holds offices and equipment closets.

Having security is weird. I don't think Shep and I need bodyguards, until suddenly we get swarmed on the street or at a restaurant. We still feel like a couple of kids from Oklahoma, but the rest of the world knows us as celebrities.

I stand in the cold, sterile space with my four sisters, and Dad, Shep, Emerson, Matthew, Dean, and the other guy. Dad and the men talk among themselves in hushed tones. Everything feels tense and strange.

"Susan, what's going on?" I whisper.

"Hell if I know," she says, her voice low and cutting. She's not normally one for that tone. I haven't seen her in weeks and . . . she looks awful. She's lost weight, her eyes are sunken, and her shoulders are even hunched over a bit. Susan Canton, future CEO, does not hunch over.

I glance around. "Wait, where's Adam? I haven't seen him since the family photo op at the beginning."

"Yeah, did he leave?" Sam asks, picking up on the defeat in Susan's countenance.

She sighs, looking off into the distance. She turns to us and shrugs before saying plainly, "Adam and I got divorced."

"Wait, WHAT?!" I say in unison with Skye, Sam, and Sal.

"Ladies," Emerson says, interrupting us before Susan can elaborate. Though it doesn't look like she's planning on explaining further. She looks . . . done. Just done.

"Here's the situation," Dean starts. "Don't be alarmed, but a situation has escalated. A stalker of yours, a significant criminal, has made it to Dallas. We had him on our radar, but we lost him, at the same time he posted *explicit* death threats against each of you. Mr. Canton and your husbands have been briefed, and Fergus here, Mr. Clark's head of security, will take it from here, since they have a bigger staff." He nods at Emerson's head bodyguard.

The Clarks are based in London, but while we have millions and a couple bodyguards, the Clark family has billions and employ a private security company across the whole globe. As Dean finishes his sentence, a very good-looking guy in tactical gear bursts through the door.

"Clear," he says.

Fergus nods at the guy and then turns to Sally. "Miss Canton, since you are unmarried and headed to school, Nate has been assigned to guard you specifically. He will stay by your side until the threat is neutralized."

"Sally *Canton*?" Nate says to Fergus, as if the idea of Sally being a Canton is incomprehensible or something?

I turn to Sally to ask if they know each other, and the moment I do, as if on cue, she faints.

———

If you are struggling with alcohol use, my personal advice is to tell someone, out loud, that you have a problem. If you can, tell someone who loves you. If not, try finding an AA meeting near you at *aa.org* or calling one of the hotlines below.

I found support online. Thank you Belle, my sponsor, whose website, Tired of Thinking About Drinking, changed my life.

- Al-Anon and Ala-teen hotline line: 1-800-356-9996
- Substance Abuse and Mental Health Services Administration (SAMHSA): 1-800-662-4357
- Drugfree.org: Call 1-855-378-4373 or text 55753

IF YOU ENJOYED THIS BOOK

Thanks so much for reading! If you enjoyed reading *Things I Wrote About,* please consider leaving a review on Amazon or Goodreads. For indie authors, the most important things in life are coffee and book reviews. Okay, I'm mostly kidding. But if you have a minute, leaving a rating or review will help me find more awesome readers like you.

PLAYLIST & EXTRAS

**Find playlists, photos, and inspiration for
each Heartlanders book at**
kelseyhumphreys.com/heartlanders

WANT MORE CANTONS?

Read the Canton sisters' parents' swoony love story for FREE!
Things I Always Wanted:
An Introvert/Extrovert Best Friends To Lovers
Romantic Comedy

If you're just now joining the Canton sisters,
be sure to go back for these:

Skye and Matthew's story in *Things I Should Have Said,*
An Introvert/Extrovert Romantic Comedy

Samantha and Emerson's story in *Things I Overshared,*
An Extrovert/Introvert Grumpy Sunshine Romantic Comedy

STORIES OF LOYA

Read the epic fantasy romance series the Canton sisters
are obsessed with! Think *Hunger Games* meets ACOTAR.
Written by Kelsey Humphreys under the pen name
K. A. Humphreys
kahumphreys.com

FREE BOOKS!

If you loved *Things I Wrote About,* would you like all of Kelsey's releases in advance and for free? Join her launch team:

kelseyhumphreys.com/launch

ACKNOWLEDGMENTS

My first thank-you will always be to Jesus for my salvation, my sobriety, and my creativity.

My second thank-you will always be to Christopher, my high school sweetheart, my "fortress" and the inspiration for all my hot, sweet fictional men.

To my family, thank you for your unwavering support through all my many creative endeavors. To my early rom-com readers: Mom, Anita, Mattie, Morgan, Courtney, and Andi. To my team on this series: Shayla Raquel, Meredith Tittle, Theresa Oakley, and Shana Yasmin.

To my fans and followers who have been with me through my nonfiction writing and speaking, my YouTube talk show, my musical work, and finally my comedy sketches, and most recently "The Sisters." Your love and support for those comedy sketches brought this series to life.

ABOUT THE AUTHOR

After tens of millions of video views, comedian Kelsey Humphreys has captured her hilarious, heartwarming characters in book form. Her steamy stories dig into deep truths about love, identity, purpose, and family. When she's not writing romance or creating comedy videos, she's reading, running, moming and wife-ing in Oklahoma.

Ask your local bookstore to host her for one of the most fun - and funny - book signing events you'll ever attend.

Follow her funny posts on Facebook, Instagram, and TikTok **@TheKelseyHumphreys**.

Made in the USA
Las Vegas, NV
15 November 2024

11870846R00218